THE GALLERY

a C.R. Allen novel

Edited by Christine Leninger

Cover art by C.R. Allen

Independently Published by Boundless Horizons LLC

1st edition 2024

Paperback ISBN: 979-8-3304-4123-5

E-Book ISBN: 979-8-3304-4124-2

STORIES FROM C.R. ALLEN

For Artists Everywhere

For your boundless creativity, unwavering dedication, and the sacrifices you make to bring beauty, truth, and emotion into the world. Your passion often goes unseen, your struggles unspoken, but through every stroke, note, and word, you shape the very soul of humanity. This is for your perseverance, your courage, and the art that makes life more than survival.

PROLOGUE

The modern downtown office building that was the corporate head-quarters for PaySphere was visible as soon as Javier ascended the subway station staircase and stepped into the bright morning light. It wasn't the tallest building downtown, but its sleek, modern design stood out amongst the historic buildings that surrounded.

Javier had almost missed his first day of work at PaySphere, sleeping through his first alarm, and only waking in time thanks to a loud and boisterous owl outside his window. Two bus trips and a subway ride meant a long and tedious commute to work, but a crummy studio apartment outside the city was all he could afford.

He hadn't even had time to make coffee. Thankfully, because of the broken hot water heater in his building, the cold shower before work was equivalent to a shot of espresso. It would all be worth it, though. This internship at PaySphere was going to change everything for him.

"I'm sorry, I think you have the wrong building," the woman behind the front desk said as he approached the elaborate lobby desk.

He immediately felt embarrassed, his baggy suit from the neighbor-hood thrift store completely meager looking compared to the handsomely dressed men and women walking in behind him.

"Good morning," Javier began, after taking a deep breath. "My name is Javier Alvarez. Today is my first day of work here."

The woman looked up at him, puzzled for a moment, then back to her screen, adjusting her glasses.

"H-A-V," she repeated as she typed. "How do you spell it?"

"J-A-V...," he began instinctively. It wasn't the first time someone had trouble spelling his name.

"Javier," she stopped him, content she had found his appointment. "Here's a visitor badge. You'll need to wear it until security sets you up with a permanent one. Take a seat and Haley will be down shortly."

"Gracias," Javier said before correcting himself. "Thank you." He wanted to kick himself for almost speaking Spanish, something he often did when he was nervous.

"Sure," the woman gave him one more look with her wrinkled, furrowed brow before returning her gaze to the computer.

Javier clipped the visitor badge to his jacket's front pocket.

The lobby of the prestigious downtown office building looked like it came straight from a modern art magazine. The skylight in the center was larger than the entire floor of his apartment building and bathed the space in warm, natural light. A small atrium carved into the floor at the center showcased exotic flowers and plants from all over the world.

The ultra-modern chairs weaved a squiggle pattern through the room instead of straight lines, like most lobbies. Some chairs sat in open space, soft and round over-sized eggs that looked about as comfortable as sitting on the ground. He elected to sit on the nearest sofa.

A magazine lay unclaimed next to him: THE GLOBAL MERIDIAN QUARTERLY. On the front page was a very good-looking but clearly older man on a jet ski, accompanied by a headline: 'GLOBAL MERIDIAN ROCKETS INTO THE NEW YEAR".

The issue date was last year, April. Wasn't the new year in January? Also, the old man was riding a jet ski, not a rocket. However, considering it was a company magazine, he understood why the almost laughable content held so little appeal to him.

As the minutes stretched on, waiting for someone to come collect him, his legs began to go numb - he looked at his watch and realized fifteen minutes had already passed.

"These sofas and chairs were not made for sitting," he thought to himself.

Standing up, he felt immediate relief as the blood flow was restored to his legs. Not wanting to look silly standing in the middle of the room like an army private at attention, he walked over to the nearby wall and gazed at the art.

The abstract painting featured eyes at the top, made with purple and red strokes. Below that, a pair of hands, reaching out with open palms towards the bottom. In between them, a pyramid with a strange bronze symbol at its peak. A vast arrangement of people amassed at the base of the pyramid. They were shapes and colors of all sorts, no two of them the same.

"It must have taken the artist forever to paint this," he thought.

The sense of unease at viewing the painting waned in him, replaced by another feeling entirely. The hairs on his arms stood up. He felt flush in his face and neck, and beads of sweat formed on his brow. It almost felt like he was having a panic attack.

"Interesting isn't it?" A soft voice pierced the lobby music.

Javier flinched as he noticed the beautiful woman standing next to him, as if she had appeared out of thin air. She had short blond hair and green lipstick that matched the color of her eyes. She wore a blue pantsuit that flowed down her long and thin figure.

"I'm sorry. Did I startle you?" She purred at him.

"No, not at all ma'am," he croaked, panicking inside as a bead of sweat splattered onto the marble floor.

"It is warm in the lobby," she said, her mouth shifting into a slight smile.

"It... it is," Javier stammered.

They stood together in silence, Javier afraid to take his eyes off the painting.

"I know the artist who made this piece," the woman's voice could have lulled a bengal tiger to sleep. "He was commissioned to paint it by a friend of mine. They paid him a million dollars."

Javier's eyes grew wide. The simple mention of a million dollars ignited thoughts of all he could do to help his family with such an ample sum.

"In the end, it took him over 5,000 individual brush strokes to finish it," she continued. "Over a period of a year and a half, working tirelessly."

"Wow," Javier said, the first thing to come to mind. "That's a lot."

The woman shifted her weight away from him slightly. Javier could not avoid following her every little movement.

"It's shit," she said with a laugh. "That's a little over nine brush strokes a day. Can you imagine crawling into bed at night feeling satisfied that you moved your brush nine times total? But I guess that's art."

Her eyes narrowed as she examined him.

"You look familiar," she commented. "Have we met before?"

"I don't think so," he said. He certainly didn't think he had.

"Are you sure?" She asked. "I feel like I've seen your face somewhere."

"Maybe I just have one of those faces?" Javier said.

"Perhaps," the woman sighed.

"Lady , Mr. Henricks will see you now," said the receptionist.

"Good luck on your first day," Lady Gianni said to Javier with a wink.

"Thanks," Javier said, finding himself hypnotized watching her glide gracefully towards the elevators.

"How did she know it was his first day?" He thought. She had a visitor's badge, same as his, so she didn't work there. It was probably painfully obvious from his nervous nature and ill-fitting clothes. He stood out like a fish out of water.

An odd sound interrupted his thoughts. It took him a moment to pinpoint it.

Psst...

It was coming from a doorway just off the lobby.

Javier saw a girl standing there, dressed in a black skirt with a red button down top. She wore stylish red glasses that matched the shade of her lipstick and her auburn hair was tied neatly into a bun. She held a clipboard and beckoned him over.

Javier turned and pointed at himself, trying to confirm if she was talking to him.

She rolled her eyes at him and nodded.

"Come here," she whispered loud enough to reach him.

Javier hurried over to her. She practically pushed him through the doorway and closed it behind them. They were in a large room lined with cubicles where men and women in white button-down shirts typed away silently on keyboards.

"Hello my name is..." Javier began, trying to remember his manners.

"Javier, I know," the girl said with a sigh. "I'm Haley. I've been assigned your orientation."

Javier breathed out a sigh of relief.

"Great, I've been waiting for over..." he didn't get to finish his sentence.

"What were you thinking?" Haley practically snarled at him.

"What?" Javier asked, genuinely puzzled.

"Talking to her," Haley clarified before hushing her voice. "Talking to Lady Gianni."

"Oh, she introduced herself so I..." the flustered Haley cut him off again.

"We do not talk to Lady Gianni," she said with frustration in her voice. "Period, end of story."

"I'm sorry, I didn't know," Javier replied. "Who is she?"

"She is Mr. Henrick's personal art consultant," Haley explained.

Javier gave her a stare.

"You do know who Mr. Henricks is, right?" she asked.

Javier hesitated. He was afraid to .

"PaySphere is a subsidiary of the Exostic Group," she began. "Exostic is part of Berry Industries, which is wholly owned by..."

Javier was more confused than ever.

"Global Meridian Holdings," Haley answered for him. "Jeremiah Henricks is the CEO of Global Meridian. He's like the fourth richest man in the world, and he does whatever Lady Gianni tells him to."

"I'm sorry I didn't know," he replied.

"Forget it," she said with a sigh. "Just don't do it again, or it'll be both our jobs. Shit, we're late."

"But I got here fifteen minutes ear..." he tried to say, but Haley held up her hand, stopping him.

She hit the button on the nearby elevator.

"We belong on the fifteenth floor," she stated.

The door dinged, and the doors slid open. Several tall men in business suits walked out. One smiled and winked at Haley. She nervously smiled back at him.

As the elevator door slid closed, her smile disappeared and turned to a frown.

"I just wanted to tell you," he began. "That I really appreciate the opportunity to be here. This is such a great company and I can't wait to be part of its success. Thank you."

"Ugh," Haley groaned. "Don't thank me. I did nothing to get you here. Somebody in HR picked you. I'm just the one who got stuck doing your orientation."

They rode the rest of the elevator ride up in total silence.

"15th floor," Haley said as the doors opened. "Executive offices."

The dark marble of the grand hallway reflected the bright lights like a full moon's glow on the surface of a still lake. Javier tried to read each placard as they walked past the glass offices that flanked the corridor but quickly lagged behind as each title became longer and more complex.

They stopped at a corner office, the placard indicating it belonged to Dennis Smith, Executive Vice President of Account Management and Customer Relations.

Inside were three men dressed in suits huddled around the desk, their attention focused on the object at its center.

Haley knocked on the door twice and the man sitting behind the desk gestured them in.

"One moment," the one with brown hair instructed.

Javier thought they must have interrupted a very important business meeting.

"You see this right here," the man continued. "That's the stitching made by hand. They have this village in Italy where these old ladies who've been doing this their entire lives stitch the leather into the case."

The object they were referring to was a solid shell attaché case. The brown-haired man rapped on the exterior of it hard with his knuckles.

"Feel how tough the lining is, military-grade aluminum," he bragged. "This thing could stop a bullet."

"Wow," said the blond man. "But I thought hard shell was out of style, like ten years ago."

"Style is cyclical," the brown-haired man retorted. "My buddy at GQ says next season, this is going to be what everybody has. Retro is in."

"You convinced me," the man with black, slicked-back hair commented. "I'm going to go pick one out at lunch."

"Me too," said the blond-haired man.

"Shit, what time is it?" The brown-haired man asked before checking his watch. "I have to take care of this if I want any chance of making my massage this afternoon. Come on in, Haley."

"Good morning sirs," she said with a forced smile and Javier following her inside. "I wanted to introduce you to the new intern. This is Javier Alvarez."

"Javi!" the brown-haired man said, walking forward.

"Dennis Smith," he introduced himself. He had short, spiked brown hair and a graying beard. Javier smiled and shook his hand enthusiastically, noticing the large bulky rings on his fingers that made it difficult, almost painful, to grasp.

"Like the rings?" Dennis asked rhetorically. "Two state football championships in high school and a college Division II championship."

"Wow," Javier remarked. "Nice to meet you, sir. What's the fourth one for?"

"Oh that," Dennis said, making a fist and holding it up to his shoulder so all the rings could be on full display. "That's for being the company's fantasy football champion for five years running."

He high-fived with both the other men in the room.

"See you guys at the Peregrine later?" he asked them.

"You got it," the black-haired one said as he walked past Javier, as if he wasn't even there.

The other was following close behind him, but stopped and leaned in close to Haley.

"Heard you are going out with Tim from finance," the man said to her.

"I'm just meeting him for a drink," she replied, looking uncomfortable. "Nothing more."

He held his arms to the frame of the door and leaned in close until only a few inches separated their faces.

"Well, when you're ready to date the real deal," he said. "You come find me."

For several agonizing seconds, Javier watched her skin practically crawl as she tried to avoid looking at him. Thankfully, he eventually got the hint and jostled past them and into the hallway.

"Take a seat, Javi," Dennis said, gesturing to the open leather chair in front of the desk.

"Thank you, sir," Javier said, shuffling over and sitting down. "And I prefer to be called Javier."

Dennis wasn't listening. Javier hated being called Javi since he was in school.

Haley closed the office door and stood off to the side.

Dennis sat on the edge of his desk.

"You know this is a special place to work," Dennis began. "Really special. Getting an internship here, it's the big time."

"I'm excited," Javier said with a smile.

Dennis walked over to stand next to Haley, who stood perfectly still.

"You know what makes a place like this work?" Dennis asked.

"No sir," Javier replied.

"Team work," Dennis answered, weaving his fingers together until his hands formed a ball in front of him. "Everyone in this building is part of the same team. Do you know what happens when someone doesn't act like a teammate?"

"No sir," Javier answered.

"The whole thing falls apart," said Dennis as he exploded his hands and wrapped one arm around Haley's shoulder. She stood rigid.

"Haley here," he continued. "She's a good team player. Great, actually." He squeezed her tighter.

"That's what we want from you." Dennis returned to his desk to sit in his high-backed leather chair. "Listen to Haley. She'll show you the ropes, and you'll do great. Comprehendo Javi?"

"Yes sir," Javier replied, doing his best to hide his annoyance.

Haley motioned towards the door with her eyes.

Javier got the hint and hurried after her.

"One more thing, Javi," Dennis said. Javier froze. "Get yourself some new clothes, preferably a suit that wasn't manufactured in the 80s."

Javier turned bright red. He nodded in reply.

Both Javier and Haley walked down the hallway to where it split.

"The offices for the interns and assistants are this..." Haley began, but jumped backwards just in time, right as she turned the corner.

She had nearly bumped into an old man in a tweed jacket.

"Oh, I'm so sorry sir," Haley said, looking terrified.

"No worries dear," the old man said. His soft eyes and kind smile made him seem friendly, reminding him of Javier's grandfather in a lot of ways. His voice had a slight Texas droll to it. "My fault really. I wasn't looking where I was going."

"Thank you sir," Haley replied.

"Who's this?" the old man asked.

"Oh, I'm sorry," Haley stumbled with her words. "This is Javier. He's our new intern. I was just showing him around."

"Glad to have you here son," the old man said, shaking Javier's hand heartedly. "The name is Craig Bones."

"Nice to meet you, Mr. Bones," Javier replied.

"Don't let the last name fool you," Mr. Bones said. "Ain't nothing scary about me. In fact, I pride myself on keeping things free and relaxed around here."

"Excellent sir," said Javier.

"Now, if you need anything at all," the old man continued. "You see anything that don't look right, anything that don't smell right, you come to me, y'hear?"

"You got it, sir," Javier responded enthusiastically.

"Excellent," Mr. Bones said, patting Javier on the shoulder. "Doors always open."

With that, the old man walked to the office at the end of the hall with the shortest title of all on the placard, CEO.

Haley led Javier to a side door and into a shared space where she and five other assistants and interns had their desks. She motioned to an open cubicle and Javier sat down in the chair.

"This week you'll be itemizing receipts and submitting expense reports for Dennis and the other executives," Haley explained, pointing to a pile of paper stacked almost four feet high on the desk. "Not much to it, just type what you see and move on to the next one. There's an employee handbook somewhere underneath the pile. HR says you have to read that first before you do anything else. I recommend you just skim it. Nothing really important there."

She showed him how to login, use the scanner, and where to enter the data.

Javier took a deep breath. It was the moment he'd been waiting for. He was ready to get to work, and that he did.

First, he pulled the thick employee handbook from the pile and opened it. It read like a legal contract, but Javier took his time and took notes to help him remember every rule and instruction in it.

When he finally closed it after reaching the end, he looked at his watch. It was almost 2pm in the afternoon. He already was running behind, and wondered if he would have to stay late to catch up.

The job was monotonous; the expense reports from Dennis's department were mostly for the same repeated items. Plane fare, dinners, hotel rooms, taxis; the sort of things that were expected of a business trip.

He was just happy to be working. The afternoon flew by and soon the other assistants filed out one by one until it was just him and Haley left.

He wanted to get through the entire stack before leaving, show them what kind of person he was. It was still very thick, but he was determined to not go anywhere until it was gone.

But he started noticing strange things on some receipts, things that he wasn't certain about and needed help. He set them to the side, not wanting to bother Haley, but when there were over a dozen stacked up, he knew he couldn't hold off any longer.

"Haley, can you look at this for a minute?" he asked.

She groaned loudly before wandering over.

"You know I'm only here this late because I had to show you around this morning," she said, peering over his shoulder.

She read the scanned receipt he had up on the screen.

"I'm not sure what the problem is," she said.

"This hotel receipt is for a stay under someone else's name," he said.

"It's probably just a mistake by the hotel," Haley answered quickly. "When you enter it, just fix it for him."

She moved to walk away.

"I don't think so," Javier continued. "It looks like it's for a woman who stayed there. Should I call and try to get the corrected receipt?"

Haley's teeth clenched.

"No, correct it for him and move on," she said slowly and deliberately.

"But the handbook says," Javier began.

Haley leaned down until she was close to his face.

"This company makes billions of dollars a year," she said in a fierce whisper. "Things like this don't matter. Just fix it when you enter the receipt."

"There are others," he continued. "One for purchases at an adult video store, a pawnshop, and I'm pretty certain this one is for a strip club."

He cycled through the suspect receipts.

"Enter them and move on," she repeated. "It's just entertainment expenses."

"But the handbook says that anything against policy should be reported to my supervisor," Javier said, with growing confusion.

"And who is your supervisor?" Haley asked.

"Dennis," he replied.

"And whose expense report are you working on right now?" She asked.

"Dennis," he replied.

"There you go," she exclaimed. She held her fingers to the bridge of her nose. "I'm sorry, I'm just tired. It's been a long day. I'm going to go home and you should too."

"But what should I..." Javier began.

"Do what you want," Haley replied, returning to her desk and collecting her purse. "You heard what Dennis said, this place works cause people are team players. Think about that before you do anything rash, ok?"

She scurried out the door before Javier could get in another word.

Javier sat and thought for a moment.

The sun wasn't quite setting outside yet. He still had time to finish his work for the night. So he got to it.

When the stack of receipts had shrunk to nothing, Javier patted himself on the back. The only ones left behind were the suspect ones that went against the company's expense policy. They were all for Dennis and his lackeys. He decided he would sleep on it and deal with it tomorrow.

He packed up his things, pulled on his coat, and walked out of the side office and into the hall. All the glass offices were dark, their occupants long departed for the day. All except for one, the CEO's office. Through the glass windows Javier could see Mr. Bones sitting at his desk and watching a report about the Tokyo Stock Exchange on the large TV.

The handbook said he was supposed to report the receipts to his supervisor, but it was his supervisor who submitted the invalid expenses. It naturally made sense that if he couldn't report it to his supervisor, then he would have to report it up the ladder one more rung. The only problem; the next rung was the kind old man sitting in that office.

"You see anything that don't look right, anything that don't smell right, you come to me, y'hear?"

The old man's words repeated in his head as he thought hard about what to do next.

J avier ignored the rumblings of his stomach as he walked towards the subway station. His thoughts still lingered on the invalid expenses that Haley had told him to 'fix' for Dennis and his friends. He had considered just doing as she said, being a team player as she implied; however, he knew he wouldn't have been able to sleep that night if he had.

He was glad he went to Mr. Bones and shared what he had found. Mr. Bones had reassured him he took it seriously and would handle it personally. The old man had a calming presence. He knew how to smooth things over and everything would be fine. More importantly, Javier knew he was acting with integrity and everyone else would realize that. They couldn't exactly fire him for following the handbook.

Marveling at the displays in the closed stores as he walked past, he thought about the fancy attaché case Dennis had. He dreamed of one day walking down the street with one of his own; one earned through hard work and integrity.

As he walked, loud music blared from a high-end bar. He looked at the sign, THE PEREGRINE.

He stopped to peer in at the girls in shimmering cocktail dresses, laughing and flirting with men in business suits at the bar and tables. Serving large plates with lobster tails and thick juicy steaks accompanied by the pop of champagne bottles.

One day, he'd be in there too. He smiled.

In the corner by the window, three men sat at a table, and they didn't look as joyous as the other patrons. They stared into their empty shot glasses with dull eyes. At their feet sat three attaché cases, shiny and new.

It took him a minute but Javier recognized them; it was Dennis and his two lackeys.

He tried to hide his face in the collar of his jacket and continue past them.

An owl hooted loud overhead, startling Javier. Without realizing it, he had locked eyes with Dennis.

He looked away immediately and hurried to the subway station.

Javier was relieved to descend the steps and bask in the bright fluorescent lights of the platform waiting area. His train was still a few minutes out, so he stood behind the yellow line alone. However, something in the back of his mind felt ominous, like something was following him.

As the message of the train's arrival played on the loudspeaker, he took a deep breath. Glancing at the stairs that led back up to the street, they were still devoid of anyone coming or going. He was fine.

He tried to clear the feeling from his mind.

The train squealed to a halt in front of him, and the doors opened. A few passengers filed out. He rushed inside, only looking back to the station stairs at the last moment.

Three men in suits stood there. One was pointing directly at him.

They disappeared from sight as the doors closed.

Sitting in a nearby open seat, he felt eased by the several other passengers in the subway car with him until loud yelling erupted from the car in front of him. Standing up, he peered through the glass window that separated the two and his heart sank in his chest.

Dennis and his friends were busy pushing through, moving towards him. The doors that connected the cars would not open while the train was in motion, so Javier stood there reserved and watching as they approached the window and the three men stared back at him with loosened collars, disheveled ties, and rage-filled eyes.

When they got to the next station, they'd be able to switch cars. He'd be trapped. The loudspeaker announced the imminent arrival to the next station.

Javier's mind raced, pondering whether to fight or try to escape. Would anyone in the train car come to his aid? Not likely. If the city had taught him anything at all so far, it was that everyone was on their own.

The ding of the door's opening rang in his ear. He didn't dare hesitate.

Sprinting at full speed out, he hoped he could lose them on the surface streets.

His heart raced, bounding up step after step and only pausing once he was on the surface. He wasn't sure exactly where he was, but his pause was only momentary.

He heard hurried steps below him, so he returned to a full sprint down the street.

The breeze carried a heavy scent of salt. Sounds of breaking waves mixed with the pounding of his heartbeat into an uneasy background noise. The area was more industrial than the luxurious downtown office area he had come from. Most of the lights were out on the streetlights, leaving gaps of complete darkness.

He turned down street after street, praying he could escape.

Eventually, the street he had taken went no further, the water's edge blocked his path in a dead end. The glow of the urban city across the swirling body of water was the only light that he could see, lit up like hundreds of Christmas trees.

It would have been a picturesque landscape to enjoy if not for the searing terror.

Bright colors of graffiti caught his eye, belonging to a red brick building nearby.

The door of the building had brightly colored letters above it: THE COLLECTIVE.

Javier banged on it, hoping someone inside would let him in.

The window remained dark. No one was home.

He flattened himself against the doorway, hoping that in the darkness he could hide from his pursuers.

Three shadows appeared at the end of the street.

"Where'd he go? Did we lose him?" One voice asked.

"Maybe we took a wrong turn," said another.

The shadows looked like they were turning to leave when...

An owl swooped from a perch on the building opposite and straight at Javier, who dodged its sharp talons at the last moment. In his maneuver away from the bird, his foot slipped on the step and he fell into several metal trash bins that banged loudly into one another.

Javier sat up on the ground, his arms above his head ready to defend himself from the owl should it make another attack. Except as quickly and silently as it had appeared, it had departed.

"Javi," Dennis's voice echoed against the brick walls as Javier saw three shadowy figures at the end of the alley, Javier's only path of escape.

They crept slowly and methodically towards him, their attaché cases swinging playfully at their sides.

"I'm sorry," Javier said, holding up his hands in front of him. "I had to tell him, it was in the handbook."

"Oh, we're not mad," Dennis replied unconvincingly. "You just did what you thought was right."

"Integrity means a lot," one of the other men added.

They took steps closer to Javier, forming a circle tightening around him.

"Please, let me go," Javier pleaded.

"We aren't going to hurt you," Dennis said with a sinister smile. "We just wanted to have a little chat with you. You know, a pep talk. A quick team meeting."

He eerily emphasized the word 'team' as he wrapped his fingers together like he had earlier in this office.

Javier didn't know what to do. He wasn't a fighter.

"You cost us our bonuses, you little shit," one of the men said, his eyes brimming with rage. "Now I have to cancel my trip to the Bahamas."

"They are taking away our company cards too," the other added. "You know how big a pain in the ass that is?"

"Now I have to go to the ATM before taking my girlfriend out," said Dennis, the man's wedding ring glinting in the light.

Javier fell to the ground in terror as the three men inched closer and closer until their shadows blotted out the only street lamp.

It was soon hard to tell the difference between the crashing of waves against the concrete shoreline and the screams of pain as the three men beat the young intern with their attaché cases.

*A*t the exact same moment on the other side of the city...

Three men quickly worked to build a packing crate. Cutting the wood to size, nailing it together, and adding padding.

The cargo was a painting in a simple ebony frame that was a few meters away in a staging area protected from the flying saw dust by clear painter's plastic that hung from the ceiling to the floor. A nervous-looking man stood next to the van parked just outside the loading bay, smoking a cigarette in the brisk night air.

The sound of heels tapping on concrete echoed throughout the receiving area.

"They're crating it as we speak," Lady Gianni said into her cell phone as she entered.

Power saws and nail guns permeated the background noise.

"Your client will love it," she said, moving the clear plastic tarp to the side and stepping into the protected chamber. "It's been the star of the gallery for weeks now. I've had people asking to name my price since it first debuted."

She paced in front of the painting; her glances returning to it again and again as the conversation continued.

"Why didn't I sell it?" She repeated the question from the caller. "I just didn't feel it was the right time yet. It needed to sit for a while, soak in the ambiance."

She paused in front of the painting and listened on her phone.

"I'm sorry, it's just not possible," she continued. "The artist is a complete recluse. He won't come out for any reason whatsoever."

She took a step closer to the frame, examining it from only a few inches away.

"It increases the intrigue factor," said Lady Gianni. "Intrigue drives up the value, exactly what increases your finder's fee."

"Ma'am," said one of the workmen, peeking his head through the plastic sheeting. "We're ready."

"That's them," Lady Gianni said into the phone. "Courier will be on his way shortly. It'll be arriving in Italy tomorrow morning. You won't be sorry."

She hung up the phone and put it away.

The workmen shuffled in wearing white full body coveralls and nitrile gloves. They looked like a forensics team entering a crime scene.

"What's it called ma'am?" one of the workmen asked, sounding like a sci-fi villain through his N95 mask.

She didn't reply as she stared at the piece, deep in thought, and recalled the art critic Theo Argent's review in the morning paper.

"The canvas presents a haunting nocturnal tableau of an urban street, masterfully capturing a chilling narrative through evocative brushwork.

Central to the composition is a solitary street lamp, its luminous yellow aura radiating in deliberate strokes, casting an eerie spotlight on the scene below. Beneath this stark illumination, three indistinct figures emerge, their forms rendered in ominous silhouettes, void of intricate detail, yet imbued with an overwhelming sense of menace."

"Each figure wields a briefcase, using them as clubs to maul the young man at their feet. Through dynamic, slashing brushstrokes, vividly streaked with crimson, the artist encapsulates their rage. And who is the unwitting victim of their violence? Of course it is the young man at their feet, clad in a loose-fitting suit and tie. His facial features are obscured, perhaps intentionally left undefined by the artist or already obliterated by the attack itself, save for his eyes, which remain starkly expressive."

"Those eyes, rendered with painstaking detail, stand in stark contrast to the blurred and brutalized surroundings. They are wide, gleaming with an almost palpable fear, capturing the instant of helplessness and agony. The irises, glistening under the streetlamp's cold light, convey a depth of emotion that speaks volumes, drawing the viewer into the young man's plight. His outstretched arm, a desperate plea for mercy, further amplifies the sense of despair, but it is the eyes that hold the narrative together, creating an indelible impression of humanity amidst the depicted inhumanity. His arm is outstretched, a desperate plea for mercy."

"And what was his crime? You may ask. Well, I will answer for you. Daring to challenge his pursuers' entitlement."

She had been disappointed with the review, most of it being the usual senseless babble dressed up as sophistication, a common illness plaguing the world of popular art. The only thing the critic had really gotten right, was the comments about the young man's eyes.

Those same eyes that now reflected in Lady Gianni's; familiar eyes from a familiar face.

"Pack it, ship it," she snapped, turning away and lifting the plastic to exit.

"But what should we put on the crate?" the workman in the mask asked.

She paused only a moment to lean in close and whisper the answer into his ear before disappearing out of sight.

The men went to work immediately, vacuum sealing the painting and placing it inside the crate.

"Is it ready?" the man smoking the cigarette asked impatiently.

"Not yet," one of the workmen said, as he pulled out a stencil kit and spray can.

He carefully aligned the stencils before spraying the paint.

When he was done, they wheeled the crate to the back of the truck and secured it in place with tie-downs. The fresh paint glistened in the receiving dock lights, revealing the name of the piece of art, *The Intern*.

PART 1

CONSUME

CHAPTER 1

Dani was growing concerned as she walked the dark sidewalk towards the looming structure ahead. The lights of downtown glowed in the distance behind it, giving the building a halo of white and blue. None of the other houses and businesses they passed had any lights on, their windows either broken or boarded up.

"Are you sure you know where you're going?" Dani asked the skipping brunette leading them.

Bianca turned and continued skipping in reverse.

"I walked here last week," she replied. "Trust me, you're going to love this place."

Bianca was always like this, light-hearted and upbeat, regardless of the situation. Never showing the slightest hint of a fear of failure. She was the kind of person who could run into the middle of a battlefield with bullets flying in every direction and still come out unscathed. To her, everything looked damn easy.

As she bounced ahead of them, her dark, braided dreads hung to her waist, and bounced with her. How she kept her hair always lush and healthy was a mystery. Bianca was a natural beauty. Her skin was perfect, tan, and smooth as silk. With a taut, fit body; Dani too often found herself embarrassed to be caught staring at Bianca's contours, hungry with desire. But it was Bianca's eyes that held the most sway over her: large, warm, and inviting. Dani would swim in them for days if she could.

Bianca was everything Dani had ever wanted.

Dani (short for Danielle) Scotts, was tall for a girl, too tall. Her height intimidated men and made her movements clumsy and awkward. Her whisper-thin, blonde hair had never grown past her shoulders despite years of trying every product known to mankind. Nothing had ever worked. She felt stuck, trapped with hair that mocked her in the mirror every morning despite years of dedicated cultivation.

Her face was gaunt with an enormous nose, something she hoped one day plastic surgery would fix; and she was nowhere near as voluptuous as Bianca. Of course, that was also fixable via plastic surgery; but the list of what she wanted done was long and the amount of tips in the jar at the coffee shop where she worked was laughable.

The thing that Dani was most jealous of was that Bianca, at only 22-years-old, was a successful artist. Featured in several shows already downtown, her pieces sold regularly.

This jealousy, this painful envy that Dani harbored, was a problem; because Dani was also helplessly in love with Bianca. This doomed love tortured Dani's heart and soul, as she well knew that Bianca did not reciprocate it.

If life was a Disney movie, Bianca would be Belle, and Dani would be the Beast. Except life wasn't a Disney movie, and Belle would never look at Dani as more than that, a roommate.

"Aren't you cold?" Paul asked. He trailed just behind Bianca, who was wearing a little black cocktail dress.

"I'm just fine," Bianca chirped.

While the rest had to almost speed walk to keep up with Bianca's excited pace, Paul was well over six feet tall and could keep up using his natural stride.

He was the oldest of the group at almost 30 and the only one of them who had reached true stardom. He wore a t-shirt with one of his own pieces printed on it, along with brown cargo pants. His dark skin and bald head reflected the light of the moon overhead.

In his early 20s, you couldn't walk into any respectable museum or gallery and not see any of his . He sold almost a hundred paintings to collectors and collections, making a small fortune. With the money, he had started The Collective, funded their space in the warehouse district, and established a safe place for them to live and create in.

When Dani had first met him at the coffee shop, she thought he had been hitting on her. He seemed overly interested in the different chalk drawings she had added to the menu boards. When he asked her to join , she just about did a backflip behind the counter.

Dani pulled the sweater tighter over her shoulders as the night's chill fondled her skin. She had tried to dress like Bianca but couldn't muster enough willpower to go out with so much skin revealed. Without an ample bosom like her idol, her tan dress made her look like a plank of wood with arms and legs, opting to cover herself with a sweater at the last moment to avoid embarrassment.

Their escapade to this part of town, maybe the better description was a field trip, was Bianca's idea. Paul had agreed immediately. Dani thought Paul secretly had a thing for Bianca, since he almost always went along with whatever crazy idea she came up with. But Dani had never seen them share an intimate moment together, and Bianca was always seeing someone else, in and out of relationships with older men like one might jump from channel-to-channel while watching TV. Sometimes several simultaneously.

Bianca's skipping stopped at the corner.

"We're here," she said as the others caught up.

"Wow," Dani commented, standing next to her.

You would never have been able to tell as they approached. The tall building was so bleak and ominous from a distance, but now it was only 20-ft ahead of them and engulfed in the radiance of high-output spotlights.

"It used to be the biggest church in the city," Bianca said. "Then some family bought it and turned it into a nightclub."

"I remember," Paul commented. "Club Llithium I think, with two L's."

"What a stupid name," Bianca said with a laugh. "Who thinks of that kind of stuff?"

Dani laughed with her.

"Well, the club closed down," Bianca continued. "Something with satanic rituals in the basement. So now it's an art gallery."

Dani's eyes fixed onto the old cathedral. It had three steeples that reached into the sky; the tips nearly touching the clouds. Brilliant stained glass windows filled in the space between the roof of each rise and the granite stone walls. The windows were backlit with a moving light, making the pictures inside them appear animated.

Demons and angels did battle with flaming swords and bloody spears in the glass. Dani marveled at the ancient form of art. The skill required for it was difficult to learn and just as difficult to recreate. She supposed anybody with a 3D printer or water-jet cutter could make one, but something about toiling with your medium was part of what made art special to her.

Below the depiction of war between heaven and hell, large spotlights shining onto the oversized granite brick walls displaying advertisements and previews of the pieces inside.

"How the hell are we going to get in?" Dani asked, noticing the aluminum guard rails snaking onto the sidewalk crammed with people waiting in line.

"Paul can get us in, right?" Bianca said with a wink.

"I can try," he replied.

"It looks more like a Hollywood premier than an art gallery," commented Alek.

Alek Yukof was the fourth and final member of The Collective. He had been the silent caboose as they walked to the gallery. Even though he was 20-years-old, his skinny, almost prepubescent body made him look barely a day out of highschool. Wearing a gray beanie year-round, the simple cap barely hid his long, bright red hair or the rampant acne he struggled to contain. Clad in a plain white t-shirt and old, torn up jeans; he looked out of place practically anywhere he went.

His only feature that aged him were his eyes, where their deep blues seemed caught at the center of a raging storm. The dark circles that stressed them showed a lack of sleep; something Dani witnessed when waking up late at night only to see the light on in his room and the sounds of scraping on canvas.

Paul had found Alek on the street, impressed by the boy's homemade art he was selling for almost nothing. Alek had talent, far more than Dani, but his perfectionist nature got in his own way too often for him to produce much.

Paul led the way as the foursome crossed the street and walked straight to the front door, bypassing the line. Most of the older men and women waiting patiently wore suits and extravagant dresses. They shook their heads in disgust at the ragtag group as they passed.

A red carpet extended from the front door to the curb. Alek was right about it looking more like a Hollywood premier than a gallery show. Dani felt like she was trespassing on private property as she stepped on it, the soft felt making her knees wobble with inexperience on high heels.

The doorman's grimace as they approached told her that their plan to gain entry using Paul's fading fame had a slim chance of success.

"You're going to have to wait in line with everyone else," the bouncer said, holding a hand up.

"You don't understand," Paul said with a smile. He was as tall as the bouncer, but not nearly as built. "I am Paul Moreau."

The bouncer stared at him with an unamused look.

"*Flowers in the Wind*," Paul said, naming one of his most famous works. "*Dandelions in Fall*?"

Still no sign that the bouncer had any idea how famous Paul had been once.

"What about *Lillys on the Lake*?" He added, Paul's usually confident voice cracking slightly.

"Back of the line, now," the Bouncer commanded.

The men and women in line whispered to each other and snickered at them as the foursome reluctantly found their place at the back of the queue.

"Shit," Paul said with disappointment in his voice. "He must be a follower of Duchamp."

Marcel Duchamp was an artist famous for his disdain of 'retinal art,' art designed to please the eye.

"Can we at least split a cab to get home?" Dani asked. "I don't think I can make it in these heels."

"I can't believe I'm wasting time away from the studio for this," Alek said grumpily.

They all stopped talking when they heard a shrill whistle.

It was Bianca. She had slipped a ways down the street and now waved at them.

"Follow me," she said before disappearing down the alley behind the old church.

Both Dani and Alek looked at Paul for guidance, who just shrugged and moved to follow the sprightly brunette.

Like always, they followed his lead.

To say the alleyway was dark would have been an understatement. In the shadow of the immense church, it felt like it hadn't seen light from the sun or moon in years. On one side were the granite blocks that made up the church and on the other, a concrete wall topped with a chain-link fence lined with barbed wire.

The lone light was a lamp that hung on the wall above a steel door. The sign on the door read, SHIPPING & RECEIVING. Bianca was already there as the rest of them walked up, pressing on the intercom button.

From the other side of the roll-up door, they could hear the buzzing blaring like an alarm inside. After waiting several minutes, there was no indication that anyone was inside to answer their call.

"Receiving is closed right now," said a voice from the shadows next to Bianca.

They all jumped.

They couldn't see the man, they could only see a glowing orange dot hovering and swaying in the darkness. He took a step forward into the light.

He wore jeans and work boots, with a black t-shirt that had the logo for the gallery printed on it. His head was clean-shaved, and he looked unhealthily skinny. The cigarette between his lips badly needed to be ashed.

"Entrance is back the way you came," the man said. "But I think you already knew that."

Bianca looked back at Dani, Paul, and Alek. She mouthed the words: *I'll handle this*.

The rest of The Collective hung back in the darkness as Bianca talked to the gallery workman. Dani's jealousy fluttered in her chest. She couldn't help it. Watching Bianca lock eyes with the gruff-looking man, puffing out her chest and resting her foot on the concrete step to show off her bare leg; it was more attention than Dani ever could have hoped to receive.

Dani had lived her entire life with what she wanted being flaunted right before her eyes; she had learned to control her jealousy. She would vent these emotions later from the solitude of her own bedroom.

Bianca smiled as she talked to the man, Dani was too far away to hear their conversation. Whatever it was, though, the man seemed to grow more excited by the minute. Even in the chilly night air, Dani thought she could see sweat forming on the top of his bald head.

When Bianca gently touched the man's arm, Dani could see the spell being cast. Bianca had him; hook, line, and sinker.

The workman moved to the keypad next to the door and typed in the code.

In the light, Dani noticed a tattoo on his hand, five dots arranged like the face of a die. She found it curious.

Bianca motioned for them to follow.

The rest of The Collective emerged from the darkness and almost sneaked forward despite there being no reason to. They were being let in.

As the keypad beeped and the electronic lock disengaged, the man ushered them through the doorway and closed it behind them. The room was pitch black, but by the way their breaths seemed to echo inside, Dani assumed it was a vast space with a high ceiling.

The workman pulled out a flashlight.

"Follow me," he said, leading them.

They all trailed the beam of light as it shined into the darkness. They were hardly stealthy intruders, as sounds of rustling plastic and jingling fasteners filled the emptiness of space around them.

The workman's flashlight's beam landed on another steel door against a brick wall, where it grew as they approached.

"Don't tell nobody I let you in," the workman said. "If you do, it would be my job."

"Of course, Larry," Bianca replied, with her intoxicating voice. "We won't tell a soul."

She had her hand on his arm as he led the way, ensuring her seductive presence would prevent him from faltering or changing his mind.

Larry unlocked the door and pushed it open a few inches, peering out.

"Coast is clear," he said. "You'll call me, right?"

"As soon as I get home," Bianca replied, kissing him on the cheek.

His face turned visibly flush even in the dim light.

Bianca, Paul, and Alek went ahead of Dani; slinking out into the gallery's main hall. Dani was last. She followed behind, but ended up running into Alek.

"What the hell, Alek?" she said, nearly toppling over in her heels.

He didn't respond.

Dani could see why, the gorgeous Gothic architecture of the old church's interior loomed over her. The brilliant frescoes on the ceiling illuminated by recessed lighting. Over a dozen sculptures floated in mid-air, whatever lines that secured them to the ceiling, invisible to the naked eye. They rotated perfectly in time with one another. It took her a moment, but the longer she stared the more clear it became that they were letters. Letters that spelled out the words; the name of the gallery itself: GALLERY NOCTURNE.

CHAPTER 2

Alek nudged Dani, knocking her out of her trance. The ceiling frescoes, with depictions of raging battles between angels and demons, enthralled her. She found 'old art,' as she liked to call it, mystical. She was no historian, but if Dani had to guess, the old church was at least two hundred years old. That meant someone painted the hundreds of square-feet of ceiling by hand without the help of scissor lifts or laser alignment tools.

The gallery was very crowded; standing room only. Old men dressed in expensive suits meant to impress their dates boasted about their business dealings with one another. Their younger and strikingly beautiful wives or mistresses socialized and gossiped with each other. Dani hadn't seen any displays yet, but the ceiling frescoes and architecture made the building an enormous piece of art on its own. Yet none of the visitors talked about it as they drank expensive cocktails; too caught up in discussions of tax incentives and country club achievements.

Judging by the number of people already inside, Dani guessed that many still standing in the line would be waiting for an awfully long time to enter.

She saw a brochure on the ground at her feet and picked it up quickly before someone stepped on it.

"Follow Paul," Bianca said, and they marched into the crowd like a line of soldier ants heading to battle. Either because of Paul's size or rugged-by-comparison attire, many in the crowd willingly moved out of his way as he created a path for them.

After they had successfully parted the throng, Paul stopped. The rest of The Collective lined up next to him.

They stood in front of a raised platform, a stage, with a white wall behind it. It was well lit, hidden spotlights shining on it like the sun. Next to the stage on both sides were two archways blocked off by red sashes.

"It doesn't look like people are allowed inside yet," Dani said. "Everyone's just waiting here."

Dani pulled out her brochure and opened it up for the group.

Unfolded, it revealed a large map of the gallery in the shape of a cross, the old church had been built in the European style. They currently stood on the long end of the building, near the front entrance to the west. It was further divided into four wings.

The north transept was its own wing, named *The Echoes,* with a poem typed next to its name.

"In the mirror's gaze and echo's call, our truths and whispers find their way to us all," Alek said, reading it aloud. "Sounds cool."

The opposite transept on the south emblazoned with the words *The Veil* and another poem.

"Beneath the veil of night, our dreams weave tales untold, in threads of shadow and light, a tapestry of the soul," Dani read it. "That's where I'm heading."

She smiled.

The apse on the east end, entitled *The Remnants,* was smaller than the others.

"The remnants of the past whisper through time's vast hall, a mosaic of memories, the last standing wall," Paul read its poem for the group. "My kind of place."

The center of the gallery was the largest space on the map with the name *The Horizons.*

"On the brink of the horizon, new thoughts dawn like the sun, casting light on ideas unborn, where endless possibilities run." Bianca read its poem.

"This place is huge," Paul commented. "There's no way we can check it all out in one night."

"I'd have to actually go on a date with that Larry guy if we tried to come back again," Bianca said with disgust.

"Sounds like we have to split up," Paul said. "And I think we each already chose our areas. Unless someone wants to trade?"

Everyone shook their heads.

"After they let us in," Paul continued, he always took command of the situation. "We each get two hours, then meet back in the center."

He perused the map for a moment.

"Here," he pointed to a spot almost dead center of the church.

"Gotcha," Dani said.

The lights everywhere other than the stage dimmed, and the crowd hushed.

Dani, Alek, Paul, and Bianca turned their attention to the platform, where a woman in a beige dress walked to the center. She had short, blond hair and brilliant diamond earrings that hung almost to her shoulders. Thin but healthy looking, she was absolutely elegant. Her head floated as she moved with no bobbing, like a seasoned runway model.

"Ladies and gentlemen," the woman began. She didn't appear to be wearing a microphone, but everyone could hear her voice loud and clear. The old building had been constructed with acoustics in mind, designed for an age before electronics.

"For the few of you who do not already know who I am," she said. "My name is Lady Gianni. I am the owner and director of Gallery Nocturne."

Polite clapping briefly interrupted her.

"Tonight," Lady Gianni continued, the command in her voice evident. "You will find paintings, drawings, sketches, sculptures, and displays that will speak to you in ways you've never experienced before. Every artist, every work here was personally chosen by myself because they have tapped into at least one fundamental aspect of the human spirit."

As she spoke, Lady Gianni glided effortlessly around the stage. Passing by Dani, the younger woman felt butterflies flap wildly in her chest. She wasn't sure if it was the woman's words or allure that put them there; her very presence affected everyone in the room.

"If you walk out of here without feeling anything," said Lady Gianni. "Well then, you might be missing a soul."

The crowd chuckled.

"In this former house of worship," she continued. "We worship something else. In *The Veil*, we pay homage to our dreams and fantasies. *The Remnants* is the realm of reflection of our past. While *The Echoes* explores the intangibility of our very souls. And in *The Horizons*, we look forward to the bright future that awaits us."

Dani felt short of breath, like her heart was swelling and competing for space with her lungs inside her chest.

"I promise you," Lady Gianni said. "You won't find another gallery like Nocturne. The sounds, smells, and textures of each section have been curated specifically to enhance your experience. Art should appeal to more than just one of your senses. I encourage our artists to embrace the avant-garde. Some of the art you will see tonight will push your mind and hearts to their limits. Some of you may even find it disturbing. Do not be afraid, none of it can hurt you.”

She paused for a moment, surveying the room.

“Please, just enjoy yourselves,” she added. “Give in to the emotions that you feel. Let the art take you to new planes of existence you never knew existed before.”

Dani felt like she was speaking directly to her.

“We do not allow photography of any kind inside,” said Lady Gianni. “If you do attempt to take any pictures of this beautiful church or any pieces, you will be asked to leave and your phone confiscated until a member of my staff has deleted them.”

The crowd murmured slightly. Dani knew this was common practice in most galleries, however, from the woman’s tone, it sounded like the Gallery Nocturne took it seriously.

“You won’t need them,” Lady Gianni said. “The art leaves an impression that is best relived through memory. Thank you for coming. Welcome to Gallery Nocturne.”

She nodded to men dressed in black t-shirts next to the archways then waved to the crowd, who applauded her with excitement, before disappearing down the stairs and off stage.

As the densely packed crowd dispersed and formed lines to pass inside, Dani could feel herself able to breathe freely again.

“This is going to be fun,” Paul said before they joined the tidal current of visitors streaming into the open halls.

The entrance to *The Veil* was narrow and brightly lit, an opening no bigger than Dani's shoulders that forced entrants to walk in one at a time. With the habits of the pandemic world still fresh in their psyche, those waiting to enter naturally stood five feet apart in a line.

Dani waited patiently as those in front of her took nervous steps forward and disappeared into the white light. Dissolving into nothing after entering the small space.

When it was her turn, she had to hold her hands above her eyes to shade them.

"1, 2, 3," she counted off in between breaths nervously, then stepped forward into the seemingly impenetrable radiance.

Her eyes took their time adjusting. Slowly, a new world unveiled itself in front of her.

She was standing on a Plexi-glass catwalk. The floor underneath, the walls on her sides, and the ceiling above her consisted of a single, seamless, brilliant white material as smooth as pearl. There were no corners, but the room didn't feel like a cylinder either. With the clear floor, it was like she was walking on clouds high in the sky.

The person in front of her must have ran through it quickly, no one was on the catwalk ahead of her. She took a step and something caught the corner of her eye. She stepped backwards and then forwards, she saw it again.

Standing perfectly still, there was nothing, but when she moved, it would appear. She walked down the catwalk slowly; concentrating on the object.

It was a faint shape in the paint, but not of a different color. Three-dimensional depth that was both clearly there and absent simultaneously. It could have been a bird or a shooting star, its existence too momentary to be observed fully.

Dani remembered the long line to enter behind her and picked up her pace. Giggling as she jogged, more shapes flew by and gave her the sensation of flying in the sky.

At the end of the catwalk was another incredibly bright opening, and she didn't hesitate this time when she went through it; almost hitting it at a run.

She stumbled at the end, not realizing there were several steps down once you went through it. Her balance in sneakers was poor, her balance in high-heels was worse. She felt herself falling forward and braced herself.

To her relief, she landed on something soft. She felt it against her face at first. Opening her eyes, her vision filled with an array of bright green. It was grass, soft, freshly mowed grass.

Hoping no one saw, she quickly stood up and brushed herself off.

Apparently, no one did; the other visitors were lost in the wonders of the hall that reminded Dani of the first candy room from Charlie and the Chocolate Factory.

The Veil was a long hall, easily a hundred feet long and about a third as wide. Narrow and cramped on the brochure map, the space looked deceptively bright and open once inside.

Grass ran the full length and by the smell and feel of it against Dani's face, it was real. There was even a small pond built halfway down where several visitors skipped pebbles. The walls painted in murals of blue sky with wisps of cloud and green rolling hills gave her the impression she had landed in the middle of an immense rural meadow with miles of open land in every direction.

Dani looked to the ceiling, expecting high rafters and rows of LED illumination. Except there was only one light, high in the sky. It was large and round, so bright that Dani had to shield her eyes from its warm rays.

It looked like the sun.

Much like the church, the setting of *The Veil* was one extensive work of art itself, the walls lined with paintings floating on the horizon.

Approaching the first, it depicted an elderly woman resting in a hospital bed. Through the window above her bed, she could see the sun shining over a park with children playing. The sleeping woman had dozens of wires coming out of her, connected to a wall of monitors and machines behind the bed.

Dani stood there just watching, examining each detail of the piece. The brush strokes were exquisite, each one gave a feeling of purposefulness and planned. But something about it bothered her, a detail she couldn't quite put her finger on.

Her heart raced when she realized what it was. The straight lines of the painting were perfect everywhere, except around the window, which had the most subtle of waves and softness to its edge. There was no window. It was like many hospital rooms, more a jail cell than a place of healing. The wall was blank as the others in the painting. The window being just a peek into pleasant dreams of a dying old woman.

Dani scanned the rest of the painting, there were so many other details to explore: the magazine on the chair left by a relative or maybe a friend, the woman's face which was open in either gasp, a scream, or a satisfied final breath. She checked her phone. Almost twenty minutes had already elapsed just staring at this one work and there were at least two dozen left in *The Veil*. She needed to keep moving.

At most art shows, especially the for-profit ones, you'll hear a steady buzz of people chatting quietly in the background. They are usually critics, magazine writers, agents, etc. who are more interested in the business side of the show than the art itself. Not to say they don't appreciate the artistic, but for them, business came first.

Aside from them, you'll also usually find small clusters of people discussing the art with each other. Saying things like "How does this make you feel?" and "Or what do you think the artist was trying to say?".

As Dani cruised from painting to painting on the outer wall, she was stunned by how devoid of voices the hall was. The sounds of buzzing bees and chirping birds were unchallenged as she strolled. Even the grass muffled the footsteps of the onlookers. Everyone in attendance seemed to be happy just enjoying the art, content to stare in silence.

It was a testament to how powerful each piece was.

As she straddled the line between hurrying along and trying to soak in each painting, she noticed the art growing darker. Her emotional responses to each piece shifted to sadness, grief, and longing. She was only halfway down the hall when the light of the artificial sun overhead dimmed. A gray fog had rolled into the sky, dark clouds that blotted out the warming rays.

Dani felt cold, and something else tickled up her spine. It was a twinge of fear.

She quickly understood why. The painting in front of her was no longer a dream. It clearly depicted what could only be a grotesque nightmare.

A naked man on his knees, hunched over the ground, his head buried in his hands, writhing in pain. The skin on his back split open down the spine, long fingernails like claws grasped the flaps and pulled the open wound wide. A face was trying to emerge from inside the person's body. It had no eyes, or mouth, or nose; almost like the painter had given up painting their own nightmare and fled in horror.

Rivers of crimson fell down the person's back and flowed onto the ground.

Dani had dreams like this one her entire life, but like all dreams, it was hard to match up the details exactly with what she stared at now. Staring was the right word, like watching a car accident in slow motion, too afraid to blink and miss a moment.

CRASH!

The room lit up with bright light as a lightning bolt from the ceiling hit the pond. Several women in the gallery let out startled shrieks. It scared away the sounds of the birds and the bees. The pitter-patter of rain engulfed the hall.

Blotted out by the clouds of the rainstorm, the warming rays of the sun were nothing but memories.

It wasn't really raining. Dani could see the raindrops falling from the sky, but none of them ever reached the ground or her. They seemed to evaporate just a few feet above her head, but she could see them. It was a brilliant spectacle of artistic ingenuity.

Very thin strings of LED lights hung from invisible wires in the ceiling, so thin they were completely translucent under the sun and with the rain they were...

"Enjoying *The Veil*?" she heard a voice next to her.

Dani almost jumped out of her skin. If her body hadn't been frozen in place, she would have collapsed to the ground.

"Sorry to startle you," the voice said. "I forget how easy it is to get lost in the art sometimes."

"You're, you're," Dani stammered.

"Lady Gianni," the woman said. Dani had gotten a good look at her on the front stage, and she looked even more beautiful and radiant up close.

Dani would have replied if she could just remember how to speak again.

"And you are?" Lady Gianni said, facing her and holding out her hand.

"I'm Dani," she replied after a long pause. That took more effort than she realized.

She shook Lady Gianni's hand, which was small and petite compared to Dani's.

"What do you think of my body?" Lady Gianni asked, returning her gaze to the painting.

Why on earth would she ask me that?! Dani's mind raced to think of something, anything, that would be appropriate.

Then her eyes glanced at the placard under the painting.

My Body.

The artist's name was not listed.

Dani breathed a sigh of relief.

"I, uh," she struggled to find something profound. "I like it."

"You like it?" Lady Gianni said, slight confusion in her voice.

"Yes," Dani responded, wanting to kick herself for not thinking of something clever.

"The artist had hoped to unearth a more complex response than that," Lady Gianni commented, placing her hand to her face.

"I mean," Dani stuttered. "I like that the creature inside is able to come out. Like it belongs in the world, like it deserves to have a face of its own. Maybe even a name."

"Go on," Lady Gianni said, her lips curved into the most subtle of smiles.

"I guess," Dani continued. "There's someone inside all of us trying to get out, and maybe our dreams are the only time they get to."

"Or maybe our nightmares," Lady Gianni added.

Dani nodded, doing her best to keep her eyes on the painting and not the beautiful woman next to her.

"Tell me Dani," the woman said. "Are you enjoying the storm?"

"I am," Dani said. "It's amazing."

"I find my own dreams sometimes take a darker turn to nightmares," Lady Gianni continued. "As fast as a thunderstorm hitting on a warm summer's day."

A loud crack of thunder rang through the room.

"It feels almost real," said Dani.

"Almost real?" Lady Gianni asked with a smirk. "We don't do almost at the Gallery Nocturne."

"I mean it feels like a real storm," Dani added quickly. "Even the walls look like rain is falling on them."

"Touch one," Lady Gianni commanded.

"What?" Dani said, confused.

"Touch the wall," Lady Gianni repeated.

She couldn't explain it, but apprehension filled her mind, freezing her movements. As if discovering the secret behind the art would somehow ruin the dreamlike wonder that was embedded into every detail of *The Veil*.

"Touch the wall Dani," Lady Gianni said again, her voice more forceful in Dani's ears.

She didn't want to do it, but she also felt like she had to, no matter what.

Reaching out with one hand, she touched the tips of her middle and pointer fingers to the wall. She expected to feel cold glass to her touch, or maybe the soft liquid of an LCD screen.

She felt neither. Pulling her fingers away, she held their tips close to her eyes. Beads of water clung to them, cold liquid water as fresh as an actual storm.

"How did you do that?" Dani asked.

But there was no one there to listen. When Dani turned back, Lady Gianni was gone.

The pattering of rain slowed, a few sparse rays of sun emerged from the ceiling onto the meadow. One ray shined on Dani, and cast a shadow onto the painting of the beast tearing itself out of the person's body, *My Body*.

Dani didn't get to finish viewing the rest of the art in *The Veil*. They were all too good to rush through. However, she had run out of time, so she exited through the illuminated doorway at the end of the hall. Unlike the entrance, the exit was rather abrupt. Re-emerging into the main gallery felt like waking abruptly from a dream after having cold water splashed on your face.

The Horizons hall buzzed with the voice of the bustling visitors. Unlike *The Veil*, this large central space was an open plan with several diagonally arranged walls about ten feet high, each featuring one or two paintings, photos, or sketches. From the ceiling, where the fresco demons and angels looked down, the scene might have looked like a swarming beehive.

Dani saw Bianca first. She was talking to an older gentleman. She approached slowly, not wanting to interrupt.

"Dani, come here," Bianca said excitedly, noticing her. "Let me introduce you to my new friend. Jeremiah, this is Dani, Dani, this is Jeremiah."

"Pleasure to meet you," Dani said, shaking his hand.

He seemed slightly put off. Maybe her larger than expected hands had surprised him. Or maybe it was something else. His eyes seemed to look over Dani's shoulder at someone beyond her.

"Jeremiah Henricks," he said, letting go of hers quickly.

"She's an artist too," Bianca said, her charming smile on full display. "Beautiful flowers and sunsets."

"I'm sure it's wonderful," Jeremiah said in a suddenly rushed tone. "I fear I must be going. It was lovely to have met you, Bianca."

He said it almost nervously.

"You as well, Dani," he added.

He shuffled off quickly past them and into the crowd.

"Damn," Bianca said, letting out a big breath. "That guy was something. He runs some global conglomerate, has a huge art collection too. Says he takes a particular interest in young new artists like myself."

"I'm sure he was very interested in your art," Dani said sarcastically.

Bianca winked back at her.

"Well, that was something," Paul said, walking up to join them. "I don't know how to describe it. It was pretty awesome."

"So was mine," Dani replied. "Felt like I was walking through a dream and then there was a storm."

"A storm?" Paul asked.

"Didn't you hear the thunder crack?" said Dani. "It was as loud as the real thing."

"Nothing," replied Paul. "It was quiet in *The Remnants*, not a sound other than the person next to you."

"Alek, over here," Bianca yelled at the youngest of the group, who seemed to look confused as he wandered *The Horizons* gallery looking for them.

"Sorry I'm late," Alek said as he approached. "I lost track of the time in there."

"What was *The Echoes* like?" Dani asked, excited to learn more.

"I can't, I can't explain it," Alek replied. "It was beyond description. Are you guys ready to go? I need to get back to my work. I have so many ideas."

"Slow down, speed racer," Paul said. "We got one more to go."

Indeed, they did. There was a thick wall of people surrounding the central piece of *The Horizons* hall. So thick that they could only see part of the main attraction.

Paul led the way as they jostled their way towards the front. It was more difficult this time than it had been in the crowd by the stage, but not because people were pushing back. Most people didn't even notice their approach. Instead, they stood motionless, unmoving, zombified; their eyes glued to the central piece.

Paul worked his magic, and eventually they found the front where they joined the entranced masses.

The sculpture was a long oval basin built into a stone platform, maybe nine or ten feet long and about six feet wide. It was impossible to determine its depth as it was filled with a thick black liquid with small bubbles oozing on the surface. Emerging from the liquid was the figure of a man, reaching up towards a green branch that hung from the ceiling. Coated in the black substance, every so often a drop would slowly form from his outstretched arm and fall to the basin floor with a loud, rhythmic plopping sound. It took her a few minutes to recognize the smell. The substance was oil, and the man was drowning in it.

Dani examined his face. The thick, viscous liquid clogged his eyes, ears, mouth, and nose. There was a visible scar running down his cheek, the ridges of it glistening in the overhead lights.

It was a brilliant piece, whomever had made it was truly gifted. Dani looked down at the placard at the base, eager to discover the name of this master of sculpture, but no artist was included. Instead, only the piece's title was listed. It read:

Consume

High above Dani, Paul, Bianca, and Alek, perched on metal scaffolding amongst the spotlights, was a brown owl. It watched the members of The Collective carefully with obsidian eyes.

CHAPTER 3

Dani stirred as the morning sun reached her bed. Most people like her, who were not morning people, would install blackout curtains over their windows to avoid this. Unfortunately for Dani, the window where the sun came through was a bright skylight that illuminated the entire warehouse that housed The Collective.

Checking her phone, she had an hour before she had to leave for work. She grabbed her toiletry bag, picked an outfit, and slipped on flip-flops before heading out her bedroom door. Shoes were a safety precaution. The downstairs stairwell designed for industrial workers in steel-toed boots was sharp with rusty grates.

The warehouse had been Paul's idea; a place where artists ate, slept, socialized, created, and displayed together. He joked that *Dandelions in the Fall* (his most famous piece) paid for the space. He had gotten a good deal on the property since the warehouse district had fallen on hard times in the wake of the last recession.

The group had each painted or sprayed the exterior walls of the old warehouse in their own style. It was a bright cornucopia of color in a sea of drab red brick buildings next to the shipyard.

"Good morning," Dani said, reaching the bottom floor.

Paul was sitting on the couch near the front entrance, working on his laptop. He just waved back, his brow furled into an expression that indicated he was concentrating on something important, probably going over the plans for their next 'field trip' scheduled for that night.

"I got the shower for fifteen," she yelled.

"All yours," Paul yelled back.

She appreciated him. She was forever in his debt, after all.

Dani was happy to be there, happier than she had ever been in her entire life. Her parents acted loving when she was a child, but high school was a difficult time for all of them. They didn't speak anymore. Dani had been on her own since she before she turned eighteen. It had been tough, jumping from displaced teen halfway house to halfway house.

When Paul had come in for a mocha latte, it was an incredible twist of fate in her favor. That was over a year ago. This was the longest she had lived in one place since leaving her parents. She loved it at The Collective. There were only a few hiccups, her hopeless preoccupation with her roommate Bianca being one.

The downstairs space was part studio, part gallery. Bianca worked in the center of the room on one of her color field paintings; it had the best light. It was a style that Dani didn't quite understand, but it was popular. Bianca's never seemed to have any issues with selling them.

That morning, Bianca sat elegantly stroking her paintbrush onto a canvas made up of circles, squares, and triangles. Her long hair hung past the seat of the stool, She wore nothing but overalls, which left little to Dani's surging imagination.

Dani hustled through the locker room door before Bianca noticed her staring.

The building itself was the perfect place for them to set up shop. Upstairs were a half dozen offices that they converted into bedrooms for each artist. There were two toilets, one upstairs and one downstairs, and then a separate locker room in the basement with private showers.

The water was cold at first; it took a bit of time for it to warm up because of the old industrial water heater. Dani leaned against the wall, a towel wrapped around her.

She thought back to the last halfway house she had stayed at, where some girl fresh out of juvie had taken umbrage with her simply for the way she looked and tried to smash her head in against the shower tiles. Dani had fought back before the other girls separated them, but it was too late. She was gone the next day, on her way to another home. Dani was always the one who had to leave when this kind of thing happened, and it always happened to her.

Even at The Collective, a safe place for her, she did not let her guard down. She did not enjoy being naked, the feeling itself made her feel too vulnerable. An inadequacy from her lack of feminine features that she had lived with her whole life. A stark comparison to Bianca, who flaunted her body, clothed and unclothed, whenever she wished.

Steam billowed out from above the shower curtain and Dani stepped inside before pulling off her towel and hanging it on the peg outside.

Feeling the hot water run down her head and body, she tried to think about what she was going to work on later that night. She had just finished her latest painting, a wildflower patch growing through cracks in the pavement between two concrete buildings. Now she needed to be inspired. A fresh idea. Maybe she'd think of something while at work.

Dani hadn't grown up an artist, earning a meager few awards in elementary school art classes, but they were hollow, meaningless merits. Every kid eventually got awards for their work in art class at that level. The teacher had a round robin system of handing them out. Neither her parents nor art teachers thought she was capable of anything other than mediocrity.

In a way, they were right.

Dani was by far the least talented artist at The Collective. Paul is, or rather was, a gifted genius. Bianca obviously had enough talent to get her own shows. And Alek's would be prolific if he actually released the hundreds of works in progress hiding in his room.

Finishing her shower, she hurried back upstairs. Alek's door was closed like always, but the bright light on inside meant he was working on something.

He liked to work in his room alone, Dani would get a glimpse inside every so often. Alek, who had spent years alone on the streets, refused to opt for a bed and slept on a beat up red couch they had found on the side of the road one day. He said it gave him more room to work. Canvases hung all around the room. Some were just blank, with no paint applied at all. Reserved for concepts he was not ready to begin.

Dani finished getting dressed, nothing fancy, jeans and a blouse was all. Working at a coffee shop didn't require that much.

"Everyone downstairs!" Dani heard Paul yell.

She groaned, hoping she could sneak away to work before he had the chance to brief them on their next 'field trip'.

She passed by Paul's studio on the way to the stairs.

Paul didn't produce anymore. After his initial success, he tried to hit it big again, but the art community would lambast everything he made. The most voracious of which was the critic Theo Argent. A picture of whom Paul left pinned to a dartboard on the wall. The squirrelly looking man with flat hair and square glasses had several darts embedded into his prominent nose.

These days, Paul cared about two things and two things only. The first being, he had a personal crusade against any corporation that polluted the environment. No one quite knew why. Dani thought maybe it was because he just loved nature, much of his original success being simple works of flowers and lakes. However, intuition told her something else may have fueled his raw fanaticism for environmentalist causes.

His other love was The Collective, where he managed the books, the shows, and most importantly, the sales. Selling their art online, he handled each artist's individual pay-outs, and made the business run smoothly so the others could focus on their creativity.

He was pretty good at it. The shows were fun, gritty parties in a dangerous part of town attracted thrill seeking yuppies with loads of cash. But the internet was where he sold a majority of their work. There was a large secure storage area under the warehouse where he kept a lot of their paintings, including Dani's. He was the only one with a key. He could be a little paranoid, but that was just how it worked at The Collective.

Downstairs Alek, Bianca, and Paul stood around the table that doubled as their dining room most nights. Papers were scattered on top of it. Dani dreaded it but she knew exactly what this was about.

"Can this wait? I'm going to be late for..." Dani said as she reached the bottom of the stairs.

"It can't," Paul said dryly, ignoring her. "The caffeine addicts will have to live with their espressos being a few minutes behind schedule. I'll give you a ride in the van. Come on."

Dani knew better than to argue with him and joined them at the table.

Front and center was a newspaper page with a big headline across the top: 'ENVIRONMENTAL THINK TANK REPORT SHOWS BIG OIL NOT THE CAUSE OF GLOBAL WARMING'.

"You see, this is the problem," Paul said, jabbing at the article with his finger. "This is why we are doing this."

"Because you read a newspaper?" Bianca asked.

"Since when do you read newspapers?" Alek added.

"What's a newspaper?" Dani joked.

Paul held back his temper.

"They delivered it to our door by mistake," Paul said. "It doesn't matter. I looked into it this morning. This is just another PR stunt by Summit Petroleum. The whole think tank is funded and staffed by their scientists. Their stock is up 10% and they just issued a press release yesterday saying they were going to open up another refinery."

He caught his breath.

"So we're going through with it, then?" Alek asked.

"Absolutely," Paul replied. "Tonight, we're going to go in there and make them pay."

"Are you sure this is a good idea?" Dani questioned. "We're just a bunch of artists. What can we really do?"

Paul gave her a dull stare.

"You're right," he began. "We are just a bunch of artists. We try to impact the world with paint and canvas. But what if we could do more, much more? Summit Petroleum is literally profiting off the wholesale rape of mother nature. I got us the site map. I know the guard schedule; if we stick to the plan, no one is going to be there. We get in, sabotage the place, get out before anyone is the wiser."

Dani had her apprehensions. She loved the environment as much as anyone. She didn't own a car, hating how those things damaged the planet, and was vegan. However, her desire to avoid ending up in jail surpassed those convictions.

"I can't tonight," Bianca said. "I have a date."

"A date that's more important than this?" Paul said with frustration clear in his voice.

"Actually, yes," she replied in her tone that showed there was no way in hell she was going to go.

Paul clutched at the bridge of his nose.

"What about you Dani?" Paul said, turning to her.

"I don't think I should," she replied tentatively. "This is bigger than just some march or rally. We could be arrested."

"We won't be," Paul said, putting his hands on her shoulders. "I've got it all planned out, every angle accounted for. I just need you there to keep the van running until Alek and I are done."

"I don't know," Dani waffled.

"Dani, please," he pleaded. "I need you."

Dani didn't want to go. She trusted Paul's plan, but the risk just felt too great. Then again, if it wasn't for him, she'd still be out there fending for her life at the halfway houses. She didn't want to disappoint him; he did save her after all.

"Ok, I'll go," she said.

"Thank you," Paul said. "Let's go over it one more time."

Paul's van ran on vegetable oil recycled from local restaurants, a fact he was very proud of.

"It's the only carbon neutral fuel around," he would remind her every time he gave her a ride. It also stank to high heaven, but if she didn't get a ride now, she'd be really late to work.

As they puttered out of the roll-up door and onto the road, Paul halted the vehicle.

"There it is again," Paul said, looking into the sky.

Dani looked up too.

"What is it?" She asked, seeing the strange shadow perched on the building across from them.

"An owl, I think," he replied. "Big sucker too. I've seen him every day for the last week."

"Don't owls sleep during the day?" Dani questioned.

"I don't know," said Paul. "Maybe ones in the city don't."

He put the car back into gear and they continued down the road.

"Paul," Dani began, almost afraid to ask.

"I'm sorry I had to ask you, but with Bianca bowing out, I didn't have any options," Paul said, anticipating her question. "It is important to me that we do more than just make art."

"No," Dani clarified. "Not that, I understand. I'm going."

"What is it then?" Paul asked.

"Have any more sold?" Dani's question hung in the van's air.

Paul seemed to mull in his mind how to respond.

"Not quite," Paul answered.

"Not a single one?" She asked, holding back the tears forming in her eyes. She didn't want to ruin her mascara.

"I'm afraid not," he didn't take as long to answer this time. "It's just a weird time of year. You'll bounce back in the summer."

Dani put her head down, not wanting him to see her cry.

"I haven't sold anything at all this year," she said. "Maybe I should give it up."

"No!" Paul said immediately. "You can't. You're too good to put it down."

"You're the only person who thinks that," Dani said. "Hell, Bianca's kindergarten shapes sell more than me. What if I'm not any good?"

"You'll get there," Paul said, rubbing her shoulder. "It just takes longer for some."

Dani stared at her feet.

"I believe in you," Paul said. "I've believed in you since the day I saw you in that coffee shop. You are an amazing artist. The world will figure that out too one day."

"Thank you," Dani said, wiping away a tear.

The van's brakes squealed as it came to a stop.

"Made it," Paul said triumphantly.

Dani opened the car door, nearly knocking over the fold-out chalk sign for ESPRESSO EXPRESSIONS.

"Damnit," she cursed to herself.

"Hey," Paul said, his voice calm and collected. "You got a job to do tonight. Focus on that. I'll work on getting your stuff sold."

"Alright," Dani replied. "Thank you for the ride."

"See you tonight," Paul replied with a wink.

She closed the car door, and the van emitted a putrid smell of burning oil as it disappeared around the next corner.

Dani took a deep breath before stepping towards the coffee shop door, but something was in the corner of her eye that made her stop in her tracks.

There it was again, the owl.

It perched on a telephone pole, staring at her.

She pulled out her phone to take a picture. Was it the same one from the warehouse that just followed them there?

Then she noticed the time and realized she was late.

"Shit," she said and walked inside.

CHAPTER 4

Working at Espresso Expressions was not a bad gig. After the morning rush was over and the day slowed down, all she had to do was make the occasional drink, help customers figure out the Wi-Fi password (it was BrewtifulVibes), and wipe down the tables. When those three things didn't demand her attention, she would grab the chalk pencils and draw on the menu wall behind her.

There was only one other person in the shop. Dani could tell she was a mother preparing for a virtual job interview for a couple of reasons. First, her phone wallpaper was pictures of her children. Second, she dressed in a nice top with her makeup and hair done up; but she wore sweat pants with sneakers. And lastly she asked for help with the Wi-Fi twice (Dani really needed to suggest to management they change it to something easier to spell). Despite how visibly nervous the woman was, she was still very nice to Dani, so she wished her good luck on getting the job.

Dani went to work on the menu board that plastered the back wall, standing on a steel step stool with her knees resting on the counter. She carefully wiped away her drawings from last week, an ivy border. Then thought for a moment about what to replace it with.

Maybe Roses, no, definitely not. They were thorny, temperamental and difficult.

Tulips sounded nice. Then again, tulips were so easy to draw that she could do it almost with her eyes closed.

She needed something else, something more challenging.

Then it caught her eye.

One of the other baristas had left flyers on the counter advertising for a Chinese New Year Festival at the cultural center downtown. The management didn't strictly allow advertising at the shop like this, but they also couldn't afford to pay much in wages either, so they turned a blind eye to workers who tried to promote their side gigs while on the clock.

In the flyer, a beautiful red, yellow, and silver dragon puppet weaved across the page. The feet of the puppeteers were visible underneath it, their pants adorned with stringy, white tassels. Below the dragon was a snapshot picture of an Asian-looking temple. Springing up its pillars were green vines with tiny purple, lavender, and cobalt flowers bunched like foam accumulating on the crest of a wave.

She had to use her phone to find its name; it was Wisteria.

"Challenge accepted," Dani said out loud as she taped the flyer to the board and drew.

The vines were the simple part. It was those hundreds of little flowers on each bunch that took the longest. She had another few hours on her shift, plenty of time to finish.

The woman in the shop must have started her interview, Dani could hear her speaking in business jargon, words about forecasting and sales projections that meant little to her uneducated mind. Dani never much cared for the world business. All she wanted to do with her life was draw and paint.

The soft acoustic guitar playing on the speakers filled her mind with notes as she just let the images flow onto the board. When she entered the artistic zone, she didn't have to concentrate. The part of her mind controlling her hand would go on auto-pilot while the rest of her brain would wander off on its own.

Right now there was only one thing on her mind, the 'field trip' for that evening to Summit Petroleum. Paul had been planning it for months, while Dani and had put together every excuse they could think of not to go. However, something in that newspaper article triggered Paul and there was no more delaying the inevitable.

She was reaching near the top of the menu board to finish a few details on a leaf when Dani heard the ding of the front door.

"Be right with you," she said to the person who had just entered.

"Take your time," a soft voice responded.

Dani finished the leaf and began to step down off the short stool. Somehow in the process, her foot got caught, and it tipped. She could feel herself falling in slow motion.

"Ouch," Dani yelled, landing on the rubber mat floor with a thud. It wasn't anything serious, just a sore lower back that didn't hurt nearly as much as her injured pride.

"Are you alright?" The customer asked.

"I'm fine," Dani said, standing up and rubbing her spine. "What can I..." The words hung in the air.

Lady Gianni from Gallery Nocturne was standing in front of the glass counter filled with baked items, peering down at the selection. She wore a gray pantsuit with a shirt underneath and white designer high heels.

Dani quickly brushed the chalk from her apron.

"Hello ma'am," Dani said, standing up straight behind the counter. "What can I get for you?"

"I'm not sure yet," Lady Gianni said, clearly not recognizing Dani from the night before. Maybe it was better that way. "I was thinking something sweet."

"The Danishes are vegan," Dani began, figuring that someone with such a fine figure as Lady Gianni probably didn't eat animal products. "The muffins are as well, freshly baked by a shop down the street."

"I think I'll have a blueberry scone," said Lady Gianni.

"Great choice," Dani said. "Though I'm partial to cranberry myself."

She pulled the pastry with the tongs from the display case.

"Can I warm that up for you?" Dani asked.

"Yes, please," Lady Gianni replied.

Dani did her best to smile naturally. Lady Gianni still hadn't recognized her as far as she could tell.

She popped the scone into the warming oven.

"What about something to drink?" Dani said.

"A regular coffee with cream would be fine," said the art director.

Pouring her a cup, Dani did her best to etch a little flower with the little cream pour into the top.

Lady Gianni didn't even look at it, opting to put a lid on her little personalized piece of art immediately. She held out her credit card and Dani ran the payment. She handed her card and receipt back to her.

"Thank you for coming into Espresso Expressions today," Dani said as cheerfully as she could muster. "We hope to see you again."

"And do you like working at Espresso Expressions, Dani?" Lady Gianni asked.

The woman's eyes met Dani's for the first time. They were the most unique shade of emerald Dani had ever seen before.

"Um," Dani sputtered, surprised. "I guess so. The people are nice and it's not too stressful."

"So you don't like to be challenged then?" Lady Gianni asked. She was examining Dani closely.

Dani's throat swelled as she panicked.

"No, not at all," she said. "I love challenges."

"Where do you paint and draw?" Lady Gianni asked again quickly.

"At my studio near the shipyards," Dani replied, just as swiftly.

"And how long have you been drawing?" The art director questioned.

"Since I was a little girl," Dani replied.

Lady Gianni gave her a raised eyebrow.

Shit, Dani thought to herself. Every little girl draws. She meant how long had I been drawing serious art.

"I mean," Dani tried to clarify. "I started drawing stuff like this about two years..."

"Did you draw all of these?" Lady Gianni interrupted her, gesturing with her hand towards the various drawings throughout the café. The owners had agreed to put up a few of Dani's works around, mostly because she offered to them for free.

Dani had always harbored a dream that some art agent would walk in, notice them, and inquire who the brilliant artist that made them was.

Lady Gianni floated over to the nearest one. It was of a sunset over the water. The city flanking the sun as it disappeared over the horizon.

Dani waited, wondering if she should say something. Should she mention she was already part of an art collective? Divulge to Lady Gianni that actual sales of her work were abysmal? Should she reveal every deepest, darkest secret she still clings to?

Her anxiety was trying to take the reins.

The woman had an aura that engulfed you, muddling your brain until you weren't sure if it was a dream or a reality.

Lady Gianni stood in front of the ing a long time before moving to the next. An old man fishing off the dock in the harbor.

It was based on a real person, someone who Dani had seen out the window at The Collective angling into the muddy water of the bay every day. She had studied him for weeks, he of course, being completely unaware he had been sitting for his . He never caught anything, not in any of the times she watched, but he still returned every day without fail. Well, at least he used to. It had been a month since she last saw him.

She wondered if he had given up on fishing in that spot, but that didn't seem like the right . When you paint someone, you learn every little detail of their entire being. Those little details give away who the person deep inside is. She knew the old man had ironclad determination. The only thing that would have stopped him was death.

"Your drawings are," Lady Gianni said. Dani hung on that last word like a drowning person clinging to a flotation device.

"Charming," Lady Gianni continued.

Dani could breathe again.

Charming wasn't what she had been hoping to hear, but it was better than a long list of alternatives that had gone through her mind.

"I'm glad you like them," Dani said, feeling the satisfaction run through them.

"I didn't say that," Lady Gianni replied. "I said they were charming, which they are. Perfect for little coffee shops that sell stale baked goods and overpriced coffee."

The lump forming in Dani's throat was almost choking her.

"But you have potential," said Lady Gianni. "I'll give you that."

"Thank you," Dani said, not sure if that was the right response.

"," the woman clarified. "I expect your arrival at eleven am tomorrow morning. Do not make me wait."

Dani couldn't speak. She was far too confused.

Lady Gianni left the coffee shop, leaving her coffee and scone behind.

"Congratulations," said the other coffee shop visitor, the mother on the job interview, placing her empty coffee cup and tray onto the counter.

Dani almost jumped, startled by the stranger who had approached without her noticing.

"For what?" Dani asked.

"Well, forgive me for listening in," the woman replied. "But that sounded to me like a job interview. And based on how it ended, you got the job."

She left the shop soon after, leaving Dani alone.

The only thing Dani could think about the rest of the day was, "What job?"

CHAPTER 5

Larry Sellers's head pounded as the bright light of the sun burst through the blackout curtains of his double wide. He reached for his phone but couldn't find it on his bedside table, knocking over half-drunk beer cans and an ashtray to the ground.

"Shit," he yelled, not that there was anyone there to hear him.

It was his mother's place, at least it had been. She had passed away, leaving it to him. It was one of two things she had left him, a double-wide and a stockpile of Marlboro Reds.

After his night shift at the gallery, he had stayed up hoping that the little tease who he had let in would have called him. He should have known better. Hell, she hadn't even told him her name. Disappearing inside with her friends before Larry could ask it.

Larry walked to the refrigerator, all ten steps that it took from his bed, and opened it, finding it mostly empty except for a few cans of beer left over from the 30-pack he had grabbed on his way home. He popped one and chugged it. Nothing like the hair of the dog to get your brain functioning again.

He found his phone on the counter, 1% battery left. Emergency battery saver mode on.

Twelve missed calls from his boss, Tom, and he was over three hours late for his shift at the Gallery Nocturne.

The screen went black as it died, the last bit of electricity inside used up in just turning the bastard on. He had no idea where the charger was.

Shit, he couldn't even call in sick.

Larry considered knocking on one of his neighbor's doors and asking to use their phone, but knew better. They would no doubt recognize him from the sex offender notice that was mailed to everyone in a few square mile radius when he had moved in. One of those laws designed to inform the community but also made it near impossible for him to find a job. Being an ex-con was difficult enough, being an ex-con sex offender was near impossible.

He knew only one neighbor who might help him, the crazy gun-lover next door. However, he also owed the man money, something Larry wasn't able to repay yet.

The only option was to walk the mile and a half to the convenience store and use their pay phone. He owed it to Tom at least, after all the man had done for him.

Putting his jacket on and pulling the hood over his head, he ventured out his door and down the road.

He had met Tom a few years back, part of a parolees job placement program. Though they had both served time at the penitentiary upstate, Tom had been out almost ten years and was now one of those rare success stories. Someone who had beaten the system and was living a normal life.

Larry had only been out of prison over a year and if his mother hadn't passed and left him the home, he probably would have done something stupid to get himself sent back.

He didn't serve time for doping, but it was a problem he developed while on the inside. You'd be surprised how easy it was to get drugs in prison in exchange for goods or services.

Several welfare moms shut the curtains of their windows as they saw him walk past. As if Larry would suddenly drop his trousers and swing his dick around at the sight of a child. He had been that stupid once, many years ago. Stalking that poor teenage girl and then assaulting her while fueled by cheap vodka and cocaine. But he had served his time. He felt he deserved a clean slate.

Walking out the front gates of Sunny Meadows mobile home park, he hit the main road. The park nestled itself in the shadow of an affluent neighborhood, only separated by a short greenway and a row of tall, bushy trees. Most of the families that lived in the neighborhood of upper middle-class houses never even knew Sunny Meadows existed. There was never a reason to go further up the road unless you took a wrong turn, then you'd known in an instant that you weren't in Kansas anymore.

Larry walked down the sidewalk, vapor escaping from his mouth with each breath in the chilly air. Placing his hands in his pockets for warmth, he thought, "Damn, I forgot my smokes at the house," then shrugged—he could always pick up another pack when he got there.

The sidewalks of the neighborhood were freshly manicured, their winter rye grass mowed tightly to the edges of the concrete. Signs with the words "Home Sweet Home" hung from the porch awnings.

He was crossing the street when a strange sound caught his attention. It sounded like a bird, an owl most likely, high in one of the trees. It was hooting and hollering up a storm.

He stopped to look for it, holding his hand over his eyes to shade them from the bright morning sun.

Larry didn't notice the minivan barreling down the street.

He only saw it after he heard the screech of the brakes and the squeal of tires.

It was too late; it was sliding on the wet road.

Larry froze in place, watching his death approach in slow motion right before his eyes.

The van hit him in the leg and knocked him to the ground, but the rest of the vehicle came to a stop before he could be run over.

Larry lay on the ground not moving, his chest heaving, as little clouds puffed out of his mouth like an old-fashioned locomotive.

It was hard for him to tell how long he lay there, the minivan still running just a few feet away.

"Oh my god," said a brown-haired woman emerging from the passenger side of the car. She was probably in her mid-40s. She looked fit and athletic for her age. "Are you ok, sir?"

"I'm fine," Larry said, standing up and brushing off his pant legs. "Just pushed me a little, landed on my ass."

"Should I call 911? Get an ambulance?" She asked. "Do you have a concussion?"

Larry wanted to laugh. He had endured much worse while in prison. By comparison, this was a gentle love nudge.

"I really am fine," he replied.

"I'm so sorry," the woman continued. "It's my teenage daughter. We were just trying to do a quick driving lesson, and we started talking and you know, you look away from the road for one second and..."

Her frantic voice trailed off.

"I promise I'm ok," Larry said. "No harm, no foul..."

Larry got a look at the young girl sitting behind the wheel of the minivan. She couldn't have been more than fifteen years old with long brown hair, just as pretty and attractive as her mother.

"Please don't press charges," the woman pleaded. "She's not technically old enough to be driving yet. She doesn't even have her learner's permit. I just thought it couldn't hurt for a quick lesson around the neighborhood while it was quiet out."

Larry's mind ticked back into gear. His attention shot back to the mother.

"I understand," he said.

The woman began rummaging in her purse, tearing a piece of paper out of a notebook and writing on it with a pen.

"Here's my name, phone number, and address," the woman said, handing it to him.

He took the paper and stared back at it, not sure why she had given it to him.

"If you feel sick or hurt," she said, looking nervous. "Please call and talk to us first before going to the police. We can arrange something."

"Sure thing," Larry said with a nod.

"Thank you so much," the woman said, smiling.

Larry smiled and made his way to the sidewalk.

The woman got back into her van and Larry heard the gear shift move into drive.

Larry looked back at them and waved.

The woman in the passenger seat waved back at him, but he didn't notice. He could only focus on watching the girl in the driver's seat. The girl was white as a sheet and looked like she had just seen a ghost.

It reminded him of someone.

The van pulled away and was soon out of sight.

Larry looked down at the scrap of paper in his hand: 'Patti Johnson 3493 W. Oak Ln. 555-9203'.

He put it into his pocket.

It was another mile to the convenience store. He walked quietly with his head down. His mind focused on the face of that teenage girl. The resemblance was uncanny. She looked just like the girl who was the reason he spent four years of his life in prison.

Of course, that girl had been blond with blue eyes, but it was the facial expression that drew the parallel between the two. That look of existential fear a person had when they realized they were completely and utterly helpless. It always came after they pleaded for their life, as if their words gave up the last shreds of hope they had of safely returning home. Then came their tears.

He tried to force the thoughts out of his head, but every time he did, they only dug in deeper. He had been out for a year; going back was not an option. Going back meant only suffering and death, of course being on the outside wasn't too much different.

Arriving at the convenience store, he went to the pay phone on the side and slid in the coins from his pocket. There was a man leaning against the wall nearby smoking a cigarette, which only made him want to go in and buy a fresh pack more.

He put his fingers to the pay phone buttons, then realized he didn't know the number for the gallery or Tom. It was programmed into his phone, which was dead back in the doublewide.

"Shit," he said aloud.

He hung up and pulled the returned coins from the dispenser.

"That kind of day, huh?" The man smoking the cigarette asked.

"You have no idea," Larry replied, wishing the face of the girl in the minivan wasn't still playing on a loop in his brain.

"You need a little help with that?" The cigarette man asked.

Larry looked at him.

"You got anything to help me sleep?" asked Larry.

CHAPTER 6

Hank Marlowe was determined to not screw it up this time. It was his fifth placement in as many months with the security staffing agency, and that typically meant it was the final straw or else they'd let him go. He couldn't help that people didn't like the way he looked, but he also couldn't afford to lose this job.

Despite over two decades in private security, work was tougher than ever to find. Younger men were applying for the same jobs and willing to work for less. Adding to the challenge, Hank had a big black mark on his record for breaking protocol one time, and suddenly he found himself having to take whatever jobs he could get his hands on.

He drove his beat up old Toyota Camry to the front gate of Summit Petroleum's refinery. A kind-eyed old black man peered at him out the window, as Hank pulled out his driver's license and showed it to him.

"I'm Hank," he said out his window. A faint dribble of rain fell from the darkened sky. "I'm the new guard."

"Nice to meet you, Hank," the man said. "I'm Terrance. I'll be getting you started tonight. Go ahead and park out behind the guardhouse over there."

Inside the guardhouse, it was warm and toasty. There were about fifteen black and white CCTV monitors on the wall above a desk, along with an antiquated 16" television with an internal slot for VHS tapes.

"Nice setup," Hank half-joked.

"You kidding me?" Terrance said. "I've seen liquor stores with better security cameras. Fact is, this place is forty years old. They won't spend a dime on renovations until the government tells them they have to."

"I just thought an oil refinery job would have a bit more to it," Hank replied.

"Nah," Terrance said, waving his arm. "There's nothing to this place. I've been here twenty years and not once has there ever been an incident. We're too far away from anywhere with people for it to be a bother. Consider this the most boring job on the planet."

"I'm good with boring," Hank said.

"I bet," said Terrance. "I read your background. I know what happened."

"Let me explain," said Hank.

"No need." Terrance didn't let him finish. "As far as I'm concerned, you were the victim. Just some underpaid security guard trying to do his job to stop some gang banging shoplifter. It was a damn shame that you got blamed for that bastard shooting up that store like he did. You were just trying to stop him from stealing, what was it?"

"A case of beer," Hank said solemnly.

"And from that scar on your face," Terrance continued. "I see you paid your dues. You didn't deserve to be sued."

"Violating protocol, they said," Hank added.

"You did what you thought was right," Terrance said. "That's good enough for me. I think here you'll find none of that crap to worry about."

"Good," Hank said with a sigh of relief.

Terrance had read Hank's file, but he wouldn't know what else had happened. How his lawyer had recommended he and his wife get a paper divorce.

"It would protect your house and cars from being taken from you in the lawsuit," the lawyer convinced him. "It would protect your family."

Except that after the divorce finalized on paper, he came home one day to find the locks changed and a voice mail from his ex-wife telling him she was sorry, but it was over.

When Hank called his lawyer to see what his options were, the man had refused to help him, citing a conflict of interest. That conflict being Hank's lawyer was now sleeping with Hank's ex-wife.

Virtually penniless, Hank had tried to blow his own brains out with his handgun. He wasn't even able to do that right, missing and permanently scarring his face. Now he endured phone calls three times a day from the hospital pestering him about bills he couldn't afford to pay, and a disfigurement most people found disquieting; he was doing whatever he had to do to survive.

At least he had work right now, and unlike the last four places he had been at, Terrance didn't seem to have a problem working with a man missing chunks from his face. The night shift sucked. Hank had always hated it, but it would keep his complexion out of sight of anyone that might call to complain.

"Thank you Terrance," Hank said, and he meant it.

"No problem, my man," Terrance replied. "Let's get you situated."

He pulled the chair out from the desk. It was once a fine red leather chair. However, years of being sat in day and night had cracked the leather. The yellow cushioning inside was overflowing out of rips in the side. Terrance smacked the back of it and gestured for Hank to sit.

Sitting down at the desk, he found a map of the facility with several hand-written triangles inscribed with numbers. He looked up at the monitors that filled the wall, and noticed that each one had matching numbers written on masking tape stuck to them.

Hank pulled his glasses from his pocket and put them on. He had a hard-time seeing out of his left eye since the surgery to remove the bullet fragments caused "irreversible damage to his optic nerve" the doctors told him. They were cheap frames, sliding off easily, but they were all he could afford.

"Now this map here tells you where each camera is located," Terrance explained. "The job is pretty much to take a seat and watch 'em all night. If you see anything funny, don't go thinking you're Shaft or something. Don't be a hero, just call the police like anyone else would. They don't issue us guns or tasers, we are here to observe and report only."

"Got it," Hank replied.

"There's a mini fridge by your left leg," Terrance continued. "A fan on the floor by your right. You'll need that for the summers. The thermostat on the wall works, but the old A/C unit ain't too good when it gets hot. That door behind you leads to a bathroom. Try to take it easy on the plumbing. It's older than the security system."

Hank nodded.

"The refinery staff is minimal at night," Terrance said. "A few maintenance workers and what have you. They all leave around midnight."

Hank could see several cars approaching the gate from the facility, the gate opening on its own to let them out.

"You won't see another soul till about six in the morning," continued Terrance. "They'll have their own key cards to come in, just wave at 'em."

Hank felt a tinge of nervousness; he had hoped to avoid face-to-face contact as much as possible.

"If you're worried, just wear a face mask," Terrance said. He must have noticed Hank's apprehension. "Thanks to Covid, you'll just be another health conscious person."

That made Hank feel a little better.

"I'm not sticking around," said Terrance after an enormous yawn. "So this will conclude the in-person part of your orientation. For insurance purposes, you'll now spend the next two hours watching a series of orientation videos from corporate. It's required and no, you can't fast forward. The button is broken."

"Not a problem," Hank replied.

"You say that now," Terrance was smiling. "Tell me tomorrow if you don't feel the urge to blow your brains out halfway through. Oh, sorry."

"I don't get offended," said Hank quickly, not wanting the kind old man to feel bad. Hank had come to terms with what he had done.

"Well, that's it," Terrance said, and he clapped his hands together. "I'm heading home. Phone directory is next to the phone. Hit 9 to dial an outside line. My number is on a note pinned to the wall. Call me if you need anything."

Terrance yawned again. He looked exhausted.

"Hey Terrance," Hank began. "What's this line with a dot at the end on the map? It looks right next to the guard shack."

Terrance laughed.

"The coverage here is spotty," Terrance answered. "There's more than a few blind spots around the property. That is one of them, and it's close enough to the shack that it's the perfect place to grab a smoke."

He winked.

Hank laughed.

"Thank you, Terrance," Hank said, extending his hand.

"My pleasure, Hank," Terrance said, taking it in a firm shake.

The old man shambled to the guardhouse door and opened it. The rain was falling in sheets outside, a chilly wind filled the small room. Terrance paused.

"It's just a job, Hank," Terrance said, with some genuine feeling in his voice. "Don't be some hero. You see anything, just call the police. It doesn't look too good to have a false alarm, but it's better than putting your ass on the line."

Hank nodded to him.

Terrance closed the door and left.

Hank took a deep breath. Pulling the first VHS tape from the stack piled on the desk, he stuck it into the gaping mouth at the front of the small television.

The screen clicked on automatically; it was a bunch of white noise.

Hank said an affirmation to himself, an affirmation of thankfulness, then pressed the play button.

Just past midnight, Dani was behind the wheel of Paul's van while Alek was in the back rummaging around in a toolbox, with Paul watching over his shoulder.

"I told you I brought them," Alek said.

"I didn't see them," Paul replied.

It was making Dani nervous.

"Maybe we should call the whole thing off," Dani commented, her last hope of getting Paul to abandon his fool's crusade.

"Not a chance," said Paul without even considering it.

"Got it," Alek said, pulling a pair of wire cutters from the box.

"Good," Paul said, nodding. "Let's go."

He and Alek piled out the back and walked to the chain-link fence lit up by the van's headlights.

Dani had driven them almost an hour outside of the city to this remote forested area where the Summit Petroleum refinery was. Alek and Paul had been reciting the plan back and forth to one another the whole ride, which made her more anxious.

Link by link, the two of them cut through the ten foot tall fence.

Despite the deluge of rain, Dani kept the window open.

Click, click, click. Each snap of the metal by the wire cutters sounded like the ticking of a grandfather clock.

It took longer than expected, but Alek and Paul had cut out a hole large enough for the van to roll through. Eager to get out of the rain, they piled back inside and shut the door.

"You sure we won't get caught?" Dani asked for probably the hundredth time.

"Not a chance," Paul replied, cool and calm. "The new security guard starts tonight. My buddy told me he'll be watching a two-hour orientation video until about 2am. That gives us over an hour to get in and back out."

"Ok," Dani said, but didn't dare move.

"Now drive," Paul commanded.

Dani slowly put the van back into gear and pulled through the opening.

"**D**id you know that Summit Petroleum is one of four petrochemical companies owned by Global Meridian Holdings?" the overly enthusiastic middle-aged man on the video asked.

"No, I didn't know that," Hank replied to the training video in an extremely bored voice.

Pulling off his glasses, he rubbed the bridge of his nose.

He had been watching videos for only twenty minutes, but he knew exactly what Terrance was saying about it making you feel like blowing your brains out.

They were barely instructional. It was mostly this guy named Jeremiah Henricks in a plaid jacket talking about every company owned by the parent company, Global Meridian Holdings. None of it applied to his job.

He took another deep breath, reminding himself he needed this place. What was another hour and a half of boring video in the big scheme of things when it came to earning enough to afford rent?

Hank watched Mr. Henricks drone on, explaining the overly complicated corporate structure of Global Meridian and how important the employees were to him.

"Ya, right," Hank said aloud.

He felt elated when the Global Meridian logo filled the screen and the instructions to input training tape #2 appeared across the monitor.

Hitting the stop button, the old miniature television set went black, and Hank saw his reflection in the glass. The scar that ran from his cheek up to his eye was almost half an inch deep and half that distance wide.

He didn't feel that way at the time, but he was actually kind of lucky. A few degrees difference and it would have killed him.

He fumbled with the stack of tapes until he found the second one, when he looked up for a split second at the cameras.

Something was moving on the grounds.

The storm had grown stronger. Trees and branches thrashed violently in the camera video. The black and white feed was too grainy and low definition for him to make out much more.

He put his glasses back on and moved his face closer to the screen, but saw nothing.

It was probably just the storm, something blowing across the screen.

He fed the second tape into the TV, then it caught his eye again. It looked like a person had run across the field of view. However, by the time he had focused on the monitor, there was nothing there except blowing branches.

His finger hovered over the play button on the old VHS player, but something inside him wouldn't let him press it. He could have sworn he had seen someone. No, he knew he saw someone. Where did they go?

Then he remembered Terrance mentioning there were blind spots all over the place.

He rolled his chair over to the phone and lifted it to his ear.

The dial tone roared as loud as the storm outside. He moved his finger to the number 9 but hesitated, his finger hovering over the button.

What if he had imagined it?

His first night on the job and a false alarm already. It wouldn't look good. There was nothing on the monitors now.

He put the phone back down.

Hank couldn't afford to mess this up.

His eyes darted to the rain hat and jacket hanging from the wall by the door.

He really should check it out, just to be safe. If he sees anyone, he'll hurry back and call the police. Nothing heroic, just observe and report.

13-B was the monitor where he had seen movement. He located it on the map. It was the camera near the crude oil storage tanks.

Standing up, he put the rain jacket on and grabbed the flashlight from his belt.

Observe and report.

Dani sat in the cab of Paul's van alone, shivering. It had been fifteen minutes since Paul and Alek had run into the storm. She knew what they were doing, or at least what they planned to do. Nearby were four large silo-like reservoirs that stuck out of the ground. Each was about half full of crude oil.

A shallow depression lined with concrete was between the four reservoirs at the center. In the event of catastrophic pressure in the silos, they had a relief valve that would pop and spill the oil into the depression that then would channel the flow away from the forest and towards emergency overflow tanks. It was a safety measure that only a refinery built over half a century ago would have designed; not passing modern EPA regulations.

Dani imagined what the small lake of oil would look like if it ever was full, a surface dark as a moonless night that would consume anything that was unlucky enough to fall into it. A safety precaution, it might have never been used, as lush trees grew on the banks of the reservoir, oblivious to the danger they would be in should the tanks ever blow.

The storm was doing a number on them; the wind had blown several branches down. A strike of lightning flashed in the distance. This illuminated the trees for a moment, just long enough for Dani to see a shape in the branches. It looked like the owl she had seen earlier. She squinted as the windshield wiper swept beads of water from the glass, allowing her a better view. There was nothing there. It had been a figment of her imagination.

Dani checked her watch. She wasn't sure when she should panic. She flipped on the radio, hoping some music would calm her nerves.

Paul liked the old stuff. "I Can See Clearly Now" by Johnny Nash played from the crackling speakers. Even with the nervous waves clinging to her every thought, she couldn't help but laugh at the irony.

The plan was for Alek and Paul to dash inside and turn on the water cleaning system. Paul had explained that the company used high pressure jets of water every few years to clean the tanks before refilling them. They dumped this contaminated water into the river even though they weren't supposed to, being grandfathered in under old rules thanks to millions of dollars worth of corporate lobbyists.

Paul would turn the valves to start the system, then water would mix with the oil, diluting it until it was worthless. So it was as simple as turning the valves and getting the hell out of there.

A simple job. She shouldn't be this nervous.

Even though it was pouring outside, Dani felt the urge to go searching for them. Just to make sure they were alright. They might be lost in the storm, unable to find their way back to the van. She pulled on a disposable rain fly that Paul had packed and put it on. He had ordered large male sizes, and it hung loose over her like the oversized sweaters her grandmother had always given her at Christmas. As long as it kept the rain out, it would do. Steeling herself with a deep breath, she opened the door and prepared to face the icy rain and wind.

"Alek!" she yelled first. "Paul!"

The wind and the rain almost gobbled up all the sound, but there was another sound she didn't recognize. It was a rumbling sound; she didn't just hear it. She felt it in the ground under her feet.

It only made her more worried.

"Alek, Paul," she repeated, trying to scream as loud as she could.

Then she saw a light in the distance. It was a flashlight. It was bobbing like whoever was holding it was running.

Hank found the reservoir area after getting turned around twice. The entire complex was confusing, especially at night. He hoped he could find his way back. Beginning to doubt he had seen anything at all, he was glad he hadn't called the police.

However, as he turned the corner, those thoughts slipped from his mind.

Up ahead of him were two figures with a crowbar trying to turn a valve on pipes that ran out of the ground. Hank could tell immediately they weren't supposed to be there. He considered running back to call the police like he had originally planned, but what would he tell them? He saw two men who ran off before he could see their faces?

They could be saboteurs or even terrorists; planting explosives on the tanks. By the time the police arrived, it would already be too late.

What could Hank really do to stop them? He didn't have a gun, a taser, or even a can of mace.

But they didn't know that.

"Freeze," he said, like had heard police officers yell in the movies.

Both of the figures stopped what they were doing immediately.

"I've got a gun," Hank yelled, as convincing as he could.

He approached the two slowly until he was only a few feet from the shorter one. He grabbed the figure's shoulder and spun him around.

It was just a boy, couldn't have been more than a year out of high school. He looked terrified.

"What the hell do you think you're doing?" Hank yelled at the kid.

He was having a hard time seeing, rain clung to his glasses. Hank pulled them off, trying to wipe them on his uniform.

The boy pushed Hank hard, and his foot slipped on the slick mud. He fell backwards and landed on the ground with a thud.

"Shit," Hank cursed aloud. Both the boy and the other man had taken off at a full sprint towards the concrete reservoir.

Hank scrambled to his feet and pursued them. The beam of his flashlight danced in front of him like a symphony conductor's baton.

The concrete incline into the bowl at the center reservoir between the four tanks was pretty steep, but both the boy and the man ahead of him stumbling only slightly as they slid down the rain soaked banks.

His adrenaline was pumping, Hank didn't dare stop to think if he should turn around. The only thought in his head was catching them and bringing them to justice.

One step, then another. He almost made it down before the slippery ground won out and he felt his feet fall out from underneath him. He slid the rest of the way down the embankment.

"Argh," he yelled, the rain falling onto his face as he winced in pain. The rough concrete had shredded his rain jacket. He pulled it off.

He could barely see. His glasses had fallen off in the scuffle with the boy.

By the time his left eye got back into focus, the two figures were ascending the ridge at the opposite end of the overflow pit. The headlights of a vehicle above them, their way out.

Hank knew he would not catch up to them, but maybe he could get close enough to get the license plate number. That would be redeemable.

Why hadn't he called the police back at the warm, dry guardhouse?!

Getting to his feet, his legs felt strange, but it wasn't from the fall. He realized the ground was rumbling. Something was happening. It must be whatever those two were up to by the pipes.

He ran, sprinting as best he could on the shaking ground towards the van.

Hank was halfway, at the center of the overflow pit, when he heard the first valve pop. It sounded like a rifle firing, but louder. Then he heard a second pop, and then a third, and finally a fourth.

He kept running, trying to ignore the alarming sounds long enough to get close to the van. The figures had already finished scrambling up the side of the concrete incline. Hank needed to hurry if he wanted a chance.

His legs were getting tired, they were feeling heavy, and without his glasses, they were just blurry shapes.

Each step he took felt like he had weights attached to his feet. He couldn't go on any further, he had to stop. The criminals disappeared inside the van, yet it was still idling, just sitting there. He wiped his eyes with his sleeve, hoping to get a better look. Maybe if he was lucky, he could read the van's license plate.

Then his calves felt strange, they felt wet. The sensation was growing too, rising to the base of his thighs. He looked down.

He was almost waist deep in a thick black liquid; the smell was strong enough that he could make it out through the rain. It was oil.

Panicking, he used every ounce of energy he had to move while he still could towards the closest edge where a tree hung over the concrete. His muscles burned, but he trudged on until they no longer listened to him. He was almost to the edge.

The oil was up to his navel.

His soaked clothes weighed him down.

He desperately tore at the thin material of his pants.

It was up to his chest now. He paddled his hands through the viscous liquid, trying anything to help move him faster. It stuck to his fingers and hands. He pulled his shirt off; the buttons popping almost effortlessly until he was almost naked.

The oil was up to his shoulders.

He kicked and pushed on his tiptoes to keep his head above the rising oil; it felt like a lead weight was around his waist.

Almost there, another twenty feet.

His chin was barely above the surface.

Five feet, maybe more, until the edge of the overflow pit.

The sounds of his grunts went silent as his head went under.

"**D**rive now!" Paul yelled at the top of his lungs.

"No, I just saw him go under," Dani pleaded through sobs. "We have to help him."

"I said drive," Paul said. "We have to get out of here."

"I'm going to go help him," Dani opened the driver's side door.

"The hell you're not," Paul replied. "Get in the back with Alek."

"But," Dani said, but the words barely escaped her mouth when Paul yanked her by the shoulder towards the back seat. She fell to the floor of the van. Alek rushed to her side.

Paul pushed himself into the driver's seat and put the van in gear. Dani stared out the back window, looking at the pool of black that had formed faster than she could ever had imagined in the overflow pit. A flash of lightning illuminated it for a split second, and in that moment frozen in time, Dani saw the figure of a man drenched in oil reaching out of the water towards a downed branch hanging over his head. A branch she knew he would never reach.

PART 2

THE DOLLHOUSE

CHAPTER 7

The morning after the field trip to the refinery, The Collective was quiet.

Dani's alarm woke her. She slipped out of bed and went downstairs to shower and change. Bianca's bedroom door was wide open, but she wasn't downstairs. Dani's jealous side knew that meant she had stayed over at the man's house after her date. Alek's light was off, still sleeping. He was probably exhausted.

Paul was gone too. He took the van, the mud tracks still visible on the pavement.

Dani took her time in the shower, not concerned about using up all the hot-water that day. She shaved her legs and washed her hair thoroughly, trying to get the smell of vegetable oil out of it. Then did her makeup in the locker room mirror.

She heard the roll-up door open. That meant Paul was back.

Dani walked out of the locker room in her outfit; a white shirt under a black jacket and a black knee-length skirt. She hoped she looked professional enough for Lady Gianni.

She found Paul with the hose, spraying the mud tracks into a drainage grate on the street.

"Little fancy for the coffee shop," he said as she approached.

It was chilly that morning, mist from the sprayer lofted into the air. Dani avoided the spray so her hair wouldn't get wet.

"Can we talk about what happened last night?" Dani asked.

"Talk about what?" Paul said.

"You know," Dani replied. "At Summit."

Paul glared at her, then peeked in both directions of the street as if nervous someone was eavesdropping.

"I don't know what you're talking about," said Paul, his tone urging her to let it go.

But she wasn't going to.

"I know what I saw," Dani insisted. "That man was drowning in all that oil."

"It was dark," Paul replied, still glancing around them nervously. "You were scared. You don't know what you saw."

"I saw a man," Dani repeated. "It was exactly like that sculpture we saw at Gallery Nocturne. *Consume*, remember?"

"Did you now?" Paul asked, his face giving her a peculiar look.

He turned off the hose and walked over to the open driver's side door, fishing for something inside.

Paul tossed a newspaper at her, Dani caught it.

"Deliveryman, drop this one off by mistake, too?" Dani chided.

"Nope," Paul replied with what Dani thought was an unusual level of calm. "I went out and picked this one up."

The headline article title read: 'SABOTAGE AT SUMMIT REFINERY'.

"Late last night," Dani read the opening paragraph out loud. "Persons unknown deliberately sabotaged the Summit Petroleum's refinery just outside of the city using the site's emergency overflow system. Thankfully, the facility had minimal staffing at the time of incident and no one was harmed."

She paused.

"Keep reading," Paul said.

"Summit has yet to release a statement yet, however industry insiders have already started weighing in. The clean-up costs alone will number in the millions, not to mention the loss of raw material. However, given the strategic importance of Summit and its parent company Global Meridian as key military suppliers, many believe that the government will step in to assist. Their stock is expected to rebound sharply once announced."

"No one was hurt?" Dani repeated as a question.

"Nope," Paul confirmed. "Whomever we saw chasing us must have gotten out before the tanks burst."

Dani should have felt relieved, but she didn't.

"I'm more pissed off that they are going to get a bailout," Paul sneered. "But I supposed I should have expected it. Global Meridian has its fingers in all the politicians' pockets."

"Right," Dani said. She glanced at the time on her phone. "I got to go."

"To work?" Paul said with raised eyebrows.

She wasn't sure if she should tell him where she was going. He might blow a gasket. She wasn't even certain it was a job.

"I'll tell you later," she said instead, heading back inside.

Alek was waiting for her, the bags under his eyes darker than ever. He looked like he hadn't slept at all.

"You saw it too, didn't you?" Dani asked him.

Alek nodded.

"But the paper said no one was hurt," added Dani. "If that's the case, then we just imagined it. A trick of the light."

"A trick of the light," Alek repeated her words.

Dani didn't want to be late.

"I've got to go," she said, skirting towards the exit. "We can talk later."

The old church that held Gallery Nocturne was just as impressive in the daylight as it was at night. The details of the architecture exploded under the bright sunshine in ways that a spotlight could not do it justice. Several gargoyles stared down at her from overhangs on the roof, their pupil-less stone eyes unflinching. Those weren't the only carvings. The original stone masons carved faces of men, women, and children into some of the granite bricks. At night, they would have looked like just simple imperfections on the rocky surfaces, but with the shadows formed by the daylight, their facial features were recognizable. No two appeared alike.

Dani couldn't help herself. She reached her hand out and touched one of them, feeling the indents that formed the eyes and mouth. It was of a child, the cheeks bulbous and full with a button nose.

"No one knows how many there are," Lady Gianni said from behind her.

Dani was growing used to the woman's uncanny ability to approach her virtually undetected.

"Good morning," Dani said, brushing strands of hair away from her eyes, escapees of her hair-tie.

"The stones are carved of various people and creatures," Lady Gianni replied. "Some are from the Bible, some are from older religions and lore. Moses, Dragons, Succubus, Chimera, plus so much more."

"Who built it?" Dani asked.

"It's uncertain," said Lady Gianni. "The records are incomplete. I've heard the freemasons built it, but who knows for certain?"

Dani rubbed the stone cherub's face and felt the smooth granite underneath her fingertips. Years of weathering storms and smog from the city, yet it still felt immaculate, as if just erected. There was something mystical about the old church. Every detail only uncovered another seemingly endless layer of intrigue.

"I'm excited for us to get started," Lady Gianni said with a smile. "Follow me."

She set off towards the front door to the gallery, Dani rushing to catch up.

Inside, the light from the sun shot blues, orange, red, and yellow tinted rays through the stained glass; filling the church with vibrant beams of multicolored sunshine. Dozens of workmen shuffled about the floor carrying tool boxes or pushing dollies. They all wore black t-shirts with Gallery Nocturne printed on them, the same uniform as Larry, who Bianca had seduced in order to let them in.

Dani wondered if he'd recognize her if they crossed paths again.

"The gallery is open to the public two nights a week," Lady Gianni said as they walked past the stage where Dani had first seen her. "That doesn't mean there isn't plenty to do in between. Our last showing saw a record number of pieces purchased by collectors. We are packing and shipping them out today."

"Are most of your clients here in town?" Dani asked.

"A few," Lady Gianni replied. "Most are overseas, old acquaintances of mine who pay a premium for quality."

The sounds of power saws, nail guns, and squeaky roller wheels orchestrated themselves into a chaotic symphony of background noise. It sounded more like a construction site than an art gallery.

"Of course, with most of our stock depleted," Lady Gianni continued. "I'm responsible for refilling the floor with additional works from new artists. Thankfully, because of my connections, I have plenty to choose from."

They walked through the archway next to the stage and entered *The Horizons* showroom.

"*The Veil, The Echoes,* and *The Remnants* are the only exceptions," said Lady Gianni, her pace slowing only slightly to allow for Dani to keep up. "I reserve selling works from them only for our most elite clientèle."

"Excuse me," Dani said in a mouse-ish voice.

"Of course everyone who can get in thinks they are elite," Lady Gianni either didn't hear her or ignored her. "But the scarcity drives up prices."

"Excuse me," Dani said again, a little louder.

Lady Gianni stopped and turned.

"Yes?" she said, looking almost annoyed.

"I'm sorry but," Dani wasn't sure how to ask now that she had gotten the woman's full attention. "I don't know why I'm here."

Lady Gianni stared at her for a long moment. Those enormous emerald green eyes made Dani feel warm, like they were infrared lasers frying her from the inside out.

Dani was growing more nervous by the second. Did she already screw this up?

Lady Gianni let out a loud, full laugh. She closed her eyes, putting her hand over her face.

"I'm sorry, my dear," she said through her own cackling. "Sometimes I do this. I get ahead of myself. You've been selected for the internship position. Congratulations!"

"But I didn't apply for it or even know one was open," Dani replied.

"There wasn't one," Lady Gianni said with a grin. "I just created it yesterday after seeing your charming work at the coffee shop."

There was that word again, charming. It still felt like an insult.

"You'll be working here every day," Lady Gianni's hand twirled like she was trying to gather the right word from thin air. "Maybe personal assistant might be a better job title. I don't know, I'm still working on it. I'm sure we'll figure out exactly what use I'll have for you, eventually."

"Ok," Dani said wide-eyed. She wasn't certain how to act around Lady Gianni, who could be sweet and kind one moment but fierce and demanding the next.

"Where was I?" Lady Gianni said with her hand to her chin. "Oh yes, *The Horizons* is the only hall that I plan on selling to the masses..."

"Lady Gianni!" A man's voice abruptly ended her sentence.

"Jeremiah my dear," Lady Gianni replied.

An old man in a fine business suit appeared from the exit to *The Echoes*. A woman holding a binder and wearing a pink turtleneck hurried after him.

He kissed Lady Gianni on both cheeks.

"I didn't think I'd see you this morning," Lady Gianni commented. "After what happened on the news, I thought you'd have more pressing matters to deal with."

Dani remembered him from the first night at the gallery. It was Jeremiah Henricks, the man who Bianca had been talking to. He didn't seem to recognize Dani at all.

"Pressing? Not at all," the man said with a scoff. "Damn thing is turning into a blessing in disguise. Stock is up, my boys in D.C. are working on something for me already. Eco terrorists should attack my refineries more often. But that's not why I'm here."

His voice became suddenly quieter and less boastful.

"I've got a friend of mine," Jeremiah continued. "Mr. Bones runs one of my subsidiaries. He's curious about buying something, but skittish. Not sure that the value will be there for him in the long run."

Jeremiah was picking his words carefully.

"As you know, firsthand," Lady Gianni said, her eyes narrowing slightly. "I guarantee the appreciation of everything we sell. However, maybe it's best we talk in private."

She darted a glance at Dani and the young woman in the pink top, who both were listening quietly.

Lady Gianni took Jeremiah's arm and led him away, leaving the two younger women alone.

"I'm Dani," Dani said, introducing herself.

"Haley," the other woman replied. They shook hands quickly. "This place is…"

"Amazing," Dani finished her sentence for her.

"Are you Lady Gianni's PA?" Haley asked.

"PA?" Dani repeated back in question form. She wasn't sure what it stood for.

"Personal assistant," Haley clarified.

"Um, maybe," Dani answered. "I think so. Not sure yet."

"First day?" Haley asked.

"How'd you know?" Dani wondered.

"Your hands," Haley said with a nervous facial expression. "They are really sweaty."

"Oh," Dani squeaked, suddenly feeling self-conscious.

"Don't worry about it," Haley said encouragingly. "To tell you a secret, it's my first day too."

"Wow," Dani replied. "You certainly look natural doing it."

"Thank you," Haley said before adding. "I guess."

They stood in silence, both swinging their shoulders back and forth and looking around.

"Who is he?" Dani asked.

"You've never heard of Jeremiah Henricks?" Haley said in disbelief.

"Should I have?" asked Dani, feeling a bit out of touch.

"He's one of the richest men on the planet," Haley explained. "CEO of Global Meridian, which owns companies in just about every industry out there, from textiles to petroleum."

Dani remembered the newspaper article from that morning. It was an eerie coincidence that she had just met the owner of Summit Petroleum after being an accomplice to its sabotage less than twelve hours ago.

Haley was giving her an odd look. Dani must look guilty.

"How do you get to be Mr. Henrick's PA?" Dani asked, hoping to volley the attention off herself.

Haley leaned in close.

"It's hard to explain," she whispered. "I used to be an intern at Pay-Sphere. Have you heard of it?"

"No," Dani replied.

"Well, one of my coworkers had an incident," Haley continued. "A pretty bad one. I think they promoted me so I wouldn't talk about it with anyone."

"Anyone like me?" Dani said.

"Anyone like the media," Haley said in a whisper. "But let's just keep that between us, please?"

"Scout's honor," Dani said, holding up three fingers.

They exchanged numbers as Lady Gianni and Mr. Henricks walked back to join them.

"I promise," Lady Gianni told him as they approached. "I'll get right on it, finding the right piece for your friend."

"Just something to wet his beak," Mr. Henricks commented. "Nothing crazy like what I just bought. He's a bit more old school, a softer soul than most."

"My assistant will be in touch," Lady Gianni replied.

He kissed her on the cheek and then went stomping towards the exit.

Haley nodded at Dani and put her finger to her lips.

Our little secret.

She hurried away after him.

"Funny little man," Lady Gianni said once they were out of earshot.

"He seemed nice," Dani commented, forcing herself to say something kind.

"Oh, he's a right horrible bastard," Lady Gianni replied. "All men are really. Too busy following their dicks and their bank accounts to recognize the true beauty of this world."

Her face changed into a scowl.

"And his taste in art is horrible," she added with a giggle. "Then again, if it weren't for men like him, there wouldn't be jobs for gals like us."

"Like us?" Dani muttered. She didn't feel like she was anywhere near the same league as this beautiful, successful woman.

She turned to see Lady Gianni staring at her with those piercing eyes.

"You know exactly what I mean," Lady Gianni said slowly, her voice almost hypnotic. "Neither of us are what we seem."

Lady Gianni smiled, a smile that made Dani very nervous.

Lady Gianni directed her to a side door where a series of nicely furnished offices were tucked away. The rooms, which were built into the old church's storage area, had no windows. But there was plenty of light, high-output fluorescents made it feel like a bright summer day.

Lady Gianni showed Dani her desk, right outside the largest office that belonged to the director herself. The desk contained a work cell phone, a security badge, and a laptop. What she was supposed to do with them yet, she wasn't certain.

They discussed wages. Her salary would be double what she had been making at the coffee shop. They went over job duties, everything from taking calls and messages to sorting through potential art for the gallery.

She filled out an application with her personal information for payroll and Lady Gianni locked it in a filing cabinet behind her desk.

"There's one thing we haven't discussed yet," Lady Gianni began, flattening her hands together in front of her face. "I thought it was implied, but probably best we get it out in the open early."

Dani felt nervous.

"The real reason I want you here is so you can paint for the gallery," Lady Gianni stated.

It was both what Dani wanted with all her heart and dreaded at the same time.

"Your work at the shop was quaint," Lady Gianni began. "But you can only go so far painting and drawing flowers. I see your potential, but you need a new environment that will allow you to embrace more carnal artistic urges."

Dani knew what she needed to tell Lady Gianni, but held back.

"At the Gallery Nocturne, I'm certain I can unlock the dormant creature inside you," the woman said with a strange flair at the end.

Dani knew it was now or never.

"I'm sorry that I didn't tell you this sooner," Dani said as she sat uncomfortably in the chair in front of Lady Gianni's massive mahogany desk.

"Hmm," Lady Gianni said with interest in her voice. She leaned forward and rested her chin on her folded hands. "What's that, my dear?"

"I'm part of a place," Dani explained. "We call ourselves The Collective. We live together, we make art together, we show our work together. I should have said something earlier. I feel like this is a conflict of interest."

Lady Gianni leaned back and seemed to think about it for a moment.

"I think I've heard of them," she said.

The comment surprised Dani.

"Paul Moreau set it up, right?" She asked.

"Yes, he's the one that…" Dani almost let it slip that she had been practically homeless before Paul found her.

"That discovered you?" Lady Gianni said in a sly voice.

"In a way," Dani answered. "I love living there. I couldn't just leave."

Lady Gianni began laughing.

"Oh Dani," she said. "I don't see a conflict at all. I don't want you to leave The Collective."

"You don't?" Dani said, feelings of relief flooding over her.

"I hired you," Lady Gianni began. "Because I see someone chasing something, chasing a beautiful, fantastic, extraordinary dream. Much like myself."

Dani sat silently, unsure of what to say.

"Do you know how many men have told me what to do in my life?" She asked rhetorically. "Since the day I entered this world, it's been a man's world."

"Men like Jeremiah Henricks?" Dani asked.

Lady Gianni scoffed.

"Mr. Henricks is a chihuahua by comparison," she said. "All bark and no bite."

She stood up and walked around the desk until she was standing right behind Dani. Dani couldn't help but feel strange as Lady Gianni's slender fingers wrapped themselves tightly around her shoulders. She couldn't kick a vision from her mind, a feeling they were the long and slender arms of an octopus.

"I'm just about sick," Lady Gianni said as she squeezed Dani. "Of men telling me what to do with my business, my family."

A long pause.

"With my body," Lady Gianni squeezed tighter, Dani withheld the urge to recoil despite the pain.

Her grip relaxed.

"I've been dealing with that for longer than you could ever know," Lady Gianni sat on the edge of her desk. "I'm sure you have too."

She leaned forward, staring into Dani's eyes.

Dani tried not to think about her own estranged father.

"Whatever you paint at The Collective," Lady Gianni continued. "It belongs to The Collective."

"Thank you," Dani said, forcing herself to smile. Her shoulders felt sore.

"But whatever you paint here," Lady Gianni said, holding her arms up. "In this glorious monument to the gods of divine beauty and inspiration, they belong to us."

A cell phone suddenly rang. It was the one Lady Gianni had given her.

Dani just stared at it, not sure what to do.

"Are you going to get that?" Lady Gianni asked with a grin.

"Oh my god, sorry," Dani said, fumbling to pick up the vibrating device. "Lady Gianni's office."

Dani heard the person on the other line.

"Be right there," Dani said, before hanging up. "It's the loading dock. They want you to approve the new layout of *The Horizons*."

"Excellent," Lady Gianni said.

They left the offices and Dani followed Lady Gianni to *The Horizons* gallery, where a man wearing a hard hat was waiting, holding a clipboard.

"Dani, this is Tom," Lady Gianni said, introducing them. "He's the head foreman. He handles the logistics of this place."

"Nice to meet you," Foreman Tom said. He was Dani's height and built like a day-laborer. Dani shook his hand, noticing a tattoo on his wrist of five dots arranged like the face of a die, the same one that had been on Larry's hand.

"You as well," Dani replied.

"Shall we?" Tom asked.

He took Lady Gianni down each row of *The Horizons,* where men were busy installing new canvases and frames on the walls, refilling the empty spaces. Lady Gianni barked out notes and instructions to Tom, who jotted it on his clipboard.

She demanded that walls, lighting, and placements be moved, adjusted, and swapped in almost every section. Tom never showed the slightest bit of annoyance at the endless orders being passed to him and his team.

Lady Gianni's attention to detail was extraordinary. When they were done, Tom gathered several more workmen to make the changes as she oversaw the activities. Dani watched each closely, trying to see if she could recognize one of them as Larry from the other evening. In the process, she noticed several of the workers also had the same five dot tattoo.

As they worked away, Dani got to see how every suggestion made was an improvement. It was like the whole gallery was a giant jigsaw puzzle, and only Lady Gianni knew how to make the pieces fit together just right.

"No, no, no!" Lady Gianni yelled, storming off to scold one of the workers who was hanging sash drapes on a new exhibit. "Budala! Amadan! Estúpido!"

Dani was left alone with Foreman Tom, who chewed gum while watching his co-worker get chewed out in foreign languages neither of them understood.

She worked up the courage to ask a question.

"What's with the matching tattoos?" Dani questioned. "Are you all part of the same board game club or something?"

"Board game club?" the foreman said with a laugh. "It's the quincunx."

Dani must have appeared very confused.

"Prison tattoos," he clarified. "The four dots symbolize the four walls, and the center is the man on the inside."

"You've been to prison?" She asked.

"Twice actually," Tom said with a chuckle. "Drugs and theft. Don't worry, I didn't kill nobody. Of course, that's exactly what a murderer would say."

He winked.

Dani couldn't exactly say she felt relieved. In her experience, the girls from the halfway house that had been to juvie came out violent.

"But don't you sweat it," Tom continued, sensing her unease. "I'm reformed, been out almost fifteen years now. Most of the guys here are also ex-cons. Lady Gianni gets a nice tax break for hiring us."

Dani remembered Larry's tattoo. Bianca had dodged a bullet by blowing him off.

"But don't you worry," Tom said, trying to be reassuring. "I keep a pretty close tab on everyone. You have nothing to worry about."

He laughed out loud.

"What is it?" Dani asked.

"Just that life is funny sometimes," he explained. "You're here all nervous about being around these ex-cons, while they are all more scared of you."

"Why would they be afraid of me?" asked Dani.

"You're the director's new protégé," he said. "One word and you could probably have any of them fired. They all need the job. Life ain't easy out there for people like us."

He scribbled something onto a piece of paper on his clipboard and tore it off, handing it to Dani.

"Here's my number," Tom said with a smile. "Think of me as your friend on the inside. Call if you need anything."

"Thank you," she said, smiling back.

They watched as several workmen hustled to Lady Gianni's orders.

"I did have a question," Dani asked, her curiosity getting the better of her. "I haven't seen Larry anywhere. Is he in the back?"

"Larry didn't show up today," Tom replied. "Tried calling him, didn't answer."

"Oh," Dani said, something bothering her about it.

"You know him?" Tom asked.

"Friend of a friend," Dani said quickly.

Tom raised an eyebrow at her but turned back to Lady Gianni who was approaching with green eyes tinted red with anger.

They continued their inspection, working their way down the rows until they were in the center space, the showcase where the sculpture *Consume* was. Dani was getting nervous as they approached, though the day at the gallery had taken her mind off of the previous night's events. She didn't relish seeing it again.

Her fears proved unfounded.

"Where did the sculpture go?" Dani asked. The basin and everything about *Consume* were missing, the workers constructing something else with lumber and walls in its place.

"*Consume*?" Lady Gianni asked. "It shipped out this morning. The buyer wanted it delivered immediately."

Dani wasn't sure how to respond.

"It was a moving piece," Lady Gianni commented.

"Society's addiction to oil," Dani said.

Lady Gianni peered at her strangely.

"If that is what you got from it," said Lady Gianni. "Then you missed it entirely. Anyone can produce a piece that highlights some social movement. What separates the artist from the marketer is something else."

Dani listened close.

"It was about self destruction," Lady Gianni continued. "Man's inability to avoid his own human nature. That's what separates women from men. A woman may want something, may desire something with all her heart..."

Dani's thoughts drifted to images of Bianca.

"Yet we have the self-control to not pursue it if we know it to be a treacherous path. Men know full well the consequences of their actions. They know the path may lead them off a cliff. Yet they travel it regardless, unable to resist their own shortsighted desires."

The foreman looked uncomfortable standing nearby, listening to Lady Gianni talk.

"It's amazing what art can make you feel," Dani said.

"You speak as if it's the art that exudes emotion," Lady Gianni said. "The energy of emotion is like any other energy in this universe. It can be neither created nor destroyed, only transformed or channeled."

She stared Dani straight in the eyes.

"If you learn one thing while you are here, dear girl," Lady Gianni said, her voice deliberate and direct. "Let it be that a painting is just a painting. A sculpture is just a sculpture. They are merely vessels, no different from the gas tank on a car. It is us, our energy, our emotion, that they capture and store inside."

"So what happens to all that energy when we crate them up and send them off to some collector's warehouse where they'll sit in darkness until they appreciate?" The foreman asked, his voice betraying skepticism.

"They sleep," Lady Gianni answered.

CHAPTER 8

The blood vessel on Paul's neck looked like it was about to burst. Dani could see it pulse with his heartbeat. He was trying to take deep breaths, but they weren't working. He wanted to yell, to scream at her.

All four of them were sitting on the couches in The Collective warehouse. Dani had called a meeting to tell everyone the news.

"Let me make sure I understand this," he said deliberately, slow and steady. "You took a job at a rival gallery and didn't think to talk about it with us first?"

"I didn't know it was a job," Dani explained. "She came into the coffee shop and then started asking me questions, then told me to come see her the next day."

"I can't believe it," Paul said with exasperation. "My artists are being poached by Gallery Nocturne. How can I compete?"

"I'm not being poached," Dani replied. "I told her I couldn't leave this place, not after everything you've done for me. She said it wasn't a problem, I could do both."

"But I didn't say you could do both," Paul snarled.

"Didn't you just tell me the other day how business was down because we didn't have enough exposure?" Alek jumped in. "Dani's job could help us with that."

"What about your paintings and drawings? Who gets to show them?" Paul asked.

"She said anything I painted there belongs to her gallery," Dani explained. "Anything I paint here belongs to The Collective."

Paul was about to reply when Bianca placed her hand on his shoulder.

"Paul, baby," Bianca said, her touch immediately mesmerizing him. "Calm down and think about this for a moment."

Though he was almost double her weight, she gently pushed him into his chair. He fell without resistance.

"This is a colossal opportunity for Dani," said Bianca, before adding with a smile. "And for us."

She took a deep breath.

"I didn't want to tell you guys about it yet," Bianca began. "But the other night while you were out, I was on a date with Jeremiah Henricks."

"The guy you met at Dani's gallery?" Paul asked.

"Yes, him," Bianca replied. "After a few drinks, he started talking about Gallery Nocturne. Apparently, he buys art from there for millions of dollars, acting as a broker for other rich friends of his around the world. He only buys what Lady Gianni tells him to buy."

"What does this have to do with Dani?" Paul asked.

"At Lady Gianni's side," Bianca continued. "She'll be able to push some of our work in front of the gallery's director. Think about it, what would a million dollar sale do for any of us right now?"

"We could get a bigger space," Paul replied, the anger in his eyes replaced by what would have been dollar signs if he were a cartoon.

"We can't leave, I love this place," Dani commented, but Paul wasn't listening.

He stood up and paced to the wall.

"We could open up another location," Paul continued. "In the cultural district, where the real money is."

Dani peered over at Alek, who was sitting stone-faced.

"Is it just about the money to you, Paul?" Alek asked.

"It's about the enterprise," Paul said, turning to him. "And the enterprise needs money to survive. No more scraping by with sales on eBay and Etsy. We could bring in more artists, more artists like us who just need a chance and a place to stay."

Paul stopped to think for a long moment, then faced Dani.

"Bianca's right," he said. "This is a great opportunity for you and for us. Think you could get us in for a private meeting with Lady Gianni?"

Dani's eyes grew alarmed.

"I don't know. I just started yesterday," Dani replied. "It's a bit early for me to be doing things like that."

"What about inside for their show tonight?" Bianca asked. "I tried texting Larry, but he never texted back."

Dani thought about it and if she would be overstepping by asking Lady Gianni to let her friends in tonight. Then she got an idea.

"Actually, I may know someone," she said.

Dani convinced the rest of them to dress nicer for their next visit to Gallery Nocturne. Alek put on a collared shirt (Dani helped him wash the drops of paint out of it first), Paul wore a swanky suit, and Bianca an elegant dress. Dani also did her best to look dolled up, spending longer than usual on her makeup.

When she walked out of the locker room, Paul and Bianca were chatting while Alek was sitting on the couch, tugging at his collar.

"Took you long enough," Paul said, noticing Dani.

"Ignore him," Bianca said, hugging Dani. "Thank you for this."

Dani didn't want the moment to end. She wanted to feel her roommate's body close to hers and never let go. Her hopes were dashed when Bianca pulled away quickly and left Dani with that feeling of longing.

A horn honked outside.

"Car's here," Paul said.

"No subway tonight?" Alek asked.

"I figured if we want to look like we belong," Paul replied. "We should arrive like we do."

Dani walked to the front door and reached for the handle, but before she could grab it, Alek had already beaten her to it.

"Ladies first," he said with a smile, one of those rare smiles that snuck out of his usually melancholy face.

He opened the door for her.

"Thank you Alek," Dani said.

It was still only February, and the night air was cold. If they were walking, Dani would have rushed back inside to grab her sweater.

"Whoa," Dani said, seeing the car. "Paul, you sure about this?"

"Absolutely," he said, appearing next to her.

All four of them piled into the limousine.

The driver had left them on the red carpet that stretched from the street to the front door of the Gallery Nocturne.

Dani was almost blinded when a flash of a camera went off to her left. Then another, then another. The press were there, but why would they take a photo of her?

"Paul, Paul!" a voice yelled from behind the aluminum barrier. "Where have you been?"

Paul walked over to the man and shook his hand. They chatted for a few moments as the cameras took more photos.

Bianca also seemed at home on the red carpet. She strutted around, posing in her dress for various cameramen.

Only Alek and Dani hung back, feeling like they didn't belong.

"Crazy right?" Alek said.

"I still can't believe it," Dani replied.

It took much longer than expected to reach the front door.

Paul urged Dani to the front of the group.

"Hi," Dani began. "I'm Dani…"

"Dani Scotts, yes," the doorman finished her sentence for her. "We've been expecting you. Come in, please."

He pulled the red sash to the side and opened the door for them.

The crowded front hall overflowed with people sipping on cocktails and wine. Dani knew Lady Gianni would take the stage soon, so she urged the rest of them to the side.

"Can I get you guys something to drink?" Paul asked them.

"I'm fine," Dani replied. She was nervous, unsure if Lady Gianni would welcome her attendance. More importantly, she didn't want to get foreman Tom in trouble. He had been kind enough to arrange their entry without hesitation.

"I'll have a glass of white," Bianca answered him.

Alek mumbled something that indicated he wasn't drinking either.

Paul disappeared into the crowd.

"Oh, there's Jeremiah," Bianca said, waving at someone behind Dani. "We should go say hi."

"You go ahead," Dani replied, remembering how Haley's boss had reacted the first time she met him.

"Suit yourself," Bianca ran out of sight.

This left Dani and Alek alone. Alek was fidgeting and looking more nervous than usual.

"Why are you so nervous?" Dani asked him.

Alek looked around.

"I don't know," he whispered, barely loud enough for Dani to hear him over the crowd. "I guess I'm worried about seeing it again."

"Seeing what?" Dani asked.

"You know, , the sculpture," he said.

"It's already gone," Dani told him. "Sold and shipped."

"Oh," Alek said. "Well, did you get another look at it?"

"No, it was already being crated up when I came in," Dani replied. "Why are you so concerned?"

"It's just that," Alek looked for the right words. "I know what Paul told us and what the paper said. That the guy must have gotten out before the tanks blew. But something inside me doesn't believe it. I haven't been able to sleep. His face, covered in oil, plays a loop in my head whenever I close my eyes. I was hoping to get one more look at it, see if it's just my imagination keeping me up or if it really looked exactly like what I saw."

"I saw it too, remember?" said Dani, putting her hand on his shoulder. "But it was dark. We were both way out of our element. The mind plays funny tricks on us."

"I know," Alek replied. "But I'd sure like to talk to the guy, just to be sure he's ok."

"Sure, who's ok?" Paul asked, returning with drinks in hand.

Alek got quiet.

Dani considered dropping it too, but she also didn't quite believe what the paper said about no one being hurt.

"Do you still have that guard schedule from the other night?" Dani asked.

Paul's smile disappeared entirely.

"What guard schedule? What other night?" He said through his teeth.

"We just want to talk to the guy," Alek jumped in, feeling emboldened by Dani. "Put both our minds at ease."

"Absolutely not," Paul replied. "Even if I had it, either of you talking to him would be a dead giveaway. Best you pretend it never happened."

"But," Dani began, but someone brushed past her, startling her before she could finish.

"I never thought in a million years I'd see you out and about again," a man with thick square glasses said to Paul.

He wore a black-and-white checkered suit, one designed to garner attention from anyone and everyone around him. His belt and shoes were both white leather. His short hair parted down the middle accentuated ears that were far too big for his head. With his hair and bowtie, he reminded Dani of Pee-wee Herman.

"Theo Argent," Paul replied. "My number one fan."

They shook hands, but their grasp seemed to linger as they stared into each other eyes with fierce glares.

"Still riding on the laurels of your work from almost a decade ago?" Theo asked with a smirk.

"Still pretending you have any artistic taste?" Paul replied.

Theo laughed as they released each other's hands.

"And who are these little followers?" Theo asked, resting his cheek on his hand.

"Dani Scotts and Alek Yukof," Paul said, gesturing to them with his arm.

Dani put her hand out to shake Theo's, but he did not reciprocate.

"I'm sorry," Theo said. "I don't shake hands with people I've never heard of."

"Don't be rude, Theo," Paul said. "It's unbecoming, especially for someone of your diminutive stature."

Paul looked intimidating, standing over the little man.

"I do suppose you have me there," Theo said, looking up at him. "But based on your most recent work, I've found the tallest fall the farthest."

Paul's fists clenched. He seemed ready to knock Theo's glasses right off his face.

Theo must have noticed it too.

"Alas, I can not stay and chat with the plebs all day," he said. "I have a personal tour of the hottest new exhibit in town, with none other than Lady Gianni herself. I mustn't keep her waiting, ta-ta."

He disappeared quickly into the crowd of people.

"You ok?" Dani asked Paul, his knuckles were turning white.

"I'm fine," he replied.

"Don't let him get to you," said Dani.

But something about Theo did get to Paul.

Lady Gianni began her introduction to the gathering. Dani slouched and hid her face behind Paul's shoulders as the woman spoke, hoping to avoid detection.

When Lady Gianni was done, the doormen removed the sashes, and they joined the horde, bustling to see the new exhibit first.

"What is it?" Alek asked her as they moved with the crowd.

"I don't know," Dani replied. "They were still building it when I left."

The crowd came to a sudden stop, and them along with it.

"What the hell?" Paul said with a grunt.

He tried to muscle through the people in front of them, but none of them would concede an inch. They were all standing up on their tippy-toes, trying to get a better look at what had halted the crowd.

"Holy shit," Paul said aloud, tall enough to see over the others.

"What is it?" Alek asked.

Dani could see it too.

In the center of *The Horizons* hall, where *Consume* had once stood, was a two story building. A house, with a full-size garage, a grass lawn out front, a mailbox, and a station wagon parked in the driveway. In the center of the yard was a large oak tree, stretching almost to the ceiling. Bright lights illuminated the inside of the house, the yellow glow of light bulbs showing through the windows. Behind it, a wall stood painted to show a night sky with a full moon.

"It's a house," Dani told Alek.

The crowd began to shift and move again.

The Dollhouse was its name, etched into the sidewalk in front of the enormous piece. where Dani and the rest walked up to join the queue of eager patrons. Her heels clapped on the hard walkway, which to her surprise wasn't plywood painted gray, but real concrete. The mailbox, also cemented into the ground, had an actual address painted on it.

The Johnsons

3493 Oak Lane

She carefully walked up the driveway where the station wagon sat, the rear hatch covered in various bumper stickers. A political one, blue and white with "Clinton - Kaine 2016" printed on it. One "My Child is an Honor Student at..." and at least two for restaurants Dani had never heard of. On the back window was a little stick figure family, a mom and dad, then four stick figure kids ranging from teenager to a baby in a stroller.

Paul stumbled backwards and nearly ran into Dani.

"Sorry," Paul said, trying to keep his composure. "Do you see that in the tree?"

Dani squinted. It was dark, but there was a round silhouette sitting on the oak tree's branch.

"It's an owl," Alek said, joining them.

"An owl in a tree," Bianca said, catching up to them. "How spooky!"

The sarcasm in her voice was palpable.

"It looks just like the owl I saw the other day," Paul said, straightening his collar.

Me too, Dani wanted to say, but held back.

"Is it real?" Alek asked.

"I don't think so," replied Dani. "It's not moving in the slightest."

"It looks so real, though," Paul said.

"It's just part of the piece," Bianca said. "Come on, I want to get inside before it gets any more crowded."

An old man in front of them pulled out his phone and held it up to take a photo.

"I don't think that's..." Dani tried to tell him, but it was too late. The flash went off.

Immediately, two large security guards appeared and snatched the camera from his hands.

"No photos!" One of them yelled.

"I'm sorry," the cameraman apologized.

Without another word, the two guards grabbed the man by the shoulders and shuffled him out of the gallery.

"Whoa," Alek said, eyes wide. "That was some real gestapo stuff right there."

"He did break the rules," Dani said, peering after them curiously.

The four friends entered the open front door of *The Dollhouse* and walked into the downstairs living room. The TV was on, playing a cartoon. Two figures sat on the couch watching it, their backs to the door.

Dani rounded the couch to see they were statues, perfect recreations of a woman and a little girl sitting and watching the television. In their hands was a bowl of popcorn. Dani looked around to see if anyone else was watching, then reached out and touched the little girl's knee.

It was solid and smooth, almost like glass.

"I think they're made of porcelain," Dani said.

"Porcelain?" Paul repeated back. "Like life-sized porcelain figures?"

"I think so," Dani said, stealing another touch. "The painting on them is immaculate. If they weren't sitting so still, I would have thought they were real."

"I can even smell the popcorn," Alek said.

In the kitchen, another porcelain statue of a teenager was working on what looked like homework at the kitchen table. She wore wireless earbuds in her ears, probably to drown out the sound of the cartoon in the background as she studied.

They wandered up the stairs, which were lined with family photos in frames on the wall. The photos looked just as real as everything else, with the family at the beach burying dad in the sand and several mall photo style family portraits.

"Amazing what they can do with a computer these days, right?" Paul said, examining one.

Every detail of the house felt complete. There was a half-used roll of toilet paper on the upstairs bathroom, along with a little boy brushing his teeth in the sink with actual water running down the drain. In the nursery, a father rocked in a chair holding a baby in his arms. How the chair was rocking was a mystery, perhaps some creative use of magnets or weights by the very innovative artist.

Dani's thoughts wandered back to what her own father was doing right now, a father that once rocked her to sleep just like this porcelain man was. They hadn't spoken in a long time. Her phone calls always went to voice mail and never returned. Was that fate reserved for this family as well?

They reconvened as a group on the bottom floor.

"Whoever designed this is amazing," Bianca said. "Everything is so perfect."

Alek looked solemn.

"What do you think, Alek?" Dani asked.

He thought about his words for a moment.

"I think it's tragic," Alek replied.

"Tragic?!" Paul couldn't believe it. "This is the perfect house. You should have seen the shithole apartment I grew up in with my mother and brother."

"I don't think we've finished the exhibit yet," Alek said, nodding towards the back door in the kitchen.

"You think there's more in the back?" Dani asked.

"I know there is," Alek said.

"Who's doing the honors?" asked Paul.

They could all feel it. Something about the back door felt off. The rest of the house, which was so warm, inviting, and brightly lit, was indeed perfect. But just behind the white dusty blinds that hung over the window was utter darkness.

Bianca stepped forward.

"I don't know what you're all scared of," Bianca said. "It's just an art piece."

She grabbed the door handle and pulled.

The door didn't move an inch.

"Looks like they don't want you going back there," she said, returning to the group. "You guys got yourselves wound up into knots over nothing."

"Wait," Alek said. "I can see something in the blinds."

"What is it?" Dani asked.

"I don't know," Alek took a step forward, then another until he was standing in front of the door. He tried the doorknob, but still it didn't move.

"Let's go," Bianca said, as she trotted off towards the exit. "Jeremiah is waiting for me."

None of the others moved a muscle.

Alek reached for the solid plastic tube that controlled the blinds and twirled it in his fingers.

The blinds flattened until they could see through them and out the window on the other side.

Staring back at them were a pair of white eyes in the darkness. A man's eyes.

Alek retreated to Dani and Paul immediately.

"Creepy," Alek said.

"Agreed," said Paul.

Dani couldn't speak, she just stared with fear, holding tight to every muscle of her body.

"Quite unsettling, isn't it?" said a voice behind them.

Dani turned and whatever fear she had been feeling seemed like nothing compared to what she felt now.

Lady Gianni was standing there with her hand on her hip, staring at her.

"Lady Gianni," Dani said, her voice returning to her body. She stared at the floor, preparing herself to be reprimanded, or worse, fired.

She waited for the woman's anger to come, but it didn't.

"Are you enjoying my *Dollhouse*?" Lady Gianni asked, her voice calm.

"It's great," Paul said. "Hello, my name is Paul…"

"Moreau," Lady Gianni finished for him. "I'm familiar with your work."

"I'm glad you like it," he said as they shook hands.

Lady Gianni raised an eyebrow at him.

"This is Alek," Dani said, introducing him to Lady Gianni, knowing he wouldn't do it himself.

"Nice to meet you, Alek," she said with a nod.

"Hello," Alek replied, his hands in his pockets and his eyes staring at the ground.

"I'm assuming the little sprite I passed on my way in is also one of yours?" Lady Gianni asked.

"Yes, that was Bianca," said Paul.

"I'm familiar with her work," Lady Gianni said, stepping forward towards the back door of *The Dollhouse*. They followed her with their eyes as she glided silently and softly.

"Shapes and color," Lady Gianni continued. "How original. Jeremiah raves about her."

She let out a little laugh.

"Doesn't quite have the same impact as something like this, does it?" She asked.

"Not at all," Paul said. He was smiling, trying to be charming.

"And don't you worry," Lady Gianni said. "I won't be stealing your Dani anytime soon. She made it clear where her allegiances lay. However, I do need to speak to her in private for a moment, if you don't mind."

Dani's heart sunk.

Dani and Lady Gianni disappeared through the side door that led to the offices. She was ready for the tongue-lashing she deserved.

Instead, there were two men waiting in the conference room, both laughing and chatting while holding crystal glasses full of whiskey.

"Gentlemen," Lady Gianni said, walking in ahead of Dani. "Let me introduce you to one of our new and most promising artists. This is Dani Scotts."

Dani felt like someone had dumped a bucket of cold water on her. Did Lady Gianni just call her a promising artist?

Dani recognized one of the men immediately. It was Jeremiah Henricks. He introduced himself like it was the first time they had met, even though this was now their third meeting.

The other was a kind looking old man.

"Well, aren't you a tall drink of water?" the man said, shaking her hand warmly. "The name is Craig Bones."

"I was just telling these two gentlemen about you," Lady Gianni remarked. "How Paul had you locked away in his tower, hiding your work from the world."

"Not exactly," Dani said. "He tries to sell them on..."

"Lady Gianni has never steered me wrong so far," Jeremiah said, interrupting her and speaking to Mr. Bones. "You'll get your money's worth."

"I don't know," the old man said, rubbing his hands together. "I'm not really a believer in any of this. Art has always seemed a bit like snake oil to me."

"Not this art," Lady Gianni said, putting her arm through his and walking him around the table to show him paintings and sketches on the walls. "All the pieces I sell are one of a kind, unique."

"But I've never heard of this girl before," Mr. Bones said. "No offense ma'am."

Dani nodded nervously as she crossed her arms. She didn't like being in the room and being talked about like she wasn't.

"Exactly," Lady Gianni said. "You're getting something really special, the chance to get her work at a steep discount before anyone else knows who she is yet."

"And you're certain she's going to be big one day?" Mr. Bones asked.

"Lady Gianni has delivered for me time and time again," Mr. Henricks said, sitting down and sipping at his glass. "Her record thus far has been flawless."

"So you're certain it'll... you know," Mr. Bones said, not sure what the right word to use was.

"Appreciate," Lady Gianni said for him with a wink. "I guarantee it."

Mr. Bones stopped and stared at Dani for a long moment.

"Damn why not?" He said at last. "But start small, nothing crazy. If it 'appreciates' like you say, then I'll be back for more. Lots more."

"I'm so glad you've decided to move forward," Lady Gianni said. "You won't be disappointed."

"Come along now," Mr. Henricks said, leading Mr. Bones past Dani and out of the conference room. "I got a new friend you just have to meet."

The door slammed as they exited back into the gallery.

"Excuse me Lady Gianni," Dani began. "Were you serious when you told them I was going to be a famous artist one day?"

Lady Gianni looked at her from across the table with a grin.

"With a little help from me," she said, walking around the table, trailing her finger on its surface. "You'll be bigger than Paul or any of your friends."

"But all my work is back at The Collective," Dani said. "I promised Paul the stuff I made there belongs there."

"Not to worry," Lady Gianni said, reaching Dani. "He just commissioned $20,000 for you to make something new. You begin work tomorrow."

"$20,000?!" Dani repeated. Her eyes were wide. She couldn't believe it.

"Don't get too excited," Lady Gianni said with a laugh. "After taxes and the gallery's non-negotiable fee, it'll only be twelve or thirteen thousand. But it's a start."

Dani didn't know what to say.

"See you in the morning Dani," Lady Gianni said, escorting her out of the room.

"Thank you mam," Dani said, walking slowly away. Her legs felt like jelly, like she was about to collapse. She had sold her first piece of art and for more than she ever thought she could get.

"Oh and Dani," Lady Gianni called for her.

Dani turned around.

"You don't need to sneak your friends in anymore," Lady Gianni said. "I put them on the permanent list."

She winked.

CHAPTER 9

That damn owl. It tormented Larry all day long again. Right outside his window, just hooting and hooting and hooting. Sleeping was hard enough with his blood pressure at near boiling point, whatever junk that dealer had given him putting his body into overdrive.

Larry hadn't slept in two whole days and almost a minute didn't pass that he didn't imagine her.

He just wanted a solid eight hours of sleep, an opportunity to clear his head. An opportunity to get away from her. The teenage girl's face, the one driving the car that had nearly ended his pathetic life, followed him around the mobile home like a ghost. He saw her in the bathroom mirror, in the window's reflection, and every time he closed his eyes.

Maybe a walk could help burn it out of his system.

Pulling his coat on, he prepared to face the brisk night air.

The waxing moon was bright enough to cast a serene aura across Sunny Meadows. Reflecting brightly off the reflective metal roofs of some homes. The community pool, surrounded by a rusty chain-link fence, tinted the lunar body's reflection a sickish green.

"Shit," he mumbled to himself.

Up ahead, his neighbor sat in a lawn chair, holding a rifle across his lap. He was facing away from Larry, but if Larry tried to leave through the main gate, he would have to pass right in front of him. Larry would have to own up to not having the money he owed him, money he never intended to pay back.

Ducking to the side of the doublewide, Larry decided a walk through the forest wouldn't be a bad idea after all.

Disappearing into the tree line, Larry purposely focused his thoughts on everything other than the girl. He still hadn't called Tom yet, not sure if it was because of apathy for the shitty job working for that pompous bitch

Lady Gianni or that he was just afraid to face a friend who had stuck his neck out for him. With time, Tom would understand. He had been on the inside, just like Larry. They both knew that when men like them fall, they fall hard.

"Who," the owl said above him, watching his every movement with invisible eyes.

The forest floor announced his arrival like an amplifier, each step finding fresh twigs to snap and dried up leaves to crunch.

"Who," the owl continued, he had walked a quarter of a mile, but he could still hear it.

"Leave me alone dammit," Larry said to the owl.

"Who," it replied. "Her."

Larry stopped in his tracks.

Did he just hear it speak?

"What do you want?" He asked.

"Who, who, her..." The owl repeated its strange call.

Larry concentrated on locating the creature in the darkness. He peered all around and stopped. There she was, the face of the girl, centered in his thoughts once again. He had lasted maybe ten minutes, but her terrified face had caught up to him. She was standing naked in front of him, obscured by the shadows of the branches, but it was her. He knew it for certain.

He needed something else, something powerful, to kill enough brain cells to get rid of her for good.

The convenience store was dead aside from the group of homeless huddled in the back alley sipping from large bottles of malt liquor. Larry perused the glass windows of the beer cooler carefully. He had originally planned on buying a large bottle of cheap vodka, but thought against it, considering he hadn't eaten since yesterday. He wanted something more filling, and like the slaves that built the pyramids, beer was the best way to fulfill both his needs.

Glancing up, he could see the large wall-eyed mirror glass in the corner where the wall met the ceiling. In it, he saw the cashier's reflection as they read a comic book behind the counter. Larry knew the man wasn't reading at all. He was watching Larry closely.

It might have been the gang tattoos visible on Larry's bare forearms that gave the clerk so much suspicion. The very marks on his skin that boldly proclaimed his faction to any possible threats on the inside, that may have saved his very life, now condemned him outside the prison's walls to a permanent state as a pariah of society.

Once a con, always a con, he thought to himself.

He hadn't even gone to prison for theft, but once someone realizes you've been, they assume it was for just about every crime imaginable. People and politicians like to talk a big game about how prisons are about reforming prisoners, preparing them to re-enter the world as positive contributors to society. But when you get up close to someone, no one treats you like you're reformed. They assume the worst. Larry might as well had been Jeffrey Dahmer as far as the clerk was concerned.

It was either a bleak take on the success of our prison system at doing its job or a revelation that they exist only to punish and remove someone from society.

Recidivism, a fancy word for setting someone up for failure.

A bell dinged as the front door opened and another customer entered. Larry didn't bother to look up to see who it might be. Whomever they were, he could hear them rustling around in the candy aisle behind him.

A 30-pack should do it; a case of the cheapest, skunkiest beer the store had to offer. Larry didn't know how long his last paycheck would last. He turned to head to the front counter when he saw her. The teenage girl, the one driving the car, was there chatting with the clerk. They apparently knew each other.

"How's Marci doing?" the teenage girl asked.

"She's good, going to state next year," the clerk replied.

"Tell her Lisa Johnson says hi," the teenager added.

The clerk finished ringing her up for the candy on the counter and she paid with cash.

Larry stood perfectly still, watching her from the back of the store.

"Lisa Johnson," he said her name under his breath. The girl who had been haunting him finally had a name.

He felt disappointment fill his heart as she left out the front doors, waving goodbye and smiling at the clerk as she did. He saw her hop into a running car out front and disappear from his sight, but not from his mind. From there, she would never leave.

The beer hadn't lasted long. From the stump in the forest, under the pale moonlight, cans littered the ground at his feet as Larry hummed a song to himself.

He hadn't been the first person to drink at this stump. Stomped flat cans of fancier beers decayed around him. Teenagers from the affluent neighborhood nearby must also sneak off into the woods to this same stump to kill a few brewskis and talk about TikTok and Instagram, or whatever kids talk about these days.

Larry swayed slightly as the cold liquid chilled his throat.

"Who," the owl said. "Who, who, her."

He tossed the half-empty beer can at a branch, hoping it would hit the damn thing. Of course he missed. He didn't know where the owl was perched nor could his aim be trusted in such an inebriated state.

"Screw you," he yelled at it.

His head swirled. Without food in his belly, the alcohol hit him faster than he could have imagined. Larry was about to head home, wanting nothing more than to fall face first into his bed.

He froze instead. There was a movement in the surrounding trees.

Alarm gripped him. Was it a wolf or bear, maybe?

Unlikely, this was suburbia after all.

There it was again. He caught a glimpse this time.

It was a person's leg, running to hide behind a tree.

It must be one of those damn kids from the neighborhood messing with him.

"Leave me alone," Larry yelled. "Go back home, you punks."

He heard a girl giggle in response.

"I said leave me alone," Larry yelled again. "I just want to drink in peace."

Another shape moved from tree to tree, just outside the faint moonlight.

Larry ran after it. He was going to show them they messed with the wrong drunk.

Chasing the person into the woods, he struggled to keep up with them. They were nothing but a pale shape. Every once in a while, they would run through a beam of moonlight breaking through the thick canopy and he'd get a clue about them.

Long brown hair.

Pale skin.

Stripped completely naked

It was a girl.

Except no girl would streak through a dark forest like this on such a chilly night.

His mind wandered until it came across something else that she reminded him of, something from a tale his grandmother had told him.

A nymph, a lady of the forest.

Something about the thought excited him. He pushed his pace faster.

"Who, who, her?" the owl jeered at him as it glided silently overhead.

Larry wasn't thinking. His body was acting all on its own, his subconscious securely in the driver's seat. He lunged forward, wrapping his arms around the girl.

The nymph tried to squirm away. His fingers gripped tighter, inching closer and closer until they found her neck.

He squeezed and squeezed, his eyes clouded in a red fog. The nymph's body felt like it was melting in his hands, the soft flesh flowing through the gaps between his digits.

As the red cleared from his vision, he found nothing between his fingers but a thick wad of mud and leaves. The nymph was gone.

What had his grandmother told him? That nymphs could magically turn back into trees, branches, leaves at any moment they pleased.

A bunch of teases, he thought as he stood up and tried to brush off the mud from his shirt and pants.

Still, he longed for her, even if she was just a figment of his imagination. Not being with a woman since he got out of jail had been difficult. Even the lowliest of prostitutes had denied him, assuming the worst of his intentions as they stared with worried eyes at his shaved head and features aged behind his years. Professionals or not, they couldn't rise above their own prejudices.

"Where am I?" Larry said aloud, as if the owl overhead could tell him.

He had emerged from the forest onto the street of one of the family neighborhoods. The sidewalk was clean, freshly swept by expensive landscaping companies, and neatly manicured lawns bordered it.

He had no idea where he was, and without a working phone, he would have to find a landmark to help him find his way. Covered in dirt and leaves, he would undoubtedly be a frightening sight to any neighborhood watch group on patrol. A mud monster from the comic books of the 40s and 50s.

Walking to the first house in front of him, Larry looked at the mailbox.

The Johnsons

3493 Oak Lane

A thought popped into his head, a recollection or perhaps déjà vu.

Pulling the scrap of paper still in his pocket (he hadn't changed in several days) he saw the address matched. He was in front of the exact house where the woman and daughter who had hit him with their minivan lived. The same girl he had just seen at the convenience store.

He needed to get out of there, and fast.

"Who, who, her," the owl said to him. This time, he could see it. The large brown bird was visible from a branch in the front yard of the Johnson's home.

Then he saw her.

She was crossing in front of the living room window that faced the street; she wore a white tank top and blue jeans. Her brown hair flowed down her shoulders. Every detail of her he already knew with an encyclopedic knowledge from the hours spent staring at her in his head.

It was his forest nymph.

Lisa Johnson didn't even see him when she peered through the glass to the street. Camouflaged in mud, he was the invisible watcher. She closed the front blinds, but when the kitchen light went on, he knew where she had gone.

Larry looked up at the owl.

"Is this what you wanted all along?" he whispered. "To bring her and I together?"

The owl said nothing and only stared back at him with round coals for eyes.

The sober often laugh at the nonsensical decisions of the inebriated. The daring disregard for personal danger or consequences that the drunk embodies while pursuing something they have a momentary desire for. It's almost as if the alcohol removes one's own instinct for self-preservation, numbing it until it's mute and only one thing remains.

Desire.

Too many chemicals coerced in his body, some natural and some artificial, all jostling for control. Without thinking, Larry found himself at the kitchen window, watching the nymph through the blinds. His breath grew heavy with lust. She sat at the kitchen table with books and notebooks open in front of her. He ogled her revealing, low-cut top. He obsessed over every bite of the stringy candy that she put to her lips and chewed. Her pen moved across the paper as she listened to music, oblivious to the presence observing her.

Lisa was just as attractive and beautiful as he had remembered. Her long hair dangled down from her ears, almost touching the table. She had a few freckles, the kind that only accentuated her youth.

The image of her lying on her back in the forest with his hands wrapped around her neck filled his mind. But they were just images, fleeting things that came and went, teasing and tormenting him.

Larry wanted more. He reached down and touched the doorknob. He could be in and out before anyone else could be there.

A man walked into the kitchen.

Larry collapsed to the ground and out of sight quickly. Leaning against the wall next to the door, he dared not move. He only heard a few muffled words from inside that he couldn't make out, accompanied by footsteps, and they were getting closer.

Larry waited for the doorknob to turn and tried to consider what he would do when it did. Would he run back to the street? Would he face the man and fight?

He would do neither. The doorknob didn't turn, but, to his disappointment, the latch of the deadbolt slid into place.

His chance, his opportunity, was gone.

Larry stayed up, watching the girl until she yawned and went to bed.

Defeated, he wandered through the forest until he was back at Sunny Meadows where sitting on his roof waiting for him was the owl.

CHAPTER 10

Dani woke up early that morning, a full half hour before her alarm. Nightmares about the watcher from *The Dollhouse* dominated her sleep. Every time she opened her restless eyes, she would sit up suddenly imaging she had seen them through the skylight window, but every time it had only been her imagination. She convinced herself it was just anxiety. After a quick shower, she applied her makeup in the locker room downstairs.

Bianca came bouncing down the steps.

"Thought I heard you down here," she said, walking up to Dani, who sat in the chair wearing only her bathrobe.

Dani instinctively pulled the robe tighter around her shoulders.

"Getting ready for work?" Bianca asked, putting her hands on Dani's shoulders and rubbing them.

"Yes," Dani answered. "She's having me paint today."

"Oh, Jeremiah told me," Bianca replied, walking to the showers. Dani could see her in the mirror, Bianca was taking off her t-shirt.

"Something for Mr. Bones, right?" Bianca asked, suddenly turning to face Dani, who could see her voluptuous bare chest.

Dani quickly looked away from the mirror, embarrassed to be caught staring at her roommate undressing.

"Yes, though I'm not sure what I should paint," Dani replied as calmly as she could. She had accidentally smeared some of her lipstick. She wiped it off with a towel.

"Well, Jeremiah says Mr. Bones has no artistic taste," Bianca continued, pulling her sweatpants down to her ankles.

Dani tried to calm herself down. She was growing painfully aroused, something she could absolutely not let happen in front of Bianca.

To Dani's relief, Bianca stepped into the shower and closed the curtain behind her.

"So you can probably paint whatever you want," Bianca yelled over the roar of the water pressure. "A flower, some leaves, a tree, anything really. Jeremiah asked me to paint him something. I threw a couple squares and a triangle on canvas and he told me it was the most amazing thing he'd ever seen. Can you believe that? Art is wasted on men, especially businessmen. They have no patience for it."

No response.

"Dani?" Bianca asked, sticking her head out of the curtain. "You there?"

But Dani wasn't. She had hastily collected her things and practically ran up the stairs to her room.

S lamming the door behind her, Dani tried to calm down.

Big breaths in and out, big breaths.

She needed to get her mind off of Bianca and fast. She thought about masturbating, but she didn't have enough time for that. Regardless, it hadn't helped her appease her sexual appetite for her roommate in the past, only amplified it.

"What am I painting?" she said aloud, packing her art supplies into a duffel bag and pushing her mind to other things. "What am I painting?"

"Paint whatever you want," Bianca had said downstairs.

Dani looked around the room until her eyes settled on the flowerpot next to her bed. It was a bright yellow sunflower. Dani had grown it since it was a seedling. It was almost a foot tall and had just finished flowering for the first time.

Checking the time, she knew she was out of it.

She slung the duffel bag over her shoulder and picked up the plant. It would be awkward to hold it on the subway ride to the gallery, but she didn't have a choice. She hurried downstairs and out the front door, hoping she didn't run into Bianca again that morning.

Foreman Tom waved at Dani as she walked into Gallery Nocturne. She was glad he wasn't in trouble for helping her and her friends get in.

She waved back but then quickly realized he wasn't just waving; he was beckoning her over.

"Good morning," he said as she approached.

"Good morning," she replied. "Thank you again for last night."

"Not a problem," said Tom. "Nice flower."

"Thanks," said Dani.

"Have you heard from your friend if Larry is doing alright?" Tom asked.

Dani had almost forgotten about Larry, the dock-worker who let them in on their first adventure to the gallery.

"I haven't talked to them," Dani felt bad for lying to Tom, who had been nothing but helpful and friendly to her.

"Well, could you do me a favor and see if you can get a hold of him?" Tom began. "He missed a couple of shifts now and no one has heard from him. Ex-cons aren't always the most reliable people. They have a hard time getting their feet under them again after a stumble."

Dani thought about it.

"I think I owe you one, so of course," Dani said. "I'll see if we can track him down."

"Great, I appreciate it," he said with a smile.

"Do you know where Lady Gianni is?" Dani asked.

"Last I saw her, over by the entrance to *The Veil*," Tom replied.

"Thank you," Dani said, walking off.

"Let me know if you get a hold of Larry," Tom yelled as she walked away.

At the entrance to *The Veil*, Dani found Lady Gianni talking to one of Tom's workers about changing the layout of *The Horizons* again.

"Still not quite right?" Dani asked as she walked up, the worker quickly agreeing to the request and shuffling away as if scared off at Dani's very arrival.

"It's never right," Lady Gianni replied. "Every time they change one thing, another one seems out of place. That's a nice flower you brought today, for me?"

"Not quite," Dani suddenly felt self-conscious. "I was thinking I would paint this for Mr. Bones."

Lady Gianni stared at Dani and then back to the flower alternately, her smile gone and those narrow, keen eyes seemed to soak up every detail.

She hates it, Dani thought to herself. She should have thought of something more clever. Only Dani would think that a painting of some sunflower would be worth $20,000.

"Do you know how long a sunflower lives?" Lady Gianni asked.

"I don't actually," Dani replied.

"About 150 days," Lady Gianni said. "Less than 6 months, then it withers away and dies. Only its seeds live to sow another day."

"Do you want me to find something else?" asked Dani.

"Absolutely not," said Lady Gianni. "The sunflower is perfect."

Dani felt relieved.

"Is there a studio I can set up in?" Dani asked.

She sat the flowerpot down and pulled her duffel bag to her front, unzipping it to reveal her painting supplies. When she looked up, she found Lady Gianni wearing a scowl on her face.

"You won't be needing those primitive tools," the woman said, picking up the bag from Dani's arms and throwing it to the side. Several of Dani's paint brushes went skittering across the floor.

She moved to go recover them, but Lady Gianni stopped her with a hand on her shoulder.

"I've got something for you inside," Lady Gianni said, her mouth tight and expressionless again. "Something much better."

Lady Gianni disappeared through the doorway. Dani paused for a moment, wondering whether she should grab her duffel bag, but decided against it. Picking up the sunflower pot, she followed into *The Veil*.

The Veil was brightly lit and active. Clouds moved in the sky above the horizon that surrounded the meadow, the birds chirped over the speakers, and the grass smelled fresher than ever.

An easel, stool, and chair sat next to the pond where Lady Gianni stood waiting for Dani. Dani hurried over with her flower in hand.

The pond caught her eye. It was still as glass except for the reflections of the clouds and sun overhead that blew in the wind. The reflection was so clear it was like she was looking directly up at the sky.

Dani jumped when a pebble went skipping by on the surface, the ripples destroying the perfect mirror image.

"Sorry," Lady Gianni said. "Couldn't help myself."

She grinned playfully.

"It's so serene," Dani replied. "It's easy to get caught up in it."

"Serenity is so overrated," said the museum director. "Give me a chaotic storm instead of a cloudless sky any day."

"I like the quiet," Dani said, without thinking.

Together, they walked the last few yards to the impromptu studio, where a bag sat on the ground.

"I took the liberty of acquiring new brushes and paint for you," Lady Gianni said. "I believe you'll find these quite superior over your previous tools."

Dani pulled out the items from inside the bag. An improvement might be an understatement.

She ran her fingers through the brushes, real animal hair.

"Sable hair," Lady Gianni said as she watched. "From Siberia."

Dani pulled out several sealed containers of paint.

"All made from natural ingredients," Lady Gianni said. "None of that synthetic garbage that's made in a lab. The Tyrian Purple from sea snail shell, the Carmine from insects in Central America. Very difficult to obtain, but there's a magic to the old methods."

"The colors of these are amazing," Dani said, her eyes marveling at each. She opened one up and prepared to dip her finger inside to see the color on her skin.

Faster than a praying mantis snatching an insect from mid-air, Lady Gianni grabbed her hand, stopping her fingers mere centimeters from the paint.

"You must be careful," Lady Gianni said, releasing Dani's hand from her tight grip. "Though natural, they are still quite toxic. Many ancient artists have fallen prey to their effects on the human body and mind."

Her grip was vice-like. Though Dani was taller and more built than the older woman, she doubted she could break it if she struggled.

"Be especially careful with the brown," Lady Gianni added, letting go of Dani's hand. "I've been told it's cursed."

Dani's eyes grew wide and stared at her.

Lady Gianni let out a loud laugh and smiled.

"I'm kidding, of course," she added with a wink.

Dani laughed with her.

She went to work setting up her painting area inside *The Veil*. She set out her brushes on the tray, lined up the paint in an order like she had back at The Collective, and fussed with the other materials until everything was perfectly arranged.

Lady Gianni stood quietly a few paces away, watching the entire time.

Lastly, Dani placed the flowerpot on a stool in front of the easel. The way the lighting was in that one spot, the light side of the meadow hit the sunflower perfectly on one side and the dark clouds of the nightmare side of the meadow on the other. The sunflower showed a perfect duality that Dani found pleasing to the eye.

But something else in the background was not so pleasing.

The painting *My Body* hung on the wall just to the right of the sunflower. The creature with the sharp claws and featureless face haunting her peripheral vision.

She picked up the pot and stool, intending to move it to a new location with a less distracting background.

Something caught her eye in the painting, something she hadn't noticed before. She remembered the face of the monster trying to burst out of the man's back to be blank and featureless; no eyes, nose, or mouth. However, in that moment, she saw something else on the creature's face.

She walked closer to examine it; the shape disappeared when you stood still but was visible when you moved around the canvas.

"It's called phantom painting," Lady Gianni said, walking up to join her as Dani moved forward, backward, and side-to-side in front of the piece. "Using the same color with only the most subtle of changes to the pigment to add something that's only there when moving to a different angle of the light or distance."

Dani remembered it was a difficult method that she had heard about from Alek, who had tried experimenting with it but failed.

"I think it's a nose," Dani said. "The artist gave the monster a feminine nose."

"The monster?" Lady Gianni said. "That is no monster. It's just the creature inside."

"Sure looks like a monster to me," Dani replied.

"You should get to work," said Lady Gianni. She sounded slightly disappointed.

"You're right," Dani said, peeling her eyes off of *My Body*.

She walked over and placed the sunflower on the opposite side of the meadow, then adjusted her easel, chair, and supplies until they faced away from the haunting painting. The light wasn't as perfect, but Dani would have to make do.

Dani sat in the chair and faced the blank canvas.

"I'll leave you to it," Lady Gianni said, walking towards the exit.

"Lady Gianni," Dani said after the museum director was almost to the door.

"Yes, my dear?" Lady Gianni replied.

"Thank you for this," Dani said with a smile.

Lady Gianni smiled back.

"No, thank you," she said. "I have a feeling this is just the beginning of a long and lucrative relationship."

With one more quick and smooth movement, Lady Gianni disappeared from *The Veil*.

Dani was alone with her paint and her flower.

Dani put her ear buds in and put her Pandora on shuffle to a relaxing music station. She liked to listen to music while she painted. A synthesizer played a soothing melody that reminded her of a nursery lullaby.

She started with the brown and noticed the label on it, Mummy Brown.

"Cursed, right?" Dani said with a chuckle out loud. Lady Gianni did have a sense of humor, after all.

Dipping her brush, she scraped the soft sable hair against the canvas in what would be the brown flower pot the sunflower rested in. Filled with moist soil, rich in nutrients for the flower to grow in; it was the perfect, nurturing home for the seed to grow in. Dani its parent, tending to its watering and pruning needs.

Dani thought back to her own childhood, to her earliest memories. Her parents had built her a pot to grow in as well. They had tried to do everything right for her as a child. Getting her involved in sports early, like soccer, baseball, and basketball. She was taller than the other kids, so everyone just thought she would be a natural athlete. She wasn't.

Still, her parents had encouraged her, pushing her to grow into one.

The house she remembered growing up in was like any other on their suburban block. Her mom volunteered, as many mothers often did those days, at the local parish church. She helped organize events and services. They prayed together before meals, a special moment Dani remembered fondly where they all just sat quietly and held hands.

Her dad was a mechanical engineer, jumping from company-to-company, trying to climb the corporate ladder and ensure they had a comfortable life. He was one of those man's man types, obsessed with sports. After dinner, he would have her sit on the couch and watch whatever live event was on TV, encouraging her to cheer his teams on. She wondered if part of the reason her hair was so thin now was because she had worn baseball caps non-stop as a child.

She paused. The flower pot was coming together nicely on the canvas.

She cleaned her brush before grabbing a fresh one and dipping it into the vermilion. It was time to paint the stalk and the leaves.

Growing into her adolescent years, Dani found the other kids, especially the boys, caught up to her in height. She was no longer the tallest in her class and her performance in sports dwindled. Her father still pushed her to be a competitor. She didn't want to go, but her father insisted she go to sports camps in the summers. While her friends were home playing video games, going to the mall, and seeing movies; she was running and jumping through the air on fields and courts or swinging bats at balls. She never had the heart to tell her dad she would have preferred to be home with a book or drawing in her sketchbook.

Her mom got her involved at the church. She would ring the bell or bring up various books to the pastor during church services. Another activity she didn't particularly enjoy, but it made her mom happy. That was enough.

But every day she felt different, like she was acting like someone she was not. The pressure growing little by little each time, until the weight became heavier than she wanted to bear.

The stalk and leaves on the canvas were simple structures, not requiring much thought. A few gentle wisps of the brush and they were done. It was time for the flower itself, the most intricate part.

She cleaned her brush and dipped a fresh one in a paint that was the most brilliant yellow she had ever seen.

The sun above the meadow darkened as storm clouds rumbled over. She considered going to find Foreman Tom or Lady Gianni and asking them to reset the room so that she could keep the perfect light, but seeing the darkening background behind the flower somehow made its yellow look more spectacular, so she decided against it. She would paint it as is.

The music playlist began with a new song, this one dominated by the ambiance of falling rain. The sound of rain always would be associated with a specific memory in Dani's mind—the day she came out to her parents.

They had reacted like many parents of queer children did, with confusion, sadness, and anger. Unable to understand what she was telling them, as if the words she used to describe herself and her sexual identity were spoken in some foreign language. They had told her it was all a choice, and she could choose to be what they wanted her to be, what they expected her to be. But Dani was who she was. No one, not even herself or her parents, could change that.

Dani wasn't even paying attention to the canvas in front of her. Her hands dipped for fresh paints and brushes, almost as if they were creating on their own.

From the time she was fourteen until she left the house, her parents and her fought almost every night. Bible camps and church retreats replaced sports camps in the summers, where she was told that she was just confused.

Her mother burned the clothes she bought for herself, forcing her to wear only what her parents approved of. When she came out to her friends, she had hoped they would have been welcoming. She had been wrong.

Many didn't understand it, or couldn't understand it. Her parents shunned the friends who did, the ones who were open to the real her. Left alone in her house with her parents controlling her every move, her life grew as dark as *The Veil*'s storm that raged around her.

On the canvas, the flower's bloom stunted in the darkness. The rain, the wind, the relentless storms threatened to blow it down until it was no more.

It had at last come to a head. They gave her a choice, to conform or leave. Living on the streets was tough, but at least she would be free. Jobs were scarce and the halfway houses presented their own challenges, but no one in the city was forcing her to have identity counseling with a pastor.

It was true Dani didn't shine as bright as she would have liked; she kept her secret from her roommates at The Collective. It was nice living there, but she didn't want to risk even the slightest chance of alienating any of them.

Her hand dropped the paintbrush into the tray. She took a deep breath and stood up.

The storm was full on overhead, thunder rumbling and the false rain coming down in sheets.

She looked at her work.

But it wasn't what she had made. At least she didn't think it was.

She had planned on painting a beautiful and vibrant sunflower in a pot, cheerful and uplifting. The flower on the canvas that stared back at her was none of those things. It was sad and wilting. Little shriveled leaves dotting the surface under the pot where a crack had formed that leaked precious, life-giving moisture. The petals themselves were not the brilliant yellow she had chosen, but a dull mustard-like hue with dark blotches.

Concern immediately filled her thoughts, concern that this would not be what Mr. Bones had expected, not what he would pay for.

"Glad to see you finished it so quickly," Lady Gianni said as she approached from the open door.

"I'm sorry mam," Dani said, standing up to greet her. "I think I should start over. This isn't what I was trying to paint. It's all wrong. I can do better."

Dani tried to stand between the painting and Lady Gianni, hoping to hide her shameful work.

"Move please," Lady Gianni said, with that voice of command that was impossible to deny.

Begrudgingly, Dani shifted to the side.

Lady Gianni just stared at the canvas, her eyes unmoving, studying it closely.

Dani closed her eyes.

The silence stretched the seconds.

"It's perfect," Lady Gianni said.

Dani peered out, checking to see if Lady Gianni was being sarcastic.

She wasn't. She looked completely serious.

"I didn't think this is what Mr. Bones wanted when he commissioned me for it," Dani said.

"Trust me," said Lady Gianni. "He's going to love it."

CHAPTER 11

Foreman Tom's crew removed the painting from the easel, placing it in a pre-made crate, and secured it delicately.

"Don't you worry Dani," Tom said as she watched the men nervously. "They'll take it back to prep it, then straight to Mr. Bones's office. His assistant has been calling to ask about it all morning. Apparently, he's antsy to see it."

Dani didn't know what to make of it.

She watched quietly, holding her sunflower in her arms with Lady Gianni by her side.

Something about watching the sunflower painting being taken away didn't sit well with her. She hadn't felt that way when her dozens of other works went into Paul's storage room back at The Collective, but something about this painting left her feeling empty inside.

But it wasn't an emptiness of longing like one might have for a long-lost pet or dear friend. The closest she could make sense of it was that somehow, during the process of creating it, the painting, or maybe the canvas itself, had absorbed some of the emotion of traumatic memories. The memories were still there, easily accessible in her mind, but how they had made her feel was gone, like food absent of flavor. It was a silly thought, a ridiculous thought.

"They are merely vessels," she remembered Lady Gianni's words.

If so, why did she feel sad for that pain to disappear into the old church's backroom? Maybe it was her trauma and pain that helped define who she was, and without it there was a vast space left behind inside her heart. Even painful memories are better than emotionless ones.

With the morning's painting session complete, the gallery's occupants went about their daily activities as if nothing had happened. The workmen hustling through *The Horizons,* packing up pieces and replacing them with new ones. After giving Tom new instructions, Lady Gianni and Dani whisked away into the secluded offices, away from the sounds of hammering and sawing.

"Can you make reservations tonight at eight for me and three others at Bar Fly?" Lady Gianni asked as soon as they were inside. "Some old friends are mine are in town."

"Yes, Lady Gianni," Dani said, making a note in her phone and opening the conference room door for her boss.

"Get the private room," Lady Gianni added. "We have important business to discuss and I don't want to be..."

Her voice trailed off as she stopped dead in her tracks.

"Really, Bar Fly?" said a man sitting on a chair in the conference room with his feet on the table. "It's just so gauche."

"Salvador!" Lady Gianni exclaimed.

"Ciao," he replied, standing up and kissing her on the cheeks. "And who is this beautiful flower?"

Dani thought he was referring to the sunflower in the pot she was still holding, blushing when she realized he was actually referring to her.

"This is my new project," Lady Gianni said, putting a hand on Dani's shoulder. "Dani Scotts."

Every time Lady Gianni touched her bare skin, she couldn't help but feel a wave of calm fall over her that erased her worry and anxiety like it was nothing.

"Dani, this is Salvador Vega Caruso," Lady Gianni said, introducing them. "He's one of my oldest friends."

"Actually," Salvador said, correcting her. "I am your oldest friend."
He winked.

"And my broker in Europe," Lady Gianni added.

"Pleasure to meet you," Dani said, extending her hand.

Salvador leaned forward in a bow as he took her hand and kissed the top of it daintily.

"The pleasure is mine," he said with a grin that could deceive the devil.

Dani noticed his style of dress was quite bizarre. He wore a purple suit with white lace frill cuffs that extended past his knuckles. His high-heeled boots were black and freshly shined, giving them the appearance of seal skin. Dark hair, done up like a pompadour, accentuated his dark eye liner.

"What are you doing here?" Lady Gianni asked. "I thought you were in Milan for a show."

"I was," he replied. "But the scene has just become somewhat melancholic. No one is creating anything fun anymore. Everything is the same old depressing shit."

Lady Gianni laughed.

"Europe has been on the decline for so long," she said. "You really should come to America, to the realm of limitless possibilities."

"The wild, wild west," Salvador said with a smirk. "Alas, my family would never allow it. Too many old connections and relationships to maintain. I'm also not convinced the average American knows what art is anymore."

"True," Lady Gianni replied. "But art has a strange way of propping up out here where it's least expected. Like flowers sprouting through cracks in the pavement."

She shot a side glance at Dani.

"I see," Salvador said, raising his eyebrows.

The room settled into a contested silence for a moment.

"Dani," Lady Gianni said, breaking it. "Why don't you see to those reservations while Salvador and I catch up?"

"Of course, Lady Gianni," Dani replied.

"It was a pleasure to meet you, Dani Scotts," Salvador said, bowing once again. "I hope to see you this summer at my villa in Cinque Terra. The view of the sunset over the sea is quite magnificent, ripe with inspiration for flowers like yourself."

Dani didn't know where Cinque Terra was, but wherever it may be, she immediately felt the excitement of a possible visit.

"We'll see," Lady Gianni added.

Dani closed the conference room door behind her and sat at her desk. She felt bad for the sunflower, though brightly lit there was no natural sunlight for it down here.

"A few more hours," she said sweetly. "Then we'll be home again."

She poured some water into its soil, hoping that would hold it over until then.

Looking up Bar Fly's information on Google, she pressed the first few numbers into her phone but stopped herself.

Should she be getting a reservation for five instead of four now that Salvador was in town?

Pressing the button on the intercom that tapped into the conference room, she was about to ask Lady Gianni the same question, but the two were already deep in conversation.

"I didn't realize you were recruiting talent from around here," she heard Salvador say. "I always thought you liked artists from abroad."

"I'm trying something new this time," Lady Gianni replied.

Dani knew she shouldn't be listening in, but something about their words intrigued her, begging her to linger on the open line.

"But people like her," said Salvador. "How could they possibly create something as powerful?"

"I think our own assumptions blind us to new possibilities," said Lady Gianni in retort. "We've looked down on them for so long, we never stopped to recognize their true potential."

"You think her work will be more moving than the seasoned artists I've been recommending?" Salvador asked.

Dani felt nervous. She didn't enjoy being discussed without being certain what it was about.

"I'm almost sure of it," Lady Gianni said.

"Are you concerned about repercussions?" Salvador asked. "Your usual type has been supplying you generously for some time now. If they find out you replaced them with some girl you found at a coffee shop, you may find yourself blacklisted or worse..."

His words hung in the air.

Lady Gianni laughed.

"When I show the world how powerful her work can be," said Lady Gianni. "They won't be angry, they'll be thrilled."

"You've placed your faith in such experiments before," Salvador said. "I seem to remember that not working out so great for you."

Silence crept back into the room.

For the first time ever, Lady Gianni didn't have an immediate reply.

Dani dared a glance through the glass doors. Lady Gianni was sitting in a chair across from Salvador, her posture perfect, her face stoic, but somewhere in her eyes Dani could see that an old wound had been opened.

"As we are friends," Lady Gianni said, her voice calm and collected. "I'll let that slide for now. I think my experiment taught me and the rest of our community a powerful lesson on not underestimating them, wouldn't you say?"

Salvador must have realized he had hit a nerve.

"I completely agree," he said, trying to shrug it off.

"Very well," Lady Gianni said

The silence returned.

"And Dani," Lady Gianni said suddenly.

Dani almost fell out of her chair. How long had she known that Dani was listening in?

"Please add Salvador to the reservation tonight," she said.

"Yes mam," Dani said, not sure of what else to say, before cutting the line.

After Salvador left, Dani's day returned to one of monotony; answering calls and making bookings in Lady Gianni's calendar. Mostly they were magazine editors, newspaper reporters, publicity agents, countless media peoples all trying to get access to the Gallery Nocturne. It kept her mind off of the sunflower painting and off of the strange conversation she had overheard.

As she took a break for lunch, electing to eat her Greek salad on a bench out front of the gallery, the questions regarding both swirled in her mind. If Lady Gianni had known she was on the line, then she had, of course, chosen her words very carefully. None of it made much sense, which only added to her frustration.

Tom was waiting for her when she returned, talking and laughing with the other workers. He broke off from them when he saw her and walked over.

"Did you get a chance to reach out to your friend yet about Larry?" He asked.

Dani felt nervous. She had completely forgotten about it.

"No, not yet," she said. "I'm so sorry."

"Oh," Tom said, looking frazzled.

"But I promise I will tonight after work," Dani said with a reassuring smile.

"Thank you," Tom said.

"Oh, Tom," Dani said, remembering something nagging at the back of her mind. "Do you mind if I come take a peek at my painting real quick? I'd love to see it one last time before it's sent off."

"I'm sorry Dani," Tom replied. "The courier left with it ten minutes ago. It's already gone."

"Oh," Dani said, feeling disappointed. "What about any pictures?"

Her own memory of what it looked like had faded, like a dream evaporating in the real world.

Tom looked uncomfortable.

"Lady Gianni doesn't allow photos," he said. "Not even for records purposes."

Dani's face must have been visibly disappointed, because Tom seemed to think hard about something comforting to say.

"If it's any consolation," Tom added with a forced smile. "The guys and I thought it was great."

"Thanks," she replied.

He walked back to the other workers and joined in their spirited conversation about football.

Once she was back in the seclusion of the offices, Dani dialed Bianca on her phone.

"Hey," Dani said into the receiver. "Do you still have that guy from the gallery's number?"

She listened to Bianca on the other end explain that she had deleted it immediately, having no intention of calling him.

"Damn," Dani replied. "Thanks anyway."

They hung up. Bianca didn't have it. Dani supposed she could ask Tom for Larry's number, but if Larry wasn't answering from him, why would he answer from another random number?

She couldn't quite put her finger on it, but something about Larry's mysterious absences felt important, even if she wasn't sure how.

A sudden commotion interrupted her thoughts.

Lady Gianni was on the phone in her office, yelling at someone in a foreign language Dani didn't understand or recognize.

Her phone chimed with a message from Haley.

HALEY: OMG he loves it, can't believe u did this. It's amazing. He can't stop staring at it.

Dani smiled and texted a reply.

DANI: So glad! Do you mind snapping a picture for me?

As she waited patiently for a reply, the seconds stretched to minutes. Daring a glance at the sunflower in its pot sitting on her desk, she was surprised to notice its vibrant yellow had faded. The artificial light wasn't doing it any favors. It would be fine once she got it home, back to its bright and sunny spot next to her bed.

Her phone chimed again. Dani checked it quickly. Excited to see a photo of her work.

HALEY: There's something wrong with my camera. It won't take the photo, will try again later. G2G!

Dani sank down in her chair, disappointed.

A couple hours passed, Dani kept herself busy at her desk checking the gallery's general email box and filtering out anything that was spam.

"Dani," Lady Gianni said, appearing from the glass door. It was getting late.

"Yes mam," Dani said, turning around.

"I've got to run out," said Lady Gianni, her tone audibly annoyed. "This figlio di puttana across town is causing me a problem and I need to get it sorted before dinner."

"No problem," Dani said, assuming that Lady Gianni had just cursed in another language. "I'll pack up things and we can…"

"I'm going to go on my own," Lady Gianni interrupted her, her voice not warm and inviting as usual. "If you can call the car up, I'll be ready in five minutes."

"Yes mam," Dani replied. "Is there anything you want me to work on while you're gone?"

"Tom wrote up a letter of dismissal for Larry," she said. "Can you ensure it is mailed out certified, please?"

"Of course mam," Dani said.

"It must go out today," Lady Gianni added. "It's his last paycheck and I'm not paying that lazy loaf another dollar."

Dani nodded solemnly in return. She couldn't hold back the feeling of guilt that clung loosely to her heart. Ex-cons like Larry had few chances to return to a normal life after getting out, and here she was charged with delivering what might end up being his last one. As she mulled over in her head all the negative consequences that may befall the poor soul, she didn't notice Lady Gianni move to stand behind her. It wasn't until the gallery director's hand gripped her shoulders that she looked up at the woman.

"Everyone has a job to do," Lady Gianni said as she squeezed Dani's shoulders tighter and gazed down on Dani with those fierce green eyes. "He didn't do his. Now you need to do yours."

Dani somehow felt both fear and resolve simultaneously.

"Yes, Lady Gianni," was all she could muster to say as the woman's heels clicked in rythm against the marble floors as she departed, leaving Dani alone in the office.

Dani sat at Lady Gianni's desk, reading the letter of dismissal for Larry. It cited job abandonment as his reason for dismissal. She could see that they were planning on denying any unemployment claims he may file. Lady Gianni was shrewd at managing her financials. Business was business, after all.

Shit, there was no mailing address on the form. She would have to pull it from his file.

She considered calling Lady Gianni to ask for permission first, but decided against it. Lady Gianni had made it clear to Dani it was her responsibility to mail it out. Dani didn't want to be seen as stalling and evoke possible further anger from her sometimes difficult boss. She would just peek into the filing cabinet and get Larry's mailing address real quick, nothing else.

It didn't take long before she located his file and looked for the job application with the mailing address. Something caught her eye: POLICE REPORT, stenciled across the top. She fought her curiosity to look inside, deciding against further invading his privacy.

She compromised by skimming through various court documents until she found his application with his mailing address on it and copied it onto the envelope. Putting it back into the filing cabinet exactly as it had been when she had pulled it out, she closed the drawer and packed her things. Not forgetting her sunflower.

Her sixth sense lingered in her mind, growing concern with what had happened to Larry.

Dani reminded herself it was none of her business.

Checking the time, she knew if she didn't leave now, she would be late to the post office.

Exiting the offices, she would need to pass by *The Dollhouse* on her way out.

She couldn't help but peer at the mailbox as she did.

The Johnsons

3493 Oak Lane

The Johnsons, the perfect little porcelain family. Maybe her own family had been just like them when she was a child. Though they were far from it now.

The house wasn't lit up like it was the night before. All the lights except for the front porch lamp were off. Much like how a real family might leave it after going to bed for the evening.

A strange curiosity bewitched her, beckoning her for one last quick peek at the incredibly detailed family home. She strolled up the walkway to the front door and stepped inside.

The mother and daughter figures watching TV were gone, replaced by an eerie stillness that hung in the living room's air.

Did they move the figures out of the house during the day? She couldn't see why. Porcelain, though hard, was brittle. Any attempt to transport them would risk breaking them.

Careful to hold on tight to her flowerpot, she ascended the stairs, interested to see if the others were still there. The first bedroom door was closed. Dani opened it and peered inside. An aquarium night light sat on the dresser, the fish inside bobbing around amongst the bubbles. In the bed, the little girl figure slept under the sheets.

The artist must have created additional statues so that the piece could be displayed in different layouts. It was amazing, the time and detail required to create not one family, but possibly multiple porcelain families, would have been enormous.

She checked the other rooms. The little boy was also in his bed, along with the parents in theirs. The only statue missing was the teenage girl who she had last seen at the kitchen table.

Curious.

Dani walked downstairs and into the kitchen.

The books, pencils, and notepads were on the table, but the girl was nowhere to be found.

Dani looked to the back door, where the watcher had been. The closed blinds made it impossible to see if he was still there. She went to open them and find out.

Something brushed her foot and rattled across the floor as she walked.

Kneeling down, she picked up a small white object. It was the porcelain recreation of a wireless earbud, just like the girl had been wearing.

Was this all part of the new layout, or had it fallen out on its own when they were moving the figure?

Dani wasn't certain.

Spinning the rod that controlled the blinds, she braced herself for that unwholesome face to appear on the other side of the glass.

It didn't. The watcher had been moved too.

Trying the doorknob, she was surprised to find it no longer locked. Turning it, the door swung open to reveal a white picket fence placed behind a concrete landing littered with muddy footprints.

Lady Gianni would be irate to see the display in a state like this, the footprints of Tom's workmen spoiling her prize exhibit.

She took a step down onto the concrete landing. Still awkward in high heels, time slowed as she slipped on the wet mud of a footprint and tumbled to the ground, the flowerpot flying out of her hands.

She hit the concrete hard on her side, eyes shut tight as she felt the shooting pain in her ribs go up and down her body.

"Goddammit," she yelled.

After a minute of cursing at her own clumsiness, she got to her feet.

The side of *The Dollhouse* was a narrow alley made mostly of mud, the fence on one side and roof overhang on the other inhibiting grass from growing there except in sparse clumps. One end led to the street, where she could see the sidewalk and part of the old tree. The other led to the backyard with a thick tree line painted into the backdrop. From the muddy stoop to the tree line was a continuous streak of mud. Footprints intermingled with smoothed earth.

She was no forensics expert, but she did watch enough true crime shows for her mind to race with potential explanations; the foremost of which being that something had been dragged on the ground.

Dani hoped Tom could fix it before the next show. If not, there'd be hell to pay.

An alert beeped on her phone. She pulled it from her purse and checked it.

"Shit," she said Outloud. The post office closes in 15 minutes. Somehow she had lost track of time and spent nearly thirty minutes inside *The Dollhouse*.

Brushing off the dirt from her dress, she tried to get herself back together.

Where was her flower pot?

She had dropped it when she fell, but thankfully it landed in the muddy grass. Dani picked it up and inspected it.

Luckily, it hadn't shattered, the only apparent damage being a large crack forming at the base. She stared at the crack in the dim light; it ignited a faint memory in her mind, a freak moment of déjà vu.

The crack looked just like the one she had painted.

CHAPTER 12

Dani sat on a couch in the common area at The Collective, staring at the sealed envelope sitting on the coffee table.

She tried to get to the post office on time, but missed it by only a few minutes; arriving right as the clerk was locking the door. Pleading through the glass hadn't helped in the slightest.

Dani held back tears. It was her own fault. If she hadn't wasted time inside *The Dollhouse*, she wouldn't have missed her train and she would have been able to mail it.

The sound of a door opening upstairs preceded footsteps on the creaking metal stairwell.

"Hey Dani," Alek said with a nervous smile. He had his hand in the pockets of his dirty jeans and a brown jacket tight around his shoulders.

"Hey Alek," Dani replied, not looking up to acknowledge him.

He stood there awkwardly, having something to say but not quite brave enough to say it. Dani didn't notice.

"I was wondering," he began.

Alek continued saying something, but Dani wasn't listening. All she could think about was what Lady Gianni was going to say when she found out she couldn't complete even the most basic of assignments.

"Earth to Dani," Alek said louder. "Are you there?"

Dani snapped out of her thoughts.

"Oh sorry," she said. "What was that?"

"I asked if you wanted to go grab a bite to eat," Alek added. He looked nervous. "Like are you hungry?"

"I don't know, Alek," Dani said, putting her head in her hands. "I screwed up big today, so not much of an appetite."

"How?" Alek asked.

"I didn't mail this out," she explained, holding up the envelope. "Lady Gianni is going to be furious once she finds out."

"But it's just a letter," Alek said, his voice sounding confused.

"I know," Dani added. "It's small. It shouldn't mean anything. But I really, really don't want to get on her bad side. She's already going to be in a bad mood tomorrow once she finds out the workmen trashed part of her exhibit."

"Why is her happiness so important to you?" Alek asked.

Dani peered across the room. Paul was listening to music while typing away at his laptop on the opposite end of the room. Still, she didn't dare say anything that would upset him.

She gestured for Alek to get closer. He sat down on the couch next to her.

"I painted for Lady Gianni this morning," Dani said, whispering in his ear.

"That's outstanding," Alek said in his normal voice.

"Shh," Dani said, checking to see if Paul had noticed.

"I painted for her in the morning," Dani continued. "And she already had a client set up for delivery sight unseen. It was my first sale."

"That's great!" Alek exclaimed. "How much?"

Dani smacked his arm with the back of her hand.

"Twenty-thousand dollars," Dani whispered.

Alek's eyes got huge.

"I don't want Paul to know," Dani continued quietly. "At least not yet. It would give him a heart attack."

"We should celebrate," Alek said, standing up. "Somewhere fancy, somewhere fun, somewhere..."

"I don't really feel like celebrating," Dani interrupted him. "Cause when she finds out I didn't mail this out, she's going to be pissed. And I don't want to be fired from this job."

Dani felt like crying. Alek was right. She should celebrate, but Lady Gianni's approval mattered more to her than the money.

Alek picked up the envelope and looked at it.

"Why don't we just deliver it ourselves?" He asked.

"What?" Dani said.

"I mean, the address is just half an hour away," he continued. "We can deliver it and still have time to grab a bite after."

Dani hadn't thought of that.

"We don't have a car, though," Dani added.

"Paul will let us borrow his," Alek said.

"I don't know..." Dani began. She was still hesitant to talk to Paul, much less ask him for something when she withheld a secret from him like this. She still felt like she owed him.

"Hey Paul," Alek yelled, standing up and walking over to him.

Dani tried to grab him in time, but it was too late.

"What is it?" Paul said, pulling his earbuds out.

"Can we borrow the van for a few hours?" Alek asked.

"What for?" Paul replied.

Alek looked at Dani for a second, then back at Paul.

"Dinner and a movie," Alek said.

Paul stared at him.

"Alright," Paul said with a big grin. "Go ahead, you can use it for your date."

"Wait," Dani began. "It's not a..."

"None of my business," Paul said with a wink.

Dani held her arm at her side. She wasn't sure what to be more embarrassed about; lying to Paul about using his van for a work errand for another gallery or that she didn't want everyone to think Alek and her were dating.

"Wait, so we know this guy?" Alek asked as he drove over the bridge in Paul's van, the exhaust leaving a french fry smell in its wake.

"Kind of," Dani replied. "He was that guy that Bianca flirted with to let us into Gallery Nocturne."

"And now he's stopped showing up to work and you are delivering a letter that says he has been fired?" Alek questioned.

"Pretty much," Dani replied. "I figure we can just drop it in his mailbox and..."

"Are you even certain this is his current address?" said Alek.

"It was on his application," said Dani.

"Sure, but people move and don't always tell their employers," Alek replied. "We should probably make sure it's him first."

Dani dreaded the thought.

"Oh hi, are you Larry?" Dani mocking. "I'm Dani. Remember that person you let into the gallery when you shouldn't have? Here's your pink slip. Have a good night."

"I'm not saying we have to talk to the guy," Alek said. "Just that we should make sure it's him before we drop it and leave."

Dani knew he was right, she just wished he wasn't.

The city had disappeared behind them. They were in suburbia now. Homes packed tightly together in neat little rows, clean parks with new swing sets and slides. It was a stark contrast to the neighborhood around The Collective. The old oak and cedar trees that lined the streets a welcome reprieve from the asphalt, concrete, and brick she was so accustomed to.

Alek made a left-hand turn, following the driving directions on his phone to Larry's address.

"This is a pleasant area," Dani said aloud. "For an ex-con."

"Any idea what he was in for?" Alek asked.

Dani was thinking she maybe should have checked the file in Lady Gianni's office after all. It hadn't seemed important at the time.

"No," Dani replied. "But I don't think they would hire a serial killer or anything like that at the gallery."

Alek drove slowly as they passed the brightly lit windows with scenes of families having dinner together or sitting in front of the TV watching a movie.

He noticed it first.

"It's crazy how much these houses look just like *The Dollhouse*," Alek said. "Perfect little nuclear families."

"Remind you of your childhood?" Dani asked.

"No, not exactly," Alek replied.

Dani realized she knew little about Alek's past. He wasn't exactly forthcoming about it, not that any of the other misfits at The Collective were.

"What was your family like then?" She asked.

Alek suddenly seemed very uncomfortable. He opened his mouth, then closed it again, like he was afraid to discuss it.

"It's alright if you don't want to answer," Dani said, not wanting to push him.

"No, I do," Alek began. "I want to tell you, it's just hard to explain. I'm from Russia."

"You never told us that!" Dani exclaimed.

"You never asked before," he replied. "I grew up in a big city. My dad wasn't around much until I was a teenager. My mom drank a lot."

The van passed out of the picturesque neighborhood and through a greenbelt lined with thick trees. Up ahead, the road narrowed and wound as it climbed up a small hill.

"How did you escape to America?" Dani asked.

"I didn't escape," Alek said, his voice betraying melancholy. "They exiled me here."

"Exiled?! How did that..." Dani began but didn't finish.

"Later," he said, his tone clear that he didn't want to elaborate. "We're here."

The van pulled through the open chain-link gate where a plastic sign reading Sunny Meadows Mobile Home Park hung partially torn on one side. The asphalt pavement gave-way to loose gravel that filled the van with crunching noises from the tires as they rolled through. While the family neighborhood had picturesque homes with perfect families living inside them, Sunny Meadows was the opposite.

Old tires, cinder-blocks, beer bottles, and weeds covered almost every square inch of the yard in front of the trailers. Stained clothing hung on lines strung between rotting telephone poles. Cars with their hoods up and missing engines sat rusted and decaying in driveways. Some had wheels sunk several inches into the mud after decades of neglect.

A man holding a rifle sat outside one home on a lounge chair, a cheap cigar in one hand and a bottle of Jack Daniels between his legs. He wore a red flannel that was left open so that his beer belly hung out over the waist of his torn and faded jeans.

Alek seemed nervous as they passed him, the man staring at them with distrustful eyes. His N.R.A. hat an advertised warning to anyone who might consider crossing him.

"This is it," Alek said as the van stopped in front of the mobile home with the number that matched Larry's file.

There was a marsh of mud and grass that separated the van from the front door. Dani opened the car door, wishing she had brought more sensible shoes, having already tumbled in heels once that day.

As she stood up, the sound of the driver's side door opening and Alek popping his head out surprised her.

"I can do it," Dani said, not wanting to trouble him more than she already had that night.

"I know you can," Alek replied. "Doesn't mean you have to do it alone."

Dani wanted to tell him to get back in the car, but he wouldn't have listened. She could see that in his eyes. Secretly, she was glad.

Together, they traversed the treacherous terrain, hopping from mound to mound of dead grass to avoid the mud, almost falling over twice. At the front door, they saw the lights were on inside. It looked like someone was home.

Dani rapped on the front door twice, the thin frosted glass banging loose in its frame.

No shadow appeared on the other side.

"Maybe he's not home," Alek said, raising his eyebrows.

Dani still felt something was wrong. She just didn't know what.

She knocked again, but still no one answered.

"You think he's ok?" Dani asked Alek. "He hasn't answered phone calls. He's missed work. He could be dead."

"Only one way to find out," Alek said.

Without hesitation, he turned the front doorknob.

"It's probably locked," she said, sure she was right. Except she wasn't. The hinges squeaked and the door swung open.

Dani gave Alek a look. He just shrugged back at her.

"Mr. Sellers," Dani said, taking a step inside.

The mobile home reeked of cigarettes.

"Mr. Sellers," Dani yelled again, this time from the kitchen.

Alek came in behind her and walked down the hall.

"Rooms are empty," he said. "Bathroom too."

"This place stinks," Dani replied. "It's hard to believe someone could live here."

"I've smelled worse," Alek said, passing her and opening the fridge. "My guess, he stepped out for a few minutes."

"What makes you say that?" Dani asked.

"Front door was open, and there is a case of beer in the fridge," said Alek. "Doesn't strike me like he was planning on being away for long."

"Should we wait for him?" Dani was getting nervous.

Alek opened up several cupboards.

"Whoa," he said, standing back and opening another. "These are full of cigarette cartons. He's gotta have hundreds stockpiled."

"Who would need that many cigarettes?" asked Dani.

"I don't know," said Alek. "But he must really like the Marlboro Reds."

Alek checked the pile of papers on the countertop.

"It might be his mom's place," he said, holding up a piece of mail and handing it to Dani.

The bill was addressed to Molly Sellers and stamped in big red letters: PAST DUE.

"Oh well," Dani said with relief. "We can drop it in the mailbox and..."

She turned towards the front door, but a man blocked her way.

"What the hell do you think you're doing?" the man said.

The smell of his cigar hit Dani first, a rank scent that reminded her of how the oil smelled at the refinery. The bill of his N.R.A. hat had browned from it already. She recognized him as the neighbor that had passed earlier.

"We were just looking for Larry," Dani said quickly. Alek appeared at her side immediately.

"Well, Larry ain't here," the man said. "This is trespassing."

"I'm sorry, we didn't mean to," Dani replied.

She couldn't help but feel nervous. The man clasped his rifle in front of him. If he aimed it a few inches lower, it would be pointing directly at their faces.

"You better move along," the man said. "Cops don't like to come up here, so we tend to deal with things ourselves."

They both nodded.

He moved to the side, and they both rushed to the car.

Shit! Dani thought to herself. She forgot to drop off the letter.

She stopped and turned. Alek tried to tug on her, but she wouldn't budge.

"Excuse me," she said to the man in the hat.

"I told you to git," the man replied, spitting a brown liquid out of his mouth to the ground.

"I have Larry's paycheck here," she said, holding up the letter. "That's why we were here, to deliver it to him. Would you mind giving it to him?"

"Paycheck?" the man said with squinted eyes. "You mean that lying sack of shit has a job? He still owes me a hundred bucks."

"Yes, sir," Dani said, holding out the letter.

"I'll make sure he gets it," the man said, snatching the letter from her hand.

"Thanks," she said before retreating to the van where Alek had already started up the engine.

"**H**oly crap," Alek said, letting out a held breath as they exited the gate to Sunny Meadows. "That guy was something."

"I know," Dani replied. Her heart was still beating fast. "I'm glad that's done."

They rode in silence as the van coasted down the hill and towards the suburban neighborhood that was a much more comforting sight than the dilapidated mobile homes.

Alek looked like he was working up the courage to say something. His brow always tensed, just like he did when concentrating on painting. They passed the greenbelt.

"So, how about a late dinner?" He asked at last.

Dani didn't want to disappoint him, not after all he did to accompany her that night.

"I'm not hungry," she began.

She noticed his eyes suddenly became sad as she said that.

"But maybe we could grab a coffee?" She added, hoping that would soften the blow.

"Sure," he said, sounding a little less deflated. "That'd be great. There's that new shop over on..."

"Stop the van," Dani yelled.

The brakes screeched and the engine back-fired as Alek pulled it to the side of the road.

"What is it?" He asked. "Everything ok?"

"Look," she said, pointing to the street sign up ahead.

"Oak Lane," he read it off.

"It's the street from *The Dollhouse*," Dani said.

"So?" He said with a laugh. "It's just a coincidence. There are probably a million Oak Lanes across the country."

"I know," Dani said, feeling a little foolish, but she felt something eerie about it in the back of her mind. "Can you turn here?"

"Dani," he said, taking a deep breath. "It's getting late. I don't want to be out all night."

"I'm sorry," she replied. "But just turn here, please, just for a minute."

He looked at her, then put the van into gear.

"Sure," he said, spinning the steering wheel and softly pressing the accelerator.

They rolled down Oak Lane at a slow pace.

He was probably right. There were a million streets named after the common tree all over the place. A million that had houses with families just like the porcelain ones.

It was getting late. Most of the houses had gone dark for the evening. The street was dead still and silent except for the exhaust of the van and rolling tires.

They were almost to the end of the street.

"Told you," Alek said. "Nothing to see here."

"Oh my god," Dani exclaimed, putting her hands over her mouth. "There it is."

"There's what?" Alek asked, but she didn't need to tell him. His eyes were wide as he looked at the mailbox of the house they were about to pass.

The Johnsons

3493 Oak Lane

Alek brought the van to a stop.

"It's exactly the same address as *The Dollhouse*," Dani said.

"I wonder if the artist lives here," said Alek.

"I don't think so," Dani replied.

"There's no one downstairs," Alek said, pointing to the dark front living room window, where only the pale drapes reflected the light of the street lamp. "Wasn't there a mom and daughter watching TV or something?"

"There was the other night," Dani replied, her eyes wide as she stared. "But not earlier today when I went back inside. They were upstairs sleeping except for the teenager who was studying in the kitchen."

"That kitchen?" Alek said, pointing. There was a small kitchen window off to the side, partially blocked by the large oak tree out front. There was a light on, but from the street you couldn't see much other than a refrigerator and cabinets.

"You think she's in there?" Dani asked.

"Only one way to find out," Alek replied, putting the car into park and opening the driver's side door.

"Wait," Dani said. "I didn't tell you what else was different."

Alek stopped.

"The man from the back door," Dani began, but faltered as she struggled to find the right words to describe it.

"The one peeking through the blinds?" Alek finished for her.

"Yes, him," Dani continued. "Well, when I went back this afternoon, he wasn't there, nor was the girl."

Alek looked at her with a perplexed expression.

"I just have a bad feeling that something happened to her," Dani tried to explain, even if it made little sense to her, either.

She pointed to the mailbox.

"Ok," Alek said, rolling his eyes. "The house was real, but I bet you the people who live here look nothing like the figures from *The Dollhouse*."

Dani looked at him, not feeling so certain.

"I'll show you," he said, getting out of the car.

"No, wait," Dani said, but it was too late. Alek was already on the sidewalk next to her, opening her door.

Begrudgingly, she got out.

"What if they see us?" She asked, following him under the oak tree.

"We'll just say we were at the wrong house," Alek replied. "Not like we are going to break in or anything."

As they crossed under the shadow of the oak tree, something took off from one of the branches. The sound of wings flapping and a shadow flew off towards the street.

"Crap," Dani said, startled.

"It's just a bird," Alek whispered.

They got to the edge of the house where the dark alley that lead to the backyard began.

Alek peeked around it.

"Nothing there," he said.

Dani looked for herself. There were no signs that anyone had been in the side yard. The dirt was still pristine; no footprints, no girl, no muddy streak leading to the forest.

Alek turned the corner and carefully approached the side door to the kitchen, the only light in the dark alley.

Dani tried to follow him, both their feet sinking into the mud with each step.

Once they made it to the door, she noticed they left behind dirty footprints on the concrete, just like at *The Dollhouse*.

Alek got to the window first. Standing to its side, he put his hand on the door handle.

"Still locked," he mouthed to her.

After taking a breath, he put one eye to the corner of the window and looked inside.

"You won't believe this," he whispered.

Dani's heart raced. "Was she too late? Was the girl already gone?" she thought.

Peering through the window, she prepared herself for the worst.

She wanted to hit Alek when she saw.

The teenage girl was at the table making out with a boy. He was skinny, with a full head of hair, and looked nothing like the watcher.

"Should I bust in and stop them?" Alek joked quietly as they walked back to the van.

"Shut up," Dani replied. Even though everything looked fine, even though Alek must think she was crazy, she still couldn't shake the bad feeling that sat like an anchor in the pit of her stomach.

"Can we just go home?" Dani asked.

"Sure," Alek said, hiding disappointment in his eyes.

"You gotta get out of here," Lisa Johnson said to her boyfriend. "If my dad comes down and finds you, he's going to kill me."

"Oh, come on," her boyfriend replied. "One more kiss."

She pushed him off of her.

Lisa had been dating him for four weeks now. They hadn't had sex yet, but Lisa knew that was the only thing on his mind. Her AP Biology test was the only thing on hers. If she didn't ace it, she knew it would hurt her college applications.

She unlocked the kitchen side door and opened it as quietly as she could, hoping the creaking of the old hinges wasn't loud enough to travel upstairs.

"Two more minutes," her boyfriend pleaded.

"I'll see you at school tomorrow," she said as she closed the door in his face.

She felt the doorknob wiggling on the other end. He was trying to get back in. She engaged the deadbolt. No more distractions!

Walking back over to the table, she sat down and tried to think about anything but him. She tried to think about RNA synthesis and remembering the names of protein strands bound in the DNA helix. However, her body still felt flush, and reading about how male and female chromosomes combined to make a baby only filled her mind with more thoughts of sex.

She began to wish she hadn't been so quick to kick him out. They could have snuck outside, just for a minute or two. Enough to satisfy the urges tugging at her body.

A few more minutes passed, and she had reread the same sentence in the textbook several times, remembering none of it. She put her earbuds in, maybe some music would tune it out.

Unfortunately, it was a Cardi B song, one that did not skimp on the details. She caught some movement in the corner of her eye, a shadow moving past the window in the side door.

Lisa pulled one of her earbuds out to listen for his voice.

Then she saw the doorknob jiggle.

No one could fault her boyfriend for not being persistent.

Maybe one more kiss, maybe a little something more.

She undid the deadbolt and opened the door.

The man standing on the other side was not her boyfriend.

Lisa Johnson didn't even have time to scream before his hands clapped tightly over her mouth.

PART 3

THE
SMOKING MAN

CHAPTER 13

Larry leaned back in the resin lawn chair, the rubber medical tube that had been tightly wrapped around his arm falling to the ground. The initial rush of cold after injection hit him immediately, followed by the euphoric waves that relaxed every muscle, joint, and thought from his being. The world became but a blur around him as he sat on his back porch, facing the forest, his mind drifting off into the strange place that only opiates can transport you to.

His skin was cold. It was February and Spring was still weeks away, yet he wore only a white shirt and jeans. It didn't bother him, not when he was high like this.

His fingers fumbled to pull a fresh cigarette from the pack, numb to his commands. One fell to the ground at his feet. He steadied himself as he reached down slowly to retrieve it.

Looking up, he saw the owl was no longer hiding amongst the twilight-lit branches of the forest; it was standing on the concrete pad just a few yards away, staring at him.

What was it, some sort of spirit guide? After what it had done, more of a spirit nemesis.

"What do you want?" Larry asked it. It was just an owl, but something about its face made him think it was more human than bird.

It hadn't responded; it didn't need to. Larry knew what it was thinking.

"I don't know what you're talking about," Larry said. "It's just me. There is no one else here."

Larry sat back up in his chair. The owl hopped closer to the fire, the only source of heat on his house's desolate back porch. Weren't birds supposed to be afraid of stuff like that?

"If you insist on sticking around," Larry said, reaching into the cooler next to the chair and pulling two cans out. "Might as well have a drink with me."

He rolled one of the beers over to the bird; it rested at the bird's taloned feet but seemed all together unafraid of it or him.

"It's rude to not join your host in a celebratory drink," Larry told it, the sound of his own can cracking open a shrill break in the otherwise still night air.

The drink felt like cold liquid steam was rushing through his body.

The owl stared at him.

"What are we celebrating?" Larry interpreting for the animal. "I finally caught the nymph, the one that lives in the forest. That lusty bitch has been taunting me for days."

The owl hopped over the beer can, closer to Larry.

Its dark eyes reflected the fire, like two little smoldering flames themselves.

"Will you let me sleep now?" Larry asked it.

It shook its head at him.

Lighting his cigarette, he leaned back in his chair, unhappy with the little animal.

"What do you mean the job's not done yet?" Larry said. "She's inside, dead as dead."

The owl shook its head again.

"You want me to show you?" Larry said. "Don't think I'm letting you inside. You can watch from the window."

He stood up and flicked his cigarette into the fire.

"Ungrateful little shit," he muttered under his breath. He had been looking forward to that cigarette, but he had plenty more.

Larry swayed back and forth with each step up into his home. His legs ached, not hard to see why.

The Nymph had put him on a merry chase through the forest, prancing and dancing out of his reach. The owl hooting in encouragement as he had jogged and ran to keep up. She was fast, but he was more patient. Like a wolf chasing down a baby caribou, eventually he would catch up to his prey.

Wasn't that the purpose of the legend, anyway? At least, that's how the stories Larry's mother had told him always ended. The forest nymphs gave chase, but always fell into the clutches of the hunter.

The tease deserved it.

After years of abuse inside the walls of prison, he had yearned for nothing more than to feel like a man again. A naked forest nymph outside his home was practically an invitation.

Reaching the bathroom inside, he looked at himself in the mirror. Besides being soaked in sweat; gashes and tears in his shirt meant it was the last time he would be wearing the cheap linen. Tossing it to the ground, he focused on the dribbles of blood dripping from long scrapes on his face and arms.

Some came from the branches of trees. After all, it was dark, and she had been fast. However, she had made one critical error in her attempt to escape his clutches.

The house, leaving the safety of the forest and running inside, rendered her magical powers mute. From there, she could not shapeshift.

So it was there he waited, outside her door. It hadn't taken long, nymphs by their very nature are impatient creatures. She had opened the door and come to him. Now she belonged to him.

Larry splattered his bathroom mirror with brown and red as he tried in vain to wash the blood and mud from his face and body. The nymph's claws had been sharp as they had cut against his skin, leaving deeper gashes than the branches.

Like so many times before, he looked at the tattoo of a heart with a ribbon wrapped around it on his chest; the ribbon had the word Mom on it. What would his mother think of him if she could see him now? Her son, the mighty woodsman, hunter, of his childhood bedtime stories.

"You're a screw up," his mother's voice echoed in his head. "A grade-A jackoff like your father."

"Screw you," he told the voice, bowing his head as the world seemed to shift back to reality around him. Whatever the guy had sold him wasn't strong enough. It was wearing off already.

He turned the water off and tried to think of what to do next.

"The owl," he said, holding onto the last remaining sliver of his delusion.

But it wasn't in the window, it hadn't followed him to see him prove that he had conquered the nymph. Maybe it didn't even exist.

Turning around, he needed to see for certain.

He gripped the cheap plastic discount store shower curtain's edge and pulled. The metal rings that it hung from pinged like a wind chime as they clattered into one another.

Larry took a deep breath.

There was no nymph in his bathtub. Just a teenage girl, limp and lifeless, as she lay at an awkward angle in the shallow porcelain basin. She wore a sweatshirt and jeans, both covered in mud.

He put a hand over his mouth, holding back a gasp.

His mind struggled to meld delusion and reality together.

He kneeled closer carefully, like she was a snake that might lunge forward and bite him at any moment.

She looked unconscious enough. Maybe if he dropped her back into the forest, she would wake up on her own and be none the wiser. He could be halfway to Florida by morning.

He put his hands on the girl's neck to feel for a pulse like in the movies, but his fingers were far too numb to even attempt it. Leaning over, he put his ear up against her nose. Maybe he could feel her breath.

He could feel it. She was breathing.

Good, he thought to himself.

Then she stopped. He wondered if she had died right there.

The girl's nails dug into his shoulder without warning. She yelled like a banshee as she slashed at the flesh.

Surprised, Larry tried to stand up to get away, but he slipped on the muddy tile floor and fell forward into the bathtub.

He landed hard on top of her, his head cracking the tile of the wall above the tub. She let go of him immediately at the impact.

Larry scrambled away, rushing to the counter to grab something, anything, to defend himself from her with.

He wouldn't need it.

In the tub, the forest nymph lay with her head at a crooked angle. A bone in her neck jutted out from her skin and a steady stream of blood poured down into the drain.

Larry felt blood dripping from his own scalp, but it was nothing serious.

He heard a wild fluttering sound from outside the bathroom window. Peering over, the owl was sitting on the sill, staring at him. It nodded once before taking off silently into the night.

Kneeling on the bathroom floor, he was in shock.

Banging on the front door pulled him out of his trance.

"Larry, Larry!" a man's voice yelled angrily.

Larry washed his face and head in the sink quickly.

"Larry!" whoever it was, was being impatient.

"One second," Larry yelled back. Grabbing a red shirt and hat from his closet and tossing it on. He hoped it would be enough.

Swinging the door open, his neighbor stood on his front porch, staring at him wearing his N.R.A. hat.

"Didn't see you get back from your walk," his neighbor said. "What took you so long? Catch you with your dick out?"

"I was cleaning the bathroom," Larry said.

The man was staring at Larry with a curious look.

"You look like hell," the man said. "Is that blood?"

Larry realized a fresh drip of crimson was traveling down his scalp. He wiped at it with his shirt.

"I got into a fight," said Larry, repeating the first stupid thing in his head.

"On your walk in the forest?" the man asked. He looked skeptical.

"With a raccoon," Larry answered.

The man just looked at him, studying him from head to toe.

"Well, you should be careful," the man said to break the silence. "Those little bastards have rabies."

"I know," Larry said. "Listen, it's a bad time can we just…"

"I know you lied to me," his neighbor said, cutting him off.

Larry tensed up immediately.

"I know you still got money," the man continued.

Larry let out a breath.

"In fact, somebody was out here earlier trying to drop this off." His neighbor held up an envelope. "A couple of kids and they said it was your paycheck."

"It's my last one," Larry said.

"I'm sure it's enough to pay me back," the man snarled.

"You got it," said Larry, holding back the shakes as the adrenaline in his blood wore off.

Larry took the check from the man's hand.

"I want my money tomorrow," his neighbor said, taking a few steps back.

"You'll have it," Larry said before closing the door.

He dropped the paper onto the kitchen countertop before walking to the fridge and pulling out a fresh beer. Opening it, he chugged it down in one big gulp.

He was feeling thirsty, oppressively thirsty after his ordeal. The beer would help make it easier. Easier for what he knew he needed to do next.

Chapter 14

Dani arrived for work at Gallery Nocturne that morning with an extra large cup of coffee in hand. She had barely slept. A nightmare about a wolf chasing a fawn through the forest had replayed in her mind like a skipping vinyl record all night long.

Setting her bag down on her desk, she noticed Lady Gianni's office was empty.

She sat and tried to organize herself. Lifting a file folder full of potential buyers, she found an envelope underneath addressed to her.

Tearing it open and pulling out the piece of paper, she was stunned in shock.

It was a check addressed to her from the gallery for almost $14,000.

Included was an itemized stub of taxes, fees, and the like from the gallery subtracted from the original sale price.

She took a picture of the check and uploaded it to her banking app immediately, as if worried that if she didn't deposit it right away, the money would magically evaporate into thin air.

Someone included something else in the envelope behind the stub. A terse note written in brilliant emerald ink and beautiful cursive hand-writing.

Meet me in the Remnants.

Lady Gianni

Dani grabbed her notebook and folders, but her intuition told her she wouldn't need them, so she set them back down. She texted the rest of The Collective that dinner was her treat that night and then locked her phone and bag in the drawer of her desk before heading to *The Remnants* wing of the gallery.

The entrance to *The Remnants* wing was a rickety old shack set against a pitch black backdrop. As Dani drew closer, she could hear the faint sounds of frogs croaking in the background. It looked just like an old boathouse on a lake she used to attend summer camp at when she was little. Just the sight of it reminded her of the boys at camp, taunting her and daring her to go inside or risk being called a sissy or worse.

She had never gone inside. The fireside stories of 'Killer Bill' and 'Kenny the Escaped Mental Patient' ensured that her fear won out every time she tried. The counselors were little help, most of them more interested in each other than the campers.

After all these years, she knew better. A shack is just a shack. The only danger being stepping on a nail and getting tetanus. She mounted the rotting wooden stair that bent under her weight until she walked through the black cloth that hung from the open doorway.

In *The Veil*, the entrance had been bright and welcoming. Entering *The Remnants*, only darkness and quiet greeted her. A full moon shone brightly overhead, reflecting off the surface of the floor. Silhouettes of trees filled the horizon. She could see lanterns burning in the distance, illuminating a dozen or so little dirt islands strewn throughout the room. While *The Veil* had dozens of paintings mounted to the walls, this wing had only a few displays, maybe six in total.

She took a step across the smooth, flawless surface, and bright lights emerged beneath her shoes. They started in rings, the first being brilliant and the subsequent rings growing more dim. They were the ripples of her steps across a vast artificial moonlit lake.

Of course, it was some sort of display. Built using a vast assortment of projectors or televisions in the floor and programmed to create ripples when pressure was applied.

Regardless, the sense of feeling like you were walking on water was mesmerizing. Dani jumped forward playfully, giggling as the ripples of light dispersed in all directions. She jumped left, then right, then left again. The ripples crashed into each other in brilliant splashes of color that turned red, blue, and green.

"Having fun I see?" said Lady Gianni. She was walking up to Dani on the lake. Unlike Dani's, Lady Gianni's steps didn't create ripples, but left a wake of light behind her as she glided like a boat across the water.

"This is incredible," Dani said. "How did they do it?"

"When it comes to art, the how is never important," Lady Gianni replied.

Dani resisted the urge to jump and dance across the surface.

"Shall we begin?" Lady Gianni asked, motioning for Dani to follow her.

Dani entered the woman's wake, eager to catch up.

"It looks like Mr. Bones was happy with the piece," Dani said.

"Happy would be an understatement," Lady Gianni replied. "It absolutely floored him. He asked me to commission another one immediately."

"Really?!" Dani exclaimed. "I have a beautiful idea with daisies I could start on..."

Lady Gianni held up her hand. Dani grew silent.

"I've already arranged another artist for him," she said.

"Oh," Dani said, feeling deflated.

"Your work was a great taster, an apéritif," Lady Gianni said playfully. "It helped him overcome his initial doubt. However, I have other plans for you."

Dani wasn't certain what that meant, so she remained quiet.

They walked in silence until they emerged on the shore of one of the islands. A bare tree with white bark stood tall at its center. Leafless branches hung down from above, low enough that Dani could reach them.

"Before you begin, I wanted to show you this piece," Lady Gianni said. "It's called *The Memory Tree*, and I thought it might help inspire you."

"Inspire me to do what?" Dani asked.

"To paint, of course," Lady Gianni said with a laugh. "You think I was going to waste your talents on more flowers?"

Even in the dim light, the woman's eyes were bright and fierce. Her smile did little to comfort Dani.

Dani surveyed the tree. It looked almost real. The twigs and branches sprouted from it in the perfect randomization that only nature could produce, something the unconscious human desire for order in the chaos could almost never recreate.

"It's stunning," Dani commented. "So you want me to paint a picture of a tree?"

Lady Gianni, quick as a viper, grabbed Dani's hand and pressed it to the tip of a branch.

Dani smelled something immediately.

Peanuts. Salted Peanuts.

But it was more than a smell. Her mind wandered to a memory of going to a minor league baseball game with her father when she was little. The other kids all yelled at the batters and pitchers with insults and curses; Dani sat quietly next to them, not sure why they were so mean to the players on the field. Her father handed her a bag of salted peanuts she didn't want to eat, encouraging her to crack one open and be just like one of the boys.

As the smell faded from her senses, so did the memory.

She turned to see Lady Gianni watching her closely.

"Amazing, isn't it?" the older woman said.

"I don't understand how," Dani began.

"The how is not important," Lady Gianni stopped her.

Dani took hold of another branch and her nose became filled with a new sensation.

This time it was fish guts, and her mind flooded with thoughts of sitting on the shore of a pond, crying as her father desperately tried to get her to cut open and clean the fish she had caught. Its dead relatives splayed out on a nearby log, their insides arranged in neat piles to be used for bait.

She felt the sensation of gagging and released the branch. Relief came immediately.

"Inspired yet?" Lady Gianni asked.

"Not quite," replied Dani, rubbing her nose.

She would try one more.

Grabbing a new bud, she knew exactly where it had taken her. She could almost feel the smoke from the Swisher Sweet cigarillo clouding around her face.

She let go of the branch, but the memory lingered in Dani's thoughts like the smoke that lingered in the room.

"I don't think this is..." Dani tried to say, but stopped herself.

Lady Gianni wasn't listening. The older woman was standing there holding onto her own branch, her eyes were closed tight.

"Lady Gianni?" Dani asked quietly.

If the woman heard her, she didn't acknowledge it.

Dani was curious. What was so special about that branch?

She reached out and touched the same one.

The smell of a burning campfire filled her nose. With her eyes tight shut, she imagined herself in a forest clearing, the night sky above her filled with more stars than she could ever hope to count.

The crackle of the fire filled her ears. She could see it in her mind. Approaching it, she crouched and held her hand closer to its whipping flames; the warmth brought comfort to her fingertips.

Was this one of her father's many forced camping trips? One of the dozens of times he had dragged her into the woods to be eaten alive by bugs, hike until her feet hurt, and sleep on the uncomfortable ground. The campfire at night had always been the most enjoyable part of the trips, the only time she got to sit and just enjoy nature.

However, this wasn't any of the forests that she remembered. It looked older, much older than the forests of her childhood.

She noticed a figure by the fire. It was a woman, very thin, wearing a long old-fashioned dress. She held a fire prod almost as thick as her wrist in her hand, pushing at the coals and embers that heated an iron pot of stew hanging over the hearth. Dani tried to walk around the fire to better see the woman's face, but no matter how she moved, the woman always seemed to be on the opposite end, her face obscured by the rising flames.

This was no memory of Dani's.

On the ground next to the woman, a basket made soft cooing sounds that could only be that of a baby. The woman would sometimes reach a spare hand over to rock it lightly when the baby's noises became more agitated.

The sound of a twig snapping from the surrounding forest interrupted Dani's observations. The woman must have heard it as well. She put down her fire poking stick and reached for a knife carefully tucked into a sheath tied to her waist. The blade glimmered in the fire's light.

The source of the noise quickly revealed itself, as an immense shadow of a giant emerged from the tree line. It would have been seven feet tall and half as wide at the shoulder. The man-like silhouette filled Dani with nothing but feelings of fear and dread.

But the thin woman seemed unaffected. She even sheathed her blade and returned to tending the fire, as if this monster's presence was to be expected.

In an instant, the fire went out. The smell of the logs disappearing from Dani's nose. She opened her eyes.

Dani was still standing under *The Memory Tree*, but the branch she had been holding was no longer hanging. It had fallen to the ground at her feet.

"Oh my god," Dani said, kneeling to pick it up. "I'm so sorry. I didn't mean to break it."

She held it in her hands before looking up at Lady Gianni, who she expected to be furious. But she wasn't. The older woman wasn't even looking at her. She was staring at the branch, her breaths heavy.

"You didn't break it," Lady Gianni said. "I did."

Dani looked at her with a puzzled expression.

Lady Gianni's eyes returned to their usual collected appearance.

"Shall you begin?" she said.

L ady Gianni led Dani to another island in the lake, the one with a large shack erected on it. She opened the door and gestured for Dani to go inside, which she obliged.

The faint light from the door illuminated a blank canvas and easel set up in the center of an otherwise pitch black room. Her painting supplies laid out next to it exactly as they had been in *The Veil*.

Dani entered and walked to the easel. Lady Gianni's silhouette stood still in the doorway's light.

"You want me to paint in here?" Dani asked, feeling timid.

"It's the perfect place to let your gift flourish," Lady Gianni replied.

"It's so dark, I can barely see," Dani said.

"Take a seat," Lady Gianni commanded.

Dani did as instructed.

"We call it *The Ashen Room*," Lady Gianni began. "It's one of my favorite pieces in the entire gallery. Man's ancestors believed in the cleansing power of fire. They used it to sterilize surgical tools, close wounds, and prepare their meals. This room can do the same if you let it."

"I don't understand," Dani replied.

"You will," Lady Gianni said. "I'll come get you once you've finished."

"What?" Dani asked.

But it was too late. Lady Gianni had already closed the door, plunging the room into utter darkness.

Dani leaped towards where the door had been, hitting the wall hard. Feeling around till she found the doorknob, she tried to turn it, but it refused to yield. She pushed and pulled on the door, which, despite the rickety appearance of the building, barely shifted in the frame.

"Please let me out," she yelled, banging with her fist. "I can't see anything."

If Lady Gianni was still outside and could hear her, she showed no sign of it.

Dani felt around the wall, hoping and praying to find a light switch, but after going around the small room twice, she realized there wasn't one.

Feeling her way to the center until she found the chair, she sat in it and thought about what to do next.

Lady Gianni wouldn't leave her there indefinitely, right?

The thought crossed her mind.

She cursed loudly into the darkness. Why did she leave her phone behind?

Dani could use it at that very moment to call for help, or at least to help her see.

Lady Gianni was a serious woman, no prankster. She meant what she said.

Dani knew what she was expected to do, she was expected to paint.

She felt around till she found the paintbrush, then swiped it towards where she thought the canvas had been.

Her brush found nothing but empty space.

She felt around with her other hand and located the soft white materials, then swiped with the brush again, this time connecting.

Dani had heard about this style of art. It was heavily experimental. How she was supposed to create anything worthwhile on her first try was beyond her.

She closed her eyes and tried to imagine a picture in her head of what she wanted the painting to look like, then dipping her brush into what she hoped was the correct color, re-applied it to the canvas.

Daisies growing in a meadow under a full moon. She tried to concentrate on it in her mind's eye. Except she couldn't.

The meadow and moon were the first to disappear from her mind. Leaving only a small bundle of daisies. They grew not from the ground, but sprung from a small metal cup serving as a makeshift vase.

The vase sat on the wooden desk of a woman smoking cigarillos. She was overweight, with gray hair done up into a beehive on her head and makeup layered on thick. She wore a pink and yellow muumuu that stopped just above her ankles, revealing ankle fat that overflowed from red shoes that were far too small for her feet.

Dani's hand brushed across the canvas, the soft strokes the only sound in the room. She tried to focus on just the daisies.

Billowing thick clouds of smoke surrounded the woman. Without an open window, there was nowhere for it to go. Barely visible in the gray mist, sat a girl on a stool, her head tilted towards the floor.

No, I don't want this, Dani said to herself.

She tried to will the meadow back into existence, but the old woman's will was stronger.

Dani didn't know if what she was seeing was in her mind or if *The Ashen Room* had transformed around her into this stuffy little space of some of her worst memories. She lost track of the canvas, her brush strokes hitting the air.

She felt like she had been transported to that little closet office back at the halfway house; she was sitting on the stool in front of Ms. Dolly's desk. Her eyes watered and she coughed as her lungs rejected the smoke that was inescapable around her.

"Another fight Dani?" Ms. Dolly said in her toad-like voice. "Why can't you just be like the other girls?"

"I'm trying," Dani said as she stared at the splintered wood floor.

Ms. Dolly flicked the ash of her cigarillo into a paper coffee cup on her desk, the coffee inside sizzling as it snuffed out the hot embers.

"I've been running this place for twenty years," the woman continued. "I get the runaways, the crazies, the drug addicts, the girls straight out of juvie. Yet I've never seen anyone cause as much trouble as you."

"I didn't start it," Dani pleaded, holding back tears. "The other girls have a problem with me."

"And why is that?" asked Ms. Dolly. "Were you hitting on them? Harassing them?"

"No, I wasn't," Dani said instantly.

"That's not what they told me," replied Ms. Dolly, pulling another swisher sweet from a little plastic pack and lighting it.

"I was just trying to fit in," said Dani. "Just talking."

"But you don't fit in," Ms. Dolly said through several restrained coughs. "I'm responsible for almost thirty young persons like yourself. I can't let this kind of thing keep happening or else they'll fire me."

"I didn't do anything," Dani pleaded. "I swear!"

"Look, I get it," Ms. Dolly took a long drag. "Not everyone here is going to be your cup of tea, but here's the deal: this place runs on rules, and one of them is learning to get along—or at least pretend to."

This was a memory, Dani's memory. She knew every detail of the room, from the dusty and broken ceiling fan to every word about to come out of Ms. Dolly's mouth.

Except she was no longer looking at the floor, she was noticing something else. A spec of the ash had missed the coffee cup. It glowed hot on the cheap wooden desk, so hot that a round black burn had formed under it.

"Ms. Dolly," Dani said, a diversion from her own memory of the meeting.

"It's not about being best friends," Ms. Dolly continued her speech without flinching. "It's about keeping the peace and showing a little class, whatever that means to you."

"Mam," Dani tried again to get the woman's attention, noticing the rapidly spreading burn mark in the wood. Ms. Dolly seemed to not notice it at all.

"This halfway house keeps going because we all do what we have to," Ms. Dolly droned on. "And right now, that means you figuring out how to fit in with the rest."

The woman didn't move as bright orange flames flicked at her wrist resting at the desk. The nearby daisies in the vase wilting from the heat.

Dani stood up and backed away from the growing flames that engulfed the surface of the desk.

"It's not just for them; it's for you too," Ms. Dolly continued to speak like nothing was happening. "So, let's try to make this work, okay?"

The fire moved up her body, causing her skin to melt away as if someone had doused her in gasoline. Her dress disintegrated in the heat, the fabric falling to the floor in black, crumbling strips.

Dani tried to open the door, to escape from the flames.

It was locked tight. There would be no chance of escape. Dani pressed herself as far from the heat of the growing flames as she could.

"It's not about changing who you are," Ms. Dolly's voice continued its immutable march as it had in Dani's memory, even if the woman's lips had long melted away. "It's just about making my job a tad easier and keeping this ship sailing smoothly."

There was nowhere to go. Charred wood fell from the ceiling and walls. Dani's eyes and lungs burned. She was going to be burned alive in that awful little room, to the narration of Ms. Dolly in the background.

Closing her eyes, Dani waited.

A light appeared in her vision, a tall pillar of white light bursting forth from the distance. Maybe it was the proverbial light at the end of the tunnel that was so cliché it had become a poor joke.

Except in this light, a woman stood inside it staring back at her. It was Lady Gianni.

She walked towards Dani, extending a hand. Dani reached out and grasped it tight, feeling it pull her up to her feet.

Dani's eyes adjusted. The world around her slid into focus.

She was in a little room lined with black marble on the walls, floor, and ceiling. A canvas sat in the center with a chair and canisters of paint knocked over on the ground.

Lady Gianni led Dani out of the room and she was relieved to be free of the cramped space and the smell of Swisher Sweets at last.

Foreman Tom's men went into *The Ashen Room* behind them, oblivious to whatever ordeal Dani had just experienced. There was a small army of them, some waiting outside with a crate pre-made and ready to go. They blocked Dani's view of the entrance.

"Just breathe," Lady Gianni said, holding her hand. The woman's touch was soothing. "*The Ashen Room* can be overstimulating."

Dani coughed, and a faint gray smoke dissipated into their air in front of her.

"What was that?" Dani said as fresh air filled her chest. "The room was on fire."

"I assure you that was not the case," Lady Gianni said in a sweet voice. "There's nothing in that room except complete darkness. Anything you saw was in your mind and your mind alone."

"No, I felt it," Dani said. "I felt the heat of the flames. I smelled burnt..."

Her voice trailed off. She didn't want to say the word flesh out loud.

The workmen were carrying something out of the room; it was the canvas. They handled it with extreme care, holding it with white-gloved hands and taking each step slowly.

Dani wanted to see her painting. The painting she made in the dark while imagining herself nearly being burned alive. She had tried to paint daisies, a sweet and simple image that her memory of Miss Dolly had somehow violently taken over.

Except on the canvas, Miss Dolly was nowhere to be seen.

A bald, middle-aged man sat on a plastic lawn chair with a cigarette in his mouth. He wore a white tank top and gray sweatpants. There was very little color. It was mostly blacks, whites, and grays throughout, except for a single spec of orange where the tip of the man's cigarette was lit. There was something in the background, too. It was faint and but it appeared to be a small barrel.

The workmen were already working on the canvas, mounting it into a frame on a cart.

"Wait, can I see it?" Dani asked, trying to get closer.

"I'm afraid we are on a deadline," Lady Gianni said as she gestured to Tom. "We need to get it preserved and ready for tomorrow's show."

Lady Gianni joined the men, rolling the painting away in a cart towards the backroom. She barked orders at them in various languages as they disappeared out of sight.

"We'll take good care of it," Tom said, trying to be comforting. "I promise."

"It's not that," Dani said, not sure how to explain. "The man in the painting. I thought I recognized him."

"Well, didn't you paint him?" Tom asked with a laugh.

Dani didn't join him.

"He looked kinda familiar, I guess," Tom said, realizing Dani wasn't as jovial as himself.

The man in the painting's face had been hard to see amidst the clouds of smoke, but she knew it was someone she knew.

"Let me give you a ride home," Tom offered with a friendly smile.

"It's fine," Dani said, trying to regain composure. "I can take the subway. It's not a problem."

"Not sure you want to go on the subway like that," Tom said in a strange tone.

Dani looked down at her clothes and she could see why - she was covered in paint from head to toe.

Tom's truck was about twenty years old and well-maintained. Dani could tell he put a lot of love into it.

"Just give me one second," he said, disappearing back inside the door to the loading dock.

Dani felt strange. Lifting her hands up to examine them, she could see the thick layers of expensive paint coated over her skin and under her fingernails. It was probably worth tens of thousands of dollars. Her skin felt like electricity was coursing over it. Her senses felt acute. She could smell everything in the side alley. She could see details on the church's architecture she hadn't noticed before.

It was too much at once. Dani closed her eyes, trying to block out some of what she felt.

"Let's get you home," Tom said, reappearing from the door. He had thick plastic sheets in his arms.

Laying them carefully on the dash, seat, and door of the cab; he made a paint proof space for Dani to sit in.

"Ain't exactly a limo," he said with a smile.

"It's just fine," Dani said, taking her seat. "Thank you again for the ride."

"No problem," Tom said as hustled to the other side of the vehicle.

The engine purred to life, the low rumble of exhaust creating vibrations throughout the cab. He took off towards the street.

Dani looked at her face in the side mirror, not recognizing the person staring back at her.

"Lady Gianni is intense," Tom said as he drove. "But she knows what she's doing. That painting was pretty amazing."

"Thank you," Dani replied, looking at him.

"My pleasure," said Tom.

Dani's brow furled. She suddenly became very aware of his voice again, but it sounded different, almost like he was speaking through a long tube.

Her gaze wandered back to her face in the mirror.

"I wonder if Larry is ok," she heard Tom say in this strange voice.

"Larry is probably fine," Dani said, glancing over at him.

"Oh, good to know," Tom replied. He looked a bit confused.

"She's acting strange," she heard Tom say, except she didn't see his mouth move.

Dani stared in shock.

She wasn't sure what was going on, so she turned her face towards the road while keeping one eye on Tom.

"It's been so long," Tom's distant voice said. "What I wouldn't give to slide a hand up that skirt right now."

"Excuse me," exclaimed Dani.

"What's up?" Tom said, smiling at her with a look of innocence.

"What did you just say to me?" Dani commanded.

"Good to know?" Tom replied. "*The Ashen Room* can be disorienting. Even a few of my guys had issues installing it. Do you want me to take you to the hospital instead? You seem off."

Lady Gianni warned her the paints she was using were toxic, there could be lead or worse in them. She might have been hallucinating.

"No, no," Dani said. "I need to get home and shower."

"I bet you do, you dirty girl," she could hear his voice say as his lips stayed tightly shut.

Was she reading his thoughts? It was the only explanation, or perhaps she was just imagining them.

She sat in silence for the rest of the drive. Images of Tom's sexual fantasies about her played in her head. Her naked body was in various positions and poses, except it wasn't her body. It was what Tom imagined her body to be like, very different from the real thing.

By the time the truck was stopped outside The Collective, she could barely hold back tears of disgust.

"See you tomorrow," Tom said in a friendly tone.

Dani didn't reply. She practically sprinted from the truck to the door. Anything to distance herself from the violating images of Tom on top of her that swarmed her mind.

Alek was making a sandwich in the kitchen area as Dani slammed the front door behind her.

He dropped his plate as he saw her; it clattered to the countertop.

"Are you ok?" Alek said, rushing to Dani's side.

"I'm fine," Dani said, stumbling as the images from Tom's head dissolved.

"You don't look fine," he said, leading her by the elbow to the couch. "You're ice cold."

"It's just paint," she replied, collapsing onto the sofa.

"I can see that," Alek commented. "Was there an accident at the gallery?"

Dani took a deep breath.

She explained painting in the dark and the vision she saw of Ms. Dolly being burned alive. It was just in her mind, of course. As far as she had last heard, Ms. Dolly was still alive and running the half-way house. Still, it had been jarring. She told him about the painting she had produced without even thinking about it.

"Wow," Alek said. "That's messed up. I've heard of darkness painting being done by other artists. Usually they have controlled conditions for doing so, but to just surprise someone like that is intense."

"That's not the worst of it," said Dani. "On the drive home, I felt funny. Like I could read the Foreman's mind, and he was having sexual fantasies... about me."

Alek tilted his head as he listened.

"You can't read minds," Alek said. "It's impossible. You're probably just having a reaction to the paint."

Maybe he was right, maybe she was losing her mind. She stared back at him, but she could see more than just her roommate looking back at her. Alek seemed to be almost see-through, an opaque image that she felt like she could put her hand out and it would pass right through him.

"Holy shit," Alek's voice rang in her head as he stared back at her silently. "She's really screwed up."

Dani couldn't hold it back anymore. She burst into sobs.

"You think I'm screwed up?" She asked through the tears.

"No, of course not," Alek said, his eyes wide.

"But I am Alek," Dani said as her tears landed on the concrete floor in colorful starbursts.

"I wanted to paint daisies," Dani continued through her sobs. "Flowers, cheerful things that made people smile and feel good about life. Instead, I've been painting dying sunflowers and now that smoking man. Now I'm hearing things, maybe people's inner thoughts, I don't know."

"There's got to be a logical explanation," Alek said, but Dani knew he doubted it. She could hear it in his voice and echoing in his mind.

"Something about me always feels wrong," Dani said. "Like the real me doesn't belong in the world. I mean, who would even want to be with someone as messed up as me?"

"I would," Alek's voice said, even as his lips remained closed.

"You like me?" Dani asked, the colorful paint on her cheeks now a brownish-black color after all the tones had mixed into one.

Alek looking stunned like a deer in the headlights about to get run over by a car.

She could see his thoughts. They weren't images of Dani performing sexual acts; they weren't sexual in the slightest. He was thinking about something else entirely, Dani and him holding hands.

Dani had never felt romantic feelings for him. How could she tell him lightly that she wasn't who he thought she was?

She heard Ms. Dolly's voice in her head.

"Not everyone here is going to be your cup of tea, but here's the deal: this place runs on rules, and one of them is learning to get along—or at least pretend to."

"I'm sorry about the other night," Dani said.

"What do you mean?" Alek asked.

"I'm sorry about not wanting to grab dinner or coffee," she explained. "I had so much going on I didn't realize you were asking me out."

"Oh, I didn't mean, I don't..." he stammered.

"I want to go out on a date with you," she stopped him.

"You do?" Alek replied in shock.

"Yes, just not tonight," Dani clarified.

"Why not?" asked Alek.

"If you haven't noticed, I'm completely covered in paint," Dani said, forcing a laugh.

"I guess you're right," Alek said, scratching his head and leaving a purple blotch of paint in his hair. "Tomorrow then?"

"That works," Dani told him.

She saw a picture of Alek and her at a fancy restaurant downtown play in his head.

"Maybe not dinner," she added quickly.

"Ok," said Alek, the restaurant image leaving as fast as it had come.

Dani stood up and walked towards the stairwell. "I'm going to use the shower for the next few hours, I think. I'll talk to you tomorrow."

"Ok," Alek said, rubbing the paint in his hair and staring at her with a curious look.

She only hoped that it would be an innocent date, one that wouldn't go too far. She wasn't ready to reveal her secret, at least not yet. Dani wasn't even sure he was the right person to reveal it to.

Dani didn't look back as she went down the steps into the locker room.

Looking at herself in the mirror, she didn't recognize the person staring back at her. It wasn't just the paint.

She felt crazy, like everything that had happened to her since going to work at the gallery was a bizarre waking dream. The man in the oil, mind reading, hallucinations, her paintings creating on their own.

"There has to be perfectly logical explanations for all of it," she thought.

It had to be the paint. She could feel its effect on her skin. Something about it was causing her to act this way, to feel this way, to see and hear things that weren't real.

"Just pretend," she said aloud to herself in the mirror. "That everything is normal."

She bolted the locker room door; she didn't want anyone walking in on her. Stripping and stepping into the shower, she didn't wait for the water to warm up, braving the icy droplets as they pelted the paint on her skin.

Ms. Dolly's face had thankfully faded from her mind, but the woman's voice cajoling her echoed in her ears as the kaleidoscope of color circled the showers drain.

CHAPTER 15

A moment Dani had dreaded loomed before her. Foreman Tom was waiting outside Gallery Nocturne for her as she arrived at work the next day. She held back the urge to turn around and run, for fear that any close contact would yield another episode more traumatic than the ride home the previous day.

She braced herself for the onslaught of images as he approached.

"Good morning," Tom said with a smile. "You clean up pretty good."

He was as close to her as he had been while they had been in the truck; she waited for his first thought to play aloud.

But it didn't.

"Still waking up?" Tom asked in his regular, pleasant voice. "I can grab you a fresh coffee if you want."

"Sorry," Dani said with relief. "I'm fine, thank you."

"Your guy is up in *The Horizons* gallery," Tom said.

"Who?" Dani asked.

"*The Smoking Man,*" Tom clarified. "That's what she's calling it. Lady Gianni had us working all night long to get it ready for tonight's show. The guys kept getting distracted and just staring at it."

"Oh," Dani said, not sure how to react.

"Go check it out for yourself," he said as he disappeared inside.

She had liked Tom originally, but the memory of his thoughts and images swirling in her head had made her weary of him. Was that fair?

He had never once laid a hand on her or given her any inclination that he would harm her. Tom had been sweet, thoughtful, and helpful since she had first met him. And who knows if she had just imagined the whole thing?

She pushed it from her mind and walked inside.

The gallery wouldn't officially open for hours, but there was already quite a crowd in *The Horizons* wing.

An odd mix of sweaty workmen and finely dressed men in suits were jostling for position in front of a painting hung on the wall. None seemed to mind rubbing shoulders with the other, their sole concerns being the best view. Dani approached to see for herself, but Haley found her first.

"The sunflower was one thing," Haley began excitedly. "But whatever this is, I can't believe it. You don't belong as a PA."

"What are you talking about?" Dani asked.

"*The Smoking Man*!" Haley exclaimed. "Mr. Henricks saw it and called a bunch of his friends over immediately for a private viewing. He wanted to start an art auction style bidding war right here and now, but Lady Gianni walked him back from it. She thinks it'll be the star of the show tonight."

The Smoking Man. She wasn't sure she liked the name, despite its accuracy.

"I should go find..." Dani began, pulling away from the excited Haley, who was still talking a mile a minute.

She saw Lady Gianni just off to the side from the main crowd, talking to Mr. Henricks with a smile on her face and holding a champagne flute.

"Good Morning Mr. Henricks," Dani said, walking up to them. "Good Morning Lady Gianni."

"A good morning indeed," Mr. Henricks said with a warm smile. "I have to be honest with you, Dani. I didn't believe Lady Gianni at first when she told me you would be a star, but here we are. *The Smoking Man* is pure genius. Please tell me how you were able to..."

"Please Jeremiah," Lady Gianni cut him off. "Give her a moment. She just got here."

"Of course, of course," Jeremiah said. "Haley, be a dear and get Dani a glass of champagne."

"Yes, Mr. Henricks," Haley said, scuttling off and out of sight.

"So they like it?" Dani asked, her eyes glancing at the crowd.

"No one can take their eyes off it," Mr. Henricks said. "The smoke... it captures something ethereal. I can't even describe it. When I look at it, it feels like I can see it billowing and almost filling the painting. But then I look again and it hasn't moved. This is going to fetch a fortune."

"In due time," Lady Gianni added.

Haley returned with a full champagne flute and handed it to Dani.

"Is that why we are celebrating?" Dani asked, not sure if she should take a sip or wait.

"Partly," Lady Gianni continued. "We'll throw a proper celebration once the buzz from tonight's show gets around. Right now we are drinking champagne to celebrate another splendid victory."

"And what's that?" asked Dani.

"To *The Dollhouse*," Lady Gianni said, holding up her glass. "The most expensive single piece of art ever sold by this gallery in its short but glorious history."

"Oh," Dani said as she clinked glasses with the rest. "Who bought it?"

"An old friend of mine," Lady Gianni said. "A very wealthy private collector from Milan. He wants it delivered immediately. Speaking of which, Tom!"

The Foreman shuffled over.

"Break time is over," she said. "Get them back to work on dismantling *The Dollhouse*."

"Yes, Ms. Gianni," he said before grabbing several of the workmen from the crowd by their collars and pulling them behind a curtain draped over the passage that lead deeper into the gallery.

"I couldn't have planned it better myself," Lady Gianni continued. "With *The Dollhouse* gone, *The Smoking Man* will take its place as our centerpiece of *The Horizons*. By tomorrow, everyone will be talking about it at every museum across the country."

Dani blushed.

"And the starting price for bids will skyrocket," Mr. Henricks added with a laugh.

"We'll see," Lady Gianni said to him, smacking his arm playfully. "I prefer to be more selective with who I sell my art to."

"Sure yes," Mr. Henricks said in agreement. "Shall we break up the ravenous hoard?"

"I believe it's time," Lady Gianni replied, and the two wandered towards the crowd to lead them out of the gallery.

"It must be so exciting," Haley said. "Becoming a wealthy and famous artist."

"I'm none of that," Dani replied. "At least not yet. Can I ask you a question?"

"Of course," Haley said, smiling at her.

"Are Mr. Henricks and Lady Gianni..." Dani's voice trailed off on purpose.

It took Haley a couple of seconds to realize what she was asking.

"Oh god no," Haley said at last. "He has a significant stake in the gallery. So much so that almost his entire collection is in storage downstairs, most of it coming from artists like yourself that the director introduced him to."

"I didn't know there was a basement," Dani said aloud.

"A basement would be an understatement," Haley replied. "I haven't been down there myself but I used to know a girl who came here when it was a nightclub and she said that she heard from a friend who had been down there that there's like underground crypts and caverns and secret chambers. It's a proper labyrinth underneath our feet."

"I hadn't heard about any of that," said Dani.

"Probably not where you want to be hanging out anyway," Haley said. "Cheers."

They clinked their glasses again, and both downed the last of their champagne.

Dani left work on time for once. She had thought Lady Gianni would protest and want her to work the show since she was supposedly the spotlight, but the director felt the value of *The Smoking Man* would increase if the artist seemed mysterious.

Getting back to The Collective, she found Alek sitting nervously downstairs while Bianca and Paul chatted nearby in the kitchen.

"Hey," Alek said, standing up. He was wearing a flannel shirt and jeans with sneakers.

"Is that what you're wearing tonight?" Dani asked.

"Ya, is that ok?" Alek asked.

"Depends on where we are going," Dani replied.

"It's a surprise," Alek said quickly.

"Gotcha," said Dani. She would just have to wear something similar.

"Ow-Ow!" Paul said from behind the kitchen counter. "Big date tonight!"

"Shut up, Paul," Bianca said with a laugh.

Dani suddenly felt self-conscious. Bianca was radiant as ever and she couldn't help but wish it was her instead of Alek tonight.

"I'm going to have to keep my eye on you two," Paul continued unabated. "No more closed doors upstairs."

"Paul," Bianca scolded him. "Don't be a dick."

"Fine, fine," Paul said, laughing. "I'm kidding. Just nothing in my van, please."

"How could they, anyway?" Bianca said. "The whole thing smells like fast food."

"It's a clean bio-fuel," Paul replied. "Alek went around town all day today, collecting enough of a stockpile for the next few months. We'll be riding clean, unlike your boyfriend."

"Boyfriend?" Dani asked, unable to hide her curiosity.

"He's not my boyfriend," Bianca said.

"Don't listen to her," said Paul. "She's got that pollution mogul Jeremiah Henricks wrapped around her finger. Auditioning for the part of ex-wife number six."

"He's just a friend," said Bianca calmly.

"A friend who just built his own wing of the city's public gallery downtown," Paul added for her. "And guess who's getting the first show for the grand opening?"

"That's amazing," Dani said. "Congratulations."

She wanted to rush over and tell them about *The Smoking Man*, but the time didn't feel right.

"Thank you," said Bianca, somehow perfecting, looking humble.

Dani noticed Alek standing with his hands in his pockets, staring at the ground. He must be feeling like Mr. Cellophane when Bianca was in the room.

"I better go change," Dani said.

"A word in private real quick?" asked Paul, rushing over.

"Sure," she replied.

They walked up the stairs and into Paul's office.

"Listen," he said, sitting down at the desk. His tone had suddenly changed from friendship mode to business.

"We've got a problem," he continued.

Dani's heart dropped. Word must have gotten around to him about her paintings for the Gallery Nocturne.

"Your old stuff just isn't selling," he said. "At this point, it's a numbers game. I need more from you, at least five more pieces by the end of the month. Something is bound to gain traction."

"That's two weeks away," Dani replied. It usually took her a whole week to finish something, unless she was at the Gallery Nocturne, where she could somehow work faster.

"I know," said Paul. "But money is getting tight around here. Bianca's old stuff isn't selling since she dumped her last boyfriend. Alek won't let me touch any of his works in progress. I need you to pull me out of this mess with some volume that maybe we could sell at a discount."

"I can't tonight or tomorrow," Dani said. "I can try to paint this weekend."

"To quote my favorite alien," Paul replied. "Do or do not, there is no try."

"You got it," said Dani. She wasn't sure what other response Paul would accept.

"Great," Paul said, his friendly smile returning. "Have a great time tonight. Get lots of inspiration!"

Dani nodded and left his office.

The van sputtered down the highway that led out of town. The suspension sat lower than usual, weighed down by the dozens of recycled milk jugs that were filled with cooking oil in the back.

"Paul had me check every fast-food joint in the city," Alek explained as they drove. "I spent the entire afternoon just filtering it out in the alley, trying to get all the crud out of it."

"You didn't have to do that," said Dani, feeling bad. "We could have taken a taxi."

"No, no," Alek continued. "I wanted to do it. It wouldn't feel as authentic of a night if we were being dropped off by someone."

"Am I allowed to know where this mysterious place is?" Dani asked. "You're not taking me out into the middle of nowhere, are you?"

Alek tried to think about his answer.

"I am, in a way," he replied. "But hopefully in a fun way."

He smiled and turned on the radio. Rock music filled the van. As the song ended, the DJ came on.

"That was Ton Von Unten's latest hit," the DJ said. "They just canceled their next US tour, probably going to be awhile before we see them again. In still more depressing news, the police are still looking for leads on the missing girl."

Dani's ears perked up.

"She was taken from her kitchen while the family was still at home," the DJ continued. "Still in highschool. Police are asking anyone to come forward with information at this time. It's a travesty. What is happening to this country? And they'll probably blame rock music again. Little do they know that rock music will never die. You're listening to..."

Alek turned it off.

"Not exactly uplifting," he said with a laugh.

Dani tried to shrug it off, but something about the news report bothered her.

"We're here," Alek said with a smile.

Dani could see the bright lights in the distance, the ring of a Ferris Wheel growing taller by the second as they approached.

They passed a sign on the road: 'COUNTY FAIR NEXT EXIT'.

They walked the endless rows of game stalls that lined the fairgrounds, stopping to play one every so often.

"Young man," a barker yelled as they passed. "Why don't you show your darling how much of a man you are on the High Striker? Guaranteed to earn you a peck on the cheek."

"Oh, I don't know," Dani said to him as she tried to continue past, but Alek had already stopped.

"Sure, why not," he said, fishing into his pocket for tickets.

The High Striker was a tower, about ten feet tall. At its base was a padded button that Alek was to hit with a mallet as hard as he could to send a puck vertically to see if it would ring the bell at the top.

"The strongest of men have tried for the grand prize," the barker said as he took the ticket and handed Alek the mallet. "Let's see what you've got, shrimp."

The mallet's head was heavy. It dragged on the ground as Alek strained to carry it to the machine. His face turned red as he struggled to lift it over his head, then with a soft whoosh it came down on the cushion at the base. Alek practically tripped over himself trying to control it. The puck attached to the tower barely moved, rising a measly couple inches before dropping back down.

"Nice try," the barker yelled. "Maybe next time."

"Damn it," Alek exclaimed as he clutched at his hand.

"You did your best," Dani said, smiling.

"Game is rigged," Alek said obstinately as they walked away.

Dani rubbed his shoulder.

"At least you can say you tried," she said with a smile.

He looked up and smiled back.

"Come on," Dani said. "I want a fried pickle before the line gets too long."

He chased after her towards the food truck.

Sitting on a picnic table facing each other, they each took turns dipping their greasy fried treats into the small plastic cup of ranch between them.

"I forgot how good these are," Dani said.

"When was the last time you had one?" asked Alek.

"Not since I was maybe six-years-old," Dani replied. "What about you?"

"It's my first time," he said. "They didn't have this kind of thing back home."

"They don't have fairs in Russia?" Dani said with a raised eyebrow.

"They do, but not like this," he explained. "Think more street parades and folk dancing on stages."

"You mean you don't have bumper cars and Ferris wheels?" Dani asked.

"We do, but at amusement parks," said Alek, finishing his pickle. "I've always wanted to go to an American fair."

"I'm glad we got to pop your fair cherry," Dani said with a laugh.

Alek's face turned bright red.

"My dad used to take me," said Dani. "He'd win me a goldfish at the ring toss to take home. It always died the next day."

"That's sad," Alek remarked.

"I guess it is," she continued. "But as a kid, I thought it was always super exciting. The rides, the games, the prizes, they are pretty great."

"So, why did you stop going?" Alek asked. "Did you grow out of it?"

Dani took a drink from her oversized soda cup.

"Something happened," she said, not sure how to explain it.

"What?" said Alek.

"It's just..." Dani faltered.

"You don't have to tell me if you don't want to," Alek told her.

"No, it's just a hard memory," Dani said. "But that's ok."

She drank the last of her soda.

"I got lost at a carnival once," said Dani. "My dad and I got separated. I wandered into someplace I shouldn't have. Do you know what a sideshow is?"

"I don't think so," replied Alek.

"It's not really a thing any more in America," explained Dani. "But when I was a kid, they still had them. It's where they have people with strange deformities or abilities show them off."

"You mean a freak show?" exclaimed Alek.

"I don't like to call it that," said Dani. "I was lost and crying, trying to find my father. And this woman found me. She was one of the sideshow performers. They called her the Giantess. She must have been seven feet tall."

"Whoa, that's tall for a woman," said Alek.

"Ya, she was popular," said Dani. "She picked me up and tried to help me find him."

"Doesn't sound that traumatic," Alek said with a look of confusion.

"Well, my dad found us first," Dani continued. "He thought the Giantess was trying to kidnap me. So he started a fight with her."

"Yikes," said Alek.

"I know," replied Dani. "My dad didn't stand a chance against her, so they threw each other around a little and I was yelling. Then he pulled off her loincloth she was wearing by accident and…"

She paused to see Alek's response; he looked very interested.

"Turns out she wasn't a she," said Dani.

Alek's eyes got wide.

"We got thrown out and Dad got a black eye," Dani tried to finish the story. "Never got to take my goldfish home that day and he never wanted to take me back."

"That's crazy," Alek said with a laugh.

"People like that really freaked my dad out," said Dani.

"I bet," replied Alek.

Dani's phone beeped as a text message came in. Dani unlocked it to see.

It was a picture of Haley. In it, she could see a crowded line filled with men and women in suits and dresses waiting outside the Gallery Nocturne. On the wall behind them, projected was an advertisement for *The Smoking Man* and her name underneath it.

"Work?" Alek asked.

"Kind of," Dani said, not sure how she wanted to feel. She showed him the photo.

"All of those people just to see your painting?!" He practically yelled.

"I guess so," Dani replied.

"That's amazing," he said, smiling at her.

Whatever sensation that she could read his mind from the previous day had worn off, but she felt she could still see something behind his eyes that told her he was considering something. Maybe leaning forward to kiss her or reach for her hand. Dani didn't want to ruin the night with something like that, something that would lead him on too far down a path she couldn't follow.

"Let's go check out the rides," said Dani.

Alek seemed to snap out of his thoughts.

"Sure, let's go," he said, but she could tell he still had other things on his mind.

Dani had seen too many teen romance movies to fall for this one.

As they walked from ride to ride, she noticed Alek trying to lead them in the direction of the giant Ferris Wheel in the distance. It would be private and romantic. She had no doubt Alek would try to make a move. A move she would feel compelled to reject, throwing their entire friendship and dynamic as roommates into disarray.

Her original plan had been to show Alek how little they had in common, how little chemistry they had, as a way to get him to volunteer to see her as just a friend. She hadn't planned on them to get along so swimmingly as they had.

"Why can't you just be like the other girls?" Ms. Dolly's voice said in her head.

She panicked as she tried to think of a way out. She considered telling him she was tired and wanted to head back, but they had only been there a little over an hour. Maybe Dani could fake being sick? It might backfire, push him into knight in shining armor mode.

"Let's go on the Ferris Wheel next," Alek said, trying to hold back his excitement.

Just try to let him down easy, Dani told herself.

Then she saw her chance.

"I want to go here," Dani said, pulling him by the arm hard to the left and away from the looming wheel of romanticism.

"Ok," Alek managed to say, he sounded only slightly disappointed.

"I've never done one of these before," Dani said as they stopped outside a tent.

"Seraphina Shadowgaze," Alek read the sign out loud. "Farseer into the great beyond. She sounds like a D&D character."

"Please, I've always wanted to try this," Dani lied. She had no interest in contacting dead loved ones, but it was better than the Ferris Wheel.

"I'm not sure," Alek said.

"Pretty please," Dani pleaded.

"Alright," said Alek, giving in.

They walked inside the tent.

A red curtain hung from the front of the tent, blocking access to the rear room. A sign in front of it read, "We know you're here, but we are with another client at the moment. Please be patient and you will be served shortly."

"Looks like she's busy," Alek said. "Let's try the…"

"I want to wait," Dani cut him off.

She read the pamphlet on the table which listed the various services available: tarot cards, palm reading, etc.

Alek had his hands in his pants pockets and looked abnormally stiff.

"Come on," he tried to get her to change her mind again. "I had one of these back home. I don't really want to experience it again."

"What was it like?" Dani asked.

"Creepy," Alek replied.

"What happened?" She pushed him on it. She was growing more curious by the second.

"The lady spoke in a strange voice, weird knocking sounds, the hair on the back of my neck stood up," he said. "I didn't see anything, but it was weird."

"Don't tell me you believe in this stuff," Dani said with a smile.

"I don't, but…" Alek didn't finish his sentence.

The curtain split apart, and a couple walked out holding hands and whispering to each other. She hadn't considered it, but a lot of couples go to psychics for relationship validation. They wanted to hear someone else tell them they were going to be together forever. Maybe this wasn't a good idea after all.

"Come on in," said a voice from the next room.

"I'm not sure anymore," Dani said, making a step towards the exit, but Alek was already walking into the backroom. He might have noticed the same thing that Dani had about the couple.

Begrudgingly, she joined him.

The backroom of the tent was lit by candles arranged on tables and shelves in an oval that encircled a round, center table. Books, crystal balls, and strange glass containers lined the shelves. A prominent book sat on a display stand. Dani could read the title: CONVERSATIONS WITH DEMONS.

Interesting reading.

Sitting at the table was a woman dressed in an ornate purple dress with full sleeves. Jewels and dangles hung from the garment in zig-zag patterns. She was about Alek's height, but twice as wide. Her black hair hid underneath a turban that matched her dress. Her eyeshadow was dark and thick, stretching down her cheeks and her lipstick was black to match.

"Welcome, welcome," she said in a deep southern accent. "Welcome to Seraphina's Nexus of Psychic Power."

"Hi, I was thinking," Dani tried to say.

"Hold on," Seraphina said, cutting her off and holding up a finger. "I'm sensing you are here for your fortunes to be told, for me to look into your future and see if a happy marriage and a beautiful child await you."

Dani looked over at Alek, who seemed to be getting a kick out of it.

She tried to think quickly and remembered the pamphlet from the front room.

"Actually," Dani replied. "I was thinking of something more elaborate. How about a seance?"

She knew it was more expensive, but it would also take almost an hour. Plenty of time to cool off Alek's desires for a romantic evening.

"A seance, finally someone gives me a challenge," Seraphina said. "I've been reading nothing but palms and cards all night long. Please sit."

She gestured towards two stools at the table.

With a wave of her hand, the curtain that led to the front closed on its own.

"Neat trick," Alek said with a small laugh.

"That was no trick," Seraphina replied, narrowing her eyes at him.

Dani had noticed Seraphina's other hand, which was under the table, probably holding onto the remote control for the machine that opened and closed the curtain.

They both took their seats, chuckling to themselves as they did so.

"I know my meager station of today does little to prove confidence in my abilities as a medium," the woman began. "But I assure you, once long ago, I was famous throughout Savannah."

"I bet," Alek said, doing best to not burst out laughing.

"This won't work if you are not believers," Seraphina said in a disapproving voice.

"We are believers," Dani said, kicking Alek under the table. "Please proceed."

"I also must ask that you make your payment up front," Seraphina added. "Many a seance have been cut short by the participants running in terror from this very tent."

"I got this," Alek said, pulling out his wallet, but Dani stopped him.

"No, I wanted to do it," she said, opening her purse and handing the cash to the woman. "My treat."

She winked at him, which caused him to turn red.

In truth, she knew he hadn't sold anything in months, and it was her insistence that they were there. It only seemed fair that she would foot the bill with the added bonus it would slightly diminish Alek's antiquated manly pride for paying for everything on their date.

Seraphina dropped the cash into her cleavage and smiled.

"So, who are we contacting today?" Seraphina asked. "A long-lost grandmother, or perhaps a parent taken all too soon?"

Shit, Dani hadn't thought about what to ask for.

She looked at the woman and then back at Alek, both who stared at her, ready for her choice. Dani tried to think of anyone in her family that was dead that she could use, but suddenly found herself unable to think of anyone who's funeral she had attended.

Seraphina cleared her throat loudly. She was growing impatient.

Then Dani realized it didn't matter. This was all fake. She could make someone up entirely and then just go along with it.

"I want to contact my great-aunt..." Dani paused as she tried to think of an imaginary name. "Leslie."

"Your great-aunt Leslie," Seraphina repeated back to her.

"Yes," Dani affirmed.

Seraphina seemed to think it over in her head for a moment. Like most con artists, she was probably a great lie detector herself.

"Please join hands with me," Seraphina said.

They did as instructed, and Dani noticed Alek's hand was cold and clammy.

The candles in the room dimmed slightly until they were small flames and only the table was illuminated by the bronze star-shaped chandelier hanging overhead.

She felt Alek's hand tense up; she wanted to lean over and whisper to him that she felt Seraphina's leg move right before the candles dimmed; probably to hit a switch under the table.

"Spirits, we call out into the beyond," Seraphina commanded, her voice slowly growing louder with each word. "We call out to a relative of this girl, one known as Leslie."

Dani held back the urge to snicker.

"Spirits, help us find this loved one," Seraphina continued. "Bring them to us. Bring them to us!"

She was practically yelling.

The chandelier light flickered above them. Alek squeezed Dani's hand tighter. His palm was slick with sweat.

"Leslie, Leslie, Leslie!" Seraphina screamed. A breeze had picked up inside and swirled around them, knocking Dani's bag off the table.

Dani thought she could hear a motor whirling quietly in the background.

"Leave it, leave it!" Seraphina yelled.

The woman began chanting in an unfamiliar language. Dani could feel Alek's pulse through his hand. He was squeezing hers so tight. She was going to lose feeling in her fingers soon.

Suddenly Seraphina released both their hands. The lights immediately came back to life, and the breeze died.

"I don't know what's going on today," Seraphina said in a frustrated tone.

"You can't find her?" Alek said. He sounded worried.

"Sometimes it's just how it is," Seraphina explained. "Commanding into the beyond for a spirit is kind of like screaming someone's name at a crowd of people. Except the crowd is made up of trillions of souls. They can't always hear you."

"That's too bad," Dani said, not believing Alek was so into it.

She reached down to pick up her purse and placed it on her lap.

"Do you have anything of hers?" Seraphina asked. "A piece of jewelry, maybe, anything like that. Personal effects are like little homing beacons for finding spirits. Virtually foolproof."

"I'm sorry I don't," Dani said.

Something caught her eye, some leftover paint from the day before must have been on her bag as she noticed a smudge of orange on her wrist. It tingled slightly on the bare skin of her arm.

"Maybe we should..." Dani began.

"Do you think you could find the person these belonged to?" Alek asked, holding something out to Seraphina.

Dani's eyes narrowed. They were a pair of glasses.

"Are these Leslie's?" Seraphina asked.

"No, no," Alek replied. "They belonged to a man we met the other day, a stranger, actually. We don't know who he is, but we think he might have been hurt. I just want to know if he is, you know..."

He let his comment linger.

"Dead?" Seraphina blurted out.

Alek nodded.

Dani stared at him, but he gave no notice. She knew exactly who Alek was referring to, the man in the oil, but she had no idea he had something so personal as the man's glasses.

Seraphina took the spectacles and placed them on the table in front of her. She capped her hands tight over them and closed her eyes.

"Shouldn't be a problem," Seraphina said. "If he's in the great beyond, I'll find him. These things are just resonating with psychic energy. Hands, please."

They locked hands together in a circle again and the light and wind show repeated itself same as before.

"Stranger in the great beyond," Seraphina announced. "These earthly souls have sought you out. Are you there?"

The table rumbled again. Dani rolled her eyes. The stage show was quaint but lost its luster quickly. Alek, on the other hand, was eating it up. His eyes were closed as tight as his hand wrapped around Dani's.

"Stranger, make yourself known," Seraphina yelled. Dani was growing annoyed as her hair flew into her eyes, but she couldn't push it away.

"Come on baby, find us," she heard Seraphina's voice whisper, but like yesterday, the woman's lips did not move.

Seraphina began her foreign chants, but Dani heard another voice over them.

"By the power of shadow and flame," Seraphina chanted. "Reveal yourself to me now!"

Alek squeezed tighter. Dani could feel every part of him, every emotion. Except there was only one emotion, fear. It gripped every inch of him, every muscle, it caused sweat to drip of pore in his body.

Then it stopped.

"I'm sorry I don't know what's wrong with me," Seraphina said, the room returning to normal.

"You can't find him?" Alek asked. Dani could feel a glimmer of hope eating away at the fear inside him.

"He ain't in the beyond, that's for certain," Seraphina said, pulling a cigarette from her pocket and lighting it.

Dani could feel Alek's relief through their touch.

She broke their embrace, feeling guilty for listening to him like that without him knowing. It was like she had stolen the password to his heart and mind, hacking inside him to find his secrets.

"I think we should go," Dani said.

She leaned forward and snatched the glasses off the table in front of Seraphina.

Dani was about to stand up to leave when she felt something cold on her leg.

Looking down, the carpet floor of the tent was gone. A pool of black sludge had replaced it, and sticking out of that black sludge was a hand gripping her calf.

She screamed, trying to pull her leg away, but the hand's grip was tight. The more she pulled, the more of the hand appeared from the pitch black puddle. A wrist, then a forearm, an elbow, a shoulder. Drops of the freezing cold oil ran down her leg.

Dani fell to the ground in her scramble to get away, straining herself on her elbows as she tried to break free.

A face emerged from the pool of darkness. It was a face she had seen before in the museum and at Summit Petroleum. The man with the scar on his face, not a speck of bare skin visible with the oil leaking out of his eyes.

"Leave me alone," Dani screamed.

But the man couldn't hear. His ears were filled with the viscous liquid and so were his lungs. Unable to take a breath, he couldn't speak and only mouthed words silently.

But Dani could hear him, she could hear his every terror filled thought and the same words repeating over and over again.

"Someone, please help me," he said.

She thought he was going to pull her down with him, pull her down under the pool of oil. Dani felt herself sinking down with the man. She squeezed her eyes tight, not wanting the oil to get in her eyes though it undoubtedly would.

But it didn't.

She opened her eyes and found herself alone in the tent. Alek, Seraphina, and the man drowning in the oil were all gone. Except she wasn't really alone.

Dani heard the sounds of machines beeping behind her. She pivoted on the ground and saw a hospital bed sitting in the corner.

Dani scrambled to her feet, glad to be free of the oil soaked man's grasp.

An old woman sat in the bed, hundreds of wires coming out of the wall and wrapping themselves around like snakes strangling their prey.

"Do you know where we are?" Dani asked the woman, but the glazed look of her eyes as she stared back at Dani indicated that her mind was already gone. She mumbled words under her breath in a language that sounded something like Mandarin.

Dani fell to the ground as someone ran into her.

The person tumbled on top of Dani, moving frantically.

Dani could see the person's face only for a moment, but the moment was all she would need.

She recognized the face of the teenage girl from *The Dollhouse*.

"Please, I have to get out of here," the girl said, grabbing Dani's arms. "Is there a way out?"

"I don't know," Dani said, confused. "Just stop for a second. Tell me where I am."

"Oh my god," the girl screamed, looking behind her. "He's still follow-ing me."

The girl rushed to her feet and ran away.

"Wait!" Dani yelled after her. "Who's following you?"

Then something passed through Dani, something cold and unnerving. It made every hair on her body stand on end; her throat became instantly dry, and her stomach felt like it had turned upside down inside her.

It was a shadow, a shadow of a man following the girl. Even as just a shadow, Dani knew it was the watcher from *The Dollhouse*. The faceless man who had watched the porcelain girl, who had stolen sleep from her in countless nightmares.

Soon it was out of sight, chasing after the girl into the fog that the room was made from.

Dani had a feeling inside of her, a feeling that the girl would be back and so would the shadow man.

Standing up, she noticed a young man standing next to the old woman in the bed. He wore a stained and torn suit that was too big for his frame. He stared down at the woman in the bed, gently stroking her arm.

"Who are you?" Dani asked him as she approached.

"My name is Javier," he replied.

Behind him, against the wall of the tent outside, Dani could make out three silhouettes holding what looked like attaché cases. They were right behind Javier, the outlines of their faces revealing their focus on him as their chests heaved in what looked like anger.

"There's something behind you," Dani said to him, hoping to warn him.

"I know," Javier said. "They're always there, no matter where I go."

"Where are we?" Dani asked.

"I don't know," Javier replied. "Trapped somewhere, I suppose."

"How do we get out?" said Dani.

"I don't know," said Javier.

"What do you mean, you don't know?" Dani realized she had raised her voice.

"I don't know any more than you do," Javier replied to her calmly. "All I know is that there's no escaping this place. Our paths may cross and intertwine, but we all live through the same things over and over again; our final moments."

"Am I dead?" Dani asked, feeling suddenly horrified.

"Maybe," Javier said with a nonchalance that only worried her more.

"Well, how did you die?" asked Dani.

"I started a new job at PaySphere," Javier explained, still trying in vain to comfort the old woman in the bed with the steamy breath of the men hitting the back of his neck. "And I pissed off the wrong people."

"Them?" asked Dani.

"Si, I mean yes," Javier said.

"This doesn't make any sense," said Dani.

The tent shook violently, like an earthquake.

Dani saw something fall from a bookshelf and land on the ground with a crash. It was a flowerpot with a sunflower inside. It was her sunflower in her flowerpot, a crack forming up the side just like she had painted.

"I don't know how much more time you have," Javier said, with sudden urgency in his eyes. "If you go back, please tell my mother I love her. My father too."

"I will," said Dani, grasping the table as she tried to steady herself against the increasingly violent shaking. "But tell me your last name."

"It's..." the young man began, but didn't finish.

The tent and the world around her had crumpled away like a piece of paper.

She felt hands on her, grabbing her shoulders. She tried to break free from them.

"Dani, Dani!" Alek's voice yelled at her.

She opened her eyes; she was lying on the floor of Seraphina's tent.

"Alek, is that really you?" Dani asked, hoping that it was.

"It's me, are you ok?" Alek said, looking terrified. "You had some kind of fit or something."

"I saw," she tried to say as she sat up. "I saw..."

She didn't know how to finish her sentence.

"I really need to put up a sign warning people with epilepsy not to come inside," Seraphina said.

"I don't have epilepsy," Dani said, rubbing her head where she must have hit it on the ground.

"What you call that, then?" Seraphina said with pursed lips.

"Are you ok?" Alek asked. "What happened?"

"I don't know," said Dani. "I touched the glasses and then you guys were gone and I felt something on my leg."

The memory caused her to pause.

Alek didn't dare speak. He could see the fear in her eyes.

"Alek, I saw him," Dani said. "I saw the man covered in oil, the man from the sculpture, the man from the refinery."

"What refinery?" Seraphina asked.

"And not just him," Dani continued, ignoring her. "I saw an old dying woman from a painting at the gallery. I saw the girl from *The Dollhouse*, the porcelain girl with the shadow man chasing her. And there was someone else. He told me his name was Javier. I didn't recognize him. He asked me to tell his mother he loved her."

All three of them were silent for several moments.

"Girl, you're off your meds," Seraphina said.

"No, I'm serious," Dani pleaded. "I think they were dead. I think I was seeing into the beyond or something. They were trapped there."

"There ain't no spirits in here right now," said Seraphina. "I've been doing this longer than you've been alive, you may not believe, but I sure do. If they were dead, I would have felt them."

"Maybe they aren't fully dead," said Alek. "Maybe they were trapped somewhere in between, like purgatory."

"I've seen purgatory honey," said Seraphina. "There ain't nothing to it, just a place where people gotta live their lives over again until they get it right. Now, if you'll excuse me, I got to get myself put back together after that whole hoopla."

Dani and Alek got to their feet and left the tent.

Looking at her wrist, Dani noticed that the paint smudge on her wrist was gone; wiped away on the carpet or her clothing during her fit.

"Let's skip the Ferris Wheel," Alek said as he held her up and walked her towards the parking lot. "I think I've had enough of this place for one night."

Dani should have been relieved, but she was not.

As they got to the van, Alek opened the passenger door for her.

She grabbed his jacket tight and brought him in closer.

"I think the people I saw were dead," she said to him in a whisper, like she was afraid that someone would overhear them and send her to the nuthouse. "Except they're still trapped here with us."

"Where?" Alek asked.

"I don't know yet," Dani said, trying to make sense of it all.

She looked into his sad eyes, the eyes of the boy still making sense of the real world, much less the added burden of an ethereal one. She wished she had more of that magical paint so she could tell what he was thinking.

Asking him would have to suffice for now.

"You believe me, don't you?" She asked, filled with hope.

He took a long time to answer, each moment ticking by at a snail's pace.

"I believe you," he said. "I just don't know if the others will."

CHAPTER 16

Flames kicked up from the steel barrel that was Larry's makeshift fire pit. He had found it a month ago while wandering the woods behind Sunny Meadows and had rolled it a mile to his back porch. Who knew how fortuitous a decision that would end up being?

Some say one man's trash is another man's treasure. In this case, one man's trash was another man's means of disposing of a dead body.

It had only taken a dozen or so swings of his hatchet to separate the torso from the limbs. Lisa Johnson was a petite, stringy teenager and hadn't required nearly as much effort as he had thought it would to fit her in the rusted barrel.

Various cracks and pops emanated from the fire, like bacon simmering on the stove for breakfast. The lightly colored smoke carried whatever was left of Lisa into the sky.

Larry's back patio had afforded him plenty of privacy. Backing up to the forest, it was far too cold for anyone to be out that night for a stroll through the woods that would allow them to come upon his little funeral pyre. Blocked on the other sides by the doublewide itself, a rickety old shed, and his grandfather's truck; it was the perfect secluded location to dispose of the body.

Larry had stripped the engine, transmission, and radio from the truck months ago, selling them for parts, as they were the only parts of it that still had any value. He had considered getting it towed to a junkyard, but something about having his grandfather's pride and joy sitting there behind the house made him feel like the derelict vehicle was a sort of memorial to the old man.

He grabbed the gas can he had filled up at the corner store earlier and poured more into the barrel; the flames erupted and nearly scorched Larry's eyebrows.

He had to get it hot, really hot in there. Hot enough to turn whatever was left of Lisa to ash. Then he'd bag up whatever remains, drive it to a dumpster on the other end of town, and let the city public works department take care of the rest for him. Then the only thing remaining that could link him back to Lisa would be her student ID, that he had locked in the fireproof safe inside his house. If they had a search warrant and could get inside there, it wouldn't matter. He'd already be screwed.

Where the hell was that owl?

It was the owl's fault he was in this predicament in the first place. Keeping him up at night so that he missed his shift at work, getting him fired. It had even distracted him and nearly got him hit by a car. To top it all off, the damn thing had convinced him to go chase after whatever he thought he was seeing in the forest and led him to Lisa's door.

Larry was really a victim of circumstance.

He was determined to shoot it if he saw it again, but something inside him told him he wouldn't. His intuition told him wherever it was, it was far away from Sunny Meadows.

"Good riddance, you damn nuisance," Larry said aloud to the darkness.

"Who are you talking to?" said a voice from around the side of the house.

Larry jumped to his feet.

"Simmer down, it's just your neighbor," the old man said, coming around slowly from behind the truck. He wore a flannel jacket with a rifle slung over his shoulder.

"What are you doing on my property?" Larry asked nervously.

The old man wasn't close enough to see into the barrel, but a few more steps and he might see the girl's bones, not quite disintegrated yet.

Larry grabbed the small metal gas drum and poured more into the fire. The conflagration erupted high and hot, hopefully hot enough to stop whatever was left from being recognizable.

"Now listen here fella," his neighbor said before spitting on the ground. "I've been knocking at your front door and you ain't been answering."

"I didn't answer, cause I didn't want to be disturbed," Larry said combatively.

"Well, I hate to disturb your peaceful campfire," his neighbor began. "But we got business to attend to. Where's my money?"

Larry didn't want to tell him he had blown the last of his paycheck earlier on enough smack to last him another week and that he didn't have anything left to pay with.

"Bank was closed today," Larry lied.

"To hell it wasn't," his neighbor said, growing angry. "I told you I expected it today or did those gorillas in prison screw your ears so hard you can't hear no more."

Larry felt anger boiling inside him. He didn't appreciate being talked to like that.

"I'll get you the money tomorrow," Larry said.

"I'm sick of hearing that shit," his neighbor said as his hand grasped the stock of the rifle with one hand like he was preparing to point it at Larry. "I want it now."

Larry considered rushing the old man, but the veteran tattoos and N .R.A. hat made him think it was unlikely he could close the gap in time before his neighbor could get a shot off.

The old man took another threatening step forward, closer to flames which had died back down.

"Now hold your horses," Larry said, putting his hands in the air to stop the man's advance. "I would pay you if I had it on me, but that fact is, I don't. I can get it for you tomorrow."

He couldn't, but his neighbor didn't know that.

The old man's face looked distrustful.

Larry sat the gas drum on the ground.

"So how about a little collateral in the meantime?" Larry said. "You like beer, right?"

"Of course I like beer," his neighbor said. "This is America, ain't it?"

"Sure is," Larry said. He reached over to the cooler on the ground next to the chair and opened it.

"No funny business," the old man said, pointing his rifle at Larry.

"No funny business," Larry repeated back to him. Slowly, he lifted out an ice-cold 6-pack. "This is the last of my beer right here. I want you to have it. A peace offering, a sign of sincerity."

"You're still gonna pay me tomorrow?" His neighbor said as Larry watched the man's gears in his head turn.

"Absolutely," said Larry as he took a step forward, holding the beer in front of him.

The neighbor took the beer from him tentatively.

Shit, Larry thought to himself.

The old man had caught a whiff of Lisa's burning fat in the fire. He sniffed at the air curiously.

"What are you burning anyway?" he asked grumpily.

"Just some old junk I found in the shed," Larry lied. "Some old car parts mostly, maybe some still got motor oil on them."

"That don't smell like motor oil," the old man replied with distrust. "It smells like meat or something."

Then the old man did something Larry had been dreading. He leaned over to peer inside the barrel.

The recognition on his face was immediate. Lisa's femur, though charred, was still clearly visible amongst the rest of her. And a human femur is one of the most unique bones of the animal kingdom. It didn't take the old man more than a few seconds to realize what was really in the steel drum.

Larry didn't wait.

Larry grabbed the old man and they both fell to the ground. Larry landed on top of him, the rifle horizontal between them.

"Get off me!" the old man snarled between breaths, struggling to push the younger and heavier Larry off his chest.

Larry didn't relent. He dug his knees into the old man's ribs and grappled with the rifle stock as the old man tried to swing it around towards him.

The first shot rang out as the rifle went off. Birds in the trees scattered from their slumbering nests and took off into the night.

Larry jumped off the old man in shock as the recoil launched the butt of the rifle hard into his shoulder. He yelped in pain as he rolled to the side.

For being several decades older, the old man was surprisingly spry. He jumped to his feet quickly and pointed the gun at Larry's chest as he lay reeling on the ground.

A faint ringing sound filled the void of silence left from the tussle; lingering in the air as it slowly dissipated with each passing second.

"Don't move you piece of..." the old man couldn't finish his sentence, the need to catch his breath taking over, as his lungs worked hard to replace the lost oxygen.

Larry looked up straight into the barrel of the rifle, just a few feet from his face. The old man had him dead to rights. There was nowhere to go.

"You're a screwup," his mother's voice repeated in his head. "A grade-A jackoff like your father."

"I'm sorry," Larry pleaded with the old man. Hoping the old man would give him a break, he had screwed up, that's all. One more line on the long list of simple things he just couldn't help but fail at.

"What... Were.... You..." the old man could barely talk. His breaths growing shorter and more panicked.

"I didn't mean to," Larry said, tears falling down his face and onto his shirt. But the old man's eyes told him all he needed to know. If he dared try to run or fight back, he'd take a bullet to the skull before he even had a chance. Larry was done for. He'd be leaving in handcuffs or a body bag.

"Pathetic," the old man mumbled.

Larry barely heard him. He sobbed uncontrollably.

This must have been what they had felt like, the girls he had hurt.

"I have it... In the... Right mind... to," his voice trailed off and the muscles in his arms relaxed.

To Larry's surprise, the rifle fell to the ground in front of him. And so did the rest of the old man, collapsing like a sack of potatoes.

Larry grabbed the rifle and got to his feet quickly, pointing it at the old man's body on the ground.

"Get up," Larry commanded.

But the old man didn't move.

Larry prodded him with his toe, but the man didn't react in the slightest.

The adrenaline in his blood convincing him it was some ridiculous ruse, Larry kicked the old man hard.

The man rolled onto his back and Larry saw his second dead body of the night.

With eyes wide open, a shocked expression stuck to his face. The old man had died, probably from a heart attack.

Larry breathed out with relief.

His shoulder was already turning purple from the bruising. His body dripped in sweat despite it being winter. There was one thing he knew for certain: he was exhausted.

Collapsing into the nearby lawn chair, he looked at the fire dance in front of him. The final funeral pyre of Lisa Johnson, his forest nymph. Soon to be joined by...

Shit, he didn't know his neighbor's name.

Not that it mattered.

The sounds of the distant police sirens told him someone had called the cops, probably someone from the rich neighborhood across the greenway. There would be no happy ending for Larry on this one. In five, maybe ten minutes, he'd be in handcuffs with his face smashed against the roof of the cop car. A few months later, he'd be back in prison, fending for his life every waking moment of the day.

Pulling the smack from his pocket, he prepared it for injection.

To him, shooting up was kind of like having your ex-girlfriend over for a night of crazy sex. You know it's trouble, but sometimes all you need is that toxic comfort to get you through the moment.

As his body relaxed and those euphoric waves returned, he lit a cigarette and put it to his mouth. It felt good to get high; it felt good to smoke. For at that moment, nothing else in his world mattered.

He drifted off into his own delusions of a forest full of forest nymphs like Lisa running and playing amongst the trees for him to chase. The real world ceased to matter to him.

If he hadn't been so high, he may have felt the cold liquid pooling around his feet. The gasoline leaked from where the rifle had gone off and shot a hole into the gas can.

If he hadn't been so high, he might not have lost the feeling in the tips of his fingers.

If he hadn't been so high, he wouldn't have passed out and closed his eyes.

If he hadn't been so high, the lit Marlboro Red wouldn't have slipped out of his hands and fallen to the ground, igniting the gasoline.

The owl watched from a safe distance in the trees as the explosion rocked Sunny Meadows. He wasn't afraid; he knew that only Larry's trailer would be engulfed in the flames. He knew the fire department would arrive just in time to watch the smoldering carcass of the doublewide slowly turn to ruin, too late to save Larry's pitiful soul.

Yet he still watched in awe, curious how the events had unfolded without his involvement. It would be a strange tale to share, a strange tale indeed.

PART 4

THE HOLE

CHAPTER 17

Dani was looking forward to a few days off. After the fair and Seraphina, she had spent the rest of the night trying to convince herself that all of it was in her head. An hallucinated episode brought on by exposure to something toxic in the paint absorbed through her skin. That was the most logical and likely explanation for everything, the only other possibility, that Dani was slowly going insane.

But first she needed to make it through one more day at the office.

As she arrived at Gallery Nocturne, it was impossible to miss the flashing lights of several police vehicles parked on the sidewalk just outside the old church's front steps. An officer was at the front door to greet her.

"Mam, what's your business here?" The officer asked as she tried to walk inside.

"I work here," Dani replied.

"All employees are required to submit for questioning by the lead detective," the officer told her. "This way, please."

She followed his direction and joined the long line of workmen standing outside the entrance to the offices.

"What's this about?" she asked a man in front of her she vaguely recognized.

"Goddamn Larry," the man said, sounding extremely annoyed. "He did something bad and now they are asking us if we were involved. Just cause we are ex-cons doesn't mean we are accomplices."

"What did he do?" Dani asked.

"Kidnapped and killed some girl outside of town," the workman replied. "An old man too."

Dani grew nervous. She had just been to Larry's house a few days prior. It could have easily been her. Her mind and heart raced with dark ideas of what awful things could have happened to her and Alek. It was all too strange a coincidence.

Lady Gianni appeared out of the office doors and upon catching sight of Dani, rushed to her.

"You don't need to stand in line," said Lady Gianni, pulling Dani by the arm.

"Excuse me mam," said a short dark-haired woman in a business blouse and pants. "All employees are required to be interviewed."

"She works in a different department," Lady Gianni told the woman who Dani guessed was a detective. "And started after Larry had already left. She knows nothing."

"I'll be the judge of that," the female detective said. "Back in line."

"Detective," Lady Gianni said in a stern voice. "This woman is vital to the operation of my business. By holding her in line, you are critically damaging my ability to operate. Please question her immediately so that she can get to work."

"Very well," the detective said. "Name?"

"Dani Scotts," Dani replied.

She felt Lady Gianni's arm on her shoulder. Even through her shirt, Dani could feel a tingling sensation on her skin.

"What do you do here?" the detective asked.

"I'm Lady Gianni's personal assistant," Dani answered effortlessly even as the inside of her chest felt suddenly hot, like she could sweat straight through her clothes at any moment.

"Did you know Larry Sellers?" was the next question.

She thought for a moment. It was probably best to tell the truth that she had met Larry briefly when he had snuck her into the gallery.

"I did not," Dani answered.

Wait, did she just lie to the detective?

"Were you aware that Larry, most of the workmen, and the head foreman were ex-cons?" the detective asked next, an attempt to derail Dani.

"I was not," Dani said. "All personnel files are kept in a secure location, and I'm not authorized."

She felt like her words weren't her own, like every time she opened her mouth to answer, another person's voice came out, a human ventriloquist dummy.

"Anything around here that you find peculiar you would like to share?" The detective asked, looking skeptical that Dani was being honest.

"Nothing at all," Dani said immediately.

"Ok, that's all," the detective said, putting away her notepad.

"If that's all, we'll be off," Lady Gianni said, pulling Dani away.

"Actually," the detective said, stopping them. "I have one more question."

The detective pulled up her phone and showed it to Dani.

"Do you recognize this girl?" the detective asked.

Of course Dani did. It was the girl she had seen in Seraphina's tent the night before. The girl she had seen making out with her boyfriend through the window. The girl who had a porcelain figure in *The Dollhouse*.

"Her name is Lisa Johnson," the detective added. "She's the teenage girl that Larry kidnapped and murdered."

Dani's heart was pounding hard in her chest.

"Can't say that I do," Dani's voice said.

"Thank you for help," the detective said before walking away. She sounded disappointed.

Lady Gianni and Dani walked together, the gallery director's arm firmly around her shoulder, guiding her away.

"I'm so sorry about all this," Lady Gianni said. "I had no idea that man was capable of such an awful thing."

Dani kept quiet. She didn't know how to respond.

"Is something bothering you, my dear?" Lady Gianni asked.

"Actually," Dani replied. "I'd really like a look at *The Smoking Man*. It was crated up so quickly, I barely remember it."

"Well, I'm sorry dear," said Lady Gianni. "That's just not possible."

"Why not?" asked Dani.

"Because it's already downstairs in storage," Lady Gianni told her. "Salvador sold it, for a very handsome sum, might I add, and it's due to ship out next week to a buyer in Germany."

"I'd still like to see it, even if it is in storage," said Dani.

"I just don't have time. I'm sorry," Lady Gianni said as her fingers pressed firmly into Dani's back.

"I could go down there on my own and find it," Dani offered.

"The underbelly of the old church is just too dangerous to go down unaided," Lady Gianni explained. "You'd get lost immediately. It's like a maze down there. Plus, the Librarian would never allow it."

"Who's the Librarian?" Dani asked.

"Oh, she's not really a librarian," Lady Gianni said, carefully choosing her words. "We just call her that because she keeps meticulous records and maintains the archive. I'm not a big fan of computers, so she keeps track of everything the old-fashioned way. Nothing goes in or out without her approval. She only answer to me, and I'm afraid it would be a waste of your efforts."

"I'd still like to..." Dani began to say, but her words trailed off as a feeling of warmth traveled through her, a relaxing feeling that urged her subconsciously to let it go.

She followed Lady Gianni as they approached the north transept.

"Now you'll be painting in *The Echoes* today," Lady Gianni said.

Dani supposed it was time she entered the only wing of the gallery she had yet to visit. To her surprise, Lady Gianni stopped right outside the entrance.

"Go on ahead," she said, smiling with her hands folded in front of her. "Tom is inside, setting up an easel for you."

"You aren't coming with me?" Dani asked.

Lady Gianni glanced with a worried look at the entrance.

"I'm afraid I'm very busy this morning," she replied. "Tom will get you all set up."

She almost pushed Dani through the dark doorway.

Dani paused just inside.

Something didn't feel right. Somehow she didn't feel like it was all hallucination. Too many weird things were happening at once.

She pulled out her phone and texted Haley.

DANI: Can I ask you a favor?

HALEY: Sure, what is it?

DANI: Can you poke around on the internet for a name, someone who may have died recently under mysterious circumstances?

A long pause before the response came.

HALEY: Does this have something to do with that girl all over the news?

DANI: I don't know, maybe. Please, just see what you can find. I don't have much except a first name.

HALEY: You want me to find someone based on a first name alone?

It was a long shot, but she couldn't help but feel like Lady Gianni was in on it, on everything.

DANI: Yes, his name was Javier. He was maybe 20-years-old. He may have worked at Paysphere.

Dani didn't expect a reply, at least not for a while. However, her phone chimed immediately.

HALEY: How do you know about Javi?

DANI: You knew him?

HALEY: Yes, but I can't talk about it. He's gone. Just leave it alone. PLEASE!

DANI: What about Summit Petroleum?

HALEY: I can't talk about it either. It's owned by Global Meridian, just like Paysphere. If Mr. Henricks finds out I'm talking to you about it, I'll be fired.

DANI: Just tell me, did someone die the other night there? A security guard?

HALEY: How do you know about that?! No one does, not even the police.

DANI: What was his name?

HALEY: This conversation is over. Do not text me again about it.

DANI: Please, I think they're all connected. Something weird is happening.

There was no read receipt this time from Haley.

Dani felt lost, like she didn't know if she should run to the detective and tell her everything. Tell her that all of these dead people were connected to the gallery and Global Meridian. She would sound crazy, she would sound nuts. She'd lose her job, she'd never sell another painting in this town. All because she had told the detective about some wild idea that was flying through her head.

She really had no other choice. She stepped into the darkness of *The Echoes*. Maybe painting would get her mind thinking straight.

While both *The Veil* and *The Remnants* had been in large open spaces, *The Echoes* was a twisted maze. Long stretches of empty hallways with corridors that lead to various exhibits. How was she supposed to find anything in a place like this?

Her heels clicked on the white marble floors, but bounced back and forth along the walls, compounding the sound like there was an army on the march. Spotlights angled across the hallways produced well-defined shadows. Dani could see her own silhouette following her as she walked.

She felt something else as well, the sensation that she was being watched.

A shape dashed across her peripheral vision. Dani turned quickly. Maybe one of the workmen was behind her.

But there was no one, no one except her and her shadow in the narrow hallway.

A nearby sign read *Zoetrope* above an opening. She wanted to shake the feeling; so she went through it. Waiting just inside, she wanted to see if anyone would appear behind her.

No one did.

No sounds of boots walking down the hall, no shadows stalking her. She was just being unnecessarily paranoid.

The room she entered was circular, with a pole in the center. Painted onto the ground at the base of the pole were the outlines of shoes, an indicator she should stand there. Intrigued by the concept, she took her place. A pressure plate must have activated, as a rhythmic, mechanical whirring sound filled the room, punctuated by a soft, consistent clicking. It sounded like an old-fashioned movie projector.

More alarming was the movement along the walls, where the doors on both sides of the room closed and trapped her inside. Then the room began to spin.

She couldn't tell what exactly was moving; the walls, the floor, or everything all at once. The effect was disorienting. Dani wanted to run but had nowhere to go.

She resigned herself to leaning against the pole at the center and trying to keep calm.

A bright light shined onto the walls, which had long slats in them that allowed her to see through them. On the other side was the silhouette of a young boy, standing with his hands above his head. As the spinning increased in speed, she could see his body move. He was waving at her.

Not sure what else to do, she waved back.

The shadow boy broke into a run on the wall, playfully jumping over faint images of what looked like rocks and boulders. Dani's fear waned. It must be part of the exhibit.

Another shadow formed in the corner of her eye, approaching the boy. This one was tall and bulky, a man. Dani didn't know how she knew, but something told her this was the boy's father. Even without a face, Dani could sense the boy's fear of him grow as he approached.

Why should he fear his father?

A wolf appeared in the background. The boy cowered in fear of it. It lunged at him with open jaws. The man stepped forward and grasped the wolf by the neck before tearing it in two with his bare hands. With the wolf dispatched, Dani expected the boy to stand up and thank his parent.

Except he didn't.

He remained cowering on the ground while the man loomed over him, larger than ever.

The boy was just as afraid of his father as he was of the ravenous wolf.

She found out why.

The man grabbed the boy by the arm and yanked him to his feet. She couldn't see it, but she could feel tears falling down the boy's cheeks.

She winced in pain, knowing what came next.

The father slapped the boy across the face, sending him back to the ground.

"What are you doing?" said a voice inside the room.

Dani jumped away from it, startled.

With her feet no longer planted on the outline in the floor, the spinning slowed and the shadows on the walls disappeared.

"Whoa," said the voice. "Sorry to startle you."

"I'm fine," Dani replied, recognizing Tom.

"This one can be disorienting if you haven't been inside before," Tom explained.

"Not quite the word I'd use," Dani said, the scene still troubling her.

"I heard the machine start up and came to check out who was using it," Tom explained. "Lady Gianni gave me instructions to get you set up in the next room. Please, this way."

He was his patient and gentle self. Dani just wished she could forget about the ride in his truck.

Tom led her out of *Zoetrope*, an exhibit she never wished to return to.

"**D**id you talk to the police about Larry?" Dani asked Tom as they approached an easel and a chair set up in a small auditorium.

"I was the first one they talked to since I've known him the longest," Tom replied. "I hired the guy through the program."

"Did you find out what happened to him?" asked Dani, sitting down on the chair and setting her purse down at her feet.

"They didn't get into specifics, but I overheard the detective talking to her boss on the phone," said Tom. "His house outside of the city blew up. They think it might have been suicide."

"Suicide?!" Dani exclaimed.

"Sure seems like it," Tom continued. "Murder-suicide actually. The girl and Larry's neighbor."

"His neighbor too?" Dani remembered him, the grumpy old man in the hat.

Tom nodded.

"So the theory is Larry felt guilty or maybe knew he was going to get caught, so he doused himself in gasoline and blew himself up to avoid going back to prison. It's awful, a travesty. He had been doing so good."

"Why do you think he killed them?" asked Dani.

"I have a theory," said Tom after taking a deep breath. "Guys like Larry and me, ex-cons, we used up all our chances in life. When you are out of chances, it only takes one thing to screw us up and the whole house of cards falls. It could have been some hussie leading him on…"

Dani's thoughts drifted to Bianca, and how she had manipulated Larry to let them in.

"Or some pusher finding him at a vulnerable moment," Tom continued. "Offering him drugs when he didn't have strength left to say no. His mom had died a few months back. That couldn't have helped. It could happen to any of us. It does happen to some of us. I just hope I'm not next."

Dani thought back to his wandering thoughts from the truck ride, how his images of Dani in his mind almost crossed the border into assault.

"Anyway, Lady Gianni wants you painting in here today," said Tom like nothing happened. "We call this *The Canyon*. It's not quite as exciting as *Zoetrope*, but probably better for your artistic side."

"I hope so," Dani muttered.

She tried to work up the courage to ask one of the hundreds of questions probing her mind.

"Tom," she began. "Why isn't Lady Gianni here?"

Tom's face looked nervous immediately.

"She's probably just busy today," Tom replied. "With the detectives all over the place, it's a madhouse."

"I don't think so," said Dani. "I got a strange feeling when I talked to her that she's scared of this place."

"Lady Gianni scared?" Tom scoffed. "That woman could face down a charging grizzly bear and never even flinch."

"Still, I just know there's something here," Dani replied. "What is it?"

Tom looked around the room, as if checking to make sure no one else was around.

He leaned in close.

"It's the shadow," he whispered.

"She's afraid of her shadow?" said Dani, confused.

"Not her shadow," Tom continued quietly. "The shadow, specifically the shadow man. He's everywhere in here."

"I don't know what you're talking about," Dani replied.

"Of course you do," said Tom. "You saw him in *Zoetrope,* creeping the bejesus out of people with that weird play he puts on with his son. But he's everywhere in *The Echoes.* You can't always see him, but you can always feel him watching you."

"So, he's a ghost or something?" Dani scoffed. "Some angry spirit who haunts this wing of the gallery?"

"I don't believe in spirits or ghosts," Tom answered. "In reality, it's probably just some effect that the guy who built this place had made to give anyone who comes in an eerie feeling. Artists do crazy stuff like that all the time."

"Not sure how they could," replied Dani.

"As Lady Gianni would tell you," Tom continued. "The how is not important. Whatever he is, Lady Gianni won't step foot in here."

The conversation tapered off. Dani had hoped for answers, but his response only spawned more questions.

"Shit," Tom said, looking at the time on his phone. "In all the running around this morning, I forgot to mix the paint."

He pulled a bag from over his shoulder and set it on the ground.

"You wouldn't mind mixing your own today, would you?" Tom asked. "I'm way behind already. Those boys don't know what to do with themselves if I ain't around."

"Sure, not a problem," Dani replied. She'd been mixing her own paint for years.

"Great," Tom said as he pulled out the various tubes of exotic and expensive paints from the bag. Then he pulled out something unexpected, a musty old sack.

"This sack here is full of an additive," Tom explained. "Lady Gianni says it's extremely expensive. Don't waste a speck of dust from it. It's also highly toxic, so you should wear these gloves while you handle it."

"What is it?" asked Dani.

"No idea," replied Tom. "But she's very specific about this. Just a few pinches is enough and then mix it real good. That's all there is to it."

"I got it covered," said Dani.

"Great," said Tom. "I'll be back in three hours to check on you."

"What about Lady Gianni?" Dani asked.

"She's leaving this afternoon," Tom explained. "Heading to London to woo some new buyers. She'll be back on Wednesday."

"I didn't know," said Dani.

"I didn't know either until an hour ago," Tom said with a scoff. "She's her own woman, that's for certain. We can survive a couple of days without her. I'm looking forward to the time off."

He laughed, Dani faked a smile.

"If you need inspiration or something," said Tom, pointing towards a button on the wall nearby. "That turns the exhibit on. It's a pretty cool display. Quite a calming experience."

"Thank you," she said as she waved at him.

It didn't take long for him to disappear through the doorway marked with the orange EXIT sign above it.

She squeezed the tubes of paint onto the palette next to the easel and thought about what it had felt like to be covered in the paint. How it had given her what she thought had been telepathic abilities. Dani wondered if the effect could be recreated.

Dipping a finger into the dollop of red paint, she waited.

There was nothing. No tingling, no strange thoughts filling her head.

She felt stupid.

Wiping her finger off, she put the black nitrile gloves on and opened the sack with the additive.

It was curious.

Almost everything supplied by Lady Gianni had been new, high-quality items, from the brushes to the easel to the canvas. However, this brown sack looked like it had been found at a garage sale. The outer liner had patches where tears had been repaired, dark spots blotched it where oils had stained it.

Inside, the particles look like black sand, that faintly sparkled in the overhead light.

She grabbed a pinch with her gloved hands and sprinkled some onto the paint. They absorbed almost immediately; she took the brush and mixed the red. There was no visual change that she could see to the hue or tone. The paint looked almost exactly the same as before.

Dani repeated this until all the colors were ready, and she closed the bag. Drawing its string tight, she set it on the ground at feet.

Staring at the canvas, Dani tried to think of something, anything, she wanted to paint. Her mind refused to focus on anything other than the blank canvas in front of her. She would need some help.

As she pressed the button to start the exhibit, she could only hope she wouldn't be painting in the dark again.

Half-expecting the lights to go out, she was pleased to see the stage in front of her glow a bright blue. A humming sound filled the air, like the sound an air conditioner makes as it roars to life. The glow grew bright enough for her to see the full stage. Flanking it on both sides, where the actors and actresses would typically appear from, were two walls of speakers lining the floor to the ceiling. The backdrop was a solid wall of what may have been screens. that showed vertical blue lines vibrating with the sounds from the speakers.

A low bass sound erupted from the walls, deeper than the foghorn on a boat. The blue lines reacted, visualizing the sound waves to the naked eye. More notes followed, of varying pitches and tones.

So far, it was appealing to experience, like an ASMR video, but not as inspirational as she had hoped. The canvas was still blank, staring back at her.

The sounds slowly grew more familiar. She started hearing forks and knives clattering together, each wall launching a volley at the other. Then voices talking, slowly becoming more distinctive, chatting with one another. A man, a woman, maybe a little girl; Dani could make out only bits and pieces of what they were saying.

The blue lines on the screen had adjusted to each of the sounds, but Dani thought she saw something else in it. It was as if a section of the screen had morphed to form a 3-D shape. She rubbed her eyes, which hurt as she tried to focus on it.

It wasn't just a shape; it looked like a table with chairs. People were sitting in the chairs, featureless people holding cutlery and scraping at their plates. It was a family, a mom, a dad, and a little girl at dinner.

The picture grew more detailed with every second that passed. Dani didn't even realize that her hands were moving the brush across on the canvas.

The little girl was wearing a pink princess dress. She was very young, maybe three or four years old at most. She had pink fingernail polish that matched her dress and a sparkling tiara in her hair. It reminded Dani of one that she had when she was little, one that her father had thrown out when he caught her wearing it; he told her she could only wear baseball hats.

The mother at the table wore a white sundress with yellow flower prints on it. Dani's mother had one just like it. The woman's hair was the same shade of blond as Dani's mother too, and her eyes were the same color and...

She realized the woman sculpted from the waves of sounds on the screen was her mother, every detail exactly as she remembered.

Dani looked around, not sure if she had fallen asleep and was dreaming. Everything else about the space was the same, the speakers and the stage were still there. The paint and easel as well. The painting on the canvas was also beginning to take shape. Swirls of orange and red covered every inch, but no definitive picture yet.

She looked back at the stage, hoping that she had imagined it, but she hadn't. Her mother was still sitting there talking in muffled sounds with the girl and the man. If the woman was her mother, then that meant the man must be... Dani knew his green polo shirt well. He wore it every Sunday for golf. Her dad was one of those deeply superstitious golfers. He had worn it when he played his best round of golf ever and refused to wear anything else for a match since.

She could also see him cutting into a rare piece of steak on his plate. Dani had been forced to eat red meat on Sundays despite the fact that it disagreed with her, all meat did. Her father had accused her of making it all up. He told her any allergy to it was all in her head. Kids like her were supposed to love protein and meat. Why couldn't she be like the other kids?

Her brush seemed content with the orange and red. Without thinking about it, she dipped it into the black paint.

Dani focused on the child at the table. Was that supposed to be her? Except she had never owned a dress like that. The girl also looked nothing like her, her cheeks too thin, her nose too petite, and her hair too full.

She tried to focus on their conversations, but could only understand parts of it.

The little girl had a birthday coming up.

Her favorite movie was Frozen 2.

She wanted her party to be themed after Elsa.

A pony or unicorn were acceptable gifts.

They were all things Dani wasn't allowed to enjoy as a little girl. Princess parties were absolutely out of the question, much less a Disney themed one.

The little girl wasn't her.

She had loved Cinderella and The Little Mermaid; she hadn't watched Frozen until she was in middle school.

Her dad's mobile phone rang, and he answered it, walking off the stage.

This wasn't a memory or a dream of what could have been. It was right now.

Could her parents have had another child without telling her? It had been years since they last spoke. They didn't even have Dani's number anymore.

She didn't want to watch. The thought of having a sister who could do all the things she wasn't allowed to, tore her up too much inside. Dani pressed the button on the wall. The blue stage lights dimmed, the speakers shut off, and the humming sound faded.

Dani turned her attention to the canvas.

The painting was complete, except she didn't remember painting it.

She knew the setting; it was the center of the old church, the one that now housed Gallery Nocturne. The columns and architecture that she so admired were unmistakable. The paintings and exhibits where *The s* had been were gone, replaced by crowds of people walking towards the center hall. Sprinkled amongst them were bright braziers spewing orange and red fire; casting a hellish glow across the people's faces. At the dead center, where *Consume* and *The Dollhouse* had been, was an immense sinkhole.

Darkness was the only thing inside it, darkness that made Dani feel like the pit went on forever with no end.

It gave her the chills.

She felt afraid for the people in the painting, knowing they were walking towards the pit, that they would throw themselves into it.

She could hear footsteps in the silence of *The Echoes*. Someone was coming.

Dani tried to grab her purse from the floor so she could snap a picture before Tom and workmen carried it away. In her haste, she knocked the brown sack over, spilling some of the black dust inside.

"Shit," Dani said aloud, dropping to her knees.

She remembered Tom had mentioned how expensive the material was.

Hastily, she tried to scoop it up back inside the sack with her bare hands before Tom could see.

Zap!

It felt like she had just grabbed a power-line. The current shot up her arm and through her entire body. She fell backwards, landing on her back.

That was beyond strange, she thought as her senses returned. Something about the feeling that lingered reminded her of being covered in the paint. The tingling sensation that stuck around.

The footsteps grew louder.

Panicking, Dani put on the black nitrile glove as quickly as she could.

She was about to scoop the black dust back into the sack, but paused.

What was this stuff? Why did it have such a strange effect on her? Why did Lady Gianni want her to use it in the paint when it did nothing to the tone or luster?

Without really thinking, she rummaged through her purse until she found an old makeup powder box that was almost empty. She scooped a handful of the dust into it and closed it tight.

Then, as hastily as she could, she scooped the rest of the dust into the sack until none remained on the floor.

The footsteps were close.

She stuffed the powder box into her purse.

"What are you doing?" Tom asked behind her.

Dani wasn't sure what to say at first.

"Just looking for my phone," she said, pulling it from her bag to show him as she turned.

"I didn't get any pictures last time and I really want one of this before it goes into the gallery," she continued.

"Lady Gianni doesn't allow any photos taken inside the gallery," Tom said to her. "It's one of her rules."

"Please?" Dani asked. "I don't even remember what *The Smoking Man* looked like."

"Rules are rules," said Tom.

"Pretty please?" Dani asked again, this time she smiled and batted her eyelashes at him.

She wasn't sure if it was real, but for a flash, she thought she could read Tom's mind again. She could see a clash of his desire to follow the rules and his attraction to her battling each other out inside him.

"Just one picture," said Tom, smiling back at her. "And no posting online. If you do that, both our gooses are cooked."

"Scout's honor," Dani said, holding up a hand.

She framed her photo so that the picture filled the screen and tapped it. The phone made the artificial shutter sound, and Dani shoved it back into her bag without looking at it.

"So, what will you do with a couple of days off?" Tom asked her as more workmen appeared from the doorway behind him and shuffled forward to carry away the painting.

"I don't know," said Dani. "Hang out with my friends, probably."

"Well," Tom began, but paused. She didn't need to read his mind to see he was weighing asking her something. "If you don't have any plans, would you want to go see a movie or something?"

"Oh," Dani replied. "Actually, I think my friends and I were planning on going out of town. Sorry."

"No worries," Tom said, hiding his disappointment with a smile. "I'll be around if you change your mind."

"I'll call you if they do," Dani replied before hurrying past him towards the exit.

"One more thing," Tom said.

Dani turned.

"Before she left," Tom began. "Lady Gianni wanted me to tell you there's something for you on your desk."

"Thanks Tom," Dani said.

"Don't mention it," he replied, scratching the back of his head.

Dani left.

The rest of the church was deserted, but, just like she had felt in *The Echoes*, Dani couldn't shake the feeling that someone was following her every move. Even under the bright fluorescent lights of the offices, a shadow seemed to lurk just out of her sight. Had the shadow man followed her out?

It felt big, like it would loom over even her tall frame if it ever got close enough. It was dark, except for a glint of silver light. But Dani could feel something else about it; it was angry; it wanted to harm someone, and it wanted revenge. Yet she wasn't afraid of it, because something told her it wasn't angry at her.

She pushed the thought from her mind. Nothing was following her. The shadow and whatever it was thinking were just part of her overactive imagination. Something easily stoked by the dark mysteries of the old church and its equally fearsome art.

Dani found a letter on her desk. Inscribed on the outside of the envelope, in brilliant emerald ink, was flawless calligraphy letters that spelled out *The Smoking Man*.

She admired it for a moment, knowing it was without a doubt Lady Gianni's handwriting. Dani hoped it was pictures. She desperately wanted to lay eyes on the painting again. Her own memory barely sufficed.

Opening the envelope, she was disappointed to see plain paper inside. The disappointment was only momentary, for the paper was a check made out to her in the amount of four-hundred and eighty thousand dollars.

CHAPTER 18

"You want us to break into the Gallery Nocturne?" Paul said in disbelief.

"Not break in," Dani tried to backtrack. "Just come with me and help me find *The Smoking Man*."

"Aren't there like catacombs and tombs and stuff under the church? Dead bodies?" Bianca asked. "I don't do dead bodies."

"It's just storage down there," Dani said.

"Why can't you find it yourself?" Paul asked. "You're the one who works there."

"Apparently the storage area is huge, a maze," said Dani. "I'd never find it on my own."

"Why does it matter so much?" questioned Bianca. "It's just a painting."

"Ya," Paul said, furrowing his brow. "What's with this one?"

Dani glanced over at Alek. He was sitting on the couch with his hands in his pockets and staring into the distance. He wouldn't be much help.

"It sold for half a million dollars, and I don't even have a picture of it," she said flatly. "Now it's going to some collection overseas and I'll never see it again."

She braced herself for a tirade from Paul.

Bianca's eyes got wide in amazement.

Paul just stared at her with no emotion.

They were silent for a long time, Dani feeling herself sweat as she awaited Paul's dreaded anger at her betrayal.

"That's," he began, apparently searching for the words. "Amazing!"

"Really?" said Dani, shocked.

"I mean," Paul continued. "Who had any idea? And there's more down there, more works like yours?"

"Apparently there are thousands of collector's works underneath the church," Dani explained. "A lot of Lady Gianni's wealthy patrons use it for long-term storage. She's very old school about it. There's not even a computer catalog of anything down there, just some librarian who keeps track of it all in her head."

"That doesn't make any sense," Paul said. "No one in their right mind would store expensive art like that."

"Mr. Henricks does," Bianca said. "I've heard him talk about it. He has his entire collection down there, its gotta be worth hundreds of millions. He says he keeps them for the tax write-off."

Paul looked at her for a long moment. He didn't look quite convinced yet.

Without warning, Alek stood up.

"We're friends," Alek began. "We're a Collective. We help each other. It's the reason any of us are here. Dani is asking us for help. We should do it."

"I think you're right," Paul said.

"What are you talking about?" exclaimed Bianca. "This is insane. There's no way I'm risking going to jail for this. Alek is only doing this because he wants to get into her pants."

Alek turned bright red.

Bianca stormed off towards the kitchen.

"I'll talk to her," Paul said to Dani before following Bianca.

Alek stood next to Dani.

"I-It's not just because I want to get in your pants," Alek stuttered quietly.

"I know," Dani said, watching Paul and Bianca whisper out of earshot.

"So, why do you really want to go down there?" asked Alek. "It's not like you to take a big risk for just a picture."

Dani contemplated making up another lie, but decided against it. Alek might be her closest friend in the world right now, the only one who might believe the truth.

"I think it was a portrait," Dani said. "Of someone we knew."

"Who?" Alek asked.

She raised her eyebrows at him, hoping he would try to guess instead of making her say her crazy thought out loud.

"Larry?" said Alek with eyes of disbelief.

She nodded.

"The police said he blew himself up," Dani explained. "I think I remember seeing a gas can in my painting. If it was full, it would have been plenty. He had kidnapped Lisa Johnson and killed her. I saw her picture, the police showed it to me, she looked exactly like the girl from *The Dollhouse*. She was the girl from *The Dollhouse*."

"What are you really trying to say?" Alek said. "You think whoever you paint or get displayed in the gallery is someone who's already dead?"

"No," Dani replied. "We saw that security guard from Summit Petroleum die after we saw him in *Consume*. We saw Lisa Johnson alive after we already went through *The Dollhouse*. Based on what the police told me, Larry was still alive when I painted *The Smoking Man*."

"So your paintings or the stuff in the gallery are predicting how people die?" asked Alek.

"I thought that at first," said Dani, growing nervous. She was afraid to show him the next clue. "But I don't think that anymore. I think something else is killing these people."

"What makes you say that?" Alek asked, looking taken aback. "How could that even happen?"

She took a deep breath and pulled out her phone.

"I took a picture of what I painted yesterday," said Dani, flipping through her pictures. "I didn't look at it again until this morning. That's when I realized we needed to go back there and check *The Smoking Man*."

She held up her phone for him to see.

Alek's face froze.

It was a hole in the center of the old church, just as Dani had painted. Crowds of people were walking towards the opening from every direction. The braziers were lit, casting the orange light all around. However, rising out of the pit was something that Dani had not painted.

A black shadow with orange eyes.

"I didn't paint that shadow," Dani said plainly. "When I finished it, the shadow wasn't there. I only saw it when I took a picture. Lady Gianni has strict rules about photos in the gallery. I think this is why."

"So the painting is haunted?" asked Alek as he tried to piece it all together.

"Not a ghost. This doesn't feel human," replied Dani. "It feels like something else entirely."

"None of this makes sense," said Alek, running his hands through his hair.

"No, it doesn't," said Dani. "That's why I need to go in there and see for myself. Take more pictures. See if I can find more like this."

She considered explaining to him the special dust that she added to the paint, but decided against it. One crazy theory was enough for now.

"And do what with them?" Alek asked. "What is your end game?"

"I think I need to destroy them," said Dani with determination.

"Destroy them?!" Alek exclaimed. "You know how much trouble you'd get into?"

"Just mine," Dani replied. "I'll give back the money. I'll probably be fired. But look at this picture again. Look at the people. They aren't walking around the pit, they are walking towards the pit. Maybe they are going to throw themselves inside. That's hundreds of people, maybe more. If there's even the slightest chance that my crazy theory is true, they could be in grave danger. I need to do something. Do you believe me?"

Alek looked at her with the haggard eyes of someone who's seen more than he should have at his age.

"I believe you," he exhaled. "But what about them?"

He motioned towards Paul and Bianca, who were walking towards them.

"We just need their help to find the paintings," Dani said. "I'll do the rest."

Paul was the first to speak as they stood in a circle together.

"For the record," Paul said. "We both think this is crazy."

Dani felt any optimism that they would help deflate.

"But," Paul added with a slight smile. "We wouldn't be artists if we weren't a bit nuts. We're in. Do you have a plan?"

"I think so," Dani replied.

"Then when are we doing this?" Paul asked with his hands folded in front of his chest.

"After dark," said Dani. "Meet downstairs at six and we'll all head out together in the van."

"I have a question," Bianca asked, holding up her hand.

They all looked at her.

"What am I supposed to wear?" she asked.

Dani closed the door to her room and let out a deep breath.

Collapsing to her bed, she considered setting an alarm and trying to get some sleep. She knew it wouldn't work. Her mind was flying a mile a minute as she tried to think of every potential outcome of that night's events.

Was she thinking about this the wrong way?

Dani lived in the real world, she played by the laws and rules of science. But whatever she was going up against in the old church did not. Whether it be spirit or demon or whatever kind of entity, she would have to think about what playing by its rules would be like.

Her eyes drifted to the plant on her bedside table.

The poor sunflower was dead. It looked worse than her painting of it that now hung in Mr. Bones's office. Its crack had prevented any water from being retained in the soil, and it had died of dehydration despite Dani watering it daily.

She ran her fingers through her hair. It was dry, likely from all the soap she had used to wash out the paint after *The Smoking Man*. Who knows what kind of damage all the chemicals in the paint had done to it?

Then she got an idea.

Dani pulled the makeup powder box from her purse and opened it carefully. The sparkling black dust was still inside. Mixing it with a little black paint she had left over from her last project, she quickly prepared herself to paint something new.

As her brush traced, using only a single color on the canvas. She focused on a single thought: what might help them later that night as they delved inside the old church. No matter how hard she tried, her mind returned to the same image. So she painted it.

It was probably a stupid idea. It would probably do nothing. Still, she kept painting and when she was done; she stared at it for a long time. It was missing something; she didn't know how she knew that, but she did.

"Alek," she yelled, realizing she needed another color. "Do you have any silver paint?"

The van came to a stop with only the slight squeal of the brakes announcing their arrival at the alley next to the Gallery Nocturne. It's ancient suspension system struggling to hold up the weight of the four people plus the dozens of gallons of vegetable oil stored in the back.

Paul was the first to stick his head out the window.

"I don't see any cameras," Paul said.

"I told you," Dani replied. "Lady Gianni doesn't allow anyone to take pictures or video of any kind, not even for security."

"So how do we get in, then?" asked Paul. "I can't exactly ram the door."

"One second," said Dani, pulling out her phone and dialing.

"Hello," said a gruff male voice on the other end.

"Hey Tom," Dani replied. "It's Dani."

"Oh, Hi Dani," Tom said, his voice suddenly growing excited. "Did you change your mind about dinner?"

"Actually, I need your help," she began.

"Sure, anything," Tom said.

"I have to get on a plane tonight," she said as the others listened in attentively.

"Ah yes," Tom replied. "Going out of town with your friends."

"Exactly," Dani continued. "Except I don't have enough money to cover the hotel and everything else where I'm going. I left my paycheck on my desk by accident."

"Oh," Tom exclaimed. "That's too bad."

"I'm at the gallery right now," she said. "Do you think you could give me the code so I could run in and grab it?"

"I don't know Dani," said Tom. "That's not really something I'm allowed to do. The place is deserted."

"I know, I know," Dani continued, starting to worry if her plan would work.

Bianca leaned forward and whispered something into Dani's ear.

Dani nodded.

"I'm just so stupid," Dani said, her voice sounding like she was crying. "I was really looking forward to this trip. My friends can't afford the hotel either unless they split it with me. We're all going to have to cancel."

"I'm so sorry," Tom said on the other end of the line.

"Is there anything you can do to help me get my check?" Dani asked.

"To be honest," Tom replied. "I'm about halfway through a case of beer. I'm in no state to drive over and meet you there."

Dani knew what she had to do next. She also knew she would hate herself for it.

She began faking full on sobs into the phone.

"My friends are going to be so mad at me," said Dani between breaths. "I can't believe I messed this up. I'm such a screwup. My check is just sitting in there on my desk just a few hundred feet away from me and I can't get to it."

She really laid on the waterworks.

"Just calm down Dani," Tom said. "I really can't give you the code. It'd be breaking the rules."

"Like when I took the picture of my last painting?" Dani asked. "I promised you I wouldn't share it online or anything. I kept my promise. It would just be in and out. Don't you trust me?"

"I do Dani," Tom said before going into a long pause.

Bianca used the opportunity to whisper into Dani's ear again.

"If you let me in to grab it, you'd be my hero," Dani said. "I'd really owe you one."

"Well," Tom said, thinking about it more.

Then she knew it. She had him; hook, line, and sinker.

"Just go in real quick and get out," Tom said. "It's not safe there at night with all the lights off."

"It will be like I was never there," Dani replied.

"The code is..." Tom said and, to Dani's astonishment, somehow her plan had worked.

Paul closed the roll-up door behind them as the van pulled into the receiving area. Tool racks and wood cutting machines lined the walls of the workspace. Several pallets, stacked high with wood planks, towered over them. It didn't feel like it was part of the gallery at all.

"So what now?" asked Paul, turning the van off. He opened the back door and pulled out a soft bag full of flashlights.

"There's access to the basement from the main gallery floor behind where *The Dollhouse* was set up," said Dani, grabbing a flashlight. "It's hidden behind a curtain."

Bianca and Alek followed suit, and they headed towards the gallery.

Dani felt someone brush up against her shoulder. She expected Alek had gotten close to 'protect' her, but was surprised to find it was Bianca.

"Half a million dollars?" Bianca whispered to her.

Dani felt nervous suddenly. Bianca, being close proximity to her, always made her feel like that.

"Crazy right?" Dani whispered back.

"Imagine how long we could make that last," said Bianca. She was close enough to Dani that she could smell her perfume. "Go some place off the grid, an island maybe."

Dani's heart raced as she felt Bianca's hand on the small of her back.

"We?" Dani questioned, wanting to make sure she heard that right.

"Just us girls," Bianca said, her big dark eyes visible in the lights of the receiving area. "A beach, bikinis, and strong cocktails. The world would be our oyster."

"That sounds nice," Dani said, smiling. Just the idea of Bianca and her together made her heart swell.

"Let's see how tonight goes first, right?" Bianca asked playfully, before dropping back.

They met Paul at the door to the gallery. He paused, holding the handle.

"There are no windows in here," he explained. "So we can leave the lights on. But we can't turn the lights on out there. With the glass windows, anyone could see if someone was inside if we did."

The rest nodded.

"I'll lead the way," Paul said in his usual commanding tone. "Stay close behind me."

With that, he opened the door to the darkness that was the main gallery floor.

It was completely still inside Gallery Nocturne. Dani had never seen it like this. She was used to the constant sound of workmen or visitors that flooded the gallery daily. She felt like she was walking on a dark alien planet, unable to comprehend whatever lay just outside the beam of her flashlight.

True to his word, Paul led the group forward fearlessly. That's probably why everyone looked to him as the leader. Every action or command he gave was completely void of self doubt. It was as if nothing in the world could spook him.

They walked in single file, their flashlights focused ahead of them as they went.

"It's not the same as I remember," Paul said as he navigated the wide paths separated by walls.

"Lady Gianni changes the placement regularly," said Dani from behind him.

"How very Feng Shui of her," joked Bianca.

Paul stopped ahead of them and the rest did the same.

"Wait," he said. "Where's all the art?"

"What do you mean?" asked Dani.

She pointed her flashlight onto a nearby wall, one that had several paintings mounted on it the day before. The mounting bracket for the frame was there, but the rest of the painting was gone. A dull square left behind where the painting had once hung.

"Weird," Dani said. "Maybe they moved them to storage while the gallery was closed down."

"They're all like that," added Alek, shining his beam on the opposite wall.

Dani thought she saw something above them. A dark shape flying past.

Shining her light to the ceiling, she saw nothing except for the frescoes of angels and demons staring back down at them. It was probably just her imagination, but they looked different from what she remembered. They looked like they were watching them.

It made her stomach uneasy.

"Did you see that?" Alek said, shining his light suddenly towards the end of the path.

"See what?" asked Paul.

"I saw something move," said Alek, shrinking back slightly.

"Let me see," Paul said, stepping forward courageously.

He rounded the corner where Alek had pointed his light at.

"So scary," Paul said with a slight laugh.

He leaned over and picked up a torn piece of plastic sheet.

"It must have been picked up by the wind," Paul said, dropping it back to the ground.

"What wind?" said Alek.

"Don't get spooked," said Paul, turning to face them. "It's just an old church. Nothing in here except us right now. No reason to be..."

He didn't get to finish his thought.

A gigantic shape swooped down on him from high above. Paul dove to the ground just in time to avoid its sharp claws. Someone screamed. It might have been Bianca, or maybe Alek.

"Calm down!" Paul yelled, getting back to his feet. "It's just an owl."

He shined his beam onto the side of the church, where the owl sat perched on a ledge, staring at them.

"Who," it said to them, somehow with indignation at being called 'just an owl'.

"What is an owl doing here?" asked Dani.

"They eat mice and rats, right?" said Paul. "The old church must be infested with them. Probably a pretty good hunting spot."

"How did it get in?" asked Alek.

"Who knows," said Paul. "As long as it knows if it tries that shit again, I'm going to slam this flashlight into its beak."

"Who," the owl mocked back at Paul.

"You, is who!" Paul said, annoyed. "Come on, let's get downstairs."

The owl flew off out of the light and disappeared into the cover of darkness.

They ventured deeper through the maze of empty walls until they were near the center of the church, where *The Dollhouse* and *Consume* had been displayed. A large gray drape blocked them from advancing further.

"Behind here?" Paul asked, lifting the bottom of the long cloth up and peering inside. "It's hard to see."

"That's where it will be," said Dani behind him.

"Ladies first," Paul said with a wink.

"Thanks," said Dani, going through the opening Paul had created.

On the other side, there were no more walls to reflect the light of her flashlight. The beam seemed to go on forever until the pitch black swallowed it whole.

She was about to take another step forward when someone grabbed her shoulder.

Dani thought it was Paul at first, but was surprised to see it was Alek.

"Stop," Alek yelled, and everyone froze in place.

"What is it?" asked Dani.

"Remember your painting?" asked Alek. Then his eyes trailed from her face down to her feet.

She followed it with her flashlight.

Mere inches from where she had been about to step was an utter void. She traced the ledge with the light in a giant circle until it returned to her feet.

She was standing at the precipice of a massive hole in the floor. It was about thirty feet wide.

"How deep is that?" asked Bianca.

"Let's find out," said Paul. He fished in his pocket until he found a coin, then flicked it into the opening.

They all waited in anticipation, listening for the metallic sound of the coin hitting the bottom. It was a sound that never came.

"Must be real deep then," Paul said.

"It's *The Hole*," said Dani, her voice suddenly sounding scared.

"What's *The Hole*?" Bianca asked.

"My painting, the one I made yesterday," explained Dani. "It was of a hole in this exact spot in the church."

"You think you painted this yesterday," said Paul with a speculative tone. "And they dug it out and built it in just a few hours? It doesn't make sense. You can't exactly fit an excavator in here."

"No," said Dani. "I think they were already digging it before I painted the picture."

"So you saw it," said Paul.

"No," Dani said, her voice soft and distant. "I had no idea it was here until now."

"You probably saw it or heard them talking about it," said Paul. "And just don't remember."

Dani looked at Alek, who was staring at her with a scared look on his face. Even without the heat on in the building, he looked like he was sweating through his jacket.

"Come on," said Paul. "I can see the stairwell to the basement on the other side. Follow me."

Dani pushed her own fears aside and joined the rest as they followed Paul around the edge of *The Hole* towards the opposite wall where an open doorway would lead them down.

The steps of the stairwell were of old gray stone. They descended them carefully; years of use had polished the rock to a smooth and slippery finish. There were no electric lights on the walls or ceiling, they had to rely on their flashlights to guide them.

After descending a flight, they found themselves in a long hallway with cramped ceilings overhead. Torch sconces lined the walls, their bases sculptures of different shapes of human hands.

The air was damp, Dani could feel it heavy in her lungs and mouth. It had a slight metallic taste, combined with a musty stink of dirt and mold. Dani imagined this was what a bog might smell like.

They had gone down the narrow hallway single file about fifty feet before they came to the first intersection. It split into four corridors, all going in different directions.

"Which way do we go?" Paul asked.

"I don't know," Dani replied.

Paul stood and thought for a moment, peering down each passage with his flashlight as each revealed little about their destination.

"Well Mystery Inc.," Paul said. "It appears we need to split up."

"No way," said Alek. "That's what every idiot in a horror movie says right before everyone gets killed off, one-by-one."

"Are you calling me an idiot, Alek?" Paul said. He looked down at Alek with aggression.

"No, I'm not," Alek quickly said. "I just don't think it's a good idea."

"Isn't this why you asked us to come, Dani?" Paul asked. "So we could help you find your painting?"

"Yes, but..." Dani didn't know what to say.

"If we were all going to stay together," Paul continued. "Then you two lovebirds could have done this on your own. If we split up, each take a hallway and see what's down there. Whether or not you find the painting, come straight back here in fifteen minutes."

"If you say so," Dani said.

"I'll take this one," Bianca said almost cheerfully, as she practically skipped to the first one on the far left.

"I got this one," Paul said, taking the one next to it.

Reluctantly, Dani and Alek picked theirs as well.

"Fifteen minutes," Paul repeated. "Then straight back here."

Dani and Alek disappeared down their respective corridors.

Paul and Bianca lingered a bit longer.

"You know what to do," Paul said softly, nodding at her.

She winked back at him before heading down her hallway.

Paul was the last to leave from the intersection. All four lights slowly dimmed as they continued deeper into the labyrinth of the old church.

CHAPTER 19

Bianca didn't believe Dani for a second when that hopeless girl tried to tell them she wanted to find some painting so she could take a picture. Bianca had painted hundreds of works, forgetting more of them than she remembered.

No, Dani wanted something else.

So did Bianca; actually, it was Paul's idea. They agreed to join Dani but take back with them a few extra pieces. He'd sell them through intermediaries and they'd make a couple hundred grand each. It would give her some time away from having to date these old rich assholes in order to get by.

Jeremiah had been the latest, but it was becoming increasingly exhausting to put up with him. The man talked incessantly about all the art he had bought, how it made him feel younger, more invigorated. There was some truth to that. Most men his age needed the little blue pill, Jeremiah didn't. In fact, he was like an energizer bunny in the bedroom. If Bianca found anything about him besides his money attractive, she would have enjoyed the sex.

One thing she did like was the access people like Jeremiah provided. Without him, her last show at the public gallery downtown would have never happened. It had been a major success, selling half of the stock of art. All had sold to the same anonymous buyer whom she was determined to find out so that she might become better acquainted with them. Him or her, neither mattered to Bianca.

She was growing exhausted of Jeremiah and was eager to find someone new. He had been ineffective at convincing Lady Gianni to showcase Bianca's work.

"She doesn't have any buyers who like your style," Jeremiah had explained to her.

"Bullshit," Bianca thought. She had been listening in on their conversation from the next room.

"An aesthetic failure... Conceptually weak... Unoriginal."

Lady Gianni's words had felt like daggers through Bianca's heart; she told her buyers what they wanted, she could tell them what to like and they'd believe it.

She hoped a worse feeling awaited the impossible woman when Lady Gianni found out her own art stores were robbed. Was she a little jealous of Dani, who suddenly was Gianni's new darling? Of course not. Dani, who was about as attractive as an ogre, would never be something Bianca would desire or desire to be.

Still, Dani's newfound small fortune would be easy pickings. She had caught her staring on several occasions, her desperate crush on Bianca could be easily taken advantage of.

But first she'd have to endure this awful basement, stumbling around in the dark for Lady Gianni's secretive art hoard.

Bianca jumped as she felt something brush against her foot. Pointing her flashlight down, she saw it was the body of a dead rat.

"Disgusting," she whispered out loud. Kicking it until it was out of sight.

She continued down the corridor until she came upon a doorway. The frame illuminated in bright light, giving it the appearance of a floating passage in the void of space.

Bianca put her ear to it first, listening for any sound that might warn her of its occupancy. All she could hear was the vibrations of a climate-control unit and a faint, irregular tapping sound.

Proceeding carefully, she turned the knob and opened the door a half-inch to peer inside. Thankfully, the hinges were silent as the heavy metal gave way.

It was hard to see. Her eyes had not adjusted to the bright light. She pushed the opening wide enough for her to step inside. She watched closely for movement, but there was none. It appeared to be empty.

Thankfully, she had worn her sneakers instead of more fashionable footwear. The stone pavers were uneven, with deep divots and gaps that could easily catch a stiletto heel. Peering around, she saw the room was lined floor to ceiling with shelves aligned into a gigantic grid pattern. However, the grid was circular, the rows all leading to the center. It resembled an enormous spider's web. The shelves themselves were white. Bianca touched them, and based on their texture, was curious about what they were made from. Alabaster came to mind.

Bianca froze. She thought she had heard a sound echoing across the stone walls of the room. It had been a tapping sound, like that of a nervous student's pencil on a school desk during an exam.

The drone of the climate unit that kept the air circulating drowned out any other sound she could make out. The tapping sound was still there, but muffled and distant.

Content it was nothing she should be concerned about, she examined the contents of the nearest shelving unit. The spaces inside the shelves were deep, five or six feet at the least. Inside were frames wrapped in plastic. She slid a random frame partially out.

Through the plastic, she could see the painting inside.

In a Baroque style, it depicted a dark forest with a moon high overhead. A little girl in a dress that looked like it had been in fashion in the 1800s wandered through the trees with a fearful look on her face. Behind her, hidden in the shadows, were yellow eyes peering at her from the darkness. Barely visible were the triangular faces of demonic looking creatures.

"How unsettling," Bianca thought. There was a white tag in the top right corner with a small type on it.

TITLE: THE GIRL IN THE FOREST
ARTIST: MALACHOR
YEAR: 1824 A.D.
OWNER: BRYNWEN LLYWELYN

"Sick bastard," she thought as she pulled it from the shelf and set it down near the door. She would take it with her. There's bound to be other sick bastards who would pay top dollar for such a piece.

With her back turned, the white alabaster seemed to vibrate, starting at where she had removed the painting and carrying down the line of shelves towards the center of the room.

Bianca didn't notice.

She went down several more rows of shelves, pulling a random painting from each. The styles she found were as diverse as the subject matter.

An Impressionist painting of a man trying to coach a mule over a rotting bridge, the turbulent waters of the river underneath frothing like a rabid dog.

A Fauvist painting of a lighthouse as a violent hurricane approached, the man on the ledge of the building was about to be swept away by an enormous swell.

A Surrealist's take on a dark city alley where a man with a dagger hid in the shadows as an unsuspecting couple approached wearing the garb of old-fashioned English nobility.

She had pulled almost a half dozen when she stopped, each time a strange vibration emanating from the empty space left behind.

There was more than enough there for her and Paul to take back with them.

With the vast non-computerized inventory, the missing pieces may not be noticed for months, weeks, or even years. The longer the better.

"One more, for good measure," Bianca thought.

This time she wanted to delve deeper than the outskirts of the room, theorizing that the art in the heart of the storage space might be of higher value.

As she ventured to the center, she thought she could hear the strange tapping sound again, but since it came and went seemingly at random, she ignored it. Probably just a loose nut or bolt on the climate control unit.

Content she had gone far enough, she pulled a random painting from the shelf.

Bianca recognized the artist immediately.

She double-checked the tag.

TITLE: SUNRISE

ARTIST: BIANCA CRUZ

YEAR: 2023 A.D.

OWNER: JEREMIAH HENRICKS

Her eyes grew wide in astonishment.

It was a painting she had sold only a few weeks prior, a show Jeremiah had arranged for her.

"The anonymous buyer was Jeremiah?" Bianca thought.

She set *Sunrise* on the ground. The strange vibration was stronger this time. It rippled through the room and traveled to other shelves like a rock being dropped into a pond. Bianca was too focused on trying to make sense of it to notice.

She pulled another painting from the shelves, read the tag, and let it fall to the floor. Then another, then another, each frame clattering loudly as it hit the stone. There were a dozen on the ground at her feet by the time she was done, all hers, all from her show, all purchased by Jeremiah.

Her thoughts drifted to the show's afterparty at Jeremiah's house, how euphoric she had felt basking in the glow of a successful sales day. Bianca had thought everyone had loved her work. She had thanked Jeremiah later that evening with probably some of the best sex of his entire life; she thought she owed her success to him.

It was true. Without him, she wouldn't have sold a single piece. He had bought it all.

Tears ran down her face. She felt like a fraud.

Did anyone who wasn't trying to sleep with her like her work?

Wiping away her tears, she took deep breaths to keep her composure. She pulled more pieces from Jeremiah's collection. She was determined to steal as much as she could from him. If he thought her worth was only as good as she was in bed, she would make sure the only worth she saw in him was his money.

The shelves practically bent under the vibrations as painting after paint-ing piled on the floor at Bianca's feet. There was more there than she could carry by herself.

Maybe the rest of the group would understand and help her.

Probably not Dani, but Paul would. Alek would be more difficult to convince.

She turned to head back towards the door.

Something hard landed on her face, knocking her to the ground.

Bianca screamed, tugging at whatever it was as it wrapped itself tight around her head.

She dug her nails into its flesh, digging deeper and deeper until at last whatever it was screamed and released its hold long enough for her to throw it with all her might.

It hit the ground with a thud between her and the door that led out of the storage room. There it sat on its back, temporarily stunned, and Bianca could see it fully for the first time.

It was about the size of a football, with a small, round body where eight legs stuck out like a spider's. Unlike a spider, it was completely hairless. Wrapped in pale flesh, a head stuck out from a short neck attached to the body. It looked like a head, at least. Where the face would have been, the flesh swirled and morphed like adding food coloring to a glass of water until two dark black eyes appeared and stared back at.

Bianca screamed at the top of her lungs. The creature had regained its senses and scrambled back onto the black claw tips of its eight legs. The two front legs tapped at the stone in a strange beat. It was the exact sound she had been hearing the whole time.

Its body slowly lowered itself, its legs tensed. Bianca knew what was next. It was preparing to attack.

As it sprung itself forward, Bianca grabbed one of her paintings and swung it like a club. To both her surprise and relief, it connected, and the creature collided with the shelf hard.

She didn't wait around to see if it was dead.

Taking off at a full sprint, she rushed for the exit.

Bianca knew better than to look back or take any of the stolen paintings with her. She didn't stop until she was on the other side of the door, back in the dark stone hallway, and crouched on the ground with her body blocking the door from opening.

Her chest heaved up and down, the terror at whatever the creature was still gripping her. She wanted to yell for Paul, but the words wouldn't come. She couldn't catch a breath long enough to gather the air to speak.

Bianca focused on her breathing, trying to calm down long enough to think of what to do next. Eventually, her breathing calmed and the hallway descended into silence.

Putting her ear to the door, she listened to see if she could hear the tapping of the creature inside. She could hear the hum of the climate unit but no tapping sound.

Bianca couldn't decide if that was a good or bad thing. Either way, she would not move from that spot until she was certain the creature on the other side could not get out. She needed Paul's help to figure out how to do that.

"Paul!" she yelled as loud as she could. "Paul!"

She continued yelling as long as she could until her voice grew hoarse.

Either he was too far away to hear her or something had happened to him.

But she had no choice. She would not let that thing out to follow her.

She swallowed hard, hoping to coat her vocal cords with enough saliva to loosen them up.

"Paul!" she screamed. "Help me!"

She stopped to listen. There was a faint sound in the distance. It sounded like the running of footsteps up the hall. It only grew louder and louder.

Paul had heard her. He was coming for her.

She took a deep breath.

"Paul," she yelled as loud as she could muster. "Thank god you…"

She never got to finish her words.

From the darkness, the sound of footsteps were gone, replaced by the tapping of eight legs as they approached at a furious pace.

Bianca opened her mouth wide to scream.

The spider creature flew out of the darkness in an instant, a blur of pink that quickly engulfed Bianca's face whole and muffled any sounds.

Bianca slashed at it with her nails, trying to free herself. Except this had no effect.

Bianca struggled, pulling at it, trying to free herself so she could breathe. The creature's grip was too tight this time. As the seconds turned into minutes, Bianca's hands grew weak. Then her arms fell to her sides. Her last moments of consciousness were of a dark world around her. The only sound she could hear was the excited tapping and clicking of the creature that smothered her.

Its only way to express the joy of a fresh kill.

Content that its prey was subdued, it released itself from the girl's head. Like clay being molded in zero gravity, its round body contorted and elongated in the air, suspended by the long legs, until it was small enough that it could have fit through a water pipe.

Legs first, it stuck its pincers into the girl's mouth and pushed itself inch-by-inch inside of her. Her cheeks bulged, the blood vessels in them visible as her skin was stretched to its limits. It didn't take more than a minute before the creature had shoved its entire body inside of Bianca's mouth. Only her dead body remained in the hallway, slouched over in front of the door like a rag doll.

Motionless, but not for long.

CHAPTER 20

Dani was certain she had gotten herself lost. She had passed through several intersections and forks in the underground passageways and was kicking herself for not leaving behind a marker or sign that she could use to backtrack. Even a couple of kids like Hansel and Gretel had been smart enough to leave a trail of pebbles to find their way home.

Pulling out her phone, she checked to see if fifteen minutes had passed yet. Hopefully, the others would come looking for her. Except it hadn't been fifteen minutes, at least not according to her phone. The screen still showed the exact same time as when they had split up.

She would try to call Alek; it said she had reception, except the phone wouldn't dial. It was frozen on the call screen. Holding down the buttons to restart didn't work either. It was useless.

A thought of smashing the phone against the wall ran through her head. Even though she could afford a new one for the first time in her life, she knew it wouldn't help.

Dani sat on the ground, leaning her back against a wall and wrapping her arms around her knees. She tried to hold back tears. This was all her stupid idea.

She felt like she had walked for miles already. They would never find her. Dani buried her head in her hands.

She jumped when something ran past her. Only catching a glimpse, it was a person but short, like a child.

"Hello?" she asked in the darkness after jumping to her feet.

"Hello?" a voice asked back. It sounded familiar but distant.

She searched for its origin; believing it had come from further down the passage.

Had she imagined it? There was no way a child was running free around there.

"Are you there?!" Dani yelled.

A long moment passed with no sound.

"Are you there?" the voice replied after the delay.

Was she hearing her echo? Echoes don't usually wait that long to come back to you. At least she didn't think they did.

Step by step, she crept towards the voice.

Alert for the slightest movement or sound, but only her steps and heavy breathing accompanied her. It was not long before she found another intersection.

"Hello?" she said, hoping to hear an answer.

But none came, no echo, no response, nothing.

She felt like she was going crazy, like she couldn't trust her own senses anymore.

The blur ran past her again.

It was a little boy, maybe eight or nine. Dressed like a baseball player, he had on white pants and a red jersey. Short blond hair hid under his baseball cap. He had been too fast for her to see his face, but it didn't matter. It was a sign of life in this damp, dead, empty place; so she chased after him. Dani didn't know how many turns he led her around or how far they had gone; he was so fast. She just concentrated on trying to catch up to him. Every time he was almost within reach, he would giggle and pull away.

She ran out of breath and had no choice but to stop and rest. Breathing hard with her hands on her knees, Dani tried to figure out where the boy had disappeared to.

"Come out!" she yelled between pants. "I promise I won't hurt you."

She heard the boy's laughter echo on the surrounding walls. It was impossible to tell which direction it had come from.

"Where are you?" She called. "I'm lost. Can you help me find the way out?"

Her flashlight beam crossed over the far end of the passageway and glinted on something metallic.

It was a metal stairwell.

She saw the little boy's sneaker on the bottom step before he climbed up it, the metal tread dinging with each step that he ascended until he was out of sight.

Dani rushed over and looked up. She couldn't see the boy anymore, but she saw something else encouraging; lights.

She hurried up to follow him.

The bright lights of *The Veil* were a welcome sight. The stairwell had led straight into a hidden doorway built into the wall near the entrance. Her cold, damp skin quickly warmed under the artificial sun overhead.

Where did the boy go?

She scanned the room and was relieved to see him standing next to the pond, skipping pebbles.

"How did you get in here?" she said, running towards him. "Did you sneak in or?"

The boy paid her no notice. He just kept skipping rocks.

Dropping to one knee next to him, she placed her hands on his shoulders and turned him to face her.

"It's not safe for little boys to be here," Dani said. She was right. With the giant hole in the main hall, anybody could fall in by accident.

"I live here," the boy said with a smile.

Dani peered at him closely. His eyes reminded her of someone, but she couldn't quite trace back to who.

"You mean you live under the church?" Dani asked. "You don't have to be afraid. You can tell me the truth."

"I am telling the truth," the boy squeaked. "I live here in this meadow."

Dani grew frustrated.

"It's not right for little boys to lie like that," said Dani. "This is an art gallery. No one lives here."

"I do," the boy said. His chin was also familiar, the shape and structure of his jawline peaked at her growing curiosity.

"Where are your parents?" she asked.

"I don't have any," the boy replied, skipping another stone.

Dani noticed another recognizable feature; the boy's ears. The left one had a slight depression near the top that the right one did not. Just like Dani's mother had. That thought only triggered an avalanche of the rest.

The boy's chin and eyes reminded her of her own father. Could they be related? It was too much of a coincidence.

"Do you know me?" Dani asked.

"Not really," the boy replied in a flat tone. "I've seen you around, but that's it."

"I don't understand," Dani said. "Are you the son of one of the workmen?"

"Stop that!" the boy yelled suddenly, anger permeating his voice.

"Stop what?" Dani said, standing up and taking a step back. The boy's sudden outburst startled her.

"Calling me that," the child said. "I'm not a boy, I'm a girl."

"What? But..." Dani's voice trailed off as she caught sight of the painting on the wall over the child's shoulder.

She remembered it all too well from her first night visiting the Gallery Nocturne, the subject of several subsequent nightmares. It was the painting of *My Body*. Except something was missing from it. The man with the creature bursting from him was gone.

She sensed it first, then she saw it.

Taking several more steps back, she could only watch in terror as the boy's eyes, mouth, nose, and hair melted away until his face had the smoothness of raw clay. His body grew before her eyes, growing an inch a second until he was the same height as Dani. His clothes stretched and shredded under the rapid growth until the strips of cloth fluttered to the ground.

He was naked in front of her, staring down at her. A nose formed on the face first; then eyes, then a mouth, then ears, and finally hair. The face staring back at her did not require any stretch of thought to recognize; it was the face she stared at in the mirror every day. It was hers.

The hair was shorter, styled into a masculine, messy look. His mis-matched ears did not have any holes for piercings like hers and the face showed no signs of makeup like Dani's. If she had a twin brother, this would be him.

Without warning, he reeled his head back and screamed in pain. His face contorting in ways that filled Dani with terror. She covered her ears to protect herself from the sound, but it was useless. The man's voice of pure agony was unavoidable.

The man-like thing fell to its knees, his undulating screaming filling the room.

In her retreat, her foot stumbled on a stone, and she fell backwards. A splashing sound and the icy feeling that streaked up her spine let her know she had fallen into the pond.

Frozen in shock, she watched as the man collapsed forward until his elbows and forehead were on the floor.

She quickly learned why.

It started as a slight cut, arranged vertically along his back parallel to his spine. Nothing more than a deep scratch. But it grew, lengthwise, until it ran from his shoulder to top of buttocks. Blood gushed forth as it pried itself wider and wider in time to the beating of Dani's heart.

She thought maybe the sharp grooves emerging from the split in the man's back were bones from his spine, but the reality was much more horrific. The sharp objects grew longer and longer until they bent and formed into two hands with slender claws, expediting the split wider and wider.

Then came the head.

There was no face on it, just long blond hair hanging over a formless shape.

The gruesome scene only stopped when the creature inside the man had pulled itself far enough out that Dani could see a bare chest with breasts and a slender stomach. It stood there, half emerged from the man at the waist, staring down at her.

Surely the man was dead. No one could survive something like that. Except his screams of pain continued unabated.

Controlled by the monstrosity coming out of him, the man pushed himself onto his feet and hands. He took a step forward with one hand, then another. His crab walk propelled the monster closer to her.

It was the painting; it was *My Body*. And it was no longer confined to a canvas and frame. It was free to move and wander about.

Dani couldn't move, the fear gripping her mind tight and stopping all thoughts that might trigger her fight-or-flight response. She felt the monster's claws wrap themselves around her neck. She felt them push her backwards, deeper in the pond. She felt the cold water rush around her face as her head submerged beneath the surface. Even as her mind finally realized she was being slowly drowned, she did nothing to stop it.

When you die, some people say time slows down and your whole life flashes before your eyes. As Dani's vision blurred, as the oxygen to her brain waned; she felt like this was true. Her mind shifted not from the horrific monstrosity or the water quickly filling her lungs; but to dinner with her family.

Sunday nights were reserved for family dinners, typically after church.

The entire week, Dani had been both anticipating and dreading tonight. Most teenagers couldn't wait for the weekend to come, not Dani.

Dani spun the long strands of spaghetti with her fork, wrapping them around the prongs like a python wraps around its prey before crushing it.

"Pastor Robinson asked if you'd volunteer to help with next week's service," Dani's mother said with a smile. "His usual altar boy, Timothy, is out of town with his folks."

Dani didn't respond. She wasn't really listening.

A spot of red had formed on her shirt where a splatter of pasta sauce had escaped her bowl.

"Oh dear," her mother said. "I don't want to ruin your baseball uniform. You have a game next week. I'll go get some club soda."

She hurried to the fridge.

Dani's father diverted his attention away from trying to watch the game playing on the television in the living room.

"You gotta look sharp," he said to Dani. "While you stick it to those pansies from Central High."

Dani's mother returned with a towel and a can.

"I'm not sure that's the type of language we want to be teaching our son," Dani's mother said with a stern eye towards her father.

"I don't want to play baseball anymore," Dani said out loud. She was tired of holding back what she wanted to say.

"You'll finish the season," her father replied, his eyes drifting back to the television. "If you still feel that way after, then we can look at trying you out in another sport next year. You're pretty tall. Maybe basketball or volleyball would be good..."

"I don't want to play any sports," Dani cut him off.

This got his attention quickly.

"Danny," he said, clearly trying to hold back his temper. "Every boy at your school plays a sport. Football, track and field, something. You can't just not play anything, they'll pick on you."

"I'm not every boy," Dani replied defiantly. Her courage was growing inch by inch inside of her. Like the drip of water that quickly forms into a mighty river.

"What are you trying to say, Danny?" her dad asked. "You want to be in drama or something like some sissy? Not my son, not my son!"

His fist hit the table with a loud thud. Dani's fork fell out of her hand and hit the tablecloth with another splatter of red. Her hands were trembling.

"Honey, I don't think..." Dani's mother tried to say, but her voice disappeared when Dani stood up suddenly.

"I'm not a boy," Dani said. The last of the floodgates opened up.

"Yes, you are," her father replied, standing up to face off with her. "I was there when you were born. You are a boy."

"No, I'm not," Dani replied, staring back at him with unflinching eyes. "Not inside."

"Danny," her mother pleaded. "You're not making any sense. You are our son."

"He's been watching too much of that liberal crap on television," Dani's father erupted. "He/him, she/her, they/them. It's a bunch of bull. You are either a boy or a girl, you don't get a choice in the matter. All those boys pretending to be girls, wearing dresses and makeup on TV, they are just a bunch of freaks."

"I know who I am inside," Dani said, bolstering herself. "And it's not some freak. I'm a girl. No matter what you or society tells me, I know who I am."

"You're a teenager," her dad exclaimed. "You don't know your ass from a hole in the ground. This ridiculous farce will not happen in my house. Do you understand me?"

"You can't stop me from being who I am," Dani replied, her nostrils flaring as she held back her own temper. She started unbuttoning her baseball uniform at the table.

"What are you doing, honey?" her mom asked.

"Showing you," Dani replied. Pulling her shirt apart, she revealed a tan bra underneath.

"You think wearing girl's underwear suddenly makes you a girl?" Her father mocked her.

"It's only a start," said Dani, buttoning her shirt back up. "I'm going to take hormones..."

Her dad's face twisted into a look of disgust.

"I'm going to have the surgery," Dani continued as her mom buried her face in her hands and began to cry.

"And who's going to pay for that?" Her dad replied. "Not us, not our insurance."

"I'll pay for it myself," said Dani.

"You think anyone will give you a job?" He scoffed. "You're a freak."

"No, I'm not," Dani walked towards the doorway. "I'm sick of pretending to be someone I'm not."

"Where do you think you're going?" Her dad said, stomping after her.

"To change," she replied. "Into a dress!"

"Don't even think about it," he said.

Dani was halfway up the stairs already.

"You can't stop me," she said.

"If you come down wearing makeup, a dress, anything remotely female," his face was as bright red as a tomato. "You might as well bring your suitcase with you cause you won't be staying in this house."

"Fine," Dani yelled back and slammed the door of her room shut behind her.

Her bag was already packed, sitting on the bed. She had planned for this. Everything she had read online said it's what happened to most transitioning teens. She had only wished she had told them sooner.

Her parents had sent her to every Bible camp their parish had offered, where pastors had preached about the dangers of sinners like her. The years of hating herself, cutting herself, thinking there was something wrong with her, wishing she was dead, were over. She was stronger now than she had ever been before, and all it took was her standing up for herself to her parents.

Dani looked at herself in the mirror. She didn't recognize the face staring back at her.

She had rehearsed telling her parents a thousand times in the same mirror and every time it ended with her bawling her eyes out. Now that she had actually done it for real, there were no tears to be seen. Her eyes were fierce, ready to take on every challenge the world would throw at her.

She knew it wouldn't be easy out there on her own, but at least she would be who she was, a powerful woman.

Dani grabbed the hands of the monster that were wrapped around her neck. With a loud scream, she pulled them away from her throat; the claws' grasp were weak against her will.

Free, she pulled her head above the shallow water's surface and gasped for air.

Not wasting a moment, Dani scrambled to her feet and lunged herself at the man-woman creature as it staggered backwards.

Despite its unsettling and fearsome nature, the creature was uncoordinated and unable to protect itself. Dani yelled like an Amazon as she grabbed the clawed arms and pushed them backwards, the man's body underneath stumbling over itself as it did its best to fight back.

It was futile.

Dani knew her strength. She had conquered her worst fear years ago in that kitchen back home; the monster was nothing but a sideshow by comparison.

Foot after foot, it retreated towards the wall until Dani lost grip of its arms. Her cheeks pressed up against something flat and hard.

The monster had gone, disappeared. She took a step back.

She could still see it, except it was no longer a physical shape imposing on reality. It was back in its painting, exactly as she remembered the first night she saw it.

Dani grabbed at the frame and yanked it from the wall. It clattered to the floor with a loud smash, the corners jarring loose.

She wasn't done.

Stomping on the canvas, it tore apart under her shoes until it was nothing but thin strips of fabric.

Whatever it was had been destroyed.

Dani let herself calm as her chest heaved heavy breaths.

Who knew what horrors the others were facing? If it was anything like *My Body*, they would need her help. It was her fault they were there; she needed to save them. First, she would need to find them.

The exit on the far end still looked open. She sprinted for it.

She could hear a faint sound in the distance. It sounded like someone yelling out.

Dani stopped to listen.

"Someone, help me, please," the voice yelled.

She knew that voice; it was Bianca's.

"Please come quick," Bianca's voice continued. "I need help."

"I'm coming, Bianca," Dani yelled back as she passed through the exit of *The Veil*.

Chapter 21

It felt like Alek had walked down several flights of stairs already. The air grew thicker and hotter with each turn of the narrow stairwell, like he was delving deeper into some exotic equatorial rainforest. His only explanation being that there must be an old-fashioned boiler deep beneath the structure of the church.

He wiped a thick layer of moisture from his forehead. The endless stairwell gave way to a hallway lined with archways. He approached carefully, having seen too many scary movies to be caught unaware by some killer hiding in one of these many dark openings. His fears proved unfounded. The light of his flashlight glinted slightly against the iron bars that blocked each opening. Only sparse specks of shiny, bare metal remained where rust hadn't fully gained hold. No one was going to jump out from what he knew in his heart to be a dungeon.

"What kind of church was this?" he said out loud to the darkness, shining his light into the emptiness of the first cell. He expected a skeleton or corpse inside, but the chains still bolted to the wall were empty of any inmate.

The part of his brain where his dark humor came from kicked in suddenly and he imagined the cells filled with young altar boys and an old man in a dark papal hat pacing between them, trying to pick his choice.

Alek knew the church predated the recent issues of the catholic priesthood, but in this dark corner of the building, that little bite of humor in bad taste warded off the terror of not knowing what else was down there with him.

At the end of the hall, he noticed a faint light. It flicked red and orange in a long, thin line that lay across the ground.

A doorway.

Step by step, he walked towards the light. He could feel the temperature of the air increase with each tap of his shoes on the stone. Right in front of the door, the temperature sweltered. He grew concerned that a fire raged on the other side.

He placed the back of his hand on the door itself, bracing for a searing heat, only to find it cool to the touch..

Pushing on it with all of his might, it begrudgingly swung open on its old, rusted hinges. Expecting more dungeons, his eyes peered in shock upon a large, open room. The walls to his right and left curved perfectly, forming a gigantic circle. Lined with bare, rotted bookshelves, dust and spider webs had long established their dominance. Alek could make out elongated lines of cuts on the bare stone ceiling where frescoes had been removed. A single ray of moonlight shot out of a hole in the center of the roof, filtered by thick leaves and vines that had overgrown the narrow opening.

A boulder taller than him, a piece of ceiling that had fallen, blocked his view of the center of the room. An orange silhouette pulsed around it.

Peering around the corner of the stone, he saw a bonfire burning brightly in the middle of the underground hall. It was so vast that he couldn't see anything beyond it, but he could see the shadows it cast on the walls. The shadows were moving.

Alek pulled his head back and listened sharply.

Voices were talking, male voices. They were too faint for him to make out exactly what they were saying, but they were speaking a language he understood: Russian.

Whether they were friends or foe, he did not know. There was only one way to find out. Alek took a deep breath before emerging from his hiding space and walking towards the fire.

The firelight blurred his vision. His eyes had grown too accustomed to the dark corridors. Thinking he was close enough, he called out to the men.

"Zdravstvuyte," he greeted them in Russian, his hand blocking the bright light from his face.

The jovial voices quieted quickly, followed by a sudden clicking of metal and movement of furniture.

He figured they might be homeless, squatting where no one dared to delve. Why else start a giant bonfire?

"No need to run," Alek continued, still not able to see much other than five silhouettes facing him. "I just want to know how you got down here."

With the light of the fire behind him, his eyes adjusted faster and he could see the men in detail. They were not homeless. He could tell that from their black and gray suits with ties that hung out over well fed bellies. They faced him, each with a single outstretched arm.

"Whoa," Alek said, realizing they were pointing guns at him. He put his own hands up in the universal gesture of 'Dear god, please don't shoot me'.

He considered running for a moment, but the chances of him dodging shots from all five of the men were so slim it wasn't worth it. So he stood there, trying to avoid moving in any way that may be misinterpreted as aggression.

"I didn't see anything," Alek said, diverting his eyes to the ground. "I didn't see your faces. Please let me..."

"Sasha, is that you?" A voice asked.

Alek couldn't believe his ears. Not only was the voice familiar, but it knew him intimately enough to call him by his nickname. Looking up from the ground, he recognized one of the men immediately.

"Uncle Ivan?" Alek asked.

"Put the guns down," Ivan told the others, who lowered theirs without hesitation. "This is Sergey's boy."

Alek took a step forward, still in disbelief.

"What are you doing in America?" Alek asked first, then reconsidered. "What are you doing down here?"

"I'll tell you everything," Ivan said with a smile. "First, come sit."

His hairy hand was outstretched towards a wooden chair opposite him.

Ivan and the others took their seats on the other end of a long, antique wooden table. Unlike the shelves and the roof, which were falling apart, the table was in perfect condition. On it, immense pewter platters, plates, and bowls were laid out and overflowing with a feast of steaming meats and vegetables. Alek's stomach rumbled as it informed him it had been too long since his last meal.

"Please, eat with us," Ivan said.

Alec abstained, despite his stomach's growing demands. He felt unease at the coincidence of the entire scenario. A familiar family member he hadn't spoken to in years magically appeared at the one place no one would ever look for him.

Ivan and the other men did not share his concerns or discomfort, as evidenced by their ravenous devouring of everything in sight.

"I'm not hungry," Alek replied. "Why are you here?"

Ivan looked nervously at his companions for a moment.

"We don't work for your father anymore," Ivan said at last.

"I don't understand," Alec replied. "He's your brother. You two were best friends. You fought in the Georgian civil war together."

"Allegedly," said the man to Ivan's left. The men laughed, except for Ivan.

"You saved his life," Alek continued. "He told me that story all the time. What happened?"

"We had a disagreement," Ivan replied. Alek could tell he was having trouble figuring out how to explain things.

"He tried to have Ivan killed," the man on Ivan's left said again.

"Quiet Dmitry," Ivan hissed.

"My father would never do that," Alek pleaded. "Family was everything to him."

"Your father," Ivan began, and then took a deep breath. "He's not the same man you remember. Ever since you left..."

"Sent away," Alek corrected him.

"After what happened," Ivan said, rocking his head back and forth with a discomforting look on his face. "Your father lost sight of many things. He's convinced someone corrupted you. He's convinced that person was me."

"Corrupted?" Alek asked in a high pitch tone. "Corrupted? He asked me to shoot my nanny in the head, the woman who practically raised me my entire life, because she was allegedly a spy."

"Was that too much to ask?" Ivan asked, taking a bite from a steaming leg of roast lamb and tearing at the flesh with his teeth. A gold chain swung back and forth like a pendulum from his thick neck as his jaws mashed on the food.

"She was my nyanya," Alek replied. "Of course I was not going to do it. I wouldn't have done it anyway, nyanya or not. I don't kill people."

"Oh yes," Dmitry mocked. "You're ze artist."

Alek watched the insulting man wave his fork in the air like a paintbrush making spitting sounds with his mouth.

"That's enough, Dmitry," Ivan scolded him. "He's still Sergey's son."

Dmitry grunted before using his fork to skewer the flank of a roasted pig on a nearby platter.

"That doesn't explain what you are doing here," Alek exclaimed.

"After your father sent me to a meeting with the Italians," said Ivan. "A meeting he neglected to inform me was to be my funeral, we found a new employer and left for America promptly."

"A new employer?" Alek said with raised eyebrows. "Who do you work for now? The Greeks? The Tongs?"

His mind raced with possibilities. There were plenty of organized crime rackets to choose from.

"Oh, we stay out of those circles now," Ivan replied. "We work in the private sector."

"Private sector?" Alek asked. "Wait, do you work here?"

"Bingo," Dmitry said through a mouth full of pork.

"Why does Lady Gianni need a couple of enforcers like you?" asked Alek. It didn't make any sense.

"I don't know Lady Gianni," said Ivan, his gold chain swinging as his jowls rolled like waves across his jawline. "I've heard her name in passing only. She's a former associate of our employer."

"Then who?" Alek questioned.

"You want us to see about introducing you?" Ivan replied.

"He's here?" Alek said with slight panic. With the bright fire and his eyes adjusted, he could see just about every inch of the room. There was nowhere someone could hide. The bookshelves were the only other furniture, their shadows simmering in the bright bonfire light.

"He's always here," Dmitry said with a fiendish grin. "The poor man can't leave."

A sudden whistling sound filled the room, a rush of wind whipping at the fire causing it to sputter and shrink.

Alek jumped to his feet and spun around.

The fire roared back to life, filling the room with light. All except for a patch of darkness against the far wall where he had entered. It first looked like the shadow of the fallen rock he had hidden behind, but it was growing larger by the second. Growing larger and getting closer to the fire itself.

"Stay calm Alek," Ivan said from behind him. "His appearance can be disarming."

"Who?" Alek tried to ask, but his chest felt like all the air had been sucked from it.

The shadow drew closer, undeterred by the bright fire. Alek inched closer to the flame, praying it would provide him some protection.

"Who... Is... This?" a disembodied voice echoed throughout the room.

"Hey boss," Ivan said. "This is my nephew Alek."

Despite being right next to the heat of the fire, Alek's skin became covered in goosebumps and his hair stood on end. He was filled with the desire to run for his life.

"What... Are... You... Doing... Here?" the deep, raspy voice asked.

Alek did not dare reply. He was too scared of the mass of darkness that had formed from the floor and somehow coalesced into legs, a body, arms, and a head. There was no more detail. The darkness was absolute except for one thing.

There was a sliver of silver where the shadow man's left eye would have been. The silver speck stared at him from high above. The shadow loomed at what Alek could only estimate as seven feet tall.

"SPEAK!" The shadow man's voice erupted. Alek didn't just hear the voice, he could feel it hit him like a shockwave. So could the fire, which shrunk with each word.

"I'm here to destroy some paintings," Alek blurted out, finding himself strangely unable to lie in the shadow's presence.

The shadow man's silhouette grew more defined as it absorbed the growing darkness of the room. It began to look familiar.

"Interesting," said the voice. "What... Else?"

The fire had died down until just a few embers remained.

"I don't know," Alec said with closed eyes. He was too afraid to face the shadow anymore. He just wanted it to go away. "Please don't hurt us. I'll get the others to leave."

"Others?" the voice echoed back to him.

Alek risked opening his eyes. A fool's hope that whatever he was experiencing was over.

It was difficult to see anything; the fire was completely out. The only remaining light shined down from a faint ray of moonlight high above. He looked back to where Ivan and his friends were sitting at the table.

Without the light of the fire, the table had somehow changed. It was covered in muck and rot, no longer perfect as he had just seen it. The pewter platters were still there as well, but they were cracked and tarnished. On them, large chunks of rotted meat sat oozing with flies and maggots.

Ivan and his men were gone, their chairs now inhabited by five decaying skeletons. The one in the center still had a gold chain around its neck.

"Ivan," Alek yelled, but part of him knew it was no use. Ivan and his men were already dead, long dead in fact. What he had just experienced was either a hallucination or something that he would never be able to fully explain.

"I'll leave, I promise," Alek screamed at the voice. Hoping it would grant mercy as the darkness swirled around him.

"Do... Not... Leave," the voice snarled at him.

"What do you want me to do, then?" Alek screamed back. He just wanted this to end.

"Burn," the voice replied, then after a long pause. "Everything."

Alek felt like he was being squeezed to death as the darkness pressed all around him. He might suffocate, his lungs couldn't hold any breath. The world around him faded away.

CHAPTER 22

With any luck, Dani and Alek would be so turned around by now that they'd be lost down there for hours.

Paul had planned it that way, after all.

The church's original plans were available online. He had sent Bianca to the only room large enough to be used for art storage. The extensive permits required to keep a room at the right temperature and humidity were a dead giveaway.

By now, Bianca would be on her way back with armfuls of priceless art and he'd be ready to meet her in order to load it and get it out of there before anyone was the wiser. They'd come back for Dani and Alek, but not for a few more hours.

First, he'd need to find the hatch that led out from this passage so that he could get back to the van.

It has to be in one of these rooms; he thought.

Paul passed doorway after doorway, many of which hadn't been in the original plans, but so far all had come up empty. What he found instead was disconcerting, to say the least.

I guess you could have called them art studios;, they each had an easel and a chair. However, between the rat nests, darkness, and shackles attached to the floor next to each easel; he couldn't imagine anyone would have chosen them as a place of creativity. He wasn't going to stick around to find out if the dark puddles on the ground were standing water or blood. Whatever Lady Gianni had going on down here, it couldn't have been good.

Eureka!

It was the last room in the corridor, but he had found it. The metal hatch squealed as it opened. The rusty hinges of the folding ladder attached to it took several tugs before the rust gave way and it folded down. A cloud of crimson dust from the rusty hinge sparkled in the flashlight's beam.

Paul shook the sides of it as a first test. They felt solid. But who knew how long since this ladder had been last used? The damp and the dark can rot metal and wood alike.

Here goes nothing.

The first step felt safe, so did the second. He put his full weight on the rungs and there was no painful creaking or loud cracking sounds to indicate it couldn't hold him. He climbed up into the darkness.

When he had last been inside *The Remnants* wing of the gallery, it was full of people. Many of whom had been ridiculously hopping on the surface of the pond to create the ripple effect of the hall's largest exhibit.

With the power turned off, no ripples formed at Paul's feet with each step. The entire space was dead silent.

With just a flashlight beam to light his way, finding his direction would be difficult. Finding anything would be difficult. Maybe if he went back to the hatch, he could use it to help determine which direction to go.

SLAM!

The sound echoed around him as he dropped to his knees and began crawling in wide circles, trying to find the hatch. It must have had a spring or hydraulic system that he hadn't noticed. The thing wouldn't have closed on its own otherwise. Unless...

"Shit," Paul said out loud. The thought crept into his head that perhaps he wasn't alone.

He could do this. He knew what the exit looked like. It would just take longer than he wanted to find it. Bianca would wait for him by the van. She might even go back and get more art if she was being smart.

Just pick a direction, damnit, he thought. *It's not that big a place, and I'm not going to find anything standing here like an idiot.*

Walking forward in the direction he was already facing, he started to feel pretty good about his choice. He passed the island with *The Memory Tree* on it that had been roughly central in the pond; he considered stopping to touch one of the branches, but with the power out it probably wouldn't work.

Continuing forward, he hadn't gotten more than another ten feet when he heard a clicking sound and stopped dead in his tracks.

Ultra alert, Paul shined his flashlight beam in every direction but saw nothing to explain where the clicking sound had come from. However, he did see a faint hint of light up ahead. He rejoiced. He had found the exit.

Picking up his pace, he wanted to get the first load out of there as soon as possible. Practically running through the doorway, Paul nearly fell as he tried to stop himself in time.

On the other side wasn't the main hall like he had thought. It was a room with chairs arranged neatly in rows facing a silver screen. The screen was brightly lit up, black and white videos of people dancing played across it. A plaque on the wall proclaimed the name of the exhibit, *The Camera Man*.

"Damn," he said, pissed at himself for rushing. He would need to retrace his steps.

Turning to leave, something caught his eye. Sitting on the ground in the center of the room was a sculpture of a man.

Paul took a few steps closer, his curiosity egging him forward. He must have missed this exhibit when he had first visited. Since he was likely to never return to the scene of his little heist, he figured a few extra seconds to check it out couldn't hurt.

The sculpture's skin was gray as stone, but the level of detail of his musculature was near perfect. The man wore a gray cloth around his waist that covered his genitals, but otherwise was naked. Seated on the ground, his arms wrapped around his knees, and faced forward. There wasn't a blemish, chip, or discoloration anywhere on his body that would give it away as not real. Even seated on the floor like that, he towered over the empty red velvet chairs that sat in rows around him.

Paul probably would have thought it a real person, if not for the head. The man's face was shaped into a hybrid of a human and an old-fashioned movie projector. Half of the face a dull gray eye with an ear sticking out, the other half the lens of the projector and whirling gears. The clicking sound he had heard before was the film reels spinning on spools. With the power turned off everywhere else, it must have some internal power source.

He was close enough to touch it when the film on the screen suddenly changed. The grainy black-and-white picture was gone, replaced with a vibrant, hi-resolution color picture of a vast field of flowers next to a lake. Paul could practically smell the aromas of the flowers. It looked just like one of his paintings.

As the reel progressed and zoomed in closer, he realized quickly it WAS one of his paintings, *Lillys on the Lake.*

They had stolen his work and included it in this exhibit. If he wasn't about to rob Lady Gianni blind, he certainly would have sued the hell out of her!

Something burgundy swept across the screen. It looked like a paint-brush.

As the film's perspective zoomed out, an image took its place of a teenage boy in a studio painting *Lillys on the Lake.* The boy had an IV tube coming from his arm that ran to a nearby machine.

Cold ran down Paul's spine.

It wasn't Paul who was painting; it was his brother.

How many people had seen this? It could ruin him. No one knew the truth, no one.

The boy on the screen coughed, a streak of red flying onto the canvas that he quickly wiped away. Another boy ran forward to his aid. He looked the spitting image of the painter except older. It was Paul.

Paul tried to coax his younger brother to rest, but the boy refused. Insisting he wanted to keep painting, to put as much of his work out into the world before his time was over.

The real Paul stood there, dumbfounded. There was no camera in the room. This was just a scene from his memory. How could it be playing in front of his eyes?

Paul's brother's name was Henry.

Finishing *Lillys on the Lake*, Henry used his last few ounces of energy to scribble his signature onto the bottom right-hand corner of the painting before nearly collapsing from the effort. Screen Paul, memory Paul was quick to attend to him; to lead him to the nearby hospital bed in the room, where Henry rolled to his side in immense pain.

Memory Paul adjusted the setting on the machine that controlled the IV and Henry's pain faded until the younger boy fell fast asleep from ex-haustion. With no one watching, Memory Paul quickly scrubbed Henry's signature from the canvas and replaced it with his own before taking the entire painting from the room.

The clicking sound of the reels grew louder as the scene ended and the screen turned a bright white.

Paul only felt one emotion: immense guilt. Even if the seats were empty, he could feel the presence of ghostly figures in them glaring at him in disgust.

"He was dying," Paul tried to explain to the emptiness of the room. "I dropped out of art school to take care of him. I deserved those paintings."

The only reply he received was silence, an unforgiving absence of anything and anyone to comfort him.

Paul reached for the projector. He didn't know how Lady Gianni had made the reels, but he could never allow that film to be shown again. He would take it and destroy it.

The hand of the sculpture was fast. It grabbed his wrist quicker than Paul could react. The gray hand's grip was tight. Pain shot up Paul's arm. He yelped.

Slowly, *The Camera Man* sculpture stood up, rising to its full height and bringing Paul up with it until the tips of Paul's sneakers barely touched the floor. Paul dangled as *The Camera Man* tilted his head and neck down to stare directly into Paul's eyes.

Paul could only struggle as he saw the reflection of himself in the camera's lens, his head beaded with sweat, his eyes wide in fear, his teeth clenched.

"What do you want?" Paul yelled at the sculpture, but it didn't reply. It didn't have a mouth. The only sign it had heard him was the speeding up of the clicking sound the reel made as it spun, the lens grew white. It was ready to shine its bright light directly into him. An immense heat blasted his face, increasing with each passing second until it became an agonizing, searing pain.

In one last-ditch attempt to free himself, he swung his arm holding the flashlight at *The Camera Man*'s face. He felt the bones in his hand snap as they connected with the thick metal, but it was enough. Paul fell to the ground free at last. So did the flashlight, broken practically in two.

He had no time to dwell on how burned his face was or how to remedy a broken hand; he knew the only thing he could do was run.

Not looking back to see if he was being followed, he sprinted from the exhibit and into the darkness of the pond; hoping and praying he could find the exit. Paul didn't bother to search for *The Ashen Room*, he pushed himself into the darkness. His heavy footsteps pounded on the glass like a bear running on a frozen lake.

He slammed into the wall headfirst, feeling his nose crunch as it cushioned the rest of skull before falling backwards onto the ground.

He writhed in pain, clutching at his face as his body filled with sharp sensations. He tried to keep his focus on where he was, what he was running away from, but the need to soothe himself fought back.

After a few moments, he mustered enough command of his own body to wrestle control of his own thoughts back and stopped moving so he could listen.

There were no heavy footsteps behind him, no sign he was being followed. Maybe he was safe.

The return of the reel clicking to life changed his mind quickly; it was impossible to tell from which direction the clicking came. He jumped to his feet and slammed his body up against the wall. Sliding along the wall, he hoped he would find the exit, somehow, some way.

The clicking sped up as an image projected onto the wall opposite Paul. Even cast on a surface the size of an enormous movie screen, the image from the old-time projector was crystal clear as his own memory.

It showed him speaking at Henry's funeral. Tears streaked down his face as the casket lay before him. Displayed behind him were several pieces of Henry's paintings. They were beautiful, they would go on to be some of his most world famous works. They would plaster his name on the headline of art magazines across the country, grant him an audience with the most prestigious art collectors in the world, and fetch obscene sums of money at auction. Except in the corner of each was not Henry's name, but Paul's.

The feelings of shame returned, more painful than the broken bones or scorched skin. Even at his own brother's funeral, Paul had promoted his brother's work as his own.

The picture disappeared from the wall. Paul heard the clicking of the film reels. The sound was growing louder.

Paul squirmed along, hoping for a way out.

His hands fell on nothing. He was trapped, unable to see, waiting for *The Camera Man* to get him.

It approached slowly. He could practically see the tall, gaunt silhouette in the darkness. He had nowhere to run.

His fingers felt something in the wall, an indent.

Hope filled his heart. Paul felt inside and didn't hesitate when he realized it was the latch of a door.

Pushing it open, he scrambled inside. The door closed behind him. Paul braced his body against it with his full weight, hoping it would be enough to stop *The Camera Man* from following him.

He waited, his body taught, wedged against the door, but no attempt to open it was made from the other side.

Feeling he had waited long enough, he reached towards the walls next to the door and was relieved to feel a light switch. Paul flicked it on.

Fluorescent lights buzzed to life.

Paul may have loved his van before going to the Gallery Nocturne that night, but seeing it sitting on the concrete of the receiving dock in front of him now brought tears to his eyes.

"Sorry Dani, sorry Alek, sorry Bianca," he thought.

He had no intention of going back in for them. Paul was going to get out of there before *The Camera Man* found him. That was his only option.

Running to the roll-up door, he hit the button to open the gate. The motor made a sound like it was starting up, then shut itself down. Desperately, he pressed it again. Still nothing. Minutes passed as he tried to get the motor to open the gate for them like it had before, but nothing happened.

Then he realized he needed the keypad code in order to open the gate. Every time he tried to remember what the Foreman Tom had said on the phone, it escaped him. It was like he was trying to remember something that had happened a lifetime ago. If one of the others were here, maybe they would remember it, but he wasn't going back into the Gallery Nocturne. Not a chance.

He could only think of one option.

Hopping into the driver's seat of his van, he pulled the keys from his pocket and shoved them into the ignition. The vehicle was facing the wrong direction, but with enough speed, he might be able to reverse into the roll-up door and bring it down. It may not completely fall, but if he did enough damage, at least he could crawl out of there and run on foot. He didn't care where to, even if it would be jail. He just wanted to get away from *The Camera Man*.

Turning, he felt panic fill him as the engine turned over but did not sputter to life.

Then the fluorescent lights went out.

He continued to turn the key, cursing at the van when the engine failed to start. Paul yelled every obscenity he could think of. He slammed his fists into the steering wheel and dash; he kicked at the useless pedals at his feet. Nothing worked. The van remained as dead as he knew he would soon be.

Exhausted, he buried his head into his arms, crossed over the steering wheel, and began to cry.

Paul only looked up when he heard the film reel sputter back to life, but he was long past the terror stage of seeing *The Camera Man*'s work. What new memory could it conjure up that could somehow be worse than stealing his own dead brother's work?

He quickly found out.

On the wall in front of the man, the scene of Paul sitting at the warehouse where The Collective lived appeared on the stone wall. He was seated on a chair in the storage area, out of sight from the others, an area that he carefully guarded access to. In his hands, he held a tray of chemicals and dipped a cloth into it before carefully scrubbing the bottom right-hand corner of a painting.

Meticulously and with great focus, the Memory Paul scrubbed and scrubbed until the corner was almost bare of any paint. Content that no marks remained, he dried it with a hair dryer before producing a paint and brush. With careful and purposeful strokes, he wrote his signature in the corner.

His work complete, Memory Paul put away his materials and prepped the painting for shipment. It was a beautiful piece of art, depicting a wildflower patch growing through cracks in the concrete that separated two abandoned buildings. It was pleasant, warm, and inviting; some of Dani's best work.

Paul didn't bother to wipe away the tears as the projector clicked off and plunged the room into darkness. He had thought his betrayal of Henry had been a one-time thing, a momentary and justifiable lapse of character that wouldn't be repeated. Except when his own art never lived up to the fame Henry's had afforded him, he had turned back to this vile behavior.

Dani was an easy target. He was giving her food and shelter, after all. Was he not entitled to some just compensation for that? He didn't need the money, he just wanted to be relevant again. Yet somehow it still felt worse.

Maybe he was just getting what he deserved.

Paul flicked on the headlights. Standing in front of the van was *The Camera Man*. At his full height, he gazed downwards at Paul through the windshield with his lone, dull, dead eye.

The clicking of the reel sped up. Paul prepared for the blazing heat to his skin until it would eventually leave nothing left but ash.

CHAPTER 23

Dani followed the cries for help through the exit of *The Veil*. Passing through the archway, she was alarmed to see the lights on in the main church. The colossal new exhibit, *The Hole,* spanned almost the entire length of the room. Despite the half dozen braziers surrounding it, the darkness of its depths showed no ground to the light.

She glanced to the ceiling of the church, where the frescoes of angels and demons looked different from how she remembered. The angels, clad in white, betrayed faces of despair, as if they knew something horrible was about to unfold. Meanwhile, the demons bared ravenous, hungry teeth and eyes of excited anticipation.

"Help me, please help me Dani," she heard, and her attention shot back to her mission; saving Bianca.

She scanned the room for her roommate, her heart hoping and praying that she was still alive.

There she was!

Bianca was kneeling at the other end of *The Hole,* her face buried in her hands.

"I'm here, Bianca," Dani yelled as she ran around the ledge haphazardly.

As she approached, Dani could see blood soaking on Bianca's shirt.

"Are you alright?" Dani asked between breaths. "Did something attack you?"

She threw herself over Bianca, holding her tight.

"It's alright," Dani said, trying to comfort her. "I'm here now."

"Please help me, Dani," Bianca's voice said from underneath her.

"You're safe with me," Dani replied.

"Help me, help me," Bianca repeated. Her voice turning strange and inauthentic.

Dani noticed. Slowly, she pulled on Bianca's shoulder so she could see her face, but what she saw made her stumble backwards onto the ground.

"Help me Dani, help me," Bianca's voice came again from her open mouth. But her lips or jaw weren't moving.

Looking at her roommate, she could see inside her mouth, deep in the back of Bianca's throat where her tonsils would have been, two little beady red dots stared back at her.

Dani recoiled in horror, trying to put as much distance between herself and whatever had become of Bianca.

"Oh, don't worry about her," Lady Gianni said from behind Dani, startling her. "She's harmless."

"Her...what?" Dani tried to scramble to her feet.

"It's a bit unsettling the first time you meet the Librarian," replied Lady Gianni with a smile. "But I assure you, as long as you aren't trying to remove any art from the archives, she's as pleasant as her kind come."

"You know about..." The words were hard to form in her conscious as horror and panic gripped her.

"Tom phoned me to let me know he had given you the code to retrieve your paycheck," Lady Gianni replied. "He likes to keep me informed, and he seemed very concerned about you."

She wore a sleeveless, white, sheer dress that flowed like wisps over her legs, almost to her ankles. It was formal wear, like one might wear to a fancy ball. Is that where she had come from? There was only one out-of-place feature. Tied to a white sash around her waist was the sack of dust that Tom had given Dani to mix paints with in *The Echoes*.

"I know this is probably very unsettling to you," Lady Gianni continued as Dani remained silently dumbfounded. "It'll take you some getting used to, but I promise with my tutelage, you'll be just fine. This world will finally start to make sense."

"I don't understand," Dani stammered.

"I know you don't," replied Lady Gianni. "Not yet, at least."

She put her hand to her face for a moment and then stuck her finger in the air like she had just thought of something.

"I really must thank you, actually," the woman continued.

"Thank me for what?" asked Dani.

"For bringing me such a fine specimen for my Librarian to use," Lady Gianni explained. "Without a husk, her abilities are fairly limited, and I was dreading having to give her one of Tom's repulsive workmen. Their hands are far too clumsy and coarse for the delicate work required of her."

"Is *My Body* one of yours as well? Like her?" Dani asked.

"Oh yes," said Lady Gianni with a smile. Dani noticed she kept putting her hand onto the sack of dust at her waist as she spoke, as if she was checking to make sure it was still there. "You really think I would leave this wonderful place with nothing more than some flimsy doors to protect it? I have a security system, one of my own design."

She grinned. Dani couldn't help but think her boss was proud of the monsters she harbored.

"Is Bianca dead?" Dani asked, trying to hold back the urge to cry.

"In a sense, yes," Lady Gianni conceded. "But if you still desire her company, I'm sure I can make arrangements."

She nodded at Bianca's husk with the creature inside and winked at Dani. The thought of being close to it sickened Dani's stomach.

"What do you want from me?" Dani asked, her voice cracking.

"I already told you when I hired you," Lady Gianni replied. "Out there, beyond these walls, you're a disappointment to your family, to your friends, and if he knew your secret, even to that little puppy dog eyed boy who follows you everywhere."

She paused with her hand on Bianca's head, gently stroking the long brown braids.

"I see you as someone not so different from myself," Lady Gianni continued. "You desperately seek beauty, true beauty, that is. The type that lies beneath the surface, the type that takes blood and sweat and tears to uncover. Outside these doors, the world is obsessed with its own superficial definitions of it. It oppresses you with those expectations. Here you can be your true self. You can be a world famous, wealthy, icon of art. Here you can be whatever you want and whomever you want to be. Man, woman, or even something else entirely."

"You've killed Bianca," said Dani, her face flushed with anger. "Probably Paul and Alek too, and I don't know how many others. Just to do what? Sell art for exorbitant prices?"

"It's not about the money," Lady Gianni said with a sigh. "Why do humans always think about money!? It's true, I do charge them whatever ridiculous fee I feel like for the art. But that's only because they wouldn't trust me if I didn't."

"What is this all for then?" pleaded Dani.

"Souls Dani, souls are what we really want," Lady Gianni replied. "These businessmen like Jeremiah Henricks, they pretend they're so smart, but they never read the fine print. They pay me for a piece of art with these souls in it and it extends their lives a little bit. Makes them feel younger for a time."

"Is that why you are killing these people?" exclaimed Dani.

"First, I'm not killing anyone," said Lady Gianni. "Humans are far more successful at murdering one another than I have ever been. War, genocide, the destruction of the environment. I've watched you do it for millennia, and no one does it better. Now I may put a finger on one side of the scale or the other, but I've never pulled the trigger with any of them. If I did, it wouldn't work."

"Second, there are only a few ways to obtain a human soul," she continued. "Most common being them giving it to you willingly. Now for that, you have to trick them into it most of the time. However, humans have gotten smarter. They don't really deal with our kind like they used to. So, me being the entrepreneur that I am, found a loophole. Trap some of these souls in the earthly plane. Trade them with humans, humans who will look at them every day. Humans who will laugh and weep at the sight of them, who will pour all that emotion into them. That's what I want."

"So it's like you told me," said Dani. "A painting is just a painting, a sculpture is just a sculpture. They are merely vessels."

"To capture our energy and our emotion," Lady Gianni finished for her. "I'm glad you were listening. Everyone that comes through my gallery pays me a little of their soul. However, it's only a meager living according to some of my peers. I yearn for something more, a business expansion."

"Is that why you need me?" Dani asked.

"My kind always thinks humans are stupid," Lady Gianni answered. "Every once in a while, an individual like yourself proves them wrong. Yes, I do need you. You have an innate gift, one that I was ridiculed at first for experimenting with. However, your work has all but proven me a visionary."

She adjusted the sash around her waist.

"With your gift," she continued. "I didn't need to orchestrate anything. The souls practically came straight to me. We barely had to lift a finger. I just couldn't believe it. It was so obvious. Humans are more effective than we are at killing each other. Why wouldn't you demonstrate the same aptitude when it came to trapping each other's souls? Honestly, I'm surprised no one else ever tried it. But I think we can take advantage of that and on a much grander scale."

"I won't help you," Dani replied. "I won't be part of this."

"But you already are," replied Lady Gianni. "*The Hole* is going to prove me right. They are going to come straight to me. The entire city, they won't have a choice. They'll come to this ridiculous house of worship, this monument to man's hubris, and throw themselves into *The Hole*, a direct delivery system straight to the boss himself. Once he gets the first batch, he's going to reward me with something far more valuable than this."

She held up the pouch.

"Do you know what I had to give up for this?" Lady Gianni said, her face going from an expression of triumph to anger. "Do you know who I had to deal with? Ancient beings that would make your skin crawl, making me go through hoops just for this little bit of the old magic. The Kraft, they call it. It cost me more than I had ever thought I had to give."

Dani didn't believe it, but she thought she saw something red form in the woman's eye; a crimson teardrop of blood.

"By now you've probably figured it out," Lady Gianni said, turning away to wipe her face. "The Librarian, me, we don't belong here, but we are here."

It was so much to process at once, Dani didn't know what to say or how to say it. Somehow, deep inside, she felt like it made sense at last; she was no longer as crazy as she had seemed. Maybe this world of angels, demons, monsters, trapped souls, and old magic was a world that she understood better than the one that had rejected her.

"That doesn't mean we can't work together," she said. "Now please come with me. The old magic, the Kraft, hasn't quite finished its work yet, but it will soon. Soon the whole city will converge here, the largest trapping of souls ever attempted. It would be best if we weren't here when it does."

Lady Gianni put her arm on Dani's shoulder, filling her with a seductive warmth that made her feel intoxicated. Dani's thoughts shifted and turned in her mind.

Whatever Lady Gianni was, maybe she was right. Dani had never felt like she belonged out there. Her family had rejected her, more than willing to put her on the streets than live with her true self. They had even replaced her with a little sister, given the opportunity to embrace her femininity in ways that Dani had craved as a child.

Even other women had rejected her. They had driven her from the halfway houses. Prostitutes, drug addicts, lesbians were welcome, but not Dani. Not the woman desperately trying to express herself from inside a man's body.

It didn't feel like anyone truly wanted her around except for Lady Gianni.

Bianca, Paul, Alek had allowed her to stay with them; but would they still have if they had known the truth? If they had known, she was born into a body that wasn't hers.

"Come Dani," said Lady Gianni. "Be who you were meant to be."

"She's not going anywhere," Alek said, stepping in front of them.

"You must be the lover boy," Lady Gianni said with a smirk.

Bianca's husk hissed at him.

Alek shrunk back from the creature only for a moment, regaining his nerve and composure quickly.

"I don't know what she did to you, Bianca," Alek said, using every ounce of courage he could muster. "But we'll get you to a doctor. And Dani, I'll get you out of here."

Dani found herself unable to look away from the weapon in Alek's hands. It was an enormous broadsword, engulfed in flame. He could barely hold it up straight, wobbling from side to side as he couldn't decide whether to point it at Bianca or Lady Gianni.

"What kind of idiot gives someone like you a flaming sword?" Lady Gianni asked.

Alek swung the sword slightly towards the madam, but not near enough to be more than a clumsy threat. She didn't even flinch.

"Stay back you..." Alek struggled to find a word. "Witch!"

Bianca hissed at him again.

Lady Gianni put her hand over her face in embarrassment.

"There's only one man I can think of," she said, holding back a laugh. "Who would be that naïve to think that swords are still of use in this silly world."

A large owl swooped down from the rafters above and sunk its talons into Alek's hand. Its descent was silent and its strike effective. Alek dropped the sword to the ground, where it bounced and clattered onto the marble until falling into the pit.

"This is what I've been talking about, Dani," Lady Gianni said. "There are so few like you. Most are just like him, easily manipulated by our lessers."

"You leave her alone or I'll..." One hiss from Bianca's husk and Alek retreated once more, dangerously close to the ledge.

Dani recognized the owl, the one that had been hanging around The Collective, and her old coffee shop, and out in front of *The Dollhouse*. It made sense now; somehow it was an extension of Lady Gianni herself, bound in servitude to her bidding.

"I can still save you Dani," Alek said, peeking over the side of the pit, looking for the sword that had fallen.

Lady Gianni groaned, but not at Alek.

She was looking at the owl that was busy pecking at her dress.

"Really?" Lady Gianni said. "Right now? You can't wait?"

The owl hooted loud and kept pecking away.

"Fine," Lady Gianna said with a loud sigh. "I guess you've earned it."

Reaching into the pouch around her waist, she pulled out a handful of the black dust. The owl stopped pecking at her and stood still on the ground, closing its eyes; it readied itself.

Softly, Lady Gianni blew the dust out of her palm at the owl. A strange burst of air spun around the bird like a tornado, picking up the sparkling particles and lifting the creature into the air. The owl didn't seem alarmed at all; it stood quietly and waited for whatever process that had begun, to finish.

The tornado grew until it was taller than Dani. The owl swept inside. As it dissipated, another form replaced it, that of a man, naked, yet whole.

"Oh, it's been too long," the man said as the last of the black dust absorbed into the air.

He was of medium height, with sculpted musculature, and every inch of this skin covered with tattoos of birds, eagles, and owls. His hair was styled into a short mohawk and his facial hair a tight goatee on his chin.

"Welcome back, Harpier," Lady Gianni said with a forced smile.

"Hey, it's Harper," said the man. "No one knows the old names anymore. I have to adapt."

"What just happened?" Dani said in shock. She thought she had seen everything.

"What?" Harper replied. "Don't act like you've never seen a penis before."

Dani didn't know how to respond to that.

"Don't make me regret this," Lady Gianni said, clutching the bridge of her nose.

Bianca husk hissed.

"Hey, I clean up good, eh?" said Harper with a wink to her.

"I don't know what just happened," Alek said, his eyes wide.

"Forgive Harper," Lady Gianni explained. "He's the family servant, but some of us prefer him in his original form."

"Not a servant, I'm a familiar," Harper corrected her. "And I much prefer this form over the bird. You know how many times I had kids throwing rocks at me? And I've craved proper food. Mice are disgusting."

"Can we get back to business?" Lady Gianni said with an annoyed face.

"I don't care who or what you are," Alek said. "Let us go right now."

"Or you'll do what?" asked Lady Gianni. "You don't have your ridiculous sword."

The Librarian took a step towards him. He retreated until his heels were petering over the edge of *The Hole*.

"Maybe we should make it a fair fight," said Lady Gianni, stepping forward. "You want your sword back?"

Alek gulped.

"Yes," he said.

"Then go get it," in a flash she grasped his arm and prepared to push him. Except she paused.

A colossal noise erupted from the front of the gallery. It didn't take long for them to see its origin. A white van careened through the walls and displays at full speed. As it approached the pit, the driver slammed on the brakes and the van skidded across the slick stone floor.

The Librarian was the first one hit by the van, sending the creature and the body it inhabited hurtling into the darkness. The vehicle also struck Lady Gianni, however, she avoided the pit. Landing almost elegantly onto the ground twenty feet away, only momentarily dazed.

Dani was most concerned about what had happened to Alek. She could no longer see him, and even if he had avoided following Bianca's body down into the pit, the impact from the van might have been enough to kill him instantly. Harper was nowhere to be found, though Dani hoped he was falling to a painful death.

Paul's head burst from the van's driver side window.

"Get in and let's get out of here," Paul yelled.

"Do you see Alek?" Dani asked, trying to see around the van's hood frantically.

"I don't see him," Paul yelled back. "But there's isn't time, hurry get in."

"Not without Alek!" Dani replied.

"I'm telling you," said Paul, looking worried. "There's something wrong with this place, you need to…"

He never got to finish his sentence.

Dani moved out of the way just in time as the van flew across the room. It spun several times in the air, with the weightlessness of a child's toy, before crashing into the wall on the far side.

"Paul!" Dani yelled. She ran as fast as she could around *The Hole*.

The van looked like an enormous crumpled soda can; the side panels were torn and dented. Oil poured from the rear doors that lay crooked on their hinges. The storage tanks of extra fuel Alek had painstakingly sourced from the local restaurants ruptured in the collision. A steady flow of the dark, crud-filled liquid pooled on the ground around them while another branch of the stream disappeared down the steps that led to the tunnels under the church.

Before she could get there, Paul had managed to push open the driver's side door on his own and fell to the ground.

Dani dropped to her knees at his side. Blood poured from the wound on Paul's head, his right arm hung loose at his side. He spat red to the ground as he tried his best to just breathe.

She grabbed his arm to help him up, but he recoiled and screamed in pain.

"Oh my god Paul," Dani said with tear soaked eyes. "We need to get you to a hospital."

She tried to help him up again, grabbing him around the chest this time.

Slowly, she lifted him to his feet, accompanied by his grunting and groans through clenched teeth.

He was eventually able to support his own weight, and together they attempted a slow limping walk towards the exit.

Except something was blocking their path.

A white mist had appeared, it hung tight to the ground. It billowed as it drew closer to them. At its center was Lady Gianni, her legs and feet no longer visible. The white dress, slightly torn by the impact of the van, flowed in waves around her.

Noticeably absent was the sash around her waist and the pouch of dust she had called the Kraft. Her hair swirled, compelled by a strange current of air. However, what drew a chill down Dani's spine most of all, were Lady Gianni's eyes, which had gone completely black.

She was fearsome to behold.

Dani and Paul tried to turn around, as if they could somehow outrun her in Paul's damaged state. The mist easily overtook them. It felt heavy around her feet, like struggling through thick mud in a quagmire. Their pace slowed and slowed. Unable to proceed any further, Dani wanted to scream as she felt tentacles slither their way up her legs. Pulling with all her might did nothing, even Paul with his powerful frame was helpless against it.

Slowly, the tentacles emerged from the mist as they wrapped around Dani and Paul's waists. They had suction cups on them like that of an octopus, and appeared completely white. She felt their slimy texture against her skin and pulled at them with her hands, but could do little to release herself.

She felt Paul's body pulled away from her, as the tentacles lifted him off the ground several feet. While the arms around Dani had stopped at her waist and merely held her in place, Paul's body looked like he had been caught by an enormous albino python.

He yelped with airless cries as he struggled against the tightening grip until his eyes and lips turned red. Lady Gianni's body lifted higher off the ground until she could look him directly in the eyes.

"You cost me my Librarian," Lady Gianni said with anger bubbling in her voice.

Paul didn't respond. He was too busy desperately gasping for air.

"You could have gone in *The Hole* with the others," Lady Gianni continued. "A more dignified end to your cretinous existence. Your soul would be trapped here with theirs, but at least that would save you from the tortuous fate that awaits you."

"Please stop," Dani pleaded. "You're killing him."

"Why shouldn't I crush him right here, right now?" Lady Gianni asked. "Squeeze until every bone in his body is broken, and he's nothing but a spineless worm. Wait, he's already a spineless worm."

Dani thought about how much Paul had done for her, how she would still be travelling from halfway house to halfway house, or worse, if he hadn't plucked her from the coffee shop.

"Let him go," Dani began. "He doesn't deserve this."

Paul eyes looked to Dani, blood-red tears forming in them.

"He doesn't?" Lady Gianni said.

To Dani's relief, she relaxed her grip on Paul slightly as he gasped for a much needed breath.

"Do you hear that?" Lady Gianni asked him, her face inches from his. "She doesn't think you deserve this."

Paul tried to speak words, but struggled to do more than rasp.

"He's a good man," Dani pleaded. "Take me instead, but please let him go."

Lady Gianni stared at Dani for a hard moment, then returned her gaze to Paul.

"Paul Moreau," Lady Gianni said, Dani noticing her mouth turning into a slight grin as if she was enjoying this. "The brilliant artist, what was your most famous work? *Lillys on the Lake*? I saw it once. It was a very inspired piece of brushwork. I could almost feel the desperation in the paint, as if the artist truly knew that the sunset over the water might be the last. Tell me, Paul, what were you feeling when you painted it?"

Paul didn't reply. He only stared at Dani.

"Don't look at her," Lady Gianni said with anger in her voice. "She wasn't there, but you were."

"Talk, Paul, stall her," Dani pleaded with him in her mind. She sensed he was holding back still, as if he was more afraid of saying words out loud than of the monstrosity that held his life.

"Looks like you might need a little help," Lady Gianni said, growing impatient.

A tentacle appeared from behind Paul and, without warning, burrowed itself into his ear.

Dani screamed.

A trickle of blood formed that slowly dropped from his earlobe as he shuddered.

The pupils of Paul's grew large, and the movements stopped.

"Now Paul," said Lady Gianni. "Tell Dani who really made *Lillys on the Lake*."

Paul opened his mouth, his face showing no expression whatsoever.

"My brother Henry painted it," Paul said in a monotone voice. "He was dying of cancer and I promised him I would help him sell his work after he died, to carry on his legacy."

"And where was the money supposed to go?" asked Lady Gianni.

"To cancer research," replied Paul.

"And what did you do?" Lady Gianni continued her line of questioning, questions she already knew the answer to.

"I put my name on his art and sold it under my name," Paul said. Dani noticed the glint of shame overtake his face.

"Oh, how awful," Lady Gianni said with feigned outrage. "This was just a one-time thing, right?"

"No," Paul replied. "I've been doing it with Dani's art since she moved into The Collective."

Dani felt her heart drop from her chest to the pit of her stomach.

"That isn't true," Dani proclaimed.

"You didn't question it once," Lady Gianni began. "How none of your art ever sold yet the moment I saw it I knew you had the talent to be great?"

"I just thought," Dani's mind swirled. She was so taken aback by the revelation that the church and danger she was in had fallen to the wayside of this betrayal.

The tentacle withdrew from Paul's ear, Paul emitting a silent scream as it did.

"You might think me evil, but your 'friends,'" Lady Gianni said, emphasizing the word. "Are just as capable of committing evil."

"Paul, how could you?" Dani asked.

Paul looked at her. His eyes returned to normal, but showing nothing but deep sadness.

"I'm sorry," he managed to say, his voice barely audible.

"If I know my Dante," Lady Gianni began. "The 9th circle is where you'll end up. The most frozen over part of hell, where your neck will be gnawed on for eternity by ravenous demons, men, and dogs while you scream helplessly, unable to free yourself."

Paul coughed as the tentacles tightened around him.

Dani heard a loud crack, like that of a board splintering under immense weight, and Paul's face winced tight in pain.

She wanted to plead for his life again; she wanted to stop Lady Gianni, but she felt it was futile. Whatever she was, it was stronger than she and Paul combined.

Paul's eyes turned blood red, the streams of crimson coming from his ear hastened and the crackling of his bones.

Dani closed her eyes, not wanting to witness any more.

She heard Paul's last weak attempt at a breath before all life left his body.

Lady Gianni released him, and his body crumpled to the ground.

"You don't need them Dani," Lady Gianni said.

Dani didn't dare speak, she just sobbed to herself as she felt the tentacles slowly release her.

"Your art could be everywhere," the monstrous woman continued. "Your name muttered from the lips of millions. Every realm of existence would know who you are. We could do it together."

She extended a hand towards Dani.

Dani just stared at it.

The soft skin, the warmth she knew that it would bring to her heart. It would be easier, easier than whatever alternative this world had for her.

Something caught her eye over Lady Gianni's shoulder.

Harper had seen his chance and was running towards the sack of dust, the Kraft, that lay on the ground a hundred feet away.

CHAPTER 24

"Harper, you little rat," Lady Gianni exclaimed. She could see the man's reflection in Dani's eyes.

The mist around Dani's feet shifted as it pushed away and in the direction of Harper, who was only a few yards away from the coveted Kraft.

"I'm done with your family," Harper yelled as his hands clenched it tight. Lady Gianni stopped in place as Harper held it out over the edge of the pit.

"After all we've done for you?" Lady Gianni yelled. Immense heat hit Dani in waves with each syllable of her words, her rage burning like a furnace.

"You mean all I've done for you," Harper replied. "I'm sick of scrounging around for scraps. I should have realized a long time ago, you were all a bunch of twats."

The mist of Lady Gianni inched closer to Harper.

He let the bag drop an inch in his hand before grabbing it again.

"Keep your bloody tentacles away from me, you hag," Harper warned her.

She came to a halt immediately.

"Now I'll be walking out of here," Harper began.

Dani noticed movement at the edge of the pit next to him, but it was faint and hard to see.

"With this sack and without you trying to follow me," he continued.

"Why would I let you do that?" Lady Gianni snarled.

There it was, the movement again. Dani could see it more clearly this time. Neither Lady Gianni nor Harper seemed to have noticed.

"Because if you do," he replied. "I'll leave behind enough dust for you to continue on with this sick charade of a gallery."

"I have a better deal," Lady Gianni said. "If you give me the Kraft now, I may just let you return to your true form long enough to enjoy one final flight under the moon before I roast you alive."

The movement returned. It looked like a pair of fingers, barely gripping the ledge.

A sliver of hope formed in the core of Dani's chest.

"You got it wrong, love," Harper said defiantly. "I got the Kraft. I make the rules. And ol' Harper says the new rule is, I walk, not fly out of here."

Dani wasn't sure if Harper could see it, but Lady Gianni slowly moved forward.

"Maybe I'll break your legs and arms before I turn you back," Lady Gianni said. "Leave you in the alley to be the plaything for some stray cat."

"One more inch and the bag goes in," said Harper. "I get away, I always get away."

"I highly doubt that," Lady Gianni replied. She grinned.

Behind Harper, Alek crawled out from the pit. Harper was too busy with Lady Gianni to notice.

Alek lunged at Harper, tackling him to the ground.

Lady Gianni also sprung forward, her eyes fixed on the sack that flew from Harper's hand. She didn't get far as Dani reached into the mist at her feet and pulled hard on the tentacles. The human part of her falling forward onto the stone.

Alek and Harper continued their struggle, one clothed and one naked, rolling on the ground and taking wild swings at the other.

Dani struggled and pulled with all her might, but the slippery tentacles eventually withdrew from her grip.

Harper landed one good punch on Alek that freed him from the younger man's hold and scrambled to his feet, sack in hand.

Lady Gianni's tentacle swung with deadly accurate aim. It hit Harper hard across the chest. The man's naked body went flying across the room, crashing through displays until it was far out of sight. The sack landed next to Alek, who was still reeling from the punch.

A flurry of tentacles rushed forward to retrieve the sack.

They found only air.

In a moment of adrenaline-fueled clarity, Alek kicked the sack and its contents over the edge, where it fell into the darkness of *The Hole*.

A banshee-like scream filled the old church. It pierced Dani's eardrums as she clutched her palms tight around her head to keep it out.

When it had subsided, Dani dared open her eyes once again and found Lady Gianni standing at the ledge of the pit, staring down into it with a heaving chest. An orange glow pulsed on her face. It wasn't just her face; it pulsed against the stone walls of the church. Every surface, from the windows to the ceiling, was illuminated by the fiery glow. The light was coming from *The Hole*.

From the darkness of its depths, a colossal fire erupted.

Lady Gianni turned to Alek on the ground at her feet as a tentacle wrapped itself around his neck and lifted him off the ground. His feet dangled helplessly in the air as they both drifted towards Dani.

Dani tried to stand up to fight back, but the mist was quicker than her and she too felt the slimy flesh of the tentacles wrap around her waist and lift her up.

"You fool," said Lady Gianni. "Do you know what you've done?"

"Saved the city," Alek replied, his eyes defiant.

"You saved nothing," replied Lady Gianni. She wasn't even looking at them. She stared into the pit and the growing flame fast approaching the surface. "The Kraft's magic continues to thrive with the painting secure downstairs."

The tentacles swung them violently until they felt the back of their skulls slam into the wall of the church. Lady Gianni kept them there, pinned tight.

"I gave up my husband for that Kraft," Lady Gianni said. "I gave up my son for it. And you've used it all up to accomplish nothing. The city will still come here. Every one of their souls will be trapped inside. What were you thinking?"

"I did it to piss you off," Alek said, struggling in vain to unwrap the tentacles around his neck.

"I don't think so," Lady Gianni replied. "I think your foolhardy act was nothing more than an idiot's attempt to save your one true love."

She said the end in a mocking voice.

"Men never change," Lady Gianni continued. "They run into battle and throw themselves at one another, thinking it heroic. It's all just a vain attempt to show off. Do you even know who Dani really i"

"Please don't," Dani pleaded. She didn't want her last moments on this Earth to be filled with shame.

"Lover boy has a right to know, doesn't he?" asked Lady Gianni. "He has a right to know that, like me, you are something very different from what you pretend to be."

"Stop, please, I beg you," said Dani, but she knew Lady Gianni wasn't listening.

Alek's eyes were wide. He looked terrified. Whatever confidence he had mustered to fight Harper, it had been sapped from his soul.

"She didn't tell you?" Lady Gianni asked. "I can't imagine she would. It's not something you really advertise. Personally, if I was born a man, I would have hated myself too for it. The vile beings that they are."

Dani wanted to plead for her to stop, but she couldn't. The tears were too strong. She didn't dare look at Alek to see the disappointment in his eyes. To see the feelings of betrayal fill his face. To see his lips curled into a face of disgust.

It would break her.

"Not so chatty anymore, are you?" said Lady Gianni with contempt in her voice.

Dani sobbed.

"You could have been great," Lady Gianni said. "You could have had it all. Instead, you had to bring your ragtag misfit friends and try to destroy something I sacrificed for. Maybe you'll figure it out after you learn a little about sacrifice for yourself."

Dani opened her eyes and saw Lady Gianni smile, a devilish, evil smile that could only have been conjured by the darkest of thoughts in the woman's sick and twisted mind.

In the reflection of the woman's eyes, Dani saw Alek's face.

"No," Dani screamed.

He was choking as the tentacle tightened around his neck. He struggled for each breath.

Dani screamed and flailed, her arms unable to break Lady Gianni's grip.

"Leave him alone," she yelled.

"It's so sad really," Lady Gianni said calmly. "Knowing that in his last moments, he would be thinking about how you betrayed him."

"Please, just stop," Dani pleaded, landing futile blow after blow on the tentacle arm.

Dani looked at Alek, wanting to comfort him, at least.

Alek didn't look like he wanted any comforting, that defiant look was back in his eyes. He was still fighting, trying to draw breath, all the while mouthing something with his lips.

"Bur…" he sputtered before losing breath.

"Bur…" he repeated.

Dani just wished it would be over quick for him, that his suffering would end.

He took one final breath.

"Burn everything," he said.

Alek's eyes closed and his body went limp.

"Oops," Lady Gianni said. "Did I just kill him?"

Dani wanted to die herself. She didn't want to live in a world without Alek, Paul, and Bianca. A violent world where they had been the only ones who had been kind to her. The only ones to bring her in and make her feel accepted.

"You're a monster," said Dani.

"I'm not the monster," Lady Gianni replied.

Dani didn't want to look into Lady Gianni's eyes. She didn't want to acknowledge the truth. If it wasn't for Dani; all her would still be alive. If it wasn't for Dani; the city wouldn't be preparing to march to *The Hole*.

She looked away, not wanting to face it.

The fires of the pit roared, the flames whipping out over the edge.

There was something else there too, an enormous hand. It was just a hand at first, gripping the ledge, but it was soon followed by an arm, and then another arm, and then a body. The figure that stood up in front of the ledge, bathed in the fire's light, was a man like she had never seen before. He was at least seven feet tall, his shoulders were wide, his skin was marked all over with open cuts and festering wounds. He had long, bushy black hair on his head, beard, and eyebrows that hid his eyes well. Except one eye was clearly visible. It glinted bright silver in the light.

Dani knew who it was immediately. It was the shadow that had followed her in *The Echoes*. It was the shadow man from her painting.

"I should have known that you were nothing special," Lady Gianni continued, oblivious to the shadow man approaching from behind her.

Dani felt the tentacles tighten around her throat.

"You were a failure," said Lady Gianni. "One easily corrected."

Dani struggled to pull in each breath.

"I'll look forward to throwing your body into the fire with the rest of..." Lady Gianni stopped speaking as the shadow man's gargantuan hand wrapped itself around the back of her neck.

For the first time, Dani saw fear in Lady Gianni's eyes. The woman froze as the shadow man leaned down and put his mouth to her ear.

"Honey, I'm home," he whispered. His voice was otherworldly.

Dani felt herself drop to the ground. Lady Gianni had released her.

"What are you doing here?" Lady Gianni screamed at the shadow man. "How did you...?"

"I've come to bring you home," the shadow man said.

"No, I won't!" Lady Gianni yelled as her body twisted around on its own and began to fight back. She tore at him with her hands, her fingernails growing as long as a tiger's claws.

The shadow man took no notice as he marched towards the fire with her tight in his grip.

Her tentacles swung at him, wrapped themselves around his neck and body. Squeezing and slashing. A mass of arms and tentacles, like a python trying to constrict an elephant. She bit at his face with razor-sharp teeth. Black blood squirted from each wound.

He was not slowed; steadily drawing closer to *The Hole*.

"Morfran, stop!" Lady Gianni screamed, and pleaded. "Morfran, let's talk about this. There must be a way to bring you back."

"Kyla, my love," the shadow man named Morfran said. "Vengeance never dies."

"Please, no," she pleaded.

Dani could only watch as the two former lovers stood at the brink of the fiery pit. Lady Gianni or perhaps Kyla, as he had called her, struggled to escape, but Morfran, the shadow man from her nightmares, held the half-woman-half-demon close and refusing to let her go.

He plunged forward, throwing them both into the fire.

Dani sat in shock, unable to process what she had just seen.

Was it over? Did that stop the old magic of the Kraft?

She knew it didn't. The people of the city were all coming, all coming to do the same leap of death as Morfran and Kyla had just performed together. Dani was powerless to stop it.

Then she saw Alek's body lying on the ground.

She threw herself on top of him, holding him close to her. He didn't deserve this; he was just trying to protect her; he cared for her. Was his fate the destiny of everyone she got close to?

She thought it was footsteps at first, a rhythmic march of someone approaching. It grew louder every second; it grew stronger. She looked around trying to figure out where it was coming from, then she realized it wasn't coming from anywhere, it was coming from Alek. It was Alek's heart, still beating. Still strong.

He was still alive.

She lifted him up; he was breathing even if just faintly.

"Alek, wake up," she said, shaking him.

But his head only flopped sideways.

She tried to lift him. Maybe she could carry him to safety.

They managed only a few steps before they fell together back onto the stone.

He was too heavy and she was too weak.

She still felt the same as she had been in Lady Gianni's grasp, resigned to dying over living in a world without Alek.

"Burn it," Alek said under weak breaths. "Burn everything."

"I can't," Dani replied. "We don't have anything to burn it with."

Alek lost consciousness again, his arm falling awkwardly to the side.

It was pointing at something, Dani followed the direction.

There was Paul's van. It was still destroyed and oil drained from the rear hatch. The stairwell that led to the basement was coated in the thick, noxious liquid.

Then she noticed the brazier standing nearby. A stone bowl sat on top. White and yellow flame burned inside and flickered upwards. It would weigh hundreds of pounds more than she could lift. But the base was just three poles. They didn't look as heavy as the rest. In fact, it looked like it might be able to be tipped over.

She stood and rushed over to it. With all her might, she pushed, but only managed to shift it an inch. She tried again, and again, and again.

It was going nowhere. She just wasn't strong enough.

She had to keep trying; she placed her hands on top and felt another pair of hands join her, Alek's.

"One, two," he began the countdown. "Three!"

They both let loose a colossal shove and the bowl teetered towards the stairwell. For a moment it hung in the air, frozen at the equilibrium point, not sure if it would actually fall.

Dani didn't let out her breath until an inch more of movement somehow sealed its fate. The bowl went clattering to the ground, landing directly into the pool of vegetable oil.

The oil was slow to light at first, the thick liquid threatening to extinguish the flames. But once it was lit, there was no stopping it.

Alek grabbed Dani and pulled her away from the van, where the trail of fire was quickly approaching.

"We've gotta get out of here," he said.

Holding her arm; he led her towards the church exit.

They paused to turn only once, when the van exploded behind them. It was truly a remarkable sight.

The frescoes on the ceiling peeled as the flames devoured angels and demons alike. Fire roared from the opening to the downstairs stairwell. The pit was no longer the brightest fire in the church. *, The Echoes,* and *The Remnants* had also caught fire, the flames spreading quickly to the entire building.

Dani couldn't be certain, but she felt something in her heart. She felt like a cool wind was passing not through her, but around her. Not a wave of heat from the out-of-control fire, but something else entirely, something she didn't quite understand.

As they exited the church, they heard a colossal crash behind them. Turning just in time, they witnessed the hanging sculptures that had greeted everyone who entered the gallery aflame on the marble floor. Though still intact, the fire would soon turn them to ash. They spelled out the words: Gallery Nocturne.

EPILOGUE

Dani gripped tight as she felt every bone, muscle, and organ in her body shake violently. She knew she shouldn't be scared, but sometimes fear has a way of taking hold, regardless of what the rational mind tells it.

As the plane slowed on the runway, the violent shaking lessened, and Dani relaxed her grip.

"Um, ow," Alek said next to her.

She looked down to see her hand on his wrist, still squeezing. She let go and pulled her hand away.

"Sorry," she said, her face turning red. It wasn't as red as his hand, which had turned the color of a tomato because of the restricted blood-flow.

"After everything you've seen," Alek said, rubbing his arm. "After everything you've faced, an airplane still scares you?"

"It's not the flying part," Dani replied. "It's the takeoff and landing I don't trust."

Alek laughed.

A pleasant woman's voice played over the intercom. She was speaking in Italian, a language Dani recognized but did not know enough to know what she was saying. Dani peered over at Alek.

"Oh, I forgot," he said. "She's telling us the gates are full and we'll be waiting on the tarmac for a little while."

Dani let out a loud sigh, her heart still fluttering in her chest yearned for fresh, non-recirculated air. She looked over at the passenger across the aisle from them.

He was traveling on business; she assumed from the attaché case at his feet and the elegant tie around his neck. It had been a long plane ride from London to Milan. No one wears something so uncomfortable as that unless they had important meetings to go to as soon as they hit the ground.

She watched as he stuffed that morning's newspaper he was reading on the flight into the pouch in front of him. It stuck out enough for Dani to see the front page. A face next to the lead article was a face she recognized all-too-well along with the headline: 'BILLIONAIRE JEREMIAH HENRICKS DEAD'.

"Excuse me," she said to the businessman. "Are you done with that?"

The man looked at her and smiled.

"Be my guest," he said in a polite tone with a stiff British accent.

He handed it across the aisle to her.

"Thank you," she muttered as she unfolded it to read the article.

"You don't suppose," Dani said to Alek, who was reading over her shoulder.

"That we did this?" replied Alek quietly.

"Ya," she said, feeling guilt.

"You know what Lady Gianni..." Alek began.

"Kyla," Dani corrected him. "Her name was Kyla."

"You know what Kyla said," Alek continued. "The paintings had the power to make the owner feel younger. Most of his collection was stored in the church's basement, so when it was destroyed in the fire, its magic must have been released somehow."

"Ninety-two," Dani said aloud. "That's pretty old."

"Too old to be doing half the things he was doing," Alek replied. "Sounds like he was living on borrowed time."

"Borrowed from who knows how many people," said Dani solemnly.

Dani got quiet as she thought about the feeling that had flooded her as she watched the church burn. After their escape, they both had stopped to rest in the safety of an alley across the street. The figures in the stained glass windows shattered into millions of shards as explosion after explosion rocked the stone structure. She had worried at first that the conflagration wouldn't be hot enough to damage the stone, that some cursed and haunted structure would be left intact to create further harm.

However, as the explosions continued, the very ground under the church had opened up and the mighty stone blocks crumbled under their own weight until nothing remained but a smoldering hole that engulfed the full contents of the church and what had been Gallery Nocturne. It accompanied a strange and cool wind passing through her.

She knew it was more than just a mere wind; she felt something else entirely. A feeling of thousands of voices, all muttering words of gratefulness in hundreds of languages. It was the trapped souls in the collection under the church, passing to the next plane of existence; no longer tormented and finally at peace.

"Earth to Dani," Alek said, poking her.

She awoke from her memory like from a dream.

"Sorry," Dani said, blinking fast, trying to rejoin the here and present. "I was just remembering that night."

"I could tell," replied Alek.

He looked down and noticed Dani was clutching the wrapped canvas tight in her hands.

"I can't believe you wanted to keep that," he said. "Isn't destroying these paintings the reason we came to Italy?"

He was right. The whole reason they were stuck on the tarmac in Milan rather than figuring out a new place to live was because of her desire to finish what they started. The stored artwork underneath the church was gone, and she believed those souls were now free. However, hundreds, maybe thousands more, were dispersed across the world to various collectors in Lady Gianni's network. Without Lady Gianni's (or Kyla, as her husband called her) records, which were nothing more than ash now, it was impossible to know for certain where and how many.

But she had an idea.

The pleasant Italian woman's voice came over the loudspeaker again and this time, many passengers who understood her started standing up and bustling around to grab their bags. Dani and Alek did the same.

Soon, they disembarked from the plane and shuffled along to customs.

Dani and Alek stood in line with the other passengers, waiting for their turn to talk to a customs agent. They held hands.

She felt guilt poke at her heart.

"I know it's late to tell you this," Dani said, the line in front of them slow and long. "But I wanted to tell you I'm sorry."

"Sorry for what?" asked Alek.

"For not telling you sooner about..." Dani tried to find a delicate way to say it. "About transitioning. I hated that you found out from Kyla and not from me."

"I already knew," Alek said bluntly.

The words hit Dani like a sack of potatoes.

"What? How?" Dani asked.

"Remember when I got some of that paint in my hair?" He began. "After you got back from painting *The Smoking Man*?"

"Yes," Dani replied.

"Well, I didn't go into a trance or anything," he continued. "But I just knew something, something I didn't know before."

"And you still went out with me?" she asked.

"Of course," Alek scoffed. "I like you for who you are. Everything else is just... just..."

"Logistics?" she said.

They both laughed.

"So you think Salvador has this painting you want to destroy?" Alek continued. "The one with the guy in it?"

"Javier, yes," she answered. "I didn't feel him when the paintings were destroyed. I can still feel him trapped here in our world, unable to move on. We have to find him and free him. And Salvador was Kyla's broker for her deals in Europe. He either still has Javier's painting or knows who does."

"I still don't understand how you know all this," Alek replied. "What is that dust you keep hidden in your makeup case?"

She shushed him and looked around nervously, checking if anyone around them was eavesdropping. No one seemed to have noticed.

"What?" Alek asked.

"You don't know who might be listening," Dani said.

"You sound paranoid," he said.

"We don't know enough yet about," she tried to think of the right word. "About them. About the dust. Kyla walked amongst us like a normal person. Harper was an owl before he was a human. They could be anywhere, they could be everywhere."

"You make it sound like we are in some cold war spy novel," said Alek. "Trust no one."

He pulled the collar of his jacket up to hide part of his face and narrowed his eyes.

"Knock it off, James Bond," she said, punching him playfully.

"It's our turn," Alek said, pointing to an Italian customs agent waving at them.

They rushed forward to the station and handed him their passports.

He was thin and aging, his gray hair shining on his head as he inspected their documents, then their faces through spectacles.

Alek did most of the talking in Italian for them. Dani only grew alarmed when she noticed their discussion growing more contested.

"What's wrong?" she asked Alek.

"He wants to have the painting you are holding inspected," Alek said. "They are concerned that it's valuable and may be required to be declared."

"Tell him it's a family heirloom," she replied. "Tell him it's worthless to anyone but me."

"I did," Alek said. He looked nervous.

The customs agent lifted a wired phone from its receiver and spoke quickly in Italian into it.

"Shit," Alek said.

"What now?" Dani asked.

"He's calling over his supervisor," he answered.

Dani grew more distressed. This painting was the one she was most afraid of. Afraid of having it taken away from her. Afraid of it going into circulation somewhere that would only amplify the power of the Kraft still contained inside.

But she had no choice.

Carefully, she followed the directions of the three customs agents that ushered them into a side room and placed the canvas onto a big metal table.

Against her best judgment, she pulled the linen cover back from the canvas and slowly revealed the painting to the three men. Alek took one glance, then looked away, not wanting to gaze upon it a moment longer than he had to.

The three customs agents stopped their chatting immediately and grew quiet. The awe of the painting struck them instantly.

Dani didn't need to look at it. She had painted it. It was *The Shadow Man* painting, the one she had made in black and silver paint only on a hunch, an instinct that had saved their lives.

As the men's faces drew closer, their eyes wide and with mouths open, Dani could feel the painting absorbing their emotions, their energy, a bit of each of their souls. She felt something inside the painting stir. *The Shadow Man*'s silver eye seemed to glint and grow stronger with each second. Pulsing with the customs agents' heartbeats.

She wanted them to close their eyes, to stop immediately.

Then they did, covering the canvas back up and handing it back to her. She felt the energy within the canvas wane as she placed it back under her arm; it was going back to sleep.

Alek exchanged words in Italian with the men before they were ushered out thankfully into the main terminal, the last step being the stamping of their passports.

"What did they say?" Dani asked as they walked towards the baggage claim area.

"They were concerned about who the original artist was since it was unsigned," Alek replied.

"What did you tell them?" asked Dani.

"I told them your deranged aunt from a mental asylum made it," he said.

"You did not," said Dani, shocked.

Alek just nodded.

"I can't believe…" she began, but the buzzing and ringing of her cell phone interrupted her sentence. She checked the caller ID first, and then, seeing who it was, immediately answered.

"Who is it?" Alek mouthed the words.

"Hey mom," Dani said into the phone with a smile.

Alek nodded.

"Sorry I didn't call sooner," Dani continued. "We got stuck in customs and they don't allow phones in there. But we are through now."

Alek could hear an excited voice on the other end of the line.

"Alek and I are really excited to visit Milan's sites," Dani continued. "The Duomo, the Castello. They are all on our list."

She noticed Alek cringe at her pronunciation.

"No, not the Brera," said Dani, clenching her jaw. "We've had our fill of art galleries for the time being. Of course, I'll talk to her."

Another long pause as the phone was handed off on the other end of the line.

"Hi Stephanie," Dani said with a smile on her face. "It's so nice to talk to you again."

A pause.

"That's right," she continued. "Your big sister went on an airplane to Europe."

They walked together down the long terminal towards the station where a train awaited to take them the rest of the way to Cinque Terra. Dani talking on the phone to a little sister she didn't know she even had until recently.

It was a joy Dani hadn't felt in her heart in a long time.

She smiled at Alek by her side as they walked; he smiled back.

They were about to embark on a new adventure together, and she couldn't have been more happy to have him to share it with.

Neither of them noticed a man in a wide brim hat as they passed one of the many bars that dotted the airport. He wore a fashionable white leisure suit and sunglasses. His arm hung from a sling and his shirt was unbuttoned at the top, revealing much of the skin of his hairless chest. Images of eagles and owls watched with unmoving eyes from the tattoos covering his body.

Harper put down his drink and followed Alek and Dani deeper into the terminal.

THE END